To Jean
With my best wishes

Elisabeth R. Craft

June 21, 2001

In The
COURT
OF THE
QUEEN

In The COURT OF THE QUEEN

A Novel of Mesopotamia

Elisabeth Roberts Craft

Bartleby Press
Silver Spring, Maryland

Printed in the United States of America

Published by:

Bartleby Press
11141 Georgia Avenue
Silver Spring, Maryland 20902

Library of Congress Cataloging-in-Publication Data

Craft, Elisabeth Roberts, 1918-
    In the court of the queen : a novel of Mesopotamia   /
    Elisabeth Roberts Craft.
        p.   cm.
    ISBN 0-910155-42-9
    1. Iraq—History—To 634—Fiction.   2. Funeral rites and ceremo-
nies—Fiction.   3. Ur (Extinct city)—Fiction.   4. Women—Iraq—Fiction.   5. Queens—Fiction. I. Title.

PS3553.R213 I5   2001
813'.54—dc21

                                            00-062107

In memory of my parents,
Pauline and Harold Craft

1

O n the brown earth outside the city walls, Ur-mes sat cross-legged at the door of his new home. In irritation that matched his foul mood, he scratched the gray hair on his chest and yanked at his heavy woolen skirt. Some of it, caught underneath him, pulled uncomfortably. There. He settled down again. The midday sun glinted off the nearby irrigation canal. For an instant, it so blinded him that he couldn't see the peasants, thigh-deep in water, digging out the mud.

Short-tempered by nature, he grumbled, "If that river cartel doesn't stop opening the floodgates from the Euphrates, the canal will overflow."

He shifted his position slightly, bringing the distant walls of Ur into view. "What good do those walls do anyway?" he asked himself, venting some of his gnawing fear by criticizing the city. "Hammurabi, king of Babylon, conquered Ur the same way he conquered every other city here in the lower delta. Still, our king, Idi-Sin, keeps a standing army. I suppose it makes him feel important," sneered Ur-mes aloud.

Hunching further down, he glared into the distance across the jumble of flat roofs and narrow, twisting streets, at the high platform built into the wall of the upper city. The sprawling royal palace and adjoining temple occupied the platform. Slightly to the left, he could see the soaring top of the ziggurat at the other end of the royal road, the Processional Way, that connected the two.

Behind the city's major temple, the ziggurat rose tier on tier in a solid mass. Nannar, the most powerful god in Ur, stayed in the little blue-tile house on top. Only the high priest, the high priestess and the king visited there. A complex of temples, residential and administrative buildings, nestled at its base.

But he, himself, preferred the temple next to the palace. Looking back at the palace platform, he contemplated the graceful way the temple mimicked the ziggurat's three elegant stories. It housed sacred prostitutes on the first tier, scribes and priestesses on the second, the high priestess on the top. Every day, as part of her duties, the high priestess placed grain and beer before the many painted wooden statues of gods on a long table in the room next to hers. Ur-mes stuck out his lower lip. He couldn't think of one instance when the gods had done anything for anybody.

Vexed, he turned his thoughts back to his large, new home and the day fifteen months ago that had precipitated its construction. His grandchildren had spent the morning screaming at each other. His oldest son's wife had fought long and noisily with the wife of his third son. The two serving women, distracted by the noise, spilled a caldron of soup all over the small interior courtyard. He had exploded. Why did he live in the center of the lower city? The small, narrow houses were densely packed. The dirt streets, pounded to hardness by feet, hooves and cart wheels, smelled of rotting refuse. And the noise! If it wasn't the sound of the artisan's hammer clanging on metal, it was the whirring of the potter's wheel: more often than not, both at once.

Day and night, he heard the heavy tread of oxen pulling creaking carts, the constant drumming rotation of solid-wheeled military chariots pulled by four asses, the trampling of bronze-helmeted soldiers as their officers moved them from place to place. Crowds, both townspeople and priests, constantly passed to and fro. Inebriated men from the wineshop on the corner never failed to disturb his sleep.

The following morning, he had risen from breakfast, shrugged off the stares of his family and left the house. He walked out the market gate, past the fields of slowly waving grain, musty-smelling in the hot sun, the orchards fragrant with ripe fruit, and the cattle contentedly cropping the grass. Migrant shepherds pitched their tents in the surrounding area or built houses, some as large as the one he intended to build.

He stopped. Using both hands, he shaded his eyes and gazed across the fertile land and the canals that watered it. "This is where I will build my new house," he announced to the playful breeze.

He went back to tell his skinny, withered old wife what he had decided. Shub looked at him as if he had lost his senses, but bowed her head and said, "So be it."

Thus, he had started work on a house much like his old house, but twice the size. Why not? He didn't need to stint; he was a rich man. Enormous flocks of sheep and goats and many head of cattle grazed his land. In buildings he had erected, three of his sons and a score of paid workers carried on the family business in meat, skins and wool.

He snatched up his fly whisk and viciously swung it. An objecting buzz came from the all-pervasive flies.

He had gone to the best brick maker in Ur to place his order. He asked that each brick be twelve inches square by three inches thick. According to custom, each would have the maker's stamp in the middle. He watched the brickyard workers set the wooden forms, mix the clay with straw or sand. At one point, he snapped, "Don't use so much water. The mud will be too runny; the brick less strong."

The man retorted, "I know what I'm doing." He forced the thick, sticky mass into the corners of the form then filled in the center. Using a sturdy, flat piece of wood attached to a short handle, he pounded the dark red glutinous mixture to remove air bubbles. He straightened and looked at Ur-mes, daring him to object.

Defiantly, Ur-mes lifted his chin, but said nothing.

The worker started to measure the form for another brick. It was getting late; he was tired. He had only made ninety bricks so far, twenty short of his quota. Thanks to Nannar, the foreman had stamped the partially dried bricks so he didn't have to do that.

Ur-mes continued to hover over the workers. He watched the bricks laid, two rows at alternate angles, then one horizontal. Each day, he inspected the work. He insisted on a coating of bitumen on the outside to seal the bricks against the weather and objected to the quality of the limeplaster the bricklayers used on the inside walls. Almost at the last minute, he remembered to place miniature statues of his household gods under the doorjamb.

Finally, the house was finished. Its small front door opened onto a tiny, brick-paved lobby that contained a jar of water for footbaths. A door on one of the lobby's side walls led to the large cobbled courtyard that sloped slightly toward a central drain. The roof covering the balcony also inclined so that rain running off the overhang dripped onto the cobblestones below and trickled to the drain. The wooden, second-story balcony rested on pillars of sweet-smelling cedar imported from across the sea on his order by the trader Ea-nasir.

Stairs near the entrance door, rose over the family lavatory. Across the courtyard stretched the rectangular reception room. A handsome rug for people to sit on lay against the back wall. Everything looked comfortable and familiar. He had kept the same arrangement as in his old house. On the first floor, he had set aside a lavatory and rooms for visitors. Three of his sons and their families also resided on the first floor. His two eldest sons and their families lived on the second floor with him, his wife, and Hana-Ad, the other girls having gone to the houses of their husbands.

Pleased with the spaciousness, he decided to try an innovation. He added a large, subdivided area accessed through a courtyard door near the reception room to house the kitchen with its two fireplaces, work and storage areas, and sleeping arrangements for his servants and slaves.

From the depths of his unhappiness, he sighed. What good was this big house, what good his thriving businesses now that the old queen had sent for Hana-Ad? His stomach still fluttered from the shock of seeing the richly draped ox cart and the four palace guards in their knee-length leather pants and waistband daggers stop before his doorway.

He flung his fists into the air and shook them, snatched them back and sat on them to make sure they didn't shoot into the air again. He hung his head and glowered. An evil breath of air, a quiet rumble, a whisper in the marketplace, had come his way by accident. Many rumors flew around about the old queen. With Hana-Ad about to become one of her beautiful maidens, worry gnawed at him. Were they true?

Of all his children, his five boys and four girls, he loved Hana-Ad best. His youngest, his darling of the creamy, tanned skin and the blue-black hair that fell to her waist, his sweet, ripe pomegranate ready to be plucked, had enslaved him. He had thought long and hard about the plucking. The man had to be worthy. But a letter, written by a scribe, from Ur-Enlila, the shepherd living nearby, had taken him by surprise.

At the table after the evening meal, surrounded by his family, slowly, deliberately, he read aloud that Ur-Enlila wished to negotiate a marriage contract between his son Daid and Hana-Ad.

Ur-mes regarded his dithering daughter. "You know this boy?"

"I've seen him." She turned pink and hung her head.

"What will you answer?" demanded Shub.

"I don't know. I want to observe Daid."

As he refused to be drawn into further conversation, the family waited, not patiently on the part of Hana-Ad. Every other day, she pestered her mother until Shub, in exasperation, said, "Hana-Ad, I don't know any more than you do. When he's ready, he'll tell us his decision. You just have to wait."

Oblivious to the anxiety of his daughter, Ur-mes took his time about answering the letter.

"I'll ask Apilsin about this boy," Ur-mes told his oldest son. "He knows all the shepherd families around here."

Apilsin smiled broadly when Ur-mes asked him about Daid. "My friend, marriage into that family would be excellent for your daughter. At sixteen, Daid is an unusually capable fellow. And he's a hard worker. Two years ago when a birthing cow kicked Ur-Enlila in the hip, Daid took over responsibility for their large herds. He has done well. His future's bright. Being the oldest, he will inherit."

Apilsin's comments satisfied Ur-mes. A letter went to Ur-Enlila agreeing to the start of negotiations. Immediately upon their successful conclusion, Daid asked permission to visit his future father-in-law.

"He's not wasting any time," a slightly huffy Ur-mes commented to his wife.

Shub laughed. "He's young."

Leading a heavily laden donkey, Daid arrived promptly at the appointed time. Slaves helped him remove the bags from the animal's back. Once seated next to each other on the rug in the reception room, Daid presented three large disks of silver and beautifully wrought gold jewelry to Ur-mes.

"Did you know," said Ur-mes, "that Hana-Ad already owns property in her own name?"

"No," Daid said, trying not to show his surprise.

"She will have her own slaves when she comes to live with you, and I expect to give her more property, also to be held in her own name." He turned a quizzical look on Daid.

"You are most generous," said Daid, nodding his agreement.

An ecstatic Hana-Ad caught Ur-mes around the waist and danced him across the courtyard when he told her the gist of the interview. That had pleased him. She would be happy. He had arranged that the writing and sealing of the tablet containing the marriage lines take place in thirty days. Now, he had to tell Daid that the old queen had taken Hana-Ad, that the marriage would have to be put off until—again, worry consumed him.

He had looked forward to having Daid as a son-in-law. True, Daid followed a different religion. His family followed Yahweh, as did Apilsin. They made a contract to serve no other god than Yahweh.

Yet, Ur-mes knew that Daid's father had placed household gods under the doorjamb. Of course, Ninlil, his wife, was a woman of Ur. Her family followed Nannar, the leading god of the city. Most of those who followed Yahweh didn't deny the other gods. They kept household gods. Apilsin was the only one who didn't. Ur-mes remembered when Apilsin announced that he was going to be strict in worshiping Yahweh. He promptly terrified every family in the area by ripping his household gods from under the doorjamb and throwing them away.

One family rescued the little statues and carefully buried them beside the family's own gods. Everybody watched and waited for some dreadful catastrophe to happen to Apilsin. Nothing did. Apilsin continued to pray to Yahweh and prosper.

Ur-Enlila kept a family altar where he conducted services for his household. He also stood alone before it and talked to Yahweh. What Ur-mes couldn't understand was that Yahweh talked to Ur-Enlila. He talked to Apilsin, too, or so Apilsin said. Ur-mes often wondered how. Did a voice come from the altar, from the air around? He had never gotten up enough nerve to ask Apilsin, though they frequently discussed the power of Nannar against the power of Yahweh.

Apilsin had startled him during one of their talks by saying that Yahweh was holy. How ridiculous. Gods weren't holy, though they were big and powerful and possessed eternal life. They made mistakes like everybody else. They advised men badly causing bad things to happen. That, on top of the bad things that men did, created havoc when humans and gods came together.

Ur-mes chuckled. Let Apilsin think that. He himself would have no part of gods being holy. The only thing that concerned him was suffering, and there was plenty of that.

He screwed up his eyes and pouted. This Yahweh business was beyond him. He had a god for stomach aches, a god for the fire on his hearth, a god for rain, a god for his crops, and many,

many others. He prayed to each when necessary and never expected anything in return.

Ur-mes believed that he was put on this earth to serve the gods as their slave. For that reason, the wise god Enki, according to the great Epic of Gilgamesh, saved one man and his family from the flood.

The god Enlil, red-faced and angry, announced arrogantly, "I sent the flood because I have not been served to my satisfaction."

Enki scolded him, saying, "You were too rash when you planned total destruction. Let lions and wolves keep their numbers down, or let famine beset them. But we need men. Who will serve our needs if you kill them all?"

For a day, Enlil thought about that. At the end of the day, he admitted that Enki was right. He said, "I will give the man who was saved eternal life."

Ur-mes shuddered. He wished he could have eternal life instead of being sent to a gloomy cave where the souls of the dead were covered with feathers and had nothing to eat except the clay on the ground. He knew Apilsin expected to have eternal life with Yahweh. But if he prayed to Yahweh for eternal life, Nannar might destroy him for desertion. He felt a bit frightened for even thinking of serving Yahweh.

True, the nomadic shepherds who followed Yahweh moved their great herds of sheep, goats and cattle from area to area, choosing the outskirts of one of the city-states so that they could have access to the advantages of a stable community. Generally, however, they kept to themselves. Occasionally, like Ur-Enlila, a man settled down and built a house. Daid's family had also bought a tiny piece of property outside Ur in which to bury their dead. Thus, Ur-mes assumed they would remain in the area, Daid's mother being a citizen of Ur. He knew her family through his wool business.

Daid took after his mother's family in looks. He had the square face, high cheekbones and heavy eyelids of the Sumerians. His black eyes drooped slightly at the outer edges. And he trimmed his still-skimpy black beard as did the men of Ur, rather than having the long face, hooked nose and full beard of Ur-Enlila.

Well, whether Daid looked like his mother, whether Ur-Enlila continued to live nearby, no longer mattered. In those few minutes this morning, everything had changed. He no longer controlled

Hana-Ad's future. He resented it. Yet, he had to accept his lot. The gods ruled it. If they demanded Hana-Ad, his duty was to comply. Actually, fear made him comply. The gods might retaliate with a worse fate.

Take Nannar, for example, the moon god. Ur-mes had no recollection of Nannar answering prayer. But then, he didn't usually pray to Nannar; he prayed to his house gods. He couldn't remember them ever answering any of his prayers either.

"Help me now," burst from him.

He brushed away the tear creeping through the wrinkles of his face. Fortunately, he had kept the rumors about the old queen to himself. His wife, joyous at the honor bestowed on them, couldn't understand his sadness. He had sloughed her off by claiming to miss his daughter. Her remark rankled.

She had snapped, "You're an old fool."

Well, let her think him a fool. She wouldn't hear the truth from him. He drew his bushy eyebrows together while making a sucking noise through the space where he had lost an upper tooth. The sound of footsteps made him turn his head. Slender, stately Apilsin, his great beaked nose dominating his thin face, planted his bare feet solidly with each step. Even in his depressed state, Ur-mes noticed the food stains on Apilsin's wool skirt and the crumbs in his bushy, black beard—so unlike him. He must have risen from his table the minute he heard the news. He knew I would be sad about losing Hana-Ad. What more he knows, he'll tell me.

Apilsin crossed his legs and dropped to the ground, laying his fly whisk beside him. For a minute, the two men sat side by side without speaking.

"You know," Ur-mes said finally, "the old queen has taken Hana-Ad?"

"Yes. My manservant was returning from the market and saw a draped cart with two palace guards in front of it, two behind it, and a slave guiding the oxen. Just as my man walked by, Hana-Ad's face peeped out."

Apilsin did not add that his man had said Hana-Ad was crying.

"He was surprised and rushed to tell me." The slave had also mentioned the ugly whispering in the market about the old queen. Hearing that, Apilsin stood before his altar with bowed head and prayed to Yahweh before hurrying to his friend. Ur-mes certainly looked upset enough to have heard the rumor. Without moving, Apilsin let his support and sympathy flow over the older man.

"I must tell Daid," sighed Ur-mes.

"He may already know. The news has spread."

"Undoubtedly people are dancing with joy at the honor paid me." He scowled. "They don't understand my sadness at losing my bright spirit."

"My friend, I have prayed to Yahweh to relieve your sorrow."

"Your god, Apilsin, and mine aren't the same."

"Agreed." Apilsin nodded his head. "But as I believe explicitly that my God is faithful and will answer prayer, I have prayed."

Again, they were silent. Ur-mes broke it. "The law says, if the bride's family breaks the engagement, they have to return double the bride money. Do you think I'll have to pay Daid twice what he gave me?"

"No, the money is enough. You didn't break the engagement; Ku-bau, the old queen, did. Actually, Daid may not expect any money. They still may marry in a year or two. The queen is old."

Ur-mes cringed.

So he knew. Apilsin laid a hand on the shoulder next to him. "My friend, I shall pray unceasingly for your reunion with your daughter. God is great and performs many wondrous things."

Without comment, Ur-mes laid his hand atop the hand on his shoulder.

A male slave, dressed in a short wraparound skirt of thin wool appeared at the door. Both men looked up.

"Mistress respectfully asks about the animals to be slaughtered for the feast."

With a sigh, Ur-mes said, "I'll come." He turned to Apilsin. "My wife is warning me that I had better help prepare the feast to celebrate this honor that's been bestowed on me."

"I will leave you."

"You'll return later?"

"Yes."

The two men rose and parted. Apilsin started back across the canal, the way he had come. Ur-mes, his head held high, entered his courtyard. Servants and three of his daughters-in-law awaited his decisions. At the far side, near the door into the kitchen, he spotted Shub, his wife, anxiously pacing.

Squealing in excitement, the three girls surged around him. Wasn't it wonderful? Imagine living with Queen Ku-bau.

Laughingly, one said, "I'm jealous."

"Don't be."

She drew back, blinking. Had she said something wrong?

His eyes sought Shub's. He held up two fingers. "One calf, one large sheep," he said. "That should leave plenty for the priests."

She nodded in agreement and disappeared.

As everybody turned to a task, he shook his head. This isn't a celebration. It's a dirge. I'm the only one here who understands that.

2

"I want to go home," moaned Hana-Ad. Hidden in the fabric-draped ox cart, she squeezed a tear splotch from her green sheer-wool dress. "I don't want to be a beautiful maiden with the old queen."

Feeling the cart start up in incline, she gingerly lifted the right-hand drape. The crowded, narrow streets of the city, the flat roofs of the two and three-story tenement houses, the low, long, palm-shaded homes of the rich lay below her. She bounced to the other side and raised the drape. "Oh my," she said as her eyebrows flew up. "The mud-brick walls of the palace look just like the walls at home." Glazed potsherds thrust into wet mud made the design she had so often seen from below. From the street, these walls seemed magical. Here, next to them, they appeared ordinary.

She gave a slight upward twitch of her head, straightened her wig and ran her fingers along the gold links of the chain her father had given her.

Two palace guards, standing at attention, watched her step from the cart. "Follow us," said one guard. They marched into the vestibule with military precision. Hana-Ad hurried after them.

A slave, using a silver basin, poured water dipped from an alabaster jar over her feet. With little drops of water still clinging to the leather thongs of her sandals, she caught up with the guards at the entrance to an internal courtyard crowded with people.

Mesmerized by color and glitter, her eyes riveted on a canopied platform in the middle of the opposite long wall. Blue pillars topped by red capitals supported the white pedimented roof. Painted red animals mutely held their heraldic positions on the pediment. The clear morning light, reflecting off the blue columns, turned the edges to spun gold. Sparkling gold hung in strands around the neck of the man seated on the platform and melted into his orange robe. She couldn't see his eyes too well, as the round brim of his hat shaded them.

The king! The king! A shudder of excitement ran through her body.

Three guards stood behind him. A youthful looking man, dressed in scarlet and wearing a long gold chain, bent to whisper in his ear. One scribe sat cross-legged in the right rear corner of the platform, another in the left corner.

A massed group of men knelt on the paving before the platform. Slightly ahead of the others, a heavily bearded man, holding a clay tablet in his hand, said something to the king she couldn't hear. Other men walked quietly around the edge of the court.

"This way," said one guard, starting off across the shorter end of the audience court. In straining to hear what the man addressing the king was saying, Hana-Ad slowed down.

"Walk faster," the other guard said impatiently. "Queen Kubau is waiting for you."

She bowed her head, looked intently at the polished stone floor, and hurried. That lasted two seconds. The painted corridor walls caught her eye. A band of red ran along the bottom, then a procession of figures. Some of them carried bowls, some looked like slaves. Above the procession, a strip of bright yellow stretched up to the ceiling. Her eyes followed the wall procession as she moved along. Suddenly, the wall ended in an open doorway. Through it, she saw a seated woman, a cluster of gold leaves crowning the top of her head. Young women, in gaily colored dresses, surrounded her. Hana-Ad opened her mouth to ask if that was Queen Nin-Anna, but the guards stepped smartly along, looking neither to the right nor to the left.

They entered a small courtyard. The most elegant woman she had ever seen was coming toward them. Black hair, pulled straight back from her high forehead, formed a bun at the nape of her neck, emphasizing her large Sumerian-lidded eyes and firm chin. Her tall, thin figure, in its embroidered yellow gown, moved slowly like water flowing peacefully in a streambed.

As she came abreast of Hana-Ad, she stopped. With the barest hint of a lovely smile, she said, "You must be the tenth young virgin for my sister-in-law, Queen Ku-bau." Her words sounded like whispered music to Hana-Ad. "I'm Nanshe, High Priestess of Nannar, sister to the late king, father of Idi-Sin, the present king. You must learn to bow before me."

Hana-Ad turned deep pink, dropped her chin, and seemed to pull her upper body in on itself as she doubled over.

Quickly, a smile in her voice, Nanshe said, "You are forgiven today, but remember next time. We will see much of each other." She continued slowly toward the corridor leading to King Idi-Sin's audience court.

Flustered, clumsy, and awed, Hana-Ad bent her knees, not sure whether she should go down, watching Nanshe's disappearing back. Mortified at her indiscretion, she followed the guards along the brightly painted corridor that Nanshe had exited. Again interested in the corridor, she counted three small, rectanglar windows, high up, that broke the flow of the marching figures then almost bumped into the slowing guards. Ahead of them, two straight and stiff guards jumped to the side and opened carved double doors with great flourish.

A tiny gasp escaped her. They had entered a large open courtyard. A covered walkway ran alongside a garden. Pink blossoms fluttered on branches just above her head. Red, yellow, orange, purple and pink flowers grew in little clumps near green shrubbery. She recognized a fig tree and two tall date palms. Paths led every which way through the garden. In the middle, a little bird chirped lustily on a round pool's edge. Greedily, she drank in the color and fragrance as they walked along.

At the other end of the garden, the guards ushered her into an airy, dim room. An imposing male boomed, "Kneel before the king's mother."

She fell to her knees and bowed her head.

"Rise, Hana-Ad, and let me have a look at you," said a pleasant female voice.

With but a hint of awkwardness, she rose and glanced around. The palm trees and flowers painted on the walls looked almost real in the dim light. A group of exquisitely dressed young women holding harps stood on one side of the room, female slaves on the other. In the center, resting on white pillows piled on a bed, lay a wrinkled old lady wearing a scarlet gown. A circlet of gold leaves sat squarely on her combed and puffed black wig. Rouge covered her high cheekbones, kohl encircled her eyes, and pink tinted her lips. The smell of a spicy perfume surrounded her. Gold and gems covered her ears, neck and arms. A fluted gold tumbler and a small gold pitcher lay within reach on a low table.

A court officer dressed in short leather pants, a dagger hanging from his left hip, stood at her feet. A heavy gold chain held a round seal against his chest. With a flick of his wrist, he dismissed the guards who had brought her.

Queen Ku-bau said, "Come here, child. How can you expect me to see you way over there?"

Conscious of the intense scrutiny of the young women's eyes and her own poor grooming in comparison, Hana-Ad held her head high as she moved forward.

In silence, Ku-bau examined her new recruit, starting with Hana-Ad's wig of black hair, her large, kohl encircled, dark eyes with the typical Sumerian lids, her straight nose, her full lower lip, working her way down the slender figure, noting the intricately executed gold chain around her neck, and finishing with the leather sandals that peeped from beneath the hem of the green wool gown.

Watching the old queen's eyes travel down her body, Hana-Ad's spirits sank. Nervous and rattled by her sense of inadequacy, she perspired. That made her even more agitated.

Queen Ku-Bau looked up and said, "You are a very pretty girl. You will do nicely. Now," she raised her heavily jeweled hand and indicated the girls standing against the wall, "meet the others."

One by one, the old queen introduced nine beautiful girls. "Help Hana-Ad get settled," she said.

Hana-Ad hung back, shifted her weight from one foot to the other and glanced at the old queen, as the girls started to file out.

"Go with them." Ku-bau flung the back of her hand at Hana-Ad.

In the walkway, a short, delicate-looking girl, huge dark eyes in a cameo face, took Hana-Ad's hand. "I'm Kigal," she said. "It's hard to remember all the names at once."

"Don't go getting a crush on our new friend, Kigal."

Hana-Ad turned her head and looked into a pair of black eyes set in a beautiful oval face with an unpleasant sharpness to it. Half a head taller than herself, and large boned, the girl looked solid.

"Oh, Ashnan, I'm not." Kigal dropped her eyes and blushed a violent red, but didn't let go of the hand.

"Don't let her pester you," Ashnan said. "She'll try. She's a nuisance."

Kigal let go of Hana-Ad's hand and dropped behind.

With a slight twist, Hana-Ad grabbed the hand again. "I don't mind, Kigal. Right now, I feel a little homesick for my parents and my betrothed."

Tears shone in Kigal's gentle eyes, but she smiled.

"Your betrothed," said Ashnan, raising her eyebrows and flashing her eyes around.

"Stop it, Ashnan," came from behind them.

On her left, a step behind, walked a girl with startlingly intense dark eyes, who carried herself erect, with a modicum of arrogance. A twinge of fear passed through Hana-Ad.

"I think it's wonderful, Uttu, that Hana-Ad has a betrothed," said Ashnan, turning a broad smile on their new friend. "May they have a long and happy life together."

"Thank you." Hana-Ad's smile lit up her whole face..

Kigal looked like a startled fawn, but said nothing.

"In here." Uttu led the way into a large room. Light filtered softly through the wide doorway, as did air, fragrant from the garden. The walls, painted yellow, were decorated with dancing girls in filmy gowns. Brightly colored wool and linen cushions lay grouped around the floor, along with backless chairs of cedar and small tables inlaid with bone. A delicate blue drape interrupted the wall pattern at regular intervals.

Three middle-aged female slaves leaned against the wall. One of them, the plumper of the two standing close together, exuded authority in her squared shoulders. The third, a short, stocky woman, gave the impression of being the lowliest of this trio. The elegance. The luxury. Hana-Ad swallowed hard and clutched her gold chain. She would live here!

"This is our social room," said a voluptuous-looking girl. Hana-Ad remembered Kigal called her Nidada. "If you want to be alone, you stay in your sleeping alcove," she said. "Now that we are ten, the alcoves are all full. The one over there," Nidada pointed, "the third from the main door, is yours." Casting Hana-Ad a warm, happy smile, Nidada walked toward an alcove at the back of the room.

"You may want to spend time alone, away from the chatter," said Uttu, turning on her heel toward a close-by alcove.

"Uttu will act superior once too often," said a small-boned, ruby-lipped girl, wearing dangling gold and silver earrings and an elaborate matching necklace.

Try as she might, Hana-Ad couldn't recall the girl's name.

"You'd think she came from money, but her family is poor," said Girsu-Ad. "Being chosen by the old queen has gone to her head."

Hana-Ad had no trouble remembering Girsu-Ad's name. She thought her the most beautiful of all, perfect in form and face. Looking at her now, though, she was surprised to see nothing but emptiness in those limpid eyes.

"Come on, dear. I'll show you your alcove. But it's really more than an alcove. It's a tiny room." Kigal gently pulled Hana-Ad's hand.

"And you must tell me about your betrothed and your marriage plans," Ashnan said sweetly.

"Ashnan, can't you leave anything alone?" The girl wearing orange, lounged across a yellow pillow. A small, dark mole at the corner of her upper lip made her beauty seductive.

Hana-Ad turned a questioning face to Kigal.

"That's Ninbar and the girl sitting at the table watching everything is Nin-Ad. She's quiet and reserved."

Hana-Ad noted that Nin-Ad's soft olive skin glowed with pink highlights. She looked back at Kigal and smiled. She had a feeling Kigal never said anything mean about anybody.

"And what's the name of the girl with all the jewelry?"

"Ninti. The only other one whose name you may not remember is Shegunu. She's willowy and elegant."

"The one with the deep blue eyes?"

"Yes. They're startling, aren't they? She's Queen Nin-Anna's niece. Her mother is a princess from some distant land. I don't know where."

"She's beautiful."

"She's not around much. Nin-Anna, the queen, is sick a lot and wants Shegunu to sit with her."

Kigal pulled aside the drape from Hana-Ad's alcove.

Hana-Ad looked around. Pressed against the yellow wall stood a bed with an embroidered white coverlet. A small table with a wicker stool occupied the miniscule left-hand corner. On the table top lay a silver comb, brush, and mirror done in repousse. Four tiny alabaster cosmetic jars and three delicate shells, respectively filled with white, green and red paste, occupied the table's back edge. A small rug, a facsimile of the big carpet on the floor of their recreation room, barely covered the space between the bed and the drape.

Hana-Ad stroked the polished mirror then picked it up. "Are

these for me?" She looked closely at her own face. Not as pretty as some of the girls, but not bad.

"Aren't they nice?" Kigal beamed. "We each have a set. They're all different designs so we can always tell our own."

"Where do I put my clothes?"

"Each morning, the slaves bring a gown and whatever else we need. We eat breakfast in our alcoves or in the big room. After that, we have classes. Do you play an instrument?"

"No."

"Oh!" After a moment's hesitation, Kigal said, "You'll probably be given a harp. Each of us has a harp rather than a lyre."

"Why?"

"It's easier to handle. And if you don't know how to play, it would be simpler to learn the note progression."

"What do you mean?" Hana-Ad leaned toward Kigal, an expectant, questioning expression on her face.

"The notes follow one another in perfect upward and downward order." Kigal hummed a scale. "Seven of those notes have names and make a group. Then the names repeat, making another group."

"You're scaring me a bit. That sounds complicated."

"Don't worry." Kigal's little hand gently touched Hana-Ad's elbow. "The harp is shaped like a boat. You cradle it on your left arm. One end extends into a long pole which lies against your shoulder. The strings run from the pole to the boat. You just pluck the strings. That's all there is to it."

"What about the lyre? Is it more difficult?"

"Not really. It's more awkward to handle. For one thing, it's bigger. It's kind of square. You hold it straight out in front of you."

"Yes, I've seen people play the lyre in the city's central square. The strings run from top to bottom."

"Occasionally, the old queen asks Ashnan to play the lyre because she's tall and strong. The rest of us only play the harp. So you won't feel conspicuous."

She quickly added, "It's really important that you learn."

"I like the idea," said Hana-Ad, "but don't understand the importance. Why must I learn?"

"Well," Kigal hesitated, then said in a rush, "we entertain the old queen." She drew her brows together with intensity. "Don't you know about us?"

"No. Just that Queen Ku-bau sent for me this morning."

"Oh! Well, I'll leave now. Our slaves will probably fit dresses on you." Kigal slipped through the drape like a floating wisp.

Immediately, two slaves, who Hana-Ad recognized as two she had seen in the social room, entered. One slave carried a rainbow assortment of dresses thrown over her shoulders and across her arms. She dumped them in a jumble on the bed. The second woman toted a box which she set on the table after shoving the silver toiletries aside.

"I'm Temena," said the plumpish woman, quietly taking command. She picked up a gauzy, flame colored dress. "I think this will fit you nicely. Take off your dress."

She waited patiently while Hana-Ad pulled the green wool over her head and tossed it toward the bed. With an agile spring, the other slave caught and carefully folded it.

"Here," said Temena, "put your arm through." She dropped the vivid wool gauze over Hana-Ad, arranged the fabric properly across her small breasts and ran a finger along the garment edge under Hana-Ad's left armpit to check the tension beneath her bare shoulder. Slowly, Temena walked around, looking at the fit.

"Perfect," she said finally. "These dresses are all the same size. You may pick out six."

"They're so beautiful." Hana-Ad hung over the bed and caressed them. "I've never had so many dresses." From the pile, she drew a pale lavender linen with embroidery around the bottom.

"Oh! I love this."

"Queen Nin-Anna, who supervises all the weaving done in the palace, takes special care with what you young ladies wear," said Temena.

"The queen must be a wonderful person." Awe struck, Hana-Ad caressed the air a fraction above the dress.

The two women smiled. "Gula will help you choose jewelry," said Temena.

Gula, well-proportioned, with coarse, pock-marked skin, opened the box and picked up a gold necklace set with purple stones. "These gems will look well on that dress."

Choosing six gowns from the array of gorgeous finery became a drawn-out difficult task. She wanted them all. With patience, the two slaves helped her in and out of the dresses, held the mirror for her to see, made suggestions and sorted jewelry. Finally, six garments lay side by side on the bed. Hana-Ad sighed happily.

Temena, a little twitch playing about her lips, signaled departure. Bitar, the third slave, short, humble of attitude, who had come in during the serious decision-making, picked up the six gowns. "In the morning, I'll bring you your clothing for the day."

Ecstatic, Hana-Ad sat down on the bed, then immediately jumped up to smooth the coverlet. She ran her hand lovingly over the length of it and across. Never in her life had she possessed anything so beautiful. And to think that everything in this cubicle belonged to her. She deliberately pinched her arm. Ouch! That hurt. She was awake, not dreaming. Six dresses, all that jewelry, mine. I'll say special prayers of thanks to the gods.

Oh! An index finger went across her lips. In my rush, I forgot to bring my personal goddess. Maybe I'll pray to Nannar now that I'm in the palace. She smiled to herself. Being close to the old queen, she felt brave enough to talk to Nannar, the great god. Even so, she'd ask Daid to bring her personal goddess. She missed the little statue. Her mother was right. A marvelous thing had happened to her. Many, many unexpected advantages would come to Daid and her when they married.

Happy exclamations outside her alcove drew her attention. She heard what sounded like a large platter being placed on the floor. "What lovely fruit," someone said.

Suddenly, a hunger pang grabbed Hana-Ad. Her mouth watered. She hadn't eaten since breakfast. That was hours ago.

"Join us." Kigal spoke invitingly as Hana-Ad approached them.

"Please do," said Shegunu. "Dinner will arrive any moment."

Hana-Ad had noticed Shegunu's ripe peach complexion when the old queen introduced them. Slender, she carried herself with an easy elegance and a grace that made Hana-Ad shy before her.

"You remember Shegunu," said Kigal, "and Nin-Ad."

"Yes. Thanks." Hana-Ad eased onto a cushion. "There are so many names."

"By tomorrow, you'll know everybody," said Shegunu.

Ninti and Ninbar lifted cushions from the floor near Ninti's alcove and widened the circle around the fruit.

"I'm Ninti." The long earrings swayed as the thin-framed girl smiled at Hana-Ad. "It's nice to have you with us."

Hana-Ad smiled back. "Thank you. Everybody's so kind and everything's so beautiful, I'm a little overwhelmed. My father is going to be amazed when I tell him."

A moment of deadening silence met her comment. Ninbar reached for a date. "Where's your home, Hana-Ad?"

"A half-hour's walk outside the Market Gate."

"With all those tents and cattle?" Ninti ended on a surprised note.

Hana-Ad laughed. "It's really pleasant there. It's green. The irrigation canal is nearby. The air smells fresh. And many people live in houses. Daid does."

"Oh!" exclaimed Girsu-Ad, pushing a cushion between Kigal and Ninbar, "is that the man you're contracted to?"

"Yes," Hana-Ad said, her face aglow.

"How did you meet him?"

"I was milking goats the day Daid walked by. He didn't speak. He didn't even look at me, as far as I could tell," burbled Hana-Ad. "But he told me afterwards he knew right then he wanted me to be his wife."

"How thrilling," squealed Girsu-Ad. "I wish something like that would happen to—" She stopped. "Oh! I forgot."

Hana-Ad blinked, a baffled expression on her face.

Quickly, Kigal said, "What happened next?"

"Two days later, a slave brought my father a formal letter. Daid's father, Ur-Enlila, wanted to negotiate a marriage contract."

"And your father answered," said Nin-Ad matter-of-factly. "How nice."

"Well, not right away," laughed Hana-Ad. "My father wanted to observe Daid. At least, that's what he said. Two years ago, Daid had to take over the work of their herds when his father got hurt. He was only fourteen." A note of pride crept into her voice.

"He must be a very commendable young man," said Shegunu.

Pleased, Hana-Ad shyly dropped her eyes. "Thank you. My father thought so. He started negotiations."

A smiling Hana-Ad glanced around the circle. "I was so happy. I had liked Daid, too, that day I saw him."

"After negotiations were concluded, did Daid bring gifts?" asked Ninti.

"Naturally, he asked permission to visit. And you should have seen the heavy load on the little donkey he led."

Girsu-Ad's eyes widened. "What was it?" she asked in a hushed, avid manner.

"Three large disks of silver and beautifully wrought gold pieces."

Girsu-Ad heaved a satisfied sigh.

"Did he bring jewelry?" asked Ninti.

Hana-Ad nodded. "It's gorgeous. I can wear it on special occasions after we're married."

The faces around the circle froze. To break the silence, Shegunu said, "I'm sure it looks lovely on you."

Abruptly, Ninbar changed the subject. "Did you ever live in the city?"

"Yes. Until twelve months ago, I lived just off the main wide road through the city, four doors up from that big bordello."

"You did!" exclaimed Ninti. "I lived two streets back of you."

"I can't believe it. I never saw you."

"I constantly begged my father to take me to the central entertainment square." Ninti laughed gleefully. "Did you go there?"

"Of course."

"I loved to watch the wrestling and the games of chance. And sometimes, there would be a caged lion or bear. Once—I'll never forget—the lion roared. And the bear had that thick black fur. Half terrified, I sallied up to the cage as close as I dared. Then, if the animal lunged in my direction, I ran screeching to my father."

"I liked the storytellers best," Kigal said, "and the poets. They always accompanied themselves on a harp when they recited their poetry."

"And the bazaar," said Ninbar. "How I loved to walk around in the bazaar."

"I wish we could do that now," pouted Girsu-Ad.

"Mother always took me with her," Ninbar went on, ignoring Girsu-Ad. "We liked to walk slowly and dawdle in front of the food stands. Sometimes, she'd buy me a little ball of spicy fried vegetables. I would stand where it's cool under the awnings that shield the narrow dirt passages from the sun, munching my vegetables and smelling the wonderful aromas from the cooked food. In those days, I thought that was the very zenith of life."

She snickered, and everybody else laughed.

"Where's dinner?" Girsu-Ad sat up straight to peer out the door. "It's late."

"Twice, my father took me to a place with tables," said Kigal. "I felt very grown up eating there." Her eyes twinkled at the memory.

"After I finished eating," said Ninbar, "we'd walk along, looking at the booths on either side. Mother would comment on the display of fruit, cheese, mutton, duck, whatever was sold. Some-times, the owners would object to her comments, but she didn't care. Most of the time, we bought something for supper."

"I liked to look at the pots and pans, the dresses and im-ported luxury items," said Hana-Ad. "Occasionally, my father would buy kitchen equipment or a piece of jewelry for mother. The minute we got home, I made a big announcement. I think sometimes father bought things just to see my pleasure when we gave them to her."

"Once, outside a brothel, I saw a prostitute servicing her customer in the street," said Girsu-Ad. "I wanted to stop and watch, but my father dragged me away."

Ninti said, "One time I heard my parents talking about the water south of Ur receding. As I didn't know what that meant, I asked. Papa said that a long time ago, the whole plain where we lived was underwater."

"I don't believe that," said Girsu-Ad.

"That's what I said. Papa said, 'You've seen the marshlands south of the city, haven't you?' I bet you have, too, Girsu-Ad."

"Yes," she admitted grudgingly.

"Well, papa said, 'When I was a boy, that was all underwater. If you watch, you'll see the difference when you're as old as I am'."

Ninti giggled. "I thought I'd never be as old as he was."

Ninbar gave her a funny look.

"I like to stand on the quays," said Hana-Ad, "and watch the boats on the river."

"Don't you love the great galleys with the upturned prow and stern?" Both Ninbar's hands curved up as she spoke.

"They're so graceful as they sail up the river," said Hana-Ad. "Well, I guess they're mainly rowed up the river."

"My father says they sail out of our river into a big gulf, and way down at the other end, into a wide, wide sea." Kigal said. "They go to distant lands where they collect timber, bitumen, gypsum, carnelian, tin, copper and gold dust."

"And we send beautiful jewelry back to them, among other things," said Shegunu.

Kigal said, "Don't you think they're scared when they sail out of the gulf?"

"Sailors hang around the docked galleys all the time, looking for work," said Nin-Ad. "So they can't be too scared."

"And all the galleys don't go to distant lands," Shegunu said. "Some only go too Dilmun to exchange cargoes."

"Where's Dilmun?" said Girsu-Ad?

"It's an island in the gulf just beyond the mouth of our river. It's a huge trading center."

Girsu-Ad said, "What do they trade?"

Shegunu slightly tilted her head. "Well, we buy lapis lazuli and gold dust from traders who live on Dilmun to make the jewelry which we sell to other traders. I'm sure you've looked in the shops of the jewelers and gem cutters."

"Of course." Girsu-Ad sounded irritated and defensive.

"My point," said Shegunu, "is that, naturally, you know what they make."

"Naturally." Girsu-Ad subsided.

"The gold dust," said Hana-Ad with a soft snicker, "was always beyond my imagination. I thought if it were dust, how could they keep it from flying around? I pictured slaves jumping up and down, trying to catch sparkling golden dust."

The idea of swirling golden dust sent the girls into whoops of laughter.

"Sometimes, my father had business on the quays," Ninbar said. "Occasionally, he would take me. I loved to watch the tublike fishing boats with their flower-colored sails that dotted the river. As they came into shore, I could hear the grunts of the oarsmen as their oars slapped the water and see the beads of sweat on their backs. The minute one tied up at the quay, slaves rushed to unload the squirming catch. Ugh." She twisted her mouth in revulsion.

Ninti said, "The pleasure boats were my favorite. They kind of drifted around on the river while the rich people lolled under the awnings or rested in their cabins."

Ashnan stalked toward the companionable circle of girls. "We're just going to be eight this evening."

The others looked up questioningly.

"The old queen has requested Uttu and Nidada, who are our best musicians," she explained to Hana-Ad, "to come to her chambers to entertain her."

"How do you know?" asked Kigal.

"Temena was fixing my hair when the slave asked for them," said Ashnan.

"Where's the chancellor?" Shegunu asked.

"The king wants him."

Shegunu delicately raised an eyebrow. "She could have gotten one of the scribes to read to her."

"That surprised me, too." Ashnan slid her eyes around slyly. "She's been so eager to know what's in those records."

"What records?" demanded Girsu-Ad.

With a withering look, Ashnan said, "The records of that ancient queen, of course. What else is there?"

"Oh, calm down, Ashnan," said Ninbar. "As usual, you're dying to give information, so why don't you tell Hana-Ad what we're talking about."

Ashnan smiled sweetly and addressed Hana-Ad.

"Some time ago, workmen repairing walls in the basement of an old building on the ziggurat grounds came upon a pile of records left by administrators of a very famous queen named Shub-Ad. She lived a long, long time ago when Ur was the greatest city in the world. Queen Ku-bau is fascinated with her and has tried to copy everything Shub-Ad did."

"Each night," Ashnan continued, "she has the chancellor read the records to her."

"It hasn't been easy for him," said Shegunu, "even though he's a bright man."

"Does he have trouble reading?" asked Girsu-Ad, widening her eyes in astonishment.

"The records are written in a script that we don't use today," Shegunu said.

"How did you hear that?" demanded Ashnan.

"My dear girl, you aren't the font of all knowledge. I do have sources beyond you."

Unable to come up with a fast retort, Ashnan sniffed and turned to Hana-Ad. "Tell us about your wedding plans."

Shegunu rose with an exquisite grace, noted in deferential silence by Hana-Ad, and walked to her alcove.

"Don't mind her," Ashnan said. "She's always like that if she's not the center of attention."

"Oh, Ashnan," Kigal chided. "That's not true." She turned to Hana-Ad. "She's a lovely person. She lives with us like an equal."

"Go ahead, Hana-Ad," interrupted Ashnan.

"Well, I don't know where to begin."

"Begin at the beginning," Ashnan suggested. "How did you meet him?"

"Our parents met when my father built our new house on the edge of town. We have large herds of cattle and sheep and goats. So does Daid's father. The only thing is they follow a different god."

"What do you mean, a different god?" asked Nin-Ad. "He serves Nannar, doesn't he?"

Hana-Ad hesitated. "I guess I shouldn't say it that way. He realizes there are many gods who help us with many things, but he worships only one god. His name is Yahweh. He has no special home and no form."

"What did you say?" Nin-Ad placed both hands on the carpet as she leaned forward.

"Would you explain that?" said Shegunu, her beautiful blue eyes goggled. "I don't understand. No form?"

"Odd, isn't it?" said Hana-Ad. "They never see him. He's up in the sky somewhere."

"How can they possibly worship someone they can't see?" said Ninti. "What do they do—just sit in their temple?"

"They don't have a temple," Hana-Ad said.

Kigal's mouth fell open.

"Then where do they go?" Ninbar's head swung back and forth as she spoke.

"Daid's father has what he calls a horned altar. The family worships Yahweh there."

"What's a horned altar?" asked Girsu-Ad.

"It's square, and it has humps on each corner."

"That's a horn?" said Ninbar.

"Yes. If somebody has done something bad, he can hang onto those horns. Nobody can punish him while he stays there."

"What a funny religion," said Ninti, laughing.

The others joined the laughter. Chagrined, Hana-Ad hung her head.

"Will you have to join that religion?" asked Ashnan.

"I suppose so." Hana-Ad hesitated, sounding panicky even to herself.

"That's terrible," Ashnan persisted. "It could bring punishment by Nannar on you."

"I think Nannar would want me to be a good wife," Hana-Ad said, trying to bolster her spirits.

"He may be punishing you already," said a superior Ashnan.

"Kigal," Ashnan continued, as if she was wearying of playing cat and mouse, "tell Hana-Ad what's in those old records that Queen Ku-bau is so keen about."

"I won't," said Kigal sharply. "How can you always be so mean, Ashnan?"

"I—I'm not quite sure I understand. Is there something in those records that affects us?" asked Hana-Ad.

"Yes," Ninbar said.

"Then, please, someone tell me."

In an I-thought-you'd-never-ask voice, Ashnan said, "Those records say that Queen Shub-Ad had all her court ladies—ALL—escort her to her tomb. They played their harps in her funeral escort and had to remain in her tomb along with her chariot and guards so she would have transportation and music in the next world. Queen Ku-bau has chosen ten to escort her."

Rather than look at Hana-Ad, most of the girls fiddled with their gowns, fussed with their jewelry, smoothed their wigs, or tried to brush invisible lint from a sandal.

A little smirk on her face, Ashnan stared at Hana-Ad.

Hana-Ad sat straight without moving. The high color of her cheeks and the pink of her skin gradually faded until she became almost as white as the cushion Ninti sat on. Quietly, she said, "I'll go home tomorrow."

Ashnan's one word fell like an ax, sharp and clear. "Try."

Only then did Hana-Ad make an effort to move. She looked from one bowed head to another. No eye met hers. Nin-Ad held one hand over her face. Kigal kept her eyes glued to a spot on the rug where somebody had once spilled lamb stew.

With a shoulder shrug, Ashnan picked up some grapes, popped one into her mouth, and examined the rest.

Hana-Ad pressed her left hand to her chest, trying to calm her wildly thumping heart. The fluttering made her breathing difficult. In slow motion, she bent one knee and forced her body over onto it. Using both hands to push the floor and the leverage of her other leg, she stood up. Then, with a weaving motion, she started toward her alcove. The ten steps seemed longer than the distance between her home and the market gate. Would she never reach her alcove?

Nobody else moved. The only sound was Ashnan's teeth exploding a grape.

At last. A yank and the drape to her alcove gave a soft whoosh as it slithered into place behind her. Alone. Her body slumped. In that release, tears began to flow. She flung herself across the bed and cried away the night.

3

*B*itar found Hana-Ad in an uneasy sleep, her eyes red and puffy, her face swollen and streaked with kohl. The woman dashed out to search for Temena, who at that moment emerged from the alcove of Ninbar.

"Come quickly," Bitar called, motioning frantically.

"You need all your skill with herbs," she whispered when Temena reached her. "The girl's face is so bloated that her eyes have almost disappeared."

The two women hurried to Hana-Ad's bed and stood looking at her. She moaned and twisted in her sleep.

"She must look beautiful by the time the old queen rises," sighed Bitar.

"You wake her while I go for my potions, and tell Gula she'll have to dress all the others."

Bitar sat down by Hana-Ad's head, forced her arm under her shoulders and gathered her close.

"There, there," whispered Bitar, rocking back and forth. "Temena is bringing cooling lotion for your hot, swollen face."

"I want to go home," sobbed Hana-Ad.

"Shush. We must make you beautiful first. You can't go anywhere looking the way you do."

"What's wrong?"

"I'll let you see for yourself."

Bitar brought the mirror that lay on the table and watched the reaction as Hana-Ad peered at herself.

"Oh," she gasped. "My face is all swollen."

At that, Temena returned and set to work applying lotions to Hana-Ad's face. First, she placed bits of cloth soaked in a yellow liquid on Hana-Ad's eyelids. Then, she washed her face, rubbing gently where the kohl left black streaks. Next, she spread a cooling, rapidly hardening cream, thickly around the swollen eyes. After peeling off the mask, she applied the yellow liquid to the whole face.

From the foot of the bed, Bitar followed the process intently, helping where she could.

After a short time, Hana-Ad asked, "Is what Ashnan said true? Will we die?"

"Who knows what will happen when the time comes," said Temena, laying a soft, cool cloth across Hana-Ad's eyes. "Anyway, it'd be nice to play the harp forever with the old queen. I'd sure like that."

"I don't," Hana-Ad said flatly. "I want to go home. As soon as I see Queen Ku-bau, I'll tell her."

"I wouldn't if I were you," said Bitar as she handed a fresh cloth to Temena.

"Why? What will happen?"

"Just," Bitar hedged, "I wouldn't."

Hana-Ad lay still and let the women work on her face in silence. So she was a prisoner here.

"I think you'll do," said Temena, wielding a last pat of powder with a velvety cloth. "You have a music lesson first—more time for the swelling to go down. You come right back here so I can do a special makeup job on you. Fortunately, the old queen keeps her rooms dim. Unless she chooses to examine you closely again, she won't notice."

"Now," Bitar said, "I'll help you dress. You'll have to hurry. There's no time for breakfast. Queen Ku-bau asked her son for his best harpist to teach you. She's waiting in the room where the instruments are kept."

Hana-Ad entered the instrument room slowly and solemnly, her eyes darting from object to object.

A motherly woman, carrying a harp in her left arm, smiled at her. "Don't be nervous." She drew Hana-Ad to a rear corner and stood facing her.

"This is the way you hold it." She bounced on her toes, the harp on her arm. Handing the harp to Hana-Ad, she said, "You hold it the way I did."

Hana-Ad handled it awkwardly. "I'm sorry."

"Never mind. We are just going to pass it back and forth until you hold it properly and feel comfortable with it. Then we'll talk about the strings."

Once they started work on the strings, Hana-Ad's tongue found the corner of her lips and a frown wrinkled her brow. She looked up in surprise when the slave said, "That's all for today."

"You're looking quite normal," Temena said the moment she saw Hana-Ad. "You just need a little extra work." Temena laughed. "I don't want you to get into trouble. You've only just come. Give yourself time to—"

Bitar flung aside the drape. "Hurry. The old queen's calling for music." She gave Hana-Ad an appraising glance. "You look fine."

With Bitar leading the way, she hurried toward the knot of girls waiting in the corridor at Queen Ku-bau's door. The minute she reached them, Ashnan said, in a patronizing way, "Poor little thing. Was it ill this morning?"

Hana-Ad ground her teeth. Of course, they easily figured out how upset she had been because the slaves were switched from their regular duties to work on her.

With a deliberately disingenuous smile, she turned to Shegunu on her right. "The lesson went well this morning. At least, I can hold the instrument properly and pretend that I'm playing."

"You'll learn quickly," Shegunu said matter-of-factly. Over Hana-Ad's head, her deep blue eyes flashed a disgusted look at Ashnan.

"Line up," said Uttu.

Hana-Ad maneuvered herself next to Kigal. "I want to talk to you," she murmured. Kigal's head dropped and rose in affirmation.

Two by two, the girls paraded into the old queen's chamber, Shegunu and Nidada leading, to stand in an even double line against the right-hand wall.

Half sitting on her daybed, the old queen observed them. "Hana-Ad, change places with Nin-Ad. I want you in the front row."

"That's better." She nodded approval after again surveying the line. "That lavender dress is very becoming, Hana-Ad. You have good taste."

Hana-Ad flushed and glanced at the old queen's dress. Brilliant yellow, covered with gold beads and trinkets, the gown caught every ray of light and splayed it out again. On the floor, near her head, was a large scarlet cushion. Hana-Ad looked up to see five slaves standing against the opposite wall and a small, sunlit courtyard visible through an open door.

At the command to "Play," her attention snapped back to Queen Ku-bau.

Uttu plucked a few opening notes. The others joined. Hana-

Ad imitated as best she could. After a while, in spite of her curiosity about her surroundings, she became restless. Did the old queen really listen? While they played, she pushed food around in a golden bowl. Calling it inedible, she sent it back and demanded cucumbers, fried fish and barley bread. She nibbled at the fish. Telling the girls to sit in a group around her, she motioned to a slave. "Call the dance instructor."

"Here," she said to Hana-Ad, pointing to the scarlet cushion.

Queen Ku-bau's eyes narrowed as she scrutinized Hana-Ad's face before she turned abruptly away. "I have nothing more to report on the reading of the ancient text. My dear friend, the chancellor, was busy elsewhere last night. You will have to wait until tomorrow. I want you to dance for me today. It is my wish that your instructor teach you new dance steps."

She clapped her hands. A lithe young slave in an ankle-length gown of flowing, sheer white linen sailed light-footed into the room and knelt before the old queen.

"You have ten to teach today," said Queen Ku-bau. "Show them the steps."

She glanced at Hana-Ad. "You may have a problem; we'll see."

Though the dance steps fascinated Hana-Ad, she kept tripping over her own feet and was clumsy partnering one of the others. Her jittery nervous motions made her even more awkward.

Queen Ku-bau kept close watch, but said nothing. She slid further and further down among her pillows. As soon as she fell asleep, the dance lesson stopped. The girls tiptoed to their accustomed place and sat grouped against the wall. Slaves moved quietly in and out checking on the old queen. Once, Hana-Ad's stomach gurgled. Ashnan's head went up. Anger surged in Hana-Ad. She couldn't control her stomach growls. She was ravenously hungry. At home, in the morning, the slaves always served a big, hot meal of various meats, grain and fruit, washed down with milk. It was nearly midday, and she hadn't eaten yet.

"When do we eat again?" she whispered to Kigal who sat slightly in front of her.

"When the old queen wakes, she will demand a change of clothes. We will be dismissed to eat something light in our room," whispered Kigal, barely moving her lips.

"Light?" murmured Hana-Ad, thinking that meant fruit.

"It's plentiful."

"Do we have to come back again?"

"Sometimes when she eats later, we have to play. Sometimes the chancellor eats with her."

"Shush," whispered Nidada, poking Kigal.

"Help," screamed the old queen.

Immediately, two slaves ran to her. As they raised her to a sitting position, she noticed the ten girls springing to their feet in a flutter of arms and legs.

"Get out of here," she yelled. "I want help, and I don't need ten gawking children. Ouch! Be careful." She slapped one of the slaves.

Panic struck Hana-Ad. She tensed, ready to run from the room. A hand on her arm restrained her. Nidada whispered, "Walk with me." Two by two, Uttu and Shegunu leading the way, the girls left the presence of the old queen.

Once outside, formality ceased. Ashnan rushed down the corridor and disappeared through the door of their social room.

"It never fails," Nin-Ad pouted. "She always manages to get at our food first and grab all the choicest pieces."

"You might as well stop fretting," said Ninbar. "It always happens, and there's always plenty."

"I'm hungry, too," Nin-Ad retorted.

"Well! Go eat."

At that, Hana-Ad's stomach grumbled noisily.

"Come along," said Ninbar, stepping up her dawdling walk to a rapid trot. "We're all hungry. It's been an absolutely horrid morning, and the old queen's going to be in a foul mood this afternoon."

Ashnan was inspecting the food bowls the slaves had laid on the tables when the others entered. She plunked herself down before the bowl that contained the largest portion. After a glance as Ashnan, Shegunu pulled a chair up to a table as far from her as possible. Kigal, a bowl in one hand, a straw and a tumbler of beer in the other, sat down on a blue cushion.

Hana-Ad looked at a bowl. A thick slice of warm, crusty bread, some roast bass and roast pig, dates and a pomegranate, filled it to the brim. She picked up the bowl and started toward Kigal. Suddenly, she felt Ashnan's eyes on her. Trying to appear casual, she walked past Kigal and sat down at a table opposite Uttu who, after a cursory glance, continued eating. Uneasy, but determined,

Hana-Ad said, "You play the harp beautifully. May I stand by you and try to copy your hand motions?"

Uttu's eyelids fluttered. "You have to stand the way you were placed this morning."

"What a shame. I had so hoped to learn from you." Hana-Ad smiled half-heartedly and ducked her head.

"You'll pick it up quickly," said Uttu. She returned to her food, smiling eyes clinging momentarily to Hana-Ad.

"This palace is large," Hana-Ad found herself saying. "Yesterday, I saw the king on his throne, hearing the citizens' petitions. Do we ever get a chance to listen? I'd like—"

Uttu's hand stopped halfway to her mouth. Two midnight black eyes stared at Hana-Ad.

"You mean—" Hana-Ad cleared her throat. "You mean, we never go into other parts of the palace?"

"Why should we go into other parts of the palace?"

"To—to see what it's like. To see the people, the beautiful things." The words trailed off. What she had intended as friendly conversation sounded stilted. Uttu's stony expression flustered her. Mumbling, "Sorry," Hana-Ad applied herself to her food.

Finished, she returned to her alcove, sat down at her cosmetic table and studied herself in the hand mirror. "If you could reach the temple steps to sit with the virgins contracted to marry," she whispered to her reflection, "and if a man would choose you quickly, you would no longer be a virgin."

She intently examined her eyes and lips. "I could make you really seductive like Ninbar by drawing a little black circle at the corner of your mouth." She twisted her mouth this way and that, trying to be seductive.

Her ear caught a rustle outside her alcove drape and then she heard her name being whispered.

Recognizing Kigal's voice, she said in a quiet breath, "Come in."

Sitting beside Kigal on the bed, Hana-Ad tried hard not to cry. "I don't want to die. I want to go home."

Kigal took her hand and held it tight. "That feeling will pass."

Hana-Ad shook her head. "Never! Never! Never."

"You'll get used to the great luxury we live in. Then you'll realize that if you go home, you'd have to wash clothes, help with the cooking, have no jewels or pretty dresses. You'd be unhappy."

Hana-Ad continued to shake her head. "Do you really like all this so much?" she asked in disbelief.

"Well," Kigal strung out, "I'm used to it."

"Where's your home, Kigal?"

"Here in the city. My father is a scribe in the temple."

"Do you see him?"

"I saw him once, and I never want to see him again." Tears trembled on her lids.

"Why, Kigal?" Hana-Ad leaned toward Kigal, sympathy brimming from her eyes.

"He saw me. But he turned away as if I weren't there."

"As if you were already dead." Hana-Ad sighed audibly. "And you never saw him again?"

"No." Kigal bit her lower lip hard.

"Kigal, I'm going to get out of here. I don't know how, but I am. Would you like to come with me?"

"Oh, no." Kigal visibly paled. Her hand flew to her throat. "You'll be caught and kept in a room alone, without food, for days, until you get desperate and will promise anything."

Hana-Ad knew right then that one girl, maybe Kigal, had tried to escape. She was not alone in her desire to leave Queen Ku-bau. For a few minutes after Kigal left, she stared at nothing. Then she sat up straight, her mouth a hard, determined line. "I can't give up," she told herself, "I won't give up. I'll think of something."

With that, she yawned, lay back against the pillow and closed her eyes.

In her temple room, shortly before noon, High Priestess Nanshe picked up her hand mirror to straighten the bun at the nape of her neck. She agonized with the addition of each young woman. Her own daughter, wherever she might be, was the same age. Nanshe often looked hard at the girls, searching for characteristics that resembled either hers or her husband's. She had known when she became pregnant that she couldn't have a child by her husband. Any offspring of hers should be the god's.

She shouldn't even have been high priestess. It had all happened suddenly one afternoon. She and King Shulgi, her brother, sat talking in the royal quarters. He said, "I can't stand this constant badgering any longer. It seems as if every man in Ur who has an eligible daughter is pestering me to make the girl high priestess. They're all shy young things with no capability for the position." He brought his fist down on his knee.

"I've been secretly doing what I can for the last two months," said Nanshe. "But you really should appoint someone. The temple needs a firm hand."

King Shulgi looked at her. His eyes narrowed as he continued to look.

"Shulgi," laughed Nanshe, "stop looking at me like that."

"I'm going to appoint you," he announced.

"You can't," she half yelled, bracing her feet on the floor ready to jump up. "I'm married to Ur-Lumma."

"You've only been married two weeks. You and Ur-Lumma must live apart. I'll tell him."

"No," she pleaded, extending her right palm toward him.

"I command you. It's decided. Any child you have must be the gods'."

She had wept then, but Shulgi refused to change his mind. He announced his decision in the morning audience.

An uproar ensued. Members of the court told him it was illegal. The high priest raised both eyebrows but held his tongue. Everybody said, "The high priestess is the premier wife of the god. Only the second in the hierarchy at the temple, the god's concubine, is allowed to marry, but not bear children by her husband." They gossiped that Nanshe was a spoiled royal princess with no understanding of the position and no ability. That infuriated Nanshe. She determined to make them regret their comments.

For a short time, she and Ur-Lumma had lived apart. Then, Ur-Lumma started coming to her palace-temple bedroom. They didn't have to worry about being seen. By tradition, the king came to the high priestess once a year in the god's room atop the ziggurat, during the high spring fertility festival. He came as a substitute for the god. Shulgi, who was much older than his sister, had refused to copulate.

As her superb administrative abilities became evident, Nanshe hadn't hidden her love for Ur-Lumma. The problem had come when she found herself pregnant. Her brother would know the baby wasn't the god's. As she was unsure of his reaction to her inappropriate pregnancy, she had carefully concealed her condition and the birth. She didn't know where the tiny girl was placed. Ur-Lumma had handed the baby and a good amount of gold to a trustworthy old slave with instructions never to tell what she had done with the child. The woman had since died. Nanshe still grieved for that baby. She wanted another.

And her nephew, King Idi-Sin, always did his duty. Carrying an oil lamp, he came to her in the bedroom of Nannar's blue-tiled house, dressed in full kingly regalia. He greeted her where she lay on the bed, wearing a sheer white wool gown. Then, by the flickering light of the one lamp, he disrobed, garment by garment, which he carefully folded and placed on a chair before blowing out the lamp. Their perfunctory union over, he slept. She slid from the bed and ran to her ziggurat bedroom where Mesile, her slave, bathed her before she slept.

Thus, she could pass the baby off as the god's. The birth would make the queen's jealousy worse, but put a stop to her constantly nagging her husband Idi-Sin to make their daughter, Shara, high priestess. Queen Nin-Anna would be smarter to marry Shara, a sweet, innocent, rather passive girl, to some eligible aristocrat. She'd have a much happier life if she had a home and children rather than a temple to run.

And as for Nin-Anna's son Shulgi, brother Shulgi had burst with pride when his first grandson was named after him. Fortunately, he didn't live long enough to known the child never developed. Now, at fourteen, he behaved like a five-year old. Yet, Nin-Anna insisted that he be king after Idi-Sin. She kept him in back corner rooms overlooking the river with guards to watch him. That wouldn't prevent Hammurabi, the Babylonian king, from learning the child was an imbecile. His ambassador lived in the palace with the other ambassadors. Plus, King Hammurabi had plenty of spies around.

Laying the mirror on her cosmetic table, she rose. Her sister in law, Queen Ku-bau, napped after her light meal, giving her a chance to go see how the new young girl was doing.

After her own simple repast, the high priestess walked sedately along the palace corridor leading to the old queen's rooms. As she neared the royal suite, the king stormed out of the queen's little audience chamber, followed by the chancellor. The king bowed and rushed away. The chancellor smiled, hesitated and hurried after him.

Nanshe sighed and closed her eyes for an instant. What a nuisance. Nin-Anna had probably been twisting dagger points into Idi-Sin again to make their daughter, Shara, high priestess. He would be an excellent king, in spite of his easy-going nature, if Nin-Anna would only leave him alone.

The king stomped along the corridor, the chancellor at his heels. Seeing his aunt didn't help his mood. As soon as he reached the small, private room where he handled affairs of state, he roared at the chancellor, "Ur-Ilum, my daughter will not be high priestess now. Maybe never. The king, my father, gave the office to Nanshe for life. And she will remain high priestess." He banged the table with the flat of his hand.

"Majesty," said Ur-Ilum, "the princess is ripe. Let me spread the word quietly among the ambassadors that you would welcome a proposal of marriage from one of your brother kings. Many of them have eligible sons, some in line for the throne."

Idi-Sin's head nodded vigorously. "Good idea. Do that."

"Once a contract is signed, the marriage is an accomplished fact."

"True." After some thought, Idi-Sin said, "Queen Nin-Anna will make life miserable for me."

"You have the last word, my king." Ur-Illum bowed from the waist.

"That's all very well for you to say. You don't know what it's like. You have a beautiful, docile wife."

"One that I love dearly."

"I love Queen Nin-Anna, too, but she tries my patience."

"Send her an expression of your love. I, too, shall give her the kind of trinket she likes. We were both hard on her this morning."

Idi-Sin observed his chancellor. A good ten years younger than he, himself, Ur-Ilum exuded health and happiness. His beard was always trimmed to perfection, his clothes the latest style. Even now, he swished his fly whisk with grace. Seeing that made the king realize he had left his whisk in the queen's chamber.

"Guard," he called, "bring me a fly whisk." He flailed his arms. "These flies are a menace. They cover everything. They even sit on the eyeballs of the children I see in the street."

"Many children have sore eyes. I expect that draws the flies."

A bowing guard handed the king a fly whisk.

"Well, I'll take your advice and send my wife a present. You find out which royal house has an eligible son who will be king. I want my daughter to be queen and have sons who will rule."

"Yes, Majesty." Ur-Ilum bowed out.

Eight elegantly dressed, bored young court ladies, in wearisome discussion of what to do while Queen Ku-bau slept, looked up when Nanshe entered. Quickly, they rolled to their knees, their foreheads touching the floor.

"The clothes of our god Nannar need changing," said Nanshe, softening her regal bearing with a smile. "Collect the others." She noted that the new girl was not among those sitting on the floor.

Kigal, always the one to run errands, called softly at Ninbar's drawn drape. "The high priestess requests our presence."

"Coming," said Ninbar.

Kigal ran to Hana-Ad's drape and called, "Hana-Ad!" No answer. She called again.

"Go away," said a groggy Hana-Ad.

In ten rapid steps, the high priestess reached the alcove. She flung aside the drape with a dramatic, masterly motion. "You obey when I call."

An intense furrow between sleep-bound eyes, Hana-Ad stumbled from the bed to the floor.

Kigal, behind and to the side of Nanshe, trembled. In the middle of the room, the other girls turned rigid with fright. Two days among them and she was already in trouble with one of the powerful royals.

Nanshe observed the circles under Hana-Ad's eyes and the drawn mouth. Poor child. She badly needed comforting.

"Guard," she called.

A palace guard prostrated himself in the doorway.

"You have cleared the Processional Way?"

"Yes, Highness."

"Call two other guards, then you escort these nine ladies to the outer court of Nannar's temple at the ziggurat. Stay with them until I come."

He ran off to fetch two guards. At their entrance, Nanshe pointed accusingly at Hana-Ad. "Take her," she said, "to Nannar's temple. I will wait for you at ground level by the steps that lead to the terrace of the outer court."

Hana-Ad toppled onto her face. Beyond crying in her disgrace, she lay still where she fell at Nanshe's feet. The others, unnerved and fearful of the consequences, yet fascinated, trailed after their guard.

Hana-Ad heard murmuring, then nothing. Presently, she raised her head. The two guards stood by the door, watching her. One held a white cord that dangled on the floor.

"Stand up," he said.

Slowly, she stood up, keeping her eyes on the men.

The guard gathered up the cord and walked toward her. She backed away, wary, like a cornered dog.

"Stand still," he commanded. "And put your hands behind your back."

Terrified of what the guards were going to do to her, she complied.

Carefully, he tied the cord around her hands. The soft cord didn't bite into her flesh. It felt loose. If she shook her hands, it would probably fall off. She decided she better not try.

"Follow me," said the first guard.

Jutting her chin out in a disdain she didn't feel, she followed. The guard behind her held the end of the cord. Thus, in solumn single file, they made their way through the empty corridors of the palace.

Entering the Processional Way, Hana-Ad received a jolt. Usually, priests and townspeople crowded along it—scarlet, orange and brown-skirted priests moving in and out between townspeople dressed in brilliant earthy tones, creating a kaleidoscope of color. In the emptiness surrounding her, the footsteps of the guards reverberated noisily off the buildings. Just wide enough for Nannar's cart, the Processional Way looked like any street in the lower city, hemmed in as it was by multistoried buildings. Even the walls, like the palace walls, had lost their magic. They were just mud brick with potsherds stuck in.

She noisily drew in her breath as the guard led her into the enclosure of the ziggurat. The massive, whitewashed tower right behind Nannar's temple dominated the area. The first tier stood on a platform much higher than the platform for Nannar's temple and was accessed by a staircase rising from the outercourt of the temple. She swung her head back and forth, looking at the terraces on the sides of the tower. The second tier tower was much smaller than the first, leaving wide terraces at either end. The tops of trees peeped above the wall on both terraces and a broad passsage seemed to run across the front. The third tier tower, again, looked proportionately smaller. From where she stood, she could barely see the trees on the terraces.

A staircase ran from the platform to the little square, blue-tile house on top. Two perpendicular staircases met at the second tier. What a mountainous thing this ziggurat was, reaching almost to the sky.

Overcome by the majesty of the tower, she bowed her head in praise of Nannar, the moon god, then stumbled.

The forward guard stopped and turned to her. "Be careful."

She nodded and continued to look around. Nannar's temple stood on a raised platform a little taller than the tallest man she had ever seen. And all those buildings, which she knew housed the priests and the school where her brothers had gone, hugged the sides of the enclosure. The engineers who controlled the canal waters had offices here, the tax collectors, the husbanders of grain, the wool administrators, those who ordered the materials necessary for the temple.

Still in single file, they had almost reached the stairs to the temple platform. Hana-Ad saw Nanshe waiting. Glancing up, she noticed the other girls watching her from the raised outercourt. Instantly, she snapped her hands into tight fists and set her jaw, hating them all.

The guards stopped before Nanshe and prostrated themselves, accidentally pulling Hana-Ad face down as they did so.

"Release her," Nanshe said.

Hana-Ad felt the guard fumbling with her hands and the cord drop away.

Then Nanshe said, "You may go," and she heard the sound of booted feet walking away.

"Rise, Hana-Ad," said Nanshe. Gently, she took Hana-Ad's chin between her thumb and fingers. "Dear child, I had to punish you because the others watched. We will join them now. After we finish bathing and dressing Nannar, they will return to the palace with the guards. You and I will walk back together and talk about how you live now and your responsibility. Everything isn't as bad as it seems to you."

A wave of unspeakable sadness thundered over Hana-Ad.

As Nanshe removed her hand from Hana-Ad's chin, she caressed the girl's cheek, turned and started up the staircase. Hana-Ad adoringly touched where the high priestess' fingers had brushed her cheek. Nanshe's shadow made little dancing spots of sunlight. And the sky above suddenly seemed so blue. She gazed in abject adoration at Nanshe who strode calmly up the steps of the high platform.

Passing the nine waiting girls, without a look in their direction, the high priestess said, "Follow me."

Kigal fell in beside Hana-Ad. She lightly drew her hand the length of Hana-Ad's arm. The welcome sympathy made Hana-Ad flush, though her head remained bowed.

A priest, bowing before the high priestess, opened the temple door. In single file, the girls followed Nanshe into the presence of Nannar. In the dim light, Hana-Ad couldn't see much. She moved forward with the others. Suddenly, they stood before the moon god. In one united motion, they fell to the floor in reverence.

Engulfed by a titillating fear in the god's presence, Hana-Ad, on her elbows and knees, could hardly control the trembling of her body. A powerful god like Nannar could strike her dead here on the floor if she offended him. She had never thought much about him before. At home, she had only worshipped the family gods in the first-floor niche. She approached them on her knees and sang softly in a high voice before giving them fresh water, beer or wine, vegetables, and sometimes meat. Occasionally, she burned incense before them.

She never asked for anything. She knew Daid asked his god for help with the animals, for the health of his father, things like that. But she was afraid to ask. Suppose they asked her for something. The idea panicked her. Happily, they never had.

Gathering her courage, she peeked at Nannar.

Oh! He was only a little taller than Nanshe with long hair and great, round, all-seeing white eyes, black pupils, eyes like her family gods. He wore, she noted with her new appreciation of fine clothing, a robe of exquisitely embroidered orange wool. Bowing before him, the high priestess repeated ritual words.

Forgetting her fears, Hana-Ad watched in admiration the beautiful and polished Nanshe speak the words as if she were talking directly to Nannar. Well, she is, Hana-Ad immediately told herself.

"Rise," said Nanshe, turning to the girls.

Ungainly in his presence, they huddled together behind the small food table with its three little bowls that stood before the god.

All around the room, niches contained cult statues. Braziers near Nannar kept him warm. Braziers also heated a bench jammed with small, round-eyed statues that stared constantly at Nannar. Hana-Ad recognized the two central figures in the middle of the front row as the king and queen. The others must represent courtiers or aristocrats who could afford to send little statues of themselves to the ziggurat rather than to one of the many other city temples. Always in the presence of Nannar, the personal statue offered continuous prayer for the care and well-being of its owner, who could then go about his daily business secure in the knowledge that Nannar had him in mind. Incense perfumed the room with a musky fragrance.

"Shegunu," Nanshe turned to the queen's niece, "you have royal blood. You choose a gown for the god. Uttu and Ninbar go to the robing room with her to make sure the gown doesn't touch the floor. The rest of you help me remove this gown."

Promptly, the huddle of girls broke into two groups. Their busyness carried away some of Hana-Ad's awe. Shegunu, Uttu and Ninbar went to the robing room. The rest gathered around the god. Nanshe proceeded to slide the hem of the orange garment up Nannar's body. All around the statue, other hands took the hem and lifted it up.

"Can you taller girls get it over his head?" Nanshe stood back out of the way.

"Kigal, come away. You're too short to help. Bring me the silver ewer and two cloths from the corner." Nanshe nodded in the direction of the left corner behind the god.

"Nidada, put the god's food table against the wall so it isn't knocked over."

"Yes, Princess."

"Today, we will offer Nannar bread, sesame wine, butter, honey and salt. The priests will give him meat later."

"Yes, Princess." Nidada picked up the delicately carved cedar-wood table and slowly carried it to the wall.

The three choosing the garment returned, each holding onto part of a cream-colored heavy linen. Nanshe smiled inwardly. Naturally, Shegunu with her exquisite taste would choose that gown. At Nanshe's side, Kigal held out the ewer.

"Ashnan, you, Nin-Ad and Girsu-Ad hang that orange gown in the robing room. Come right back to help with the dressing."

Nanshe took a cloth from Kigal. She moistened it with sanctified water from the ewer and washed the god's face, neck and arms.

"Kigal," she commanded, holding out the cloth.

Kigal took the damp cloth and handed the high priestess the dry one.

After drying the god, Nanshe motioned to the taller girls to dress him. Kigal returned the ewer and cloths to their corner. Once the god stood gleaming in his garment, the food table with its three little bowls set in place for his convenience, everyone knelt. Nanshe recited closing verses.

She rose and led the girls to the base of the platform stairs where the guards waited. "Escort these nine ladies back to the palace," said Nanshe. She drew Hana-Ad aside. "I will walk with this young lady myself."

"Let us walk slowly," Nanshe said to Hana-Ad after the group had gone.

For a short time, they walked side by side without a word.

Quietly, Nanshe said, "Tell me about your family. Do you have brothers and sisters?"

Surprised by her question, Hana-Ad said, "Yes. They are all married. My three sisters have gone to live with their husbands. My brothers and their families live in our house. My father built a large house on the edge of town near our leather works."

"They are all older than you?"

"Yes, much older."

"When were you born?" Nanshe's heart beat fast.

"The third month after the New Year."

Nanshe forcefully stilled her hungry spirit, her fools' paradise. This girl could not be hers. Abruptly, she said, "I suspect you are dreaming up all kinds of plans to escape."

Hana-Ad gulped and glanced sideways at Nanshe.

The high priestess noted from the corner of her eye that Hana-Ad blushed.

"I would stop that if I were you," she said gently. "It will just make you unhappy, and you won't be able to concentrate on the lessons you must learn. That will upset the old queen. She could make life unbearable for you."

Hana-Ad hung her head. Two big tears, shining liquid spheres, splashed on her gown.

"In any case, dear child, you couldn't succeed. You must realize that."

With an aching heart, Nanshe looked at Hana-Ad. She could just offer friendship. If the girls only realized it, eternal life with Queen Ku-bau was a great prize. Unfortunately, these girls never looked beyond today. She sighed.

"Hana-Ad, you are a beautiful young woman. You have lessons to learn that will be of use to you always."

Again, she glanced at Hana-Ad to judge whether her advice would sink in. The girl had not changed her forlorn demeanor.

"In these next few weeks, you are expected to become a court lady. You will need to learn how to carry yourself with elegance so that the beautiful clothes you wear become you. That dress you have on wouldn't look appropriate on a slave."

Hana-Ad squared her shoulders.

Pleased, Nanshe said, "Hold your head up. Walk like a lady of the court. Proclaim to the world that you are one."

Encouragingly, she continued, "As a member of the old queen's ladies, you have a responsibility to uphold that position."

For the first time, Hana-Ad lifted her head. She turned wide eyes on Nanshe.

"You live in great luxury." Nanshe smiled her captivating smile. "Try and enjoy it."

"But—but—"

"Child, only the gods know what the future holds. And sometimes, I think they change their minds."

They walked along in silence. Beginning to feel more normal, Hana-Ad observed that the walls of the Processional Way hadn't really lost all their magic. They still had a little. And although for their passage, it remained cleared of people, the emptiness no longer made her uneasy. She walked beside the High Priestess of Ur. A royal princess had befriended her. She began to hold her head up and walk like a court lady.

Nanshe gave thanks to Nannar.

At the palace complex, the high priestess summoned a guard. "The lady goes to the quarters of the old queen." She turned her steps toward the temple without a backward glance.

The guard took his place before Hana-Ad. With her head up, at her own pace, she stepped forward.

Eight young women sat positioned around their room to watch the door. Seeing them, Hana-Ad bristled, tension gripping her whole body. Why didn't they leave her alone?

"All smoothed out and lovey-dovey?" said Ashnan, wiggling an eyebrow.

With perfect dignity, Hana-Ad walked to her alcove.

"Oh," laughed Ashnan, "now she's a queen."

Intense hatred shook Hana-Ad. She dropped the drape, thankful for the quiet dimness, and sat down on the bed. Her jaw set. If she had to be a court lady, she'd be the best one of the group.

Never again would she let Ashnan's barbs hurt her. There'd be barbs back. And she wouldn't give up trying to escape.

The chatter and scraping of chairs as the slaves arrived with dinner brought her to her feet. Holding her head at a determined tilt, she pulled back the drape, walked to the nearest table and slid onto the chair. With studied indifference, she put her hands around the full bowl on the table just as Ashnan rushed to examine it. Their eyes met.

"Already she's grabbing the biggest bowl," Ashnan announced in a loud voice.

Everybody stared unbelieving at Ashnan. Hana-Ad noticed that Uttu and Girsu-Ad looked amused.

"Jealous?" Hana-Ad asked, giving the word an upward lilt.

Ashnan's face went blank. The rest of the girls gaped.

"Suit yourself," Ashnan finally managed. She found a table near Ninti.

Later, Hana-Ad sauntered around in the garden. The emerging stars shone dimly in the graying blue of the sky. To the east, she saw the moon starting to rise. She smiled, pleased with her bravery in calling Ashnan's bluff.

Uttu wandered out. "Bravo," she said. "We've all wanted to do that, but were afraid to."

Hana-Ad thought Uttu lovely when she smiled. "I don't know what possessed me. I've never done anything like that before in my whole life."

"Keep it up"

The two strolled arm in arm.

"Life here is certainly different than what I'm used to," said Hana-Ad. "At home, there were times when I had to milk the goats and cows along with the hired help."

Uttu chuckled. "I've done my share of milking, too. So have a number of the others. Not Kigal or Shegunu, of course. Can you believe how lucky we are to live like this? I love it. I wouldn't think of going back. Imagine! The beyond. The beyond forever with Queen Ku-bau."

Hana-Ad deliberately said, "That was an excellent dinner we had tonight. I loved the grilled veal with date wine. And that olive and sesame pudding was the best I've ever had. Mother's was never like that."

Uttu laughed. "I heard that the king entertained over a hundred people tonight.

"What do you mean by that?

"We always eat whatever the cooks are making for the king."

"Really! No wonder it was so good." Hana-Ad licked her lips. Uttu laughed.

"Temena told me that the king asked his mother if I could play the harp to entertain the guests."

Hana-Ad stopped so suddenly that her arm, entwined with Uttu's, almost pulled Uttu over.

"Oh!" exclaimed Uttu, shifting her feet.

"And she wouldn't let you?"

"No. She said she didn't want him to get used to asking."

"Have you done it before?"

"Once. Guards took me to the banquet hall. I played some pieces, and they brought me back."

"Did the guests wear special robes? My father told me that the king gives each guest a gorgeous robe to wear at these banquets."

"Yes. I saw one made out of the very finest wool. It was so beautiful—"

Hana-Ad smiled at Uttu's dreamy expression. "I wish I could play the way you do."

"It takes a lot of practice."

"If only I could go with you."

"I don't know whether the old queen will ever let me do it again," Uttu said shyly.

"I hope we can be friends," Hana-Ad blurted out.

"I'd like that, too. I really don't have a friend here."

They stood in the moonlit garden, smiling at each other.

From just inside the room, a resentful Ashnan kept balling and unballing her fists as she watched them.

4

From beneath lowered eyelids, Kigal watched Hana-Ad and Uttu. She didn't sulk; that was not her nature. She kind of hung, crumpled and aimless. Her lip drooped when Hana-Ad, carrying her full bowl, her straw and her beer, flew as straight and unswerving as an arrow, to Uttu's side. The other seven, after the first baffled reaction to the rapidly flowering friendship, arranged themselves into camps, sat on the floor, and gossiped about the two.

Shegunu remained neutral.

Ninbar and Nin-Ad approved of whatever Hana-Ad did or said. Nidada, who played the harp as beautifully as Uttu and often performed with her, stuck by Uttu and supported her friendship with Hana-Ad.

Ashnan avoided Hana-Ad. But, desperately needing a friend herself, she courted Ninti. Flattered, Ninti responded by becoming Ashnan's staunch advocate.

Afraid, not wanting to offend Ashnan, Girsu-Ad occasionally sided with her, but only occasionally.

None of the girls did anything to disturb the superficial peace that reigned among them, least of all Hana-Ad. She wanted everyone—her nine companions, the slaves, Nanshe, the old queen—to know she had adjusted.

She went out of her way to be helpful. She arranged a cushion for Nidada when her hands were full, or for Nin-Ad when coughing overwhelmed her. Another time, she carried the game board for Ninti and earned a glare from Ashnan for her pains. She grabbed at any opportunity to ingratiate herself with the others.

One afternoon, a cool breeze fluttering the blossoms, Hana-Ad left her alcove to meet Uttu in the garden. Her eyes lit on Kigal, across the room, slumped on a cushion.

As if a blow had struck her full in the face, Hana-Ad stopped in mid-step, rocked back and forth then drew her feet together. By all the gods, how awful. Kigal, of all people to neglect. "Kigal," she called, "don't move. I'll be right back."

She flew to the garden. She didn't even come to a complete halt in front of Uttu. "I have to talk to Kigal," she said, turned and flew back to Kigal.

Slightly out of breath, she managed, "Will you come to my alcove, Kigal?"

Kigal looked up and flushed. "Now?"

"Of course."

"Everybody will see."

"So let them. Anyway, at the moment, it's only Ninbar and Nidada playing that board game." She indicated the two sitting at a table near Nidada's alcove. "Come on."

Kigal pulled up her gown, steadied herself on one knee, and hopped up.

Seated side by side on the bed, Hana-Ad said, "Kigal, because Uttu is my close friend doesn't mean you're not. You are and always will be."

"Oh, Hana-Ad!" Kigal sniffled. "I'm glad."

"So you sit with us or walk with us whenever you want to." Hana-Ad nodded her head emphatically.

"But Uttu—" started Kigal.

"Uttu likes you."

"She does!" Kigal's eyes widened

Hana-Ad threw an arm around Kigal's shoulders and gave her a squeeze. "You go sit by Uttu tonight. You'll see."

Kigal pulled back.

"No, Kigal." Hana-Ad tightened her grip. "I want everybody to see you do it. Then, they'll know you're our friend. And I'll join you the minute you sit down, so you won't have to carry on a conversation. Agreed?"

Kigal slowly nodded assent. The remainder of the afternoon, she worried about what she had to do. When the slaves brought in a large caldron of thick, delicious-smelling stew, she looked around for Hana-Ad. Not seeing her, she looked at the empty bowls winking invitingly as the light from the oil lamps flickered in the soft, flower-scented air. Though her mouth watered, anxiety made her nervous and hesitant. First, she fixed her sandal. Then she realized she had left her carnelian bracelet on the bed. Coming from her alcove, she ran to the door to see if the evening star was yet visible. Again, she glanced around the room for Hana-Ad and saw her fussing with the way her alcove drape hung. Eyes lowered, Kigal carried her bowl of lamb and pig stew near where Uttu sat. Making herself very small, she slid into a close-by chair.

Smiling, Uttu turned to her. "How nice of you to sit with me, Kigal."

Kigal's head went up. She blushed. Before she could stumble trying to say something, Hana-Ad drew up a chair and sat down.

A rustling and shifting of chairs occurred, wood scraped wood, Nin-Ad coughed; nothing more.

After that, Kigal returned to her normal gentle, friendly manner, talking to one group, eating with another, walking with Uttu and Hana-Ad, secure in her position.

Three weeks later, having meticulously counted each day and weighed the effect of her efforts, Hana-Ad tackled Bitar.

"Do you live in the palace?"

"Yes." Bitar laid the day's lavender gown on the bed.

"Where?"

"In the kitchen area with the other slaves."

"Temena and Gula, too?"

"Gula, yes. Temena is married to a free man. She goes to him every night."

"Really? Near the palace?"

"Yes."

Afraid of seeming too eager, Hana-Ad changed the subject. "How did you become a slave?"

"My parents were very poor, and there were seven children. They couldn't feed us."

"So they sold you?"

"Yes."

"And Gula? Did her parents sell her, too?"

"No. Her parents are palace slaves. Well, actually, her mother is dead. Her father helps care for the prince."

"The one who's supposed to be sick?"

"That's enough of that." Bitar cut her off, fearful somebody might be listening.

Quickly, Hana-Ad asked, "Where's the kitchen? I mean, how far do you carry our food?"

"It's a long way. The kitchen is on the other side of the palace. The slaves carry your food along the covered walkway of the audience court."

"That big room where the king sits on the throne under the white canopy with the red figures marching across the cornice?" exclaimed Hana-Ad. "Is that the room you mean?"

"Yes."

Glee swelled within her like the slowly rising river spilling over its banks. "Slaves carry our food right past all those people?"

"Not while the king's holding audience. The slaves come through at dawn while the king is eating his own breakfast. A few people, who've come early for the audience, may be around. After the audience, the king goes to the temple with his court officials, so the place is empty."

"What about dinner?"

"We bring that through the courtyard, too, but then nobody is around unless the slaves are setting tables for a banquet."

"Oh," innocently, "is that where he holds them?"

"If it's a large party."

"Is that where Uttu played?"

Bitar laughed. "Yes. And you stop asking questions. Get along to your harp lesson."

In the quiet of a lazy afternoon, Hana-Ad sat on the garden fountain's ledge, watching Temena and trying to bolster enough courage to set her escape plan in motion. Shegunu crossed the garden and said, "May I sit with you?"

"Of course." Hana-Ad shifted her position to accommodate Shegunu.

"My aunt, Queen Nin-Anna, is pleased with you."

"With me!"

"Yes. I've told her how well all of us are getting along. We think it's your influence."

Hana-Ad reddened with pleasure. "How kind of her," adding shyly, "and you."

"She plans to report this to Queen Ku-bau."

Hana-Ad dropped her eyes. "I seem to be in a little trouble with Queen Ku-bau. She's not pleased with my dancing."

"She realizes you've never done it before. Once you improve, Queen Ku-bau will stop picking at you. She doesn't hold grudges. She won't remember what she said to you."

"Oh!" Hana-Ad sounded so amazed that Shegunu burst into her tinkling laugh, stood up, and tripped lightly toward their social room, the delicate linen scarf around her shoulders floating behind her.

Hana-Ad prickled with delight. Even Queen Nin-Anna thought she had adapted. Confidently squaring her shoulders, she gazed at the flowers, the bright sky, Temena, the sky, and she purposefully stood up.

Temena sat on her haunches near the entrance to the old queen's rooms. Her head rested against the wall; her eyes closed. Though her body looked relaxed, Hana-Ad knew she wasn't sleeping.

She hurried to her alcove where she studied her makeup shells. The rouge shell contained the least. Taking the cover off her powder jar, she scooped the remaining rouge from the shell and mounded it onto the cover. Kneeling on the floor, she pushed the cover against the wall under the bed, checked for any telltale splatter of rouge, and left the alcove with the empty shell.

She walked noisily down the corridor.

Temena opened her eyes.

"Oh, Temena," said Hana-Ad, "I was looking for you. I really don't know what I've done with my rouge, but the shell is empty."

Temena looked at the extended shell.

"I'll bring you another one." She rolled onto her knees and braced herself against the wall.

Elated, Hana-Ad returned to her alcove and plopped onto the bed.

A few minutes later, Temena appeared with a fresh rouge shell.

"Thank you, Temena."

As the slave turned to leave, Hana-Ad said, "You're always so good to me, I can't begin to tell you how much I appreciate it."

Temena turned back to face Hana-Ad. "Great gods, child, there's nothing to thank me for. It's my job to help you."

"Where do you live, Temena?"

"In a little street just outside the palace."

"You mean you can leave the palace? Is that allowed?"

"Of course. I leave the palace every night. I'm married to a free man. We have a son, and he is also free."

"How wonderful for you." Hana-Ad sighed deeply.

Temena studied Hana-Ad. "Don't get any ideas, my girl. I'm here to serve the old queen."

"I didn't mean—But it would be so nice, Temena."

The slave laughed. "Stop right there. You can dream any dreams you want. But the sooner you realize you can't talk about them, the better." With a half smile and a motherly tone, she said, "Keep your dreams to yourself, child."

Temena let the drape fall into place behind her. For an instant, she stood shaking her head, then swiftly returned to the spot in the corridor where she could see everything that went on in the old queen's area.

Hana-Ad sat, her head fallen, her shoulders sagging, crumpled on the bed. She twisted and moaned. She rolled onto her stomach and pounded the bed with her fists. She castigated herself. How could she be so stupid? She had approached Temena the wrong way. What a dolt. Now all was lost. Her chest heaved in one sigh after another.

Presently, she moved to the edge of the bed and straightened her wig. Her face set, her eyes narrowed. Next time, she'd lay her plans more carefully.

5

"*I*s that the duck I caught yesterday?" Ur-Enlila looked up at his wife.

"Yes." Large boned and sturdy, a capable woman, Ninlil placed the bowl of duck pieces, lucious in their light sauce and spicy aroma, in front of him, glanced at Daid and the four younger children, and took her place at the table.

"Roast pig, too." Chirped young Buzu. Holding the alabaster pitcher of milk, she slid sideways into a chair, as the serving maid laid down cheese and the pig.

"I thought this would be a nice change from our usual lamb and grain breakfasts," said Ninlil.

Ur-Enlila smiled as he looked around the crowded table. His eyes stopped at Daid. The boy's motionless fingers held the one piece of duck he had taken from the common pot. He seemed isolated from the rest of the family, his eyebrows drawn together in a scowl, so unlike his usual genial self.

Ur-Enlila caught his wife's eye and raised a questioning eyebrow.

Ninlil shrugged one shoulder. Over the chatter of the other children, she mouthed, "I don't know."

Ur-Enlila swung his head back toward Daid. "What's troubling you, son?"

"It's been many, many days since Hana-Ad went to the palace. She hasn't sent word to anyone."

"She would contact her own family before us."

"I saw her father last evening."

Ur-Enlila jerked his head forward. "Nothing?"

"Nothing." Daid threw his eyes up to the ceiling. "I don't understand it. Can she have forgotten us so soon?"

"It's not like Hana-Ad to be impressed by luxury and glamor."

Ninlil wanted to flatten the tuft of shiny black hair that stuck straight up from the back of Daid's head where he'd slept on it the wrong way. Her first born, she adored him.

"I heard," broke in Buzu, uneasily shifting her clubfoot, "one of our shepherds say that there are some ugly rumors in the city about the old queen."

"Like what?" barked Daid.

"Oh, Daid." Unexpectedly, Buzu started to cry.

Pushing his way around the table, Daid grabbed her shoulder. "What did he say?"

"Careful, Daid." His mother shoved her chair against the wall and gathered the crying girl onto her lap. "Tell us what he said so that your father and Daid can go into the city and learn the truth."

Leaning against her mother's shoulder and twisting her hands, Buzu said, "The old queen has collected ten beautiful virgins to—" She gulped, "to go to her tomb with her."

"You mean walk in her escort?" said Ur-Enlila.

Buzu shook her head.

Daid hung over his sister, his pressed lips white around the edges.

"I don't know what that means," she sobbed. "I was with Nin-Girsu. The shepherd was talking to her."

Ur-Enlila turned to the serving girl in the doorway. "Call Nin-Girsu."

While they waited, no one spoke, no one ate. Buzu sniffled quietly in her mother's arms.

A middle-aged, pleasant-faced woman entered.

"Nin-Girsu," Ur-Enlila said, "Buzu tells us of rumors about the girls taken by the old queen. What do you know of this?"

Nin-Girsu glanced at Daid, looked directly at Ur-Enlila, and said quietly, "They are to die while playing the harp in her tomb."

"No," gasped Daid.

Ur-Enlila laid down the meat he was holding. The whole family seemed to draw together.

Daid broke the silence. "Father, may I go to the city today and find out if it's true?"

"I will go with you."

At the market gate, Daid fastened the donkey his father had ridden to a stone lying on the ground. Ur-Enlila pointed to the left. Six old men, sitting in a row, leaned against the wall. "Let us sit over there beside the old men. I know two of them."

Walking slowly, supported by his son, his massive head and prominent nose in sharp contrast to his crippled body, Ur-Enlila slid to the ground beside one of the men he recognized. Daid squatted beside his father.

When the opportunity arose, Ur-Enlila brought the discussion around to Queen Ku-bau. "Do you think our old queen will keep the new laws?"

"It won't stop her from burying alive those young beauties she is collecting," said a grizzled old fellow.

Daid let out an agonized cry. His father jabbed him with an elbow.

"The king will put a stop to that," Ur-Enlila said simply.

A derisive snort came from the old man. "He can't oppose her in anything. She rules him and, through him, the country. She lies on that bed all day long, has the girls playing their harps and rules her son through the chancellor."

"How do you know that?" asked Ur-Enlila.

"Her slaves talk in the kitchen," interrupted another man.

"What do you mean, how do I know?" demanded the old man. "It's common knowledge. Where have you been?"

Ur-Enlila ignored the question. "Once she's dead, the girls can escape," he suggested.

"Don't blind yourself with that. She's teaching them all about the joy and luxury they'll have when they accompany her to the world beyond."

"And if some don't like the idea?" mumbled Daid under his breath.

"Some may not get indoctrinated," said Ur-Enlila.

"They'll be guarded. They won't stand a chance," the man declared with an emphatic shake of his head.

Ur-Enlila said no more. He stayed to listen to them argue about the old queen's power, the poor economy in the last three years, the lavish spending of the court, the heavy yolk of Hammurabi in Babylon. Slowly rising, he pleaded that he had business to take care of in the city. Daid rose when he did.

In agony, Daid helped his father mount the donkey. He had no idea where they were going or why they were passing through the market gate.

"I don't think," Ur-Enlila said guardedly, "that fellow's right about the old queen. True, she's selfish and gets her way, but she doesn't rule her son. At least not in all things. And not through the chancellor. I've heard that he often opposes her. And the king listens to him."

Wrapped in sorrow, Daid hadn't even heard him.

"I understand now," said Daid, "why Ur-mes took us upstairs to a private room when we arrived for the feast in honor of Hana-Ad's elevation to Queen Ku-bau's maidens and offered to return the marriage settlement. He knew."

"Yes," Ur-Enlila admitted. He reined in the donkey.

The sudden stop made Daid look up. Only then when they had reached the base of the palace platform did he become aware of his surroundings. The great front door swung open. Six leather-skirted soldiers in bronze helmets marched out, two by two, to parade up and down in front of the entrance before marching back inside. A tremendous anger boiled up within him.

"My father," he said between clenched teeth, looking straight ahead, "forgive me. I want to murder the old queen. How can she do this? Somehow, I'll get word to Hana-Ad, so she can watch for opportunities to escape with my help. If necessary, I'll travel to Babylon to ask the great king's intervention. He can make Queen Ku-bau let the girls go, even if our king can't. I'll free all of them."

Ur-Enlila laid an arm across Daid's shoulders. "Let's go home where we can talk about what might be done."

He took a last look at the palace. The major ramp gave access to the palace and the temple. The other, on the long side of the platform, led to the kitchen.

"Did you know that the king has a room for his bathing and his body needs?" Ur-Enlila glanced at Daid for signs of interest.

"A room just for bathing?" Daid's head snapped around.

"The old king wanted two tubs installed, one large for cold water, one small for hot."

Daid's eyes bulged.

"And he wanted a squatting toilet that could be flushed by buckets of water. The pipes into the sewer were made large enough so that a young slave could crawl through and clean them."

Daid grimaced, then turned desolate eyes back to the ground.

Ur-Enlila sighed. "We're almost home. However, we'll stop here."

Daid, who was leading the donkey, stopped and turned, surprised.

"Let me have the little switch you carry." Ur-Enlila slid to the ground. "For some reason, I think it might be useful to draw a map of the inside of the palace. The earth here is well trodden with no vegetation and will take an outline well." He hobbled around a small area, deciding where he wanted to draw.

"You may not know that many years ago, as a very young man, while your grandparents were still alive, I worked as a plumber in the palace. I crawled all through it checking the pipes."

"You did?!" Daid managed when he could pull his dropped jaw back into shape.

Using the switch Ur-Enlila drew a rectangle. "This is the entrance ramp here. The kitchen ramp is back there on the right, the temple on the other side. The king's audience court." He drew a small rectangle near the entrance ramp. "The king's private courtyard and surrounding rooms are behind the audience court. This corridor off the audience court on the right leads to the suites of foreign ambassadors, the large kitchen area, the small courtyard of the crown prince and finally, along the river side, administrative offices. The corridor off the audience court on the left leads to the courtyard and rooms of the old queen. She uses this whole area back of the king's private quarters. There is no entrance to it except this corridor."

Ur-Enlila studied his drawing. "I think that's fairly accurate. Memorize it." After Daid studied the drawing, he brushed his foot across the lines nearest him.

"Obliterate the drawing, and we'll go on home."

Once they reached home, Ur-Enlila gathered the family together and told them what he and Daid had learned in the city. Then, for Daid's sake, although he felt sure that any plan could only bring disaster, he started the discussion on how to rescue Hana-Ad. Hours passed. The younger boys drifted off to bed. Still it went on. At last, Ur-Enlila said, "We have thought of every possible tactic."

Daid slowly shook his head.

Ur-Enlila struggled to his feet. "It's time to go to bed now, son."

6

A pilsin lackadaisically stirred the curds, rested his arm on the edge of the vat, and looked up, trying to pierce the depth of the blue dome above. Then he plunged one hand into the curds, squeezing and fondling the creamy substance. Making cheese always seemed to sooth his whirling mind. "Abraham, up north in Haran, pulls me in one direction," he muttered, "and Hana-Ad, in the palace, pulls me in another."

He wiped his hand on his apron. No word from her had reached her family. Ur-mes seemed to deteriorate by the hour, while Shub became more and more bitter.

Three days ago, he had sat with Ur-mes in the courtyard. Shub stopped in front of them, her hands on her hips. "If you two are talking about Hana-Ad, don't. She is so smitten with the palace luxury that she has already forgotten the parents who love her." Ur-mes just got up and walked away.

"Yahweh," Apilsin cried to the blue air above, "what can I do to relieve their suffering? Am I right to think he should tell Shub the truth?"

Raising his hands, he continued, "Yahweh, why don't you answer me? Since I was a small boy and lived in that big tent outside the city of Larsa, I have trusted you to guide me. Everybody in the enclave—grandparents, parents, uncles and aunts, all us children—prayed to you every day in front of the altar that stood in the tent of my paternal grandfather. We made a covenant with you. Now, I beg that you help Ur-mes and his family in their sorrow."

He caught his breath. Guilt assailed him. Irritation had crept into his voice. Humbly, he asked forgiveness. "And I do have a small request of my own I would lay before you. It has been heavy on my mind ever since the messenger arrived day before yesterday with the letter from Abraham."

He stared at the vat of curds. "Now, old Terah, Abraham's father, is dead. You have blessed Abraham and told him to seek the promised land, a land flowing with milk and honey." Apilsin rolled the phrase around on his tongue. A land given to His people. Bringing them all together in one place seemed phenomenal. A few lived here at Ur, a few on the outskirts of every city in the delta. How many more there were, he didn't know.

"I would go with Abraham, Yahweh. It would be an enormous step, and perhaps not always easy, but if you say 'go,' we go. Everybody in my family would go—my wife and children, my young brother and his family, my old mother, all of them."

He leaned over the vat, his bushy black beard almost touching the cheese, and stared deep into the moving pool of curds. Golden fields of grain stretching as far as the horizon and abundant water laid before his searching eyes. Carrying his staff, he walked forward confidently at the head of his family, the going easy. The river veered to the east, he led northwest. The earth became dry, the walking more difficult. Ankles twisted on stubble. They hoarded water. Still, he held his head high and plodded on, one foot after the other, day after day. The ground started to rise. Suddenly, from nowhere, screaming men bore down on them. Women cowered. Swords flashed. Blood. Pain. Unmoving bodies lay on the ground. He set his face forward and started to climb. On, on, on. Would it never end? A speck appeared in the distance. It grew and grew. His heart pounded. Joy made him weak. Haran. And there, coming to greet him, he could see Abraham. He dropped his staff to stretch out his arms.

The cheese paddle clattered against the side of the vat, as Apilsin dropped it, staggered, and leaped to the side.

"Apsilin," exclaimed Daid, grabbing the paddle as it started to fall into the cheese, "I didn't mean to startle you so."

Apilsin shook his head, unwillingly bringing his mind back from his meeting with Abraham. "It's all right. I was a great distance away." Again, he shook his head. He smiled. "I have wanted to see you Daid." He noted the dark eyesockets, the tight worry lines on Daid's forehead.

"Then I may talk with you?"

Apilsin winced at the sadness in Daid's voice, the absence of his usual bounce, the change in the boy. "Of course, Daid. Do you want to talk here while I work or would you prefer a quiet spot in my courtyard?"

"Here is fine. I'll help you." Daid lifted the stirring paddle and slowly pushed it through the curd mass.

Apilsin watched. A string of expressions flowed across Daid's face in quick succession—helplessness, determination, fury, inexperience, need. He raised eyes that begged for help.

"You're worried about Hana-Ad and what, if anything, we can do to save her, aren't you?"

"Yes, oh, yes," Daid cried in relief. "I've tried and tried to think of a way to rescue her. But nothing is practical. Yesterday, I stood in front of the palace and just felt so completely frustrated and helpless. I could strangle the old queen."

"Rage won't help. We must be patient. If you have faith, Yahweh won't allow one hair on her head to be harmed."

"Even though she follows Nannar?"

"Yes." Apilsin was sure Yahweh had put the phrase about harming a hair of her head in his mouth. He hadn't thought of it himself. It just came out.

"I've been struggling with my belief," Daid said, his eyes downcast. "A kind, loving god wouldn't be so cruel."

"Daid, what makes you think Yahweh is a kind, loving god? He is a severe, austere god, quick to anger, who demands obedience. If you sin, he punishes."

"I don't know what I've done, Apilsin, for Hana-Ad to be killed." In his intensity, Daid stopped stirring the cheese.

"You haven't done anything. Remember, it is you and your actions that Yahweh is concerned with, not Hana-Ad's."

Daid nodded, his eyebrows quizzical. "Can I still ask Yahweh to help me when I want to spirit her away from Queen Ku-bau?"

"Many think it a great honor to live forever with the old queen."

Daid reacted as if stung. "Do you think I'm trying to rescue her when she doesn't want to be rescued? Could she really want to die?"

"I don't know, Daid."

Daid stood motionless and quiet before saying, "Maybe I shouldn't try to rescue her." The next words rose like a cry from his inner being. "I can't stand to let her die."

"Possibly she does want help. We don't know." Apilsin reached for the paddle.

He stirred in silence, searching for a reasonable action that would help Daid. "Perhaps we could meet at my altar and pray together at sundown each day, talk to Yahweh, find out what He wants you to do."

"Yes." Daid's face reflected the first eager, natural reaction he had shown. "I'll come."

Ur-Enlila sat at his doorway. The evening breeze felt pleasant after the heat of the day. His fly whisk lay unused beside him, the ubiquitous flies having nested for the night. His glance swept the sky. "Great God," he murmured, "what can I do? Daid is restless and unhappy. He does his job automatically, his mind on other things. You are my only God. I humbly bow before you and ask you to help him in his need."

"Did you speak, Father?" Daid slid to the ground beside Ur-Enlila.

Ur-Enlila started. Not wanting his son to know the depths of his worry, he said, "I was telling myself how cool the evening was, how bright the stars."

Daid smiled. "The great gods Anu and Enki have decreed a perfect night for the soothsaying priests."

"Let's hope that the Sumerian priests are sufficiently thankful. We can do without sultry temperatures."

Daid let that pass. Looking down at the ground, he said, "Father, I want to spend some time walking around by the steps of the palace temple."

"No!"

"Please, Father. I have prayed to Yahweh for days, asking his help. This seems to be what He requires of me. I will have a chance to listen to the palace scribes and to hear the gossip of the priestesses."

"They are evil. No, Daid. Don't go. They are diseased."

"I have contracted myself to Hana-Ad. I have no wish to be with the sacred prostitutes."

"You know Naram-Sin got a disease from the fourth bordello on the King's Road. The physicians passed a tube of bronze into his penis and poured in a medication because he had been pissing pus. He's in agony."

"Those women are not the sacred prostitutes."

"They're just as bad."

"I'm not going to consort with anyone. Please believe me. I just want to listen to them to see if they have any news of the old queen."

"I forbid you." Ur-Enlila set his jaw defiantly.

Daid's whole body sagged. As long as he lived in this house, he must obey his father. In a voice pitched slightly higher by his fear, he said, "I do not intend to have any dealings with the bordello women, the sacred prostitutes or even the intended brides. My hope is solely to learn. I want, I need, your approval. I'll return each night and tell you what happened."

Ur-Enlila observed his son. For the first time, he was being challenged. Instinct warned him that Daid would not obey him.

"Please, please, Father." Daid quivered in his fear of adamant refusal.

Knowledge that Daid's pleading meant he didn't want to act against his father's wishes finally broke over Ur-Enlila.

He fussed with his fly whisk before saying, "You will still have to take care of the animals."

Daid knew that meant approval. "I will, Father."

He hurried off to sit among the fruit trees at the rear of the house and formulate plans.

Ur-Enlila watched him go. His son's step again had purpose. In his unhappiness, Ur-Enlila picked up his fly whisk and beat the air with it. He didn't like what Daid planned to do at all. He didn't know much about Nannar and his wife Nin-Gal. They were kept remote even to rich people like Ur-mes. The king and the tribe of priests conducted the god's affairs. They showed him at festivals such as the eleven days of the new year and on his own special day. On that day, they dressed Nannar in splendid new robes and took him from his temple home to parade him through the city surrounded by the priests and court officials. That's all the people ever saw of him. They stood along the route in awe before the god's great luminosity.

On the other hand, he had to admit that the followers of Nannar practiced their religion as faithfully as he did his.

Ur-mes prayed with his family as they sat down to every meal. Also, every so often, Ur-mes called his entire household together and conducted a service. Nannar ruled their lives as much as Yahweh ruled his. But Ur-mes feared the power of Nannar. Maybe he was afraid of all his gods. Perhaps fear of the gods made people offer the virginity of their marriageable daughters on the temple steps. Ur-Enlila flinched.

None of the followers of Nannar seemed to mind offering their daughters. Sex was so prevalent—in the street by the bordellos, in the fields, in the public square. Yet the Code of Hammurabi punished a man for defiling a woman. It said something about punishing men who forced a betrothed girl living in her father's house, or who lay with their son's intended. The ubiquitous sex and the code were so contrary, he couldn't make sense of it.

Ur-Enlila sat shaking his head. He simply didn't understand that religion. Yet he acknowledged that other gods existed. Otherwise, why would he have personally buried house gods under the first stones set in place for his house. He slowly scratched his head as he puzzled over it. Then his mind returned to his son.

Daid was young. He would be exposed to all kinds of inducements. Families gave unwanted daughters or daughters they couldn't afford to the god. Those girls were available to everybody for the asking. Ur-Enlila had heard they practiced anal copulation to avoid pregnancy. They lived on the second floor of the palace temple and were supported by the king. Could Daid withstand their siren call?

A sudden thought made Ur-Enlila bellow at the night. Had Apilsin helped concoct this plan—Apilsin, the faithful follower of Yahweh, Apilsin, the man the other followers of Yahweh looked to for guidance? He knew Daid had gone to Apilsin's home every night. The possibility that Apilsin had encouraged his son's wild plan angered him. He snorted, he fumed. Wait a minute. He froze.

Daid had said that Yahweh told him to listen at the temple steps. If Yahweh commanded, he must bow and obey. He covered his face with his hands.

7

"Oh, stop. I can't stand it." Queen Nin-Anna threw her head back and laughed so hard that her voluptuous body quivered.

"You've never said anything so funny." She cautiously touched a gold leaf hanging over her forehead, then smiled, pleased at the jangle of the new bracelet on her arm. "Straighten my wig. I'm sure I knocked the gold band out of place."

The two court ladies circled the queen's chair, checking the position of the wig, the gold headband and the pendant leaves. Nin-Anna's small, red-tinted mouth returned to its natural petulance. For an instant, she closed her sensual black eyes.

Her fingers played with one of her gorgeous new gold and lapis lazuli earrings. If Ur-Ilum thought they would salve her feelings, he was mistaken.

Her husband, King Idi-Sin, had sent the matching gold and lapis lazuli bracelet in a small, perfect alabaster jar—a peace offering. She deserved the jewelry. After all, he had started the argument that day. She lovingly fondled the bracelet. He did have excellent taste.

She had spent a long time considering how she could get back at him. Other than withholding herself, she didn't have any means to do it. He had stymied her wish to make her oldest daughter high priestess, so, at the moment, she couldn't get rid of Nanshe, her primary target. How she hated that woman.

Providentially, Idi-Sin didn't know her feeling about his aunt. But lately, in her exasperation, she had said unpleasant things about Nanshe that had riled her husband.

Though angry with Idi-Sin for not installing Shara by holy rite as high priestess, she realized that her second daughter might be better in the position. Luga would do just as she was told. That way, not only would she succeed in disposing of Nanshe, but with Luga as high priestess, *she* could wield the power.

She licked her lower lip. If the old queen, her mother-in-law, would only hurry up and die, she would be better placed to have some power. As it was, she found herself thwarted at every step. Fortunately, she could often persuade Queen Ku-bau to help her. The old woman still retained some influence over her son.

Nin-Anna glanced slyly around the room. If Shara couldn't be high priestess, she would marry one of the loftiest aristocrats in the land.

A guard entered to announce the approach of her husband, the king. She raised an eyebrow. "Ladies, the sun still has a way to climb. It's unusual for the king to visit me so early. Leave us."

The two ladies, looking like exotic flowers in their gowns of deep yellow and vibrant blue, their black wigs and tinted faces, ran from the room on sandaled feet.

The queen flew to Idi-Sin, kissed his cheek and slipped her arm through his.

Half a head taller and inclined to fat, he gazed sadly at her from heavy-lidded black eyes with the same hangdog expression his father used to have. His gold-embroidered yellow linen gown pulled slightly across his chest.

"My love does not smile at me," she said. "His thick, beautiful, black eyebrows are knit together, and there is a wrinkle on his high forehead. What troubles my heart?"

She led him to the cluster of chairs vacated by the court ladies.

He sank heavily onto a seat, his wide, generous mouth tightly compressed. "I won't waste words. Our son escaped his attendants and succeeded in reaching the main quay."

The queen clapped a hand over her mouth, her eyes wide and rounded.

The hand dropped to her chin. "Did the people recognize him?"

"I don't think so. The palace guards did a good job. Without making a fuss, they surrounded him. They know from his constant demands that he loves grapes. So they stuffed grapes into his mouth before he could announce that he was crown prince. They pretended he had been hurt and carried him off."

"Where is he now?"

"In his room having a tantrum."

"Poor child."

"Poor child!" The king snorted. "He is fourteen, an age when he should be assisting me in my royal duties." He sighed. "I'm afraid, my dear, we will have to invest his younger brother as my successor—and soon."

"Not while Shulgi lives." The queen stamped her foot. "We must find a physician to cure him."

The king's eyes narrowed. His jaw set as he observed his wife. Her determination made life difficult for him, especially when she sided with his mother. "Are you giving me a choice?"

"No," she said in a tone that made him shiver. "HE WILL SUCCEED YOU."

"We owe Ur better than our eldest son. His condition is our sorrow. But we have more than ourselves to consider. Unfortunately, King Hammurabi is a powerful factor. I underestimated him, as did all the other kings of the cities here in the delta. We considered him pedestrian. We answered his letters as if we dealt with the head of a grain cartel. My father told me how to deal with the king of Babylon, and I followed his advice. Look at us now— vassals, even if we're vassals with local freedom."

"That was your father's policy."

"True. But I'm the one who has to deal with King Hammurabi now. He has not changed. My succesor must deal with—"

"King Hammurabi's successor," she interrupted. "You will outlive that old man. We have nothing to fear. The prince WILL become king."

"Madam, we will leave this subject."

"Every time you get into a tight spot, you leave the subject."

"Madam," he said sharply.

She lowered her eyes submissively. This morning might be a good time to visit her mother-in-law.

With flared nostrils, disdain on her lips, Nin-Anna watched his back as he left the room. She stood tapping her foot, her head tilted in listening, waiting for him to get out of ear shot.

"Guard!" she called.

"Majesty." A guard went to his knees in the doorway.

"Ask Queen Ku-bau if I may visit."

As she sailed into the old queen's quarters, surrounded by a retinue of court ladies, she heard her favorite tune. She slightly wiggled her shoulders and gazed around. Her mother-in-law had asked the ten girls to play it to please her. Her spirits jumped at the evidence of a rare good mood. The old woman would help her.

Nin-Anna glanced in the direction of the musicians to see the new girl Shegunu had mentioned. Beautiful in a subdued way. Nice that she wasn't trying to escape. Amazing that any of these girls would want to escape when Queen Ku-bau offered them a life of luxury for all eternity. Luckily, only two had caused trouble. The others had all appreciated the honor.

Nin-Anna went down on one knee before the old queen.

"What is my son doing that you don't like?"

"The word of your son is my law," Nin-Anna said sweetly, wishing she could wring his neck.

"Honored mother, I would speak to your ears alone."

Queen Ku-bau waved, dismissing her ten young women and slaves. To her amusement, she noticed that Hana-Ad stalled to stare at Queen Nin-Anna. Her son's wife was lovely and chose her clothes with taste.

Nin-Anna sent her ladies into the corridor.

"Now, what is it?" said Ku-bau.

"I wished the girls to go out for three reasons," Nin-Anna said. "First, I wanted to speak about the new girl. Shegunu tells me what a treasure she is and how well they are all getting along."

"Really?!" Ku-bau picked up her golden tumbler and sipped. "That hasn't been my impression." So, the girl had settled down. "What else?"

"The king refuses to allow Shulgi to rule. He wants to bypass him in favor of his younger brother."

"Most of the time, I'm willing to do as you suggest. In this case, I think my son is right. What else?"

Nin-Anna pouted. Somehow, she had to force her mother-in-law to back her against the king.

"Well, what else?" the old queen repeated.

Nin-Anna leaned close and said in a hushed voice, "Majesty, I have word that one of my ladies has committed adultery."

Ku-bau jumped slightly, surprised. "Well, put her to the river test. Why come to me?"

"It's a bit delicate."

"Who is it?"

"The pretty wife of the chancellor."

Almost imperceptibly, Ku-bau flinched. That pleased Nin-

Anna. She had caught the old queen off-guard. Now, she'd more easily get her way.

"You have this on good evidence?" Ku-bau said sharply.

"Yes. And I can't bear to face him," she answered.

"So you want me to do it."

"Yes." Nin-Anna edged closer and stroked Ku-bau's arm.

"I don't promise," the old queen said. "I'll see."

Lowering her head in acceptance, Nin-Anna sat back on her heels. Smiling ingratiatingly, she said, "With your approval, I would like to begin planning the marriage of my daughter Shara."

Ku-bau nodded. "Yes, and soon. She's ripe."

"I have suggested to the king she be made high priestess."

"She can't if she marries." Ku-bau slid her eyes to the side. Another of Nin-Anna's tiresome attempts to dispose of Nanshe.

"Nanshe did."

"That was an unusual circumstance. We can't afford to flout the god again. Besides," said the old queen, her eyes boring into Nin-Anna, "Nanshe is an excellent high priestess."

Nin-Anna gritted her teeth. Nanshe, Nanshe, wonderful Nanshe. "Then," she rejoined, "I think my second daughter should be high priestess."

"Excellent idea. In due time." Ku-bau examined a large gold ring set with carnelian. "What does my son say?"

"He balks every time I want to do something nice for our children."

"Eventually, she'll be high priestess; I'll see to it."

"Eventually!"

"Yes, eventually." Ku-bau observed her daughter-in-law. She couldn't fathom Nin-Anna's opposition to Nanshe. She didn't just want the position for her daughter.

"Nin-Anna, we have been through this before. I will not be a party to forcing Nanshe out. But I thoroughly approve of your idea of arranging a wedding for Shara. I will mention your suggestion to my son."

Nin-Anna graciously bowed her head and rose. She hadn't had much success with the old crone. With slitted eyes, she examined Queen Ku-bau. She was becoming unmanageable.

"Thank you, Majesty. It is always a pleasure to serve you." Nin-Anna swept from the room.

Ku-bau remained quiet, thoughtful, worrying about the effect of the adultery charge on Ur-Ilum. They seemed so content.

After a few minutes, she stirred and turned to a slave. "Send me Temena."

Hana-Ad sat on the edge of her bed swinging her legs back and forth, impatiently waiting for Uttu.

"Hana-Ad!" Temena's voice came from the other side of the drape.

Hana-Ad stopped pulling at a hang nail on her thumb and raised her head.

"Come in Temena." She jumped from the bed to her knees and began feeling under the mattress.

"What are you doing?" asked Temena, so surprised she almost forgot her mission.

Hana-Ad smiled. "I have a lovely gold chain that my father gave me. I wanted to put it on."

"Over that heavy necklace?"

"Yes." She continued to search under the mattress.

"You keep it under the mattress?"

"Yes."

Temena eyed the chain intently as Hana-Ad drew it forth, dangled it and played with it.

"I like to have it here with me. Isn't it pretty?" She held it up.

"Yes." Temena nodded slowly, mesmerized by the swaying gold. Then forcibly looking at Hana-Ad, she said, "I came at the request of Queen Ku-bau."

The gold stopped swaying.

"Queen Nin-Anna commented that you wear clothes well."

"How nice of her." Hana-Ad flushed.

"Queen Ku-bau enjoys seeing how well her daughter-in-law dresses."

Hana-Ad became wary.

"But you must not stare at her, even when she is unaware of it. Drop your eyes. Naturally, if she speaks to you, you can look quickly, then look down." Temena went through the ritual expected at court.

"Thank you," said Hana-Ad, the lesson finished. "There's so much for me to learn."

"You pick things up quickly." Temena smiled and turned to leave. "Queen Ku-bau is not displeased with you."

"I wish I could let my father know how good she is to me and what luxury I live in." With bowed head, Hana-Ad fingered the central pendant of the intricate gold necklace she wore.

Temena turned back, intending to observe the girl. But her eyes slid to the gold chain in Hana-Ad's hands. It swayed as Hana-Ad unconsciously rocked. Temena looked back at the girl's face, trying to judge her intentions, but she couldn't keep her eyes off of the chain. Greed licked at her. She had never owned anything so lovely. She longed for it from the depths of her soul.

"She might allow you to write your father if she supervised the letter."

Hana-Ad frowned and shot a glance at Temena. "Perhaps I could write a few words to indicate what I want said, and you could give it to a scribe," Hana-Ad said diffidently, knowing Temena couldn't read.

"It costs," said Temena, her eyes burning on the gold chain.

Without hesitation, Hana-Ad said, "This is all I have. It's yours." She held the chain so it hung full length in front of Temena.

The slave cupped a hand under the dangling gold. Hana-Ad let it drop. Beside herself in ecstasy, Temena draped it over her wrist to get a better look.

Suddenly, fear gripped her. "I can't," she whispered handing back the chain.

"It's yours if you change your mind. I'll find some means of writing what I want said and will have it ready."

Temena bolted through the drape and disappeared. Hana-Ad lovingly laid the chain against her cheek. It hurt to think of giving it away, but better to do that and live.

8

"The old queen wants all of you immediately," Gula announced from the wide doorway.

"I better fix my makeup." Uttu leaped from the floor.

"Me too." Nidada hopped up, knocking over the game she and Uttu had been playing.

Frantic activity ensued as girls dove towards their alcoves, the slaves at their heels.

At her dressing table, Hana-Ad reached for the rouge shell. Her hand stopped in midair; her eyes swept the table. Carefully, she looked around the table's legs and felt under the edge of the rug for the shell. Using one hand to brace herself, she leaned way over to peer under the bed. Not even dust. She stood up, stepped away from her cosmetic table and surveyed the floor, sat back down and rearranged the containers to be sure she hadn't misplaced the rouge. The sound of hurrying feet warned her that time had left her behind. She slapped, pinched and rubbed her cheeks, trying to bring up a high color, quickly powdered her nose, checked the kohl, pinched her cheeks again, grabbed her harp, and joined the others.

Queen Ku-bau demanded an old ballad, telling of the hero Gilgamesh, ancient king of Uruk.

"Start with the part about his search for eternal life," she ordered.

Shegunu began to recite while the others played softly.

Hana-Ad, in the front row, noticed the old queen staring intently at her. She started to get flustered. She missed a beat and tried to recover.

"Hana-Ad, come here," said Queen Ku-bau.

"On your knees."

In that position, Hana-Ad looked directly into the old queen's cold, intent eyes and pouty face. Ku-bau grabbed her chin, turned her head from side to side, stared and abruptly withdrew her hand.

"First, I get good reports of you, then you misbehave. You have been told how you are to appear before me. Why have you not done your makeup properly?"

Hana-Ad stuttered.

"Answer me."

"I— I—couldn't find the rouge."

"Oh!" The old queen reared back. "So you are careless with the things I have given you out of the goodness of my heart?"

Hana-Ad felt hot. Red-faced, she didn't know what to say. Perspiration erupted on the backs of her legs.

"Go stand in the corner." Ku-bau jabbed a finger over her shoulder.

Hurt, confused, head bent toward the floor, Hana-Ad walked slowly to the slaves' side of the room and let her forehead sink into the corner.

Ku-bau turned to Shegunu. "Recite the poem about the beginning of the world. The rest of you," she said in an off-hand manner, "accompany her."

"Once upon a time, there was no *snake*. There was no *scorpion*," said Shegunu. "There was no *hyena*. There was no *lion*. There was no *wild dog*, no *wolf*. There was no *man*. There was no *fear*, no *terror*."

The soft music rose to a crescendo.

"There was only *chaos*."

Hana-Ad kept her unseeing gaze glued on a tiny floor smudge.

"Do the flood," interrupted Ku-bau.

"With the first light of dawn," Shegunu said, "a black cloud came from the horizon. The heralds of the storm led on. Then the gods of the abyss rose up. Nergal pulled out the dams of the nether waters, Ninurta threw down the dykes, and the seven judges of hell raised their torches, lighting the land with their livid flame."

"Stop," Ku-bau ordered, "I don't like that. Start Ishtar and Gilgamesh."

Shegunu thought for a second, then quietly began, "Gilgamesh washed out his long locks and cleaned his weapons; he flung back his hair from his shoulders; he threw off his stained clothes and changed them for new. He put on his royal robes and made them fast. When Gilgamesh had put on the crown, glorious Ishtar lifted her eyes, seeing the beauty of Gilgamesh. She said, 'Come to me Gilgamesh, and be my bridegroom; grant me seed of your body—'"

"Do the search for everlasting life," again interrupted the restless old queen.

"There was the garden of the gods; all round him stood bushes bearing gems," said Shegunu. "Seeing it he went down at once, for there was fruit of carnelian with the vine hanging from it, beautiful to look at; lapis lazuli leaves hung thick with fruit, sweet to see. For thorns and thistles there were hematite and rare stones, agate, and pearls from out of the sea. While Gilgamesh walked in the garden, Shamash saw him."

Queen Ku-bau threw up her hands. "Get out. All of you, get out." She pointed at Hana-Ad. "You too."

Hana-Ad followed meekly behind the others. Uttu and Kigal hung back to walk with her. Uttu circled Hana-Ad's waist with her arm, and Kigal took her hand.

"This wasn't my fault. I have no idea what happened to the rouge," Hana-Ad said. "I haven't touched it since I used it this morning. It was in its place on my table. I wasn't careless." Her eyes filled with tears. "I know the rules. You two have drilled them into me."

Kigal squeezed her hand.

Between clenched teeth, Uttu said, "We'll find out what happened; you'll see."

Hana-Ad dropped her alcove drape behind her. She looked at her cosmetics. The rouge shell lay in its usual place. She closed her eyes and quickly flipped them open. Still, there it lay. She drew her brows together. If one of the other girls had borrowed it—Why would they do that? Each of them had plenty of makeup. And then not to speak up—it was so unfair.

Temena parted the drape. On a small tray, she had a rouge shell.

"But—but I—" said Hana-Ad, startled.

"I heard the old queen scolding you, so I brought you a new rouge shell." Temena held out the tray.

"Thank you." Hana-Ad fervently hoped Temena wouldn't see the rouge shell on the table.

Temena hesitated. "May I see your gold chain again? It's so beautiful."

Her heart thumping wildly at the implication, Hana-Ad retrieved the chain from under the mattress.

She dangled the chain full length before the slave and saw greedy eyes devour it. "Does this mean—" She handed the chain to Temena.

Temena nodded. She ran her fingers over the gold links. "I can remember a few simple words if you tell me what you want me to say to the scribe."

"I'd rather you had something you could leave with him."

"I'll await your decision." Temena handed back the chain and disappeared like magic.

Hana-Ad hugged herself. She could now look for writing material and think about what she would write. Thank goodness her father had taught her basic writing, much to her mother's annoyance.

Later, Bitar came to undress her. "I noticed," she said, pulling the dress over Hana-Ad's head, "your rouge shell on Kigal's table."

"Was— was Kigal's—" She stumbled, glad that Bitar couldn't see her face.

"Hers was there, too."

For a long time that night, Hana-Ad tried to stay awake, struggling with why Kigal took the rouge shell, drifting in and out of sleep, never seeming to remember the perfect answer she found. Finally, giving up—it was all too complicated—she wiggled onto her side and fell asleep.

The following night, she lay wide awake, squirming in the bed. Clay. She needed clay. Unconsciously, she moaned. "Where, oh where, do I get a stylus and a bit of dried clay on which to write?" She lay still, flat on her back. "Would ordinary mud work?" she whispered.

Cautiously, she got out of bed and pushed aside her drape. For a moment, she stared at the patch of moonlight shining through the doorway into the darkened room. Slowly, with outstretched hand feeling for tables and chairs, she made her way toward the light.

Once outside, by the full moon, she could see clearly the flowers and shrubs in the garden. She stooped to feel the soil underneath a clump of bushes. Moist. She scooped up a handful of earth and molded it into a small oblong. It crumbled. She squeezed harder. The minute she released the pressure, it fell apart. She stared at it. Water. It needed water.

Tiptoeing to the fountain, she wet her hand and dripped water onto the dirt. Soon, the mud was pliable, wet enough to mold without being runny.

With a sense of satisfaction, she placed her neat, damp, oblong behind one of the bushes where it would get the sun it needed to dry properly. She even stood still, head raised, arms outstretched, and prayed, "Please, Nannar, don't let the gardener see it. He would probably smash it, thinking it just a clod of dirt."

Alone in the moonlight, squinting at nothing, she murmured, "I need a stylus to write with." She put her hand out and absentmindedly felt the branch of a small bush. "Oh! Oh! A sharp twig might do." In the morning, she'd examine the bushes in spots sufficiently hidden so the broken branch wouldn't be noticeable.

For the next few days, she guardedly watched her lump of mud harden and dry. And she scouted the garden for a twig with the right thickness and strength.

Her heart skipped an ecstatic beat the morning the mud looked dry. Excited and jumpy that night, she pulled out the thin blue gown she had stuffed under the pillow the minute Bitar left her, slipped it on, and lay rigid on top of the bed, listening for the silence of a dark, still room and nine sleeping girls. Once satisfied that the others slept, she flitted eagerly into the garden.

Her spirits at an unsustainable high pitch, she scooped up her dried oblong and laid it on the fountain ledge. With the tip of her tongue clamped in the corner of her mouth, she hurried to a group of three green shrubs near the room on the opposite side of the garden where the old queen confined the girls she punished.

The twig she had selected wouldn't snap. She twisted it and used her nails to try to break it off the bush. She tugged at it for five minutes, then used her teeth to bite it off. At last. It split from the branch with a little snapping sound. She spat out the shredded bits of twig in her mouth. Gleefully twirling the twig, she returned to the fountain. As she picked up her dried mud, it fell in half.

Devastated, she sat on the edge of the fountain and let tears dribble down her face. Tired of crying, she swung one leg back and forth as she tried to think. She sat a long time, numbed, before remembering that the gardener kept a tiny pile of mixed straw and dirt in the corner of the garden.

Scraping some of this mixture off the top of the pile, she worked it into another small mud oblong. She added a lot more water to this one, making it quite wet and sticky, then carefully, almost reverently, placed it behind the bush to dry.

Mud and bits of straw stuck to every finger. "Just like the flour when I kneaded dough at home," she observed.

"I can't go to bed like this." Had she gotten mud on the blue gown? With muddy fingers, she held out the gown. Oh, great gods, now she had made a mess. She hurried to the fountain. First, she washed her hands, then she washed the mud off her thin wool garment. It felt cold and wet against her body. Oops. She gingerly pulled the fabric.

The sound of a table being pushed struck her ear. Oh gods. Somebody fell over a table. She jumped behind the closest bush and squatted on the ground. For what seemed like an hour, she remained squatting. One foot went to sleep. Jerking the leg to change its position, she fell on her bottom with a thud. Terrified, she listened. No other sound reached her. She stood up. The gown, muddy all around the bottom, hit her legs.

The thumping in her chest made breathing difficult. For a minute, she patted her chest and took deep breaths, then ran to the fountain, looked at the tiny bronze fish standing on its tail and trickling water, looked at the gown, stepped up on the ledge and down into the water. She squatted slightly until the bottom of the gown submerged and she could swish it around. After rubbing her wet feet in the grass, she raced like a meteor to her alcove. She grimaced at the feel of the sodden gown as she jumped into bed. Too tired to take it off, she rolled over.

At last—the three days seemed an eternity—her new lump of mud and straw had dried. Stealthily in the silence of the night, she retrieved it from the garden. With a little anguished cry, she realized that to write on the clay, it had to be damp. Rushing to the fountain, she dribbled water across the surface, letting it absorb, until the the clay looked quite wet. Hidden under the bed without sunlight, it should still be workable tomorrow. After that, she'd have to sneak water to her alcove each time she worked at writing— just enough to make the mud damp.

Squirming on her stomach under the bed, she stored her lump behind one of the back legs. There, the slaves wouldn't see it.

For hours on end, in the quiet of the late afternoon, she worked determinedly, resolutely, at writing on the dried dirt. The twig didn't etch the lines for the words sharply in the mud, and the embedded straw got in the way of the twig. She really needed a pointed bronze stylus. This way, she had to do the strokes in two sections, one up, one down. They didn't always meet properly in the middle. And the cross strokes were even worse. The words looked messy. Biting her tongue in concentration, she struggled.

Finally, she finished inscribing the three words she had chosen: caught, death, help. She studied them. A scribe ought to be able to make enough sense out of those to compose a letter so that her father would understand she needed help.

The following afternoon, she nodded at Temena, walked slowly to her alcove, pulled the drape and threw herself onto her stomach to retrieve her bit of writing, then fished under the mattress for the gold chain. She plopped onto the bed, the oblong clay piece in one hand, her chain in the other.

She couldn't sit still. She jiggled. Her back itched. She laid the chain on the bed and scratched her back. She picked up the chain again and was admiring the sparkling gold when Temena walked in, cosmetic jars on a tray. Neither spoke. Hana-Ad offered Temena the chain first, gently swaying it in front of her. The slave placed the tray on the bed and reached for the chain. She touched the end in disbelief. Carefully, she took it from Hana-Ad's fingers and held it against her chest so she could look down and see it glitter. Then she hid it within the folds of a rag she had tied around her waist. All efficient business, she placed the dried, etched clay in an empty cosmetic jar and left the alcove.

Hana-Ad flung herself backwards on the bed, arms spread out, her face ablaze with joy, and sighed. At last, her father and Daid would know. At some point, help would come.

For the next few days, dreaming of her rescue, Hana-Ad went around in a daze of happiness. She did as she was told, but seemed to be divorced from time and place.

"Hana-Ad," Kigal grabbed her arm, "what is it? You seem so, so strange somehow."

"Nothing, Kigal. I'm just concentrating on doing everything right."

Kigal's face questioned that statement.

Hana-Ad laughed and caught Kigal's arm, "Come on Kigal. Let's just saunter around the garden."

The euphoria lasted until the night Temena arrived to undress her.

"Shegunu is staying with Queen Nin-Anna tonight, so I lightened Bitar's load," said Temena in answer to Hana-Ad's puzzled look.

Hana-Ad held up her arms for Temena to pull the lavender gown over her head. As it left her body, she felt something cold slide to her neck. She ducked to look. Her gold chain lay against her skin. She grabbed at it, jerking her body toward Temena, her eyes wide and round, her face distraught.

The slave stood rigid, a warning finger on her lips.

"My husband would not allow it," she whispered. Her eyes became moist. She wanted that chain. "I cannot."

"You didn't give the words?"

Temena shook her head. "He threw the clay on the ground and stomped on it. He said our lives would be forfeit if the old queen ever found out."

Hana-Ad began to cry.

Pulling Hana-Ad onto the bed, Temena cradled and rocked her. "Shush, shush." After a bit, she said, "You know, no girl has ever managed to escape. Gula, Bitar and I would be questioned. There are ways to find the truth." She was gone.

For a while, Hana-Ad sat like a bag of disjointed bones. Finally, she drew up her knees and curled into a ball. Most of the night, she lay that way, dry-eyed and sleepless. During the new day, she moved about expressionless, unfeeling, a wooden statue.

"Hana-Ad, are you sick?" Kigal look worried.

"I'm tired," said Hana-Ad with a dismissing shrug of her shoulder.

Uttu defied Ashnan by choosing the most succulent morsels for Hana-Ad. But Hana-Ad turned them down, not bothering to conceal her disinterest.

By mid-afternoon, the old queen said, "Hana-Ad, go to your bed and await the physician."

She turned to a slave. "Tell Temena to put the girl to bed."

The temple physician examined Hana-Ad. Afterwards, he stood looking at her. She seemed like a healthy enough young woman, though obviously worn out.

"Two days complete bed rest," he said to Temena. "Give her lentil seeds ground with myrrh and thyme dissolved in beer. You will need to get a supply of suppositories. And she is not to eat any onions or milk curd."

After preparing the dose made of lentils, Temena raised Hana-

Ad, supporting her against her own body so she could drink the brew. "Child, life has its ups and downs. Nothing is sure. Only the gods know what tomorrow brings."

Temena settled the girl comfortably before putting a forefinger under Hana-Ad's chin.

"Remember what I said."

The two women looked at each other. Then Hana-Ad nodded. Temena gave her a motherly pat.

"Sleep," she ordered.

Hana-Ad obeyed.

9

A scowling Kigal rushed up to Hana-Ad, cross-legged on the ground beside a small fig tree in the far corner of the garden.

"Hana-Ad, why did you put your hand mirror in my bed-clothes?"

"But I didn't." Hana-Ad's face reflected the confusion of Kigal's.

"I was tired and dropped onto the bed. Something hard bruised my hip, and I recognized your mirror from the design."

"How odd."

A strange expression replaced the confusion on Hana-Ad's face.

"Somehow, it might explain who took my rouge shell."

"Your rouge shell?" Kigal stuck the tip of her middle finger between her teeth as she thought. "How?"

"Bitar found it in your room."

"My room! Oh," wailed Kigal, sitting down beside Hana-Ad. "You thought I took it and didn't say anything to me." She put her hands over her face.

"I didn't say anything, Kigal, because I didn't understand. It wasn't like you to be secretive about taking something."

Down came the hands. "Of course, I'd tell you," said Kigal, incensed.

"I know. I know."

"There was no reason for me to take it," Kigal continued, her feelings hurt.

"Please Kigal, please; it's all right." Hana-Ad fervently hoped Kigal wouldn't cry.

In a minute, when no tears came, she said "If we keep still, whoever is doing it will try again."

"But why would anybody do this?"

Hana-Ad ran her hand back and forth on the dirt. "Somebody is trying to get me into trouble with Queen Ku-bau. But why involve you? Why not hide my things in her own room?"

"Maybe she wants to get me in trouble, too."

"At least, that eliminates a few of us."

"Like me." Kigal sat up straight, her face brightening.

"Yes, like you," said Hana-Ad with a fleeting smile. "And like Uttu and Shegunu."

Kigal counted on her fingers. "That leaves six."

"And I doubt Nin-Ad and Ninbar are involved."

"I think you're right. I don't believe they would do anything so mean. Or Girsu-Ad. So that only leaves Nidada, Ninti and Ashnan."

"Anyway, if any of my cosmetics are missing, can I come borrow from you?"

"Of course."

Both girls smiled as Uttu approached them.

"What are you two huddled about?" said Uttu.

They jumped up. Then, close together in serious whispers, they swore Uttu to secrecy before telling.

"Fortunately," Uttu said to Kigal, "you discovered Hana-Ad didn't put the mirror in your bed before it came to the ears of Queen Ku-bau or she would have gotten in trouble again."

All three looked up as the double corridor doors opened.

The chancellor saw them, smiled and waved. How beautiful they were—the little one exquisite in a pale yellow gown that enhanced her delicate beauty, Uttu and the newest girl in scarlet. Uttu's strong, even features and lovely mouth overpowered the brilliant color and made her glow. The other girl was beautiful, too, but lacked Uttu's presence.

The old queen had summoned him early. He hoped she wouldn't demand he return later. He wanted to go home. Too many days had passed since he had spent an evening with his wife.

"Ur-Ilum, greetings," said Ku-bau, holding out her hand to him. "Happily, you are prompt. Come sit here beside me." She indicated the large yellow wool cushion on the floor.

"What does Your Majesty want with me at this hour?" He turned on all his charm.

"I asked my guards to get your wife to come with you. She hasn't visited with me since—I can't remember when. But they told me she wasn't in the palace. Where is she?"

"She's at home, Majesty. We plan to dine together tonight to celebrate our second anniversary." His wide smile displayed his perfect teeth.

Ku-bau's eyebrows went up. Just two years and already the girl was drifting to other men—if what Nin-Anna said was true.

"You don't spend much time together."

"Unhappily, our duties keep us apart more than we like."

Ku-bau felt a pang of guilt. She and the king both kept Ur-Ilum far too busy. And now, she had to confront him on adultery. She steeled herself. "It isn't good for a young woman to be left alone."

"She isn't alone, Majesty."

"My meaning is, she needs you."

"I don't understand your inference, Majesty."

She noted that his face had become serious and expectant. So he had no inkling.

"There is talk."

"Talk, Majesty? About my wife? Am I supposedly neglecting her?"

"That isn't the talk, but the cause."

He frowned. "Please, Majesty, tell me what you know. I dearly love my wife. I will do whatever I can to make her happy."

Ku-bau shriveled on her couch. "This deeply hurts me to say."

"What is it?" He leaned toward her, troubled eyes boring into hers.

"She is dallying with another man."

"I don't believe it," he exclaimed, getting to his knees.

"I have it from the queen. The queen has dismissed her."

"Dismissed her!" When he could speak, he said, "Who is the man?"

"I don't know, Ur-Ilum. Nin-Anna wouldn't tell me. Only that she had it on good authority. She felt so badly herself that she couldn't face you."

"So she asked you to do it."

"Yes," admitted the old queen. "To my sorrow." She laid her hand on his shoulder. He covered it, sensing the depth of her sympathy.

"May I go, Majesty?"

"Yes." She sighed. "Dear man, my heart bleeds for you."

"Thank you, Your Majesty," he said with humble sincerity.

Ku-bau, upset, closed her eyes as he left the room. Nin-Anna seemed to be loading her with a lot of unpleasantness. First, her constant carping about Nanshe, and now this business with the chancellor's wife. She had asked her son why Nin-Anna seemed to hate Nanshe, but Idi-Sin had sloughed off her questions. "Of course, Nin-Anna has nothing against Nanshe," he had answered. "It's just our children's future she is concerned about." Somehow, Ku-bau didn't accept that. She groaned as she sank back into the cushions on her daybed. What burdens she had to bear in her old age.

While waiting for the slaves to bring dinner, Uttu and Hana-Ad watched Ashnan sail across the room and disappear into her alcove.

"She hasn't acted that important in ages," said Uttu as Kigal sat down on a floor cushion beside Hana-Ad. "She's bursting with some gossip."

"Funny how she thrives on those bits of scandal. They're usually false, and they're damaging, but that doesn't stop her," said Hana-Ad.

"She'll tell us as soon as everyone comes to dinner," said Kigal.

Hana-Ad nodded. "That's when she'll have the largest possible audience."

Ninbar walked into the room, hesitated before her open drape, then joined the three girls on the floor near Uttu's alcove.

"I'm starving," announced Girsu-Ad, hurrying into the room, Shegunu right behind her.

"So am I." Nidada emerged from her alcove.

"You'll get plenty to eat soon," Uttu said with a laugh.

Ashnan was the last of the group to appear. The glow and deep ecstatic delight that had attracted Hana-Ad's and Uttu's attention had faded, but her eyes still sparkled. She sat down quietly.

Ninti sat down on a nearby chair. "How was your aunt today?"

"I just came from her," said Shegunu. "She's been put to bed with a bilious attack. The high priest brought her favorite physician himself and hovered around the bed singing the whole time."

"He has so much power over evil spirits, I'm sure that did as much good as the medicine," said Nin-Ad.

"The physician put his ear against Nin-Anna's stomach. He felt her forehead, looked at her tongue, and thumped her below her navel. She's in a lot of pain and screamed. He ordered purified oil and honey ground up with sunflowers in fine beer. She drank that and vomited. Then he ordered her to eat bread with cream and honey and gave her a drink of sweet wine with two drops of nightshade."

"Ugh," said Ninti.

"Poor thing," Shegunu said. "She looked absolutely green. But by the time she released me to come back, she was resting against her pillows and allowing the slaves to freshen her bed."

"Well, I have some interesting news, too," said Ashnan. "The chancellor's wife has been taken in adultery."

Shegunu glanced at Ashnan in disbelief. His wife hadn't been caught committing adultery. It was only a rumor.

"Poor man." Uttu's cry, straight from the heart, caused Ashnan to blink at her.

"That's awful," said Nidada.

"Maybe it isn't true," said Kigal.

"The chancellor wants her to take an oath in the name of the god." Ashnan looked around, smug in her knowledge. "And he'll take her back."

Shegunu's brow furrowed. She hadn't heard anything about an oath in the queen's suite.

"I have it on good authority." Ashnan pointedly looked at the door. "Where's dinner? It's late."

The next day, hoping to obtain accurate information, Shegunu presented herself at her aunt's bedside. "I'm so glad you have come," said the queen. "I've just been subjected to the most awful experience. The chancellor was here."

Shegunu motioned a slave to lay a cushion on the floor beside the bed.

"I have ordered his wife to prove her innocence by throwing herself into the river."

"But even if innocent, she might drown," said an appalled Shegunu.

"Absolutely not," countered Nin-Anna. "The gods would not allow that. If she were innocent, she would save herself." She straightened the bedclothes. "Anyway, he came to plead for that woman. He wants to keep her. Imagine! I won't have it," she shouted, her mouth hard.

"Take care." Shegunu patted her aunt's leg. "We don't want you sick again."

"I have ordered her confined to their home until she accepts the trial of throwing herself in the river."

Shegunu continued her comforting little pats. Being a captive in that home wasn't exactly a hardship. She had once visited the house before she joined the old queen's retinue. Small, narrow windows with bars of mud brick fronted the street. Behind that facade, the large house, one of the most beautiful in the upper city, extended back, facing a garden. In the entrance, along with the alabaster water jar for guests to remove dust from their feet, a breathtakingly beautiful cup made from one piece of lapis lazuli stood on a tall stand.

Tortoise-shell inlay cast a smooth gloss over some of the furniture, while gaily colored birds sat on branches or flew across the plates of the table service. Fluted gold drinking tumblers gleamed in light from tiny oil lamps placed around the table. And the reed seats of the backless chairs looked much more attractive than carved wooden seats. All during dinner, a harpist played and a man sang from the epic stories.

But forcing that lovely woman to throw herself into the river! And the chancellor apparently believed her innocent. For some reason, Nin-Anna was insisting adamantly she submit to this cruel ordeal.

On a subsequent visit with her aunt, Shegunu learned that even Idi-Sin had objected to the river test. At one point, he had demanded to know Nin-Anna's source for the adultery charge. In answer, she shielded her eyes and said, "It's too hurtful to talk about."

Just five days later, in a great flurry, the chancellor's wife threw herself at the feet of Queen Ku-bau and tearfully declared her innocence. She had broken the queen's order of house confinement, she said, to appeal to Queen Ku-bau personally.

The old queen, taken aback, did not think to clear the room. The ten girls continued to play their harps softly, their eyes, under downcast lids, taking in every teardrop; their ears every sound.

Queen Ku-bau took the young wife's face between her knurled, ringed hands. "My dear," she said tenderly, "I believe you are innocent. But for the sake of the chancellor and his exalted position, I also believe you have the responsibility of justifying yourself by jumping into the river."

"But I will drown," wailed the woman.

The old queen looked sad and lovingly stroked the face for a few moments.

"I can do nothing, child. Queen Nin-Anna is intractable." Then, the stroking hands seemed to raise the woman up and give her a little push away.

The chancellor's wife left as quickly as she came.

Ku-bau turned to her lead slave. "Go to my son and tell him I don't approve of his wife's behavior."

Shifting her eyes to the girls, she said, "Uttu, play. The rest of you dance. Distract me. I'm upset."

They danced for a while before the slave returned. "The king can do nothing," she said. "A messenger came just as I was approaching him. The woman went from here to the river and was swept away."

For an instant, Ku-bau's hands covered her face. "Leave me," she said to the flowerlike, intertwining girls.

In their quarters, the girls could talk of nothing else. How awful. The chancellor's wife was so pretty. They loved each other. The queen was a cruel, cruel woman.

Shegunu kept still. Nin-Anna never maintained strict court discipline with her ladies. This action made no sense.

The chancellor absented himself from court. He stayed secluded in his home and saw no one. After a fortnight, longing for his company, the old queen asked her son to order him back to court. The king refused. Feeling guilty about the woman's death and his unwillingness to anger the queen, he said, "Ur-Ilum will come when he's ready."

Then, one afternoon, without warning, Ur-Ilum appeared at the old queen's door. Uttu saw him first. Unable to control her hand, she plucked a string too hard and lost the beat.

Irritated at the dissonant sound, Ku-bau looked up, saw the chancellor, and audibly groaned.

"Leave us immediately," she yelled at the girls, at the same time holding out her hand to Ur-Ilum.

With as many snatched glances as they could manage, clutching their harps, they hurried from the room.

"He looks awful," Uttu said to Kigal, as they walked along the corridor to their quarters, "and he's such a nice man."

"His face is thin and drawn, and he has deep sockets where his eyes are." Kigal shook her head.

"I do wish the queen had let his wife take the oath," said Uttu, near tears.

The ten girls dispersed to their alcoves, feeling sad and wanting to be alone. Uttu signaled Hana-Ad to follow her. Secreted behind the closed drape, Uttu said, "I don't believe his wife committed adultery. I think she was telling the truth that day she came to Queen Ku-bau. For some reason, Queen Nin-Anna trumped up the whole thing."

"What do you mean?" said Hana-Ad, all wide-eyed innocence.

"I think the queen has designs on the chancellor."

"Uttu!"

10

*I*n her personal chamber on the temple's third level, Nanshe picked up the long-spouted alabaster milk pitcher that her short, dark-skinned slave had set in front of her. Slowly, she poured milk into a fluted gold tumbler and set the pitcher back on the small wickerwork table. "Mesile, have you seen the young man who spends so much time around the first floor? He always looks so sad."

"Yes, Princess," the slave lisped through her hairlip, "I have seen him. The girls tease him and try to entice him."

"Without success?"

"Yes."

"Bring him to me."

Mesile bowed, swiftly left the chamber and returned with Daid before Nanshe had finished her meal of barley soup and garlic in sour cream.

"On your knees, boy," said Mesile, "before her highness, high priestess of Nannar."

He dropped instantly, hoping the intricate symbols of the moon god in the carpet masked his astonishment.

"Rise," said Nanshe, "and tell me what name you go by."

"Daid, Your Highness." He shifted his feet uneasily.

"Don't be afraid. I'm not going to bite you." She flashed a smile.

Observing that she had strong, white teeth like his cattle, he smiled.

"You are constantly at the temple," she said, "but you visit none of the sacred prostitutes."

"I wish to learn more about Nannar," he lied.

"Do you think you would like to be a priest?"

"I—I'm not sure."

"It takes much study, and your parents would have to support you. Could they?"

"Yes."

"While you think about it," she said, noting his hesitation, "I wish you to do something for me."

Daid started to open his mouth, found himself speechless, and flushed.

"Would you like to know what it is?" she asked gently to temper his confusion.

"Yes, Highness." Then, in a rush of words, "I'll do it if I'm able. I'm just a shepherd, trained to care for my father's flocks."

"You're a strong, bright young man. I'm sure you can do it." She signaled Mesile. "Take this food away." Nanshe sat quietly, hands folded in her lap, while Mesile, silent as a cat and close to invisible in her swift motions, telescoped the three little bowls and whisked the milk pitcher off the table.

Rapidly, Daid observed the room furnishings, the narrow, tortoise-shell inlaid bed, the gilded wood table covered with gold and silver jars containing kohl, lip color, rouge and perfumes, returning his attention to Nanshe the minute Mesile closed the door.

"Can you read and write?" asked Nanshe, fixing him with a sharp eye.

"A little, my lady. I can write some and do figures. Just what is necessary for our business."

"That's good enough for my purposes. I want you to take two letters to King Hammurabi in Babylon."

Daid gulped, shifted his feet, tried to speak, gulped again.

She suppressed a smile. What an innocent.

"One letter will go to the official of the court to be read in public. The other is for the king alone, and you will wait for a written reply. Do you think you can do that?"

"Yes, Your Highness." An excited thrill flashed through him. Fiery energy erupted across his whole body.

"Have you ever attended a public session here in the palace?"

"No, Highness."

"I suggest you do. It will show you how to act when you go to the court of King Hammurabi. The high priest of Marduk is known to me. I will give you an introduction to him. He will house and feed you and tell you when to see the king. You are not to mention my errand to anyone. Also, you are not to attempt to see me again. Do you understand?"

"Yes, Your Highness."

"The court holds the public sessions each morning. Attend them. Otherwise, stay close to home and wait for my message."

Daid rushed home. He found his father sitting alone at the dining table. Around him lay the light meal of cucumbers, cold lamb, dates, and figs.

"I have waited for you, Daid. The others have eaten."

Daid blurted out his experience at court. Ur-Enlila's expression changed from eagerness to confusion to suspicion to a closed, hard front. Seeing his face harden, Daid knew his father objected. He felt guilty, but intended to go to Babylon no matter what his father said. He was convinced this was what Yahweh wanted him to do.

However, before sundown tomorrow, he'd seek the advice of Apilsin. If Yahweh objected then, of course, he wouldn't go. But if Yahweh said, "Go to Babylon," he would have no choice.

The sun hung low on the horizon when Daid found Apilsin standing before the horned altar, his head raised in obvious conversation with Yahweh. Silently, slowly, Daid went to stand beside him.

"Welcome, Daid," said Apilsin.

"Something happened yesterday that I need to talk about with Yahweh. I ask your help to be sure of the answer."

Apilsin smiled encouragingly. "What is this thing that happened?"

"The high priestess, the royal princess, asked me to take a message to King Hammurabi in Babylon," said Daid, knowing that whatever he and Apilsin discussed with Yahweh would stay between them.

Apilsin's lower lip dangled. He pulled it back, and it dangled again before he could find words. "To Babylon! To the king! How incredible." For a moment, his face awed, his breath noisy, he stood immobile. "We will talk with Yahweh," he said. Laying his hands on the altar he raised his face to the sky. "Yahweh," he said in a loud voice, "should Daid go to Babylon as he has been requested to do by the high priestess of Nannar?"

Daid laid his hands on the altar and, in an equally loud voice, repeated what Apilsin had said. In silence, they waited. Daid staggered. He thought something had happened, but nothing was different. Yet, he thought— he looked at Apilsin. Humbly, Apilsin faced Daid.

"You must go," he said.

Daid nodded.

On returning home, a pleased but subdued Daid rejoined his father on the ground near the door.

Ur-Enlila didn't look up when Daid squatted beside him. He felt uneasy, worried that Daid would defy his wishes, and he would have to impose discipline.

"My father," Daid said, "I love you dearly."

The statement unnerved Ur-Enlila. How could he enforce discipline?

Daid continued, "I have been a dutiful son."

Ur-Enlila had no quarrel with that comment.

"Apilsin and I talked for a long time with Yahweh."

Ur-Enlila cringed, dreading what his bones told him.

"We are both convinced that I am directed to go to Babylon."

"No."

"Yahweh, help me now," Daid prayed silently. "It's your will I'm obeying."

"I believe," he said quietly, with bowed head, "that Yahweh has told me to go to Babylon. He has not promised to make my way easy. Despite whatever unhappiness I encounter, I must keep in mind the reward."

Ur-Enlila's head snapped up. He stared at Daid.

"And what if there is none?"

"I believe there will be a reward. Therefore, dear father, I must go. My brothers are well schooled to manage without me. Our overseer is excellent." He knelt before Ur-Enlila. "More than anything else in this world, I need your blessing." Daid choked.

Ur-Enlila thought his own breath was going to stop. Slowly, unhappily, he said, "I cannot let you undertake such a dangerous mission without my blessing and my prayers. So you have it."

Daid grabbed his father's hand and kissed it.

"But I'm fearful. You have so little experience of the world."

Daid hung his head but said, "This is Yahweh's will I do. He will watch over me."

With bowed head, Ur-Enlila's deep voice rumbled, "So be it."

Apilsin returned to his horned altar. He faced his own decision: whether to stay in Ur or to follow Abraham to the land that Yahweh would show them, their land.

"Daid's answer has come," he cried. "I need to know what I should do. I beg you to tell me."

Suddenly, he stepped back and looked around. Light sparkled on the canal. A bird bathed in the dust alongside his path. In the distance, men worked at one of the levies in the canal.

Somebody had been near him, listening. That made him uneasy, every nerve in his body on edge.

He sensed another presence. He trembled, he panicked. He turned, his eyes sweeping in every possible direction. Great fear assailed him. He fell on his face before his God.

A voice echoed in the stillness of the hot, sunlit afternoon. "Go to Haran."

11

"Ur-mes collapsed at the dinner table." Apilsin and Daid stood in the sunlight near his altar. "Shub said he fell forward, his arms across the table and his face in his food bowl."

"The poor man," said Daid. "That would embarass him."

"And now, he can't talk."

"He can't talk!" Daid shifted his feet to cover his consternation.

"Slaves carried him to his bed and he lies there unable to move."

"The poor man," Daid repeated. "When did it happen?"

"Yesterday noon."

"How does he eat?"

"I don't know." Apilsin blinked. "I didn't think to ask. Why don't you go see yourself?"

"I will."

On his way to the palace the next morning, Daid stopped at Ur-mes' home.

Shub came to him as he was washing his feet in the vestibule.

"How is Ur-mes?" he asked.

"A little better. To me, he doesn't seem to have improved much." She flung up her head. "But the priest says he's doing well. It will take a long time."

"You must have patience, dear mother," said Daid, following her into the paved courtyard.

"Where is he?"

"In the room on the left." She pointed to the second floor. "I will leave the two of you alone, as I must see to the kitchen."

Flat on his back, Ur-mes lay with his eyes closed.

Daid stood hesitantly beside the bed, fearful of waking him.

Ur-mes opened his eyes.

Daid hung over the bed so Ur-mes could see him and smiled.

Then he drew his brows together in pain as he watched Ur-mes struggle with his speech.

After a few seconds, in halting language, Ur-mes said, "Glad you came."

Slowly, Daid told him that he was going to Babylon. He didn't know just when.

He waited after each sentence to make sure Ur-mes understood what he was saying.

"I intend to present a plea to the great King Hammurabi at his morning audience." He paused again. "I hope what I will ask him will ease your mind and speed your recovery." He saw a spark of interest in Ur-mes' eyes. "I'm going to ask King Hammurabi to force our old queen to release Hana-Ad along with the other girls she holds prisoner."

Shub screamed. She rushed at Daid, grabbing his arms. She shook him. "What did you say? What did you say?" Her face contorted with horror.

Ur-mes groaned.

Daid tried to pull away. He didn't want to hurt her. "Please, Shub."

She started to scream again, raised her hands over her head and ran in circles around the room.

"Shub, stop." Daid caught her arm, forcing her to stand still. "I'll tell you if you stop screaming and listen."

She looked at him blankly then sat down on the floor.

Daid sat in front of her, took her hands in his, and told her as gently as possible the rumors in the marketplace. "It certainly explains why we've heard nothing from Hana-Ad," he said.

Shub's eyes teared.

"I'm going to King Hammurabi. He can make Queen Ku-bau let them go."

She began to sob in great gulps.

Daid rose and went in search of help. He found two of Shub's daughters-in-law grinding grain in the kitchen.

"Come, please," he said. "Shub needs you."

He returned to Ur-mes, the two women behind him.

They helped Shub to her feet and took her from the room with clucks of worry.

At the bedside, Daid covered Ur-mes' hand with his. "I'm sorry she heard me, Ur-mes."

"Is good. Haven't courage to tell." Shamefully, he turned his face from Daid.

Daid stroked his arm. "Now, you can talk about it."

"Call slave."

Daid walked to the balcony rail. A female domestic exited the kitchen and started across the court. "Come to your master," he called to her.

"Hana-Ad," began Ur-mes when the slave stood by him. He couldn't continue. They waited.

Painstakingly, he uttered, "No take personal goddess. Get."

"Where?" said the woman.

"Room."

The slave left the room and returned rapidly, a small, large-eyed, female statue in one of her rough hands.

"Give." Painfully raising an index finger, Ur-mes pointed to Daid.

"No, no," said Daid. "Yahweh wouldn't approve of my accepting another god."

Ur-mes' jaw set. "Personal god watches." Again, he struggled with his speech. "Take when talk with king."

He offered the statue so eagerly, so sure the little goddess would help, that refusal to accept it seemed cruel. Daid's determination not to take the statue ebbed like oil surrounding a burning wick. Yet he feared having the statue might anger Yahweh rather than help. Then his mission would fail.

The slave took Daid's hand and laid the goddess in it.

Daid inhaled sharply. He held a clay female statue with great, round, painted white eyes, huge dark pupils painted over the white. She wore a hat, a boat-shaped neck dress and held a vase for a flower sacrifice cupped in her hands. He hid it in his waistband and hurried to the court.

Daid stood at the side of the great courtyard, watching and listening. An old man, claiming that a tree in his orchard had been cut down without his consent, asked for help.

"Do you know the culprit?" the king said.

"Yes, Majesty. I found the wood cut up and hidden in my neighbor's shed."

"Why would he cut down your tree?"

"He's a maker of wooden objects, and wood has become expensive."

"You should have taken your complaint to a judge."

"I would rather come to you."

"Do you think I will reward you more than the civil judges or local magistrates established throughout the Delta area by the great Babylonian King Hammurabi?"

The old man hung his head without responding.

"I will render a judgment this time. But you are not to come to me again except as a last resort. Do you understand?"

"Yes, Majesty."

Idi-Sin motioned to a guard. "See that the woodworker pays this man half a mana of silver."

"Thank you, Majesty. Thank you." On his knees, the old man repeatedly hit his forehead on the floor.

"Next," said the king.

Begging for justice, a man came forward. He swore that he owed a debt to a merchant. He said, "I gave grain as collateral against my debt. The merchant took from the grain without gaining my consent. I ask restitution, Majesty."

"If your allegation proves true," said the king, "the merchant will have to replace all the grain he has taken and also forfeit the amount he lent you."

Satisfied, the man humbly thanked Idi-Sin.

The king heard one complaint after another. There seemed no end to them.

A veterinary surgeon appeared. "Majesty, I operated on a severely wounded ox. I saved the animal's life, but the owner refused to give me the prescribed one-sixth of a shekel of silver."

"Guard," said Idi-Sin, "go with the surgeon and see that the owner of the ox pays."

Townspeople read letters that pleaded with the king to give aid to a boy whose father had been killed in the king's service; to force the return of a woman who had fled her husband's house and taken refuge in another city; to punish a merchant who had misused the funds entrusted to him by a large landowner; to do this and that for thus and so reasons. Daid boggled at the things individuals asked of the king, as if he had the answer to everything.

Through the entire audience, the king sat regally on his throne and listened. Sometimes, he turned and whispered to the handsomely dressed man who stood at his elbow. After the petitioner finished reading, one of the two scribes on the dais, holding damp clay in one hand, a stylus in the other, crawled to the king's side. Then the king either pronounced judgment right away or dictated a response to the scribe. The scribe sprinkled powdered clay on the letter, wrapped a thin layer of damp clay over the powder to form an envelope, wrote the address, and summoned a slave to take the letter to the kiln for baking.

Daid's sharp eyes also noticed that sometimes the petitioner handed a letter to the official, and read one in public. Those read were flattering and stated the case succinctly. Daid began to get an idea of the politics involved. Nanshe played a dangerous game.

He snickered. What a peasant he was, a dullard. A whole new world opened before him, an exciting world, a thrilling world, a titillating world. He faced it openly, eagerly. He was ready.

12

A sliver of the great orange sun still hung on the horizon. Daid sat on the ground beside his father at the door of their home, watching the outlines of the trees melt into shadow, the light ribbon of the distant canal gray. Absorbed in his own discontent, he sat slumped, unmoving, expressionless. He wanted to be on his way.

"Excuse me, my Father," he said, rising as if the cares of the city suspended across his shoulders. "I'm going to my room."

Ur-Enlila watched him go. His brow furrowed, he shook his head, upset at his inability to shield Daid from hurt. Deep in his own sorrow, his glance started to move heavenward, his eyes widened, and he jumped. In the dusky light stood a temple votary, a thin slip of a girl, hardly more than ten.

"I seek Daid," said the girl.

Ur-Enlila stared, offended. A temple votary here, looking for Daid?

The girl watched him for a bit then repeated forcefully, "I seek Daid." She saw the man's bulging eyes suddenly brighten, his face become expectant.

"Wait in the garden." Ur-Enlila pointed to the side of the house. "I'll send him to you." He struggled to his feet, entered the house and closed the door.

"Daid," he called.

Daid appeared on the second-story balcony. "Yes, Father."

"You're wanted in the garden."

In that instant, the grouchy, short-tempered boy straightened his back. The position of his head announced a purpose, his face alert. He leaned forward eagerly, his hand on the railing.

Ur-Enlila smiled half-heartedly and nodded. Sadly, he hobbled toward the kitchen as Daid bounded down the stairs.

The courtyard was empty when Daid came back in. Climbing the stairs two at a time, he reached his room and opened the small leather-wrapped package he had hidden under his arm. It contained silver and three fired-clay envelopes. He laid them side by side on his bed. The votary had told him to give the one stamped with the seal of Nannar to the high priest of Marduk, to read in the king's audience the one marked "public," and to hand the other to the king's scribe. He picked up the silver and let out a low whistle at Nanshe's generosity.

By dawn, Daid deposited a sack containing the few things he would carry with him by the door—a change of clothing a water skin, goat cheese, fresh bread, dates, olives, figs, and the tiny statue.

Ninlil faced him stoically, determined not to let him know her terror, her desolation, her sleepless nights, her fear that he might never return. But she couldn't hide her eyes from him.

He drew her into an all-enveloping hug. "I'll be home before you know it. You'll see."

Well in control of himself, Ur-Enlila blessed his son. Feeling moisture in his own eyes, Daid grabbed his few belongings and hurried away toward Apilsin's. He couldn't leave without saying goodbye.

"So, the time has come." Apilsin inhaled deeply and let it out. "Whatever happens, Daid, stay close to Yahweh. I'm afraid for you. Yet, Yahweh has blessed your journey." Apilsin wrapped him in his strong arms and released him.

At the quays, ships jostled each other for space. The captains yelled invectives. Oarsmen swore, pulled and backed, trying to maneuver their loaded ships out of the pack. Slaves swarmed over those tied up, either loading or unloading the vessels. One slave, a king's guard before and behind, staggered down a gangplank under the weight of a gold ingot. A small, beautiful pleasure boat clung to the dock. A sailor standing beside it held its rope tightly. The scarlet sail gently fluttered. A pompous male walked across the quay and boarded. The sailor jumped in and pushed the little boat from the wharf. The tublike fishing boats darted between the great galleys or idled in the river. A sixty-foot transport with upswept prow and stern slid majestically toward the gulf. Men hurried in and out of the warehouses along the edge of the river, the slaves in their short woolen skirts, merchants and tradesmen in long, scarlet, yellow or blue skirts, beads dangling around their necks with occasionally the glint of gold.

Daid surveyed the ships. Which might take him to Babylon? He noticed a great lumber-carrying ship, but saw no lumber. A dozen sweating slaves, bent double under huge bales of hemp, cautiously shuffled their feet along the wet gangway, then dumped the bales on the quay where laborers stacked them. The ship's prow pointed upriver.

"Are you going to Babylon?" he called to a sailor on deck.

"Yes. As soon as we finish unloading these bales."

"Can I go with you?"

"See the captain. He's on the prow."

Daid found the captain supervising the packing of ballast. "Move that sack to the right," he yelled at someone in the hold. Wheeling, he noticed Daid. His eyes narrowed into sharp, suspicious points.

In his open, honest manner, Daid said, "I want to go to Babylon." He cautiously extended a bit of silver.

With a furtive glance around, the captain hid the silver in his clothing. "You can sleep on deck, but keep out of the way."

Daid stood on the quay until he saw the captain signal the sailors to unfurl the great sail and lift up the ship's anchor. On deck, as they left the dock, he swallowed hard time after time to keep his heart from coming up into his throat as he watched the outlines of his city fade. How long would it be before he saw Ur again? What would happen in Babylon?

With an effort, he pushed aside his uneasiness to watch the passing shore. All day, he watched the grazing cattle, the waving grain, the empty fields, the houses and little villages, the fishermen, the other ships.

One of the sailors flung himself down facing Daid and said, "We left Babylon in the spring equinox. We always go then because the wind gods blow from west to east at that time. If the winds didn't help us, the voyage would take more than twice as long. Once we find the mouth of the Indus river, we sail up it for days before we reach Mohenjo-Daro. Then, of course, we have to wait until early winter when the wind gods return to Babylon to come home." He shrugged. "We've been gone a year. I'll be glad to get home."

"Is that where you went, Mo—, Mo—?"

"Mohenjo-Daro." He laughed at Daid's confused expression. "It's a huge city, as big as Babylon, a long, long way from here."

"What's it like?"

"It's all built of hard, baked brick, not like our sun-dried brick. Their bricks are only covered with mud. The streets are wide. They're laid out in squares. Some streets all go in one direction, and others cross them. The houses are in those squares, facing the streets."

The sailor chuckled. "It's nice. I liked to walk up and down those streets and watch the people. We unloaded inlaid furniture and gems, wood. Those women really like our jewelry, " he said with a raucous laugh. "I went to the big square marketplace and watched them buying it. They crowd around and poke each other with their elbows. They have long faces and darker skin than we do. Their hair is also black, but sleek and shiny. The women wear it in braids hanging down their backs."

Daid ran a hand through his thick, wavy hair. "Do they have a king?"

"I think so. I'm not sure how that works. He doesn't have an audience the way our king does. I tried to go one day and a guard told me the priest was ruling the city that day. I think that's what he told me. I don't speak their language."

Daid started to laugh.

"What's so funny?" asked the sailor.

"I can't imagine people talking differently. Can they read?"

"I suppose some can. I can't read," he announced, "but I know what our writing looks like. Theirs is different. It's all little pictures."

"I never heard of such a thing." Daid wrinkled his nose and stared out at the occasional woman sweeping the ground in front of her little house. "How can they read something like that?" he asked, bringing his attention back to the sailor.

"How should I know?" The sailor shrugged and went right on talking. "They have a big pool of water in the center of the city."

Daid shook his head. "I can't imagine all these things you're telling me."

The sailor laughed. "It's true. They have the pool near where the important buildings are. It's as big as this ship and covered with bitumen. It's full of water. People walk down some steps and stand in it."

"Did you stand in it?"

"No." The sailor smirked. "I was afraid."

Daid laughed sympathetically, then said, "I thought you were carrying wood. I don't see any."

"It's not the great logs we get in Anatolia. This is rosewood and cedar. I like to go down in the hold and just smell the wood." He raised his head and sniffed. "We picked up copper in Dilmun, the big trading center, on our return trip. Ships bring it from Cyprus to the coast then slaves carry it over the land." He shaded his eyes then moved around to Daid's side. "I can't see with the sun right in my face."

"Have you ever sailed in a ship that brought gold?"

The sailor grinned. "Yes."

"Where does gold come from?"

"Egypt. We docked in the Land of Punt. The Egyptians bring gold down their river, the Nile, to Thebes where their pharaoh lives." The sailor became expansive, feeling worldly before this bumpkin. "From there, slaves carry it across the land to a port in the Land of Punt."

Daid took in a noisy breath and rubbed his arms. "I wish I could see some of what you've seen."

"It's interesting. They walk in long lines. Overseers with long whips walk back and forth along the line. The line straggles in. The slaves stack the gold ingots in even piles on the quay. Our captain stands guard and orders it stowed in the hold. His first officer watches that."

"What do the slaves carry back to their pharaoh?"

"I didn't see that. They are taken to a field outside of town; the overseers to a temple that looks like flower buds."

He added, "The houses are colored like flowers, too. It's beautiful."

"How lucky you are."

"Well, it isn't all that great on the ship. But at least, I'm not a slave. My father sails, so I do. Once, he went way across the great sea to a land south of the Indus river. It took almost two years. They brought back gems for the king. Now, he just goes to Dilmun."

Daid nodded. "I've heard about Dilmun. It's an island at the mouth of our river."

The sailor spread his hands. "I like to go to Dilmun. It's exciting."

"You, sailor," yelled a little, wiry man, "stop the gossiping and get up the mast. Something's caught."

At nightfall, Daid said to Yahweh, "My God, I leave everything in your hands." He stretched out on deck and slept. Once, he woke with a start, thinking someone had been tampering with the thong around his neck, but saw nobody around. The thong still seemed securely tied, and the contents of the pouch on his chest felt the same. He listened for a long time before falling back asleep and heard only the flap of the sail as it lost wind then billowed forth, and the sound of the water as the rowers dipped the oars.

For Daid, time passed, all much the same. He watched the shore and looked for changes in the landscape. When he thought they had traveled enough to have reached the sacred city of Nippur, he sauntered back and forth along one side of the ship then the other, searching for it.

The captain stopped in front of him, startling Daid. "We're nowhere near Babylon, if that's what you're looking for."

Daid flushed. "I was looking for Nippur."

"It's off to the right, a short way up the river. But you won't see much."

"Why?"

The captain answered as if he were talking to a stupid boy. "Because it's not on the river. It's some distance inland. Only on the clearest days can you sometimes make out the top of the ziggurat. So go sit down."

Daid did, on the right side of the ship, where he could observe the land in the distance.

Later, the sailor he had talked to slithered down beside him. "So you want to see the sacred city? It's like Ur without the quays."

"You've been there?"

"Sure. It's nothing—except the temple. That's the home of Sumer's greatest god." He sounded self-important. "I went in, though I'm a follower of Marduk myself."

The sailor slung his arms wide and his face glowed with excitement. "Enlil's house has gold in a band all around the top. Colored stones are set in the gold. There are whole panels of copper." He raised a hand and drew it straight down, as if showing Daid the length and magnificence of one of the panels. "And they have marble rosettes and other inlays."

Daid's eyes became round as a gaming piece.

"Votive figures of stone, silver and bronze are strewn all over one table—lions, gazelles, scorpions. And statues of people are all over another table." He smiled at Daid. "But wait until you see Marduk's temple in Babylon. It's more gorgeous than that."

"It is?" Daid bounced, unable to contain himself.

"Of course. He's the greatest god and watches over Babylon." The sailor thought a moment. "I suppose you follow Nannar?"

"No. I made a covenant with Yahweh."

The sailor considered this. "Then what did you want to see Nippur for?"

"It's the sacred city for all Sumer." His glance swept the distance.

"You can't see anything today. We're past the spot anyway. Besides, one god's as good as another. They're all alike." The sailor sneered.

Daid didn't quite believe that, but didn't feel like arguing.

Early in the morning three days later, the sailors began climbing the mast, coiling the ropes, checking the cargo. Daid sniffed the air. In spite of his nervous fear, eagerness, and impatience, hope rose. He saw city walls in the distance, the ziggurat soaring above them and the tops of green palm trees above the walls. This was Babylon, greater than Ur, the greatest city in the world. The city spread out, mainly on one side of the river. Between the two parts, the river flowed through a tile-covered channel. As the rowers maneuvered the ship through an enormous bronze gate, he spotted Marduk's house on top of the ziggurat. Streets extended as far as he could see at right angles from the street parallel to the river. And, as in Ur, priests and townspeople crowded along them.

Daid stayed glued to a small section of the ship's rail, afraid to move, afraid of getting in the way of the slaves and sailors running hither and thither, pulling at ropes, readying the gangplank.

The captain hurried past Daid. "Get off as soon as we tie up."

Daid looked around for his chatty friend, but couldn't see him.

The minute the gangplank hit the dock, Daid ran off, scared of being knocked into the water by the noisy swarm of men waiting to unload the cargo. Having seen the ziggurat on the left, he started confidently off in that direction.

A yell that he recognized came from behind him. "Good luck."

Daid turned. His chatty companion hung over the ship's rail, waving. Grinning, Daid waved back.

Soon, within the myriad cross streets, the densely packed, four- and five-story brick buildings confused him. They all looked alike. The streets ran in straight lines, crossing each other, so different from Ur. The buildings hemmed him in. He couldn't see the ziggurat over the top of them.

"Please," he said to an old man, "which way is the Temple of Marduk?"

"The streets run northwest-southeast for prevailing winds. Remember that, and you won't get lost. So, the temple is five blocks this way," the old fellow shot out a hand, then twisted his thumb, "and eight that. I don't know how close you can get. Today's Marduk's special day. The high priest and the king will take him to the river."

"Will I be able to see the king?" cried Daid, all but jumping up and down.

The old man laughed. "Maybe. But don't expect to get near him."

Daid thanked the old man and rushed off. To his disappointment, the parade had left the ziggurat grounds; the crowds had gone.

He stood transfixed, staring at the ziggurat. It was just like the one at Ur, but taller. The god's house was bigger, too. Though not by much, he decided. The outer court that gave access to the tower was much bigger, maybe twice the size of Nannar's. The whole enclosure was bigger, too. No wonder, if the men who administered Babylon and those who administered the affairs of other countries had offices here. Of course, some sections would have their offices in the palace.

Soldiers lounged in front of a building on his right. That must be the barracks. And those windowless buildings in the back could be warehouses for the merchants, the same as at Ur.

Priests in either yellow or orange skirts walked across the enclosure in every direction. Some carried small clay jars, some writing implements. One carried a lamb, a sacrifice. Some didn't carry anything. They just hurried along. Others together walked slowly, talking. Daid stopped a thin, worried-looking priest and asked where he could find the high priest.

Blinking rapidly, the priest jeered. "The high priest? You, a smelly peasant?" With flared nostrils, he flipped his eyes up and down Daid. "Go to his assistants. They work over there." He pointed behind him. "The building closest to the ziggurat in this string of buildings stretching to the street wall."

If he smelled, it was the smell of his animals. He couldn't help that. He clenched his fists and angrily watched the departing back of the priest for a minute before turning toward the building indicated.

The first person he found inside directed him to a proud, erect, immaculately robed priest, whose comportment heralded his royal breeding. Intimidated, not sure what to do, Daid dropped to his knees and touched his forehead to the floor.

"Please, I would speak with the high priest," he faltered.

"I speak for the high priest."

"Sire, my instructions were to see the high priest." Daid kept his head down and his eyes on the expensive, exquisitely made sandals on the man's long, narrow feet.

The priest snapped his fingers.

"This peasant wants to see the high priest. Take him where he can wait."

The feet turned soundlessly and moved beyond Daid's vision. A foot nudged his side. He looked up at a shriveled old priest, dark complected, but with scrubbed-pink cheeks. A bony index finger with a long, curved nail beckoned. Daid followed. They walked slowly, the old priest unsteady on his feet, down an endless, empty corridor. Daid became uneasy at the endlessness, the emptiness. He played a serious game of should he or shouldn't he run back, run into the courtyard, escape.

At the very moment he made up his mind to flee, the old man stopped and opened a door. Courteously, he stepped aside and gestured for Daid to enter.

With two steps, Daid reached the middle of a room, bare except for a mat on the floor. Light came from a small, square window cut high in the wall. The sound of wood sliding against wood made him whirl around. He faced a closed door. Grabbing the latch, he rattled it. Bolted.

Too astonished to move, he stood blankly staring at the top of the door. Stunned, his hand still on the latch, he turned to examine the window. Even if he could hoist himself up to it, only his head would go through. He could yell to people on the street.

Moving to that side of the room, he jumped to catch the ledge. The wall felt smooth with no place to anchor his foot. All his muscles straining, he slowly pulled his body up to the window. At last, his elbows out the window, his weight resting on his armpits, he peered down into an inner courtyard. He counted six other windows high up like his, but no door. He dropped to the floor and sat on the mat, both hands cradling his chin. If that old priest brought him food, he could easily overpower him and escape.

He waited. No sound came toward his cell. He got up and walked around close to the walls. Why didn't somebody come? He sat back down and waited. The morning light that had brightened the cell changed, the blue sky taking on a sultry, hot aspect.

The scrape of the bolt being pulled made him jump to his feet. Two young, husky priests in yellow skirts, opened the door. Each held a bowl. Daid leaped toward them, eager to ask why he was imprisoned. They jumped back and slammed the door. Daid stood still. The door opened enough for an eye to peer in.

"Move back," came the brusque order.

Daid backed to the middle of the room. One priest entered while the other blocked the doorway. He set the food bowl near the door against the wall. Then the two priests changed places. Their errand completed, they closed and bolted the door.

Daid salivated and automatically rubbed his stomach. The food smelled good and contained lots of meat and vegetables. The second bowl held beer. At least, the priests didn't intend to starve him. He ate quickly then just sat, waiting for the high priest to send someone for him.

Days went by. Daid became cranky from the inactivity, then depressed with loneliness, then afraid that he was losing his mind. His clothes felt dirty, his skin crawled with dried sweat, even to himself, he smelled. The room smelled of urine from the corner he used. The two priests came regularly with plenty of food, but he was losing his appetite. He begged them to talk to him, to let him wash. The shorter one smiled. They closed the door.

Daid lost the sense of passing time. How many days had he been here? He couldn't remember. The day the young priests came back in the middle of the morning, he was sprawled on the mat in hopeless despair.

"You want a bath?" the taller one said.

"Yes," breathed Daid. After the bath, they would surely take him to the high priest.

"Come with us."

With Daid shuffling between them, the two priests crossed the courtyard in front of the ziggurat to a small building tucked at the base of the temple of Marduk. There, the same speaker said, "Remove your clothes."

Quickly, Daid stripped.

"Hand them to me."

He picked up the skirt he had dropped on the floor and gave it to the priest. The smaller priest then opened a door. This time, Daid didn't care if they locked the door. In the middle of the room stood a large metal basin full of water, warm to his finger.

He luxuriated, he lingered, he lolled in the water, letting it run over his head, into his open mouth, spitting it out like a fountain. When he at last opened the door, the two priests were leaning against the wall. A charcoal-colored thin-wool skirt lay on the floor.

"Put that on," said the spokesman, pointing.

The shorter priest reached out and grasped the pouch that hung from his neck. Daid snatched it away. The other priest grabbed his arms at the elbows and pinned them behind his back. In spite of the pain, Daid struggled, but the shorter priest managed to yank the thong over his head.

Daid collapsed. The priests caught him by his armpits and dragged him to the door of the building where they handed him over to a broad, muscular man wearing the same kind of short, thin-wool skirt.

"Take this man to the palace guards' quarters," the taller priest said.

The other priest, elbows tucked into his sides, holding the pouch in front of him with both hands like a sacrifice, said, "You are a slave of the king of Babylon."

he didn't know where they led. Rushing down an unknown corridor amounted to instant death. He threw up his hands in helplessness and walked back to the door.

Before dawn, a woman crossed the courtyard. Otherwise, he saw no one until Tishrata returned.

He and Tishrata guarded the concubine's door night after night. On the seventh night—was it the seventh? Daid had lost track—a slave he had never seen before came and ordered Tishrata to attend the queen. With sideways glances sliding over Daid, the two men soundlessly walked away. Daid continued to stand at attention. Could he escape? He knew which way the two men had gone to the queen's quarters. He now knew which way the king's guard escorted the concubine.

But the fourth, the only one available to him, he still didn't know where it went. He gazed at the blackness, dreaming of rushing down it, of finding a door that opened onto an empty, dark street that he could glide along unseen until he reached the river. Right in front of him would be a boat heading toward the gulf. He pictured himself sneaking aboard and hiding behind a rope pile.

He sighed and rubbed his eyes. This tiredness caused him to see visions better not seen. They just made him sadder. When last had he slept well? Certainly not since his arrival in Babylon. He started. The woman who opened the door for the concubine stood beside him, a tall, slender slave with pale skin.

"My lady wants to speak with you," she said and led the way through the open door.

Befuddled, Daid followed. They passed into a dimly lit room containing a table, three chairs, a harp, rugs and cushions. Scarlet walls painted with trees and winged beasts cast a rosy hue over everything. He gaped. Never had he seen such beautifully made furniture. He hesitated to look closely at the furniture, but the slave continued walking, and he followed.

In the next room, a delicate perfume emanated from a bowl of white petals. Small oil lamps of painted clay shed a dim light, making the pale blue room intimate. An exquisite young woman with golden skin and dark almond-shaped eyes reclined on the bed. The sheerest of white fabric covered her perfect body. His eyes felt as if they had left their sockets, he stared so.

Her laughter erupted, low and rippling. "Come here, close to me."

She stretched out her arm. He noticed that the motion outlined her breast even more clearly.

Uneasy, hot all over, he drew near.

"Closer," she said when he stopped.

Standing beside her, he looked down into her upturned face;
full, sensual lips, excited glitter in her eyes, a short nose, and a
gentle curve to her cheek that flowed into the soft line of her neck
and round shoulders.

She ran her hand lightly up and down his leg. He quivered.

"You are gorgeous," she said. "Spend some time with me
here, just the two of us. My woman will watch outside."

His whole being collapsed with desire.

"My—my lady," he stammered, "I have a duty to perform.
Forgive me." Mustering all his strength, he turned and hurried out.

Perspiring, distracted, he sat on the floor outside her door
through the rest of the night. With morning, another guard finally
relieved him. He gladly returned to the guards' quarters, but fretted and squirmed as he lay on his mat. He couldn't make his body
behave. He prayed for strength until he fell into a restless sleep.

A hand on his shoulder roused him. He tried to focus his
eyes, making the face above him bleary, but it looked like the face
of the priest who had wrested his pouch from him. This time, he
wore a tall, cone-shaped hat. Instantly wide awake, Daid sat up.

"I've had trouble finding you," the priest whispered, looking
around. He held out an open palm. On it lay the pouch.

Daid looked up, his face a mixture of disbelief, uncertainty,
wonder.

"I have read the letter to the high priest and destroyed it. I
thought that wise. It is best that you have the others in your possession," the priest said so low Daid could hardly hear him. "As
they are addressed to the king, I didn't dare break the envelopes.
If I were you, I'd get them to the king as soon as possible."

"To the king—" stuttered Daid, his mind refusing to function.

"Of course."

Daid checked himself before becoming a complete fool by
asking how.

"Is my silver here?"

"No. The assistant high priest asked me if you had silver. I
gave it to him." The priest pushed the pouch into Daid's hand and
disappeared.

Daid quickly surveyed the area around his mat. Luckily, the sleeper nearest him was snoring and others lay motionless, turned toward the wall as they slept.

He lay down again, the pouch clutched in his hand. He had no place to hide it in this bare room where the slaves ate, played dice and slept. He couldn't secret it under his mat. An old slave taken when Babylon defeated Larsa slept on the mat at night while he guarded the concubine. He couldn't wear the pouch around his neck. That would cause too much comment. He would have to strap it to his waist beneath his short skirt and hope the bulge didn't draw attention. He fell into a rejuvenating, dreamless slumber.

That night, the king's guard came for the concubine. Daid didn't look at her as she left her apartment. The next night also, she spent with the king. The third night, a guard came to take his silent, surly companion, Tishrata, to another assignment. Daid watched the two men walk across the courtyard in the bright night and saw them disappear into the corridor leading to the king's quarters.

He waited nervously, knowing the concubine would send for him. "Yahweh," he prayed, "help me resist her. You are the only god I serve. I have come to Babylon as you told me to do, though nothing is clear to me yet, but I need your help now. Yahweh, I pray to you—"

He felt a finger on his arm.

In the bedroom, the concubine lay naked on the bed. Her nipples, brown against her skin, were standing up. The puff of black hair at her groin was fluffed. She passed her hand lightly over it. "Come," she said. "You would make me happy."

Daid started to sweat. He could feel the dampness on his arms, the backs of his thighs.

She saw his desire, his struggle. Squirming down so that her breasts trembled, she lay flat on her back, raised her knees, spread her legs, held out her arms, and said, "Come."

Pressing his eyes tightly together, his mind crying, my God, my God, help, he rushed toward the door, overturning a table in his wild dash. For a long time, he stood in agony, his body pushed hard against the wall next to the closed door of her rooms. No sound came to him from any direction. At last, his body relaxed, his skin cooled, and he crumpled to the floor, his back against the wall, one leg stretched out, the other raised. He rested his head on his knee. After a while, realizing that he must have slept, he rose and looked around. Silence filled the empty courtyard. He gave thanks to Yahweh and stood quietly until his relief arrived when he returned to the guards' quarters.

Nothing happened the next night or the next. The third night, the concubine shared the king's bed. The fourth night, as he prepared to meet Tishrata and walk to their post, the grayed, scarred old slave in charge of assignments called out to him above the noise of the room. "Daid."

Daid raised his eyes. The huge, muscular slave responsible for all the guards signaled to him from the doorway.

"Come here," he yelled, motioning with his arms.

Daid cinched his wraparound skirt before hurrying to him.

"There's been a fight in the bakery. A female slave has been killed. The cook who did it is acting like a madwoman. You are to help subdue her and stand guard in the kitchen through the night."

"Yes, sir," said Daid, glad to avoid guarding the concubine.

On his return to the room in the morning, he found men standing around in groups, sober-faced. The mats were empty. Nervousness hung over the room.

Daid, alert, glanced quickly around.

"What's going on?" asked another slave coming back from night duty.

A sturdily built, middle-aged man from Uruk, assigned to the king, said, "Our man who guarded the Egyptian concubine has been arrested and thrown into the dungeon. The rumor is he trafficked with her."

Daid's heart pounded. He was the one who was supposed to have been arrested, but they had nabbed Tishrata by mistake. He had trouble getting to sleep.

A slave kicked him awake. "On your feet, and be quick about it. You have to guard the concubine's door by yourself tonight. And don't try anything smart."

Daid snorted. "What are the chances of that?"

"None, so don't start trouble."

Daid looked the man straight in the eye. "Even if I found my way out of the palace, I have no place to go, nothing to barter for food or clothing. My skirt would instantly give me away as the king's slave."

"I don't need your back talk, so get moving." The slave lunged at Daid, his arm raised to strike.

Daid jumped back, made a face, turned and ran toward the door.

"Take care or you'll find yourself under the lash," the slave yelled after him.

Daid walked nonchalantly along the corridor, circling the flare he held. He'd get to the concubine's door when he got there. After handing the flare to the guard he relieved, he leaned against the wall beside the concubine's door. He didn't care whether she came or went, whether the king lived or died, whether he ever moved from the spot where he stood. The quiet night progressed slowly in its empty nothingness and so did the next.

On the third night, the king's guard came to take the concubine to the king. As she left her room, she raised her head and looked at him sharply. Up went her chin. She walked arrogantly passed him.

By the time she entered Hammurabi's suite, she had worked herself into a tantrum. She swept in like a roiling black cloud the instant it releases lightning.

Hammurabi sat serenely, leaning an arm on a table, a golden tumbler full of beer in his long, tapered hand, a half smile playing about the red lips almost hidden by his well-trimmed beard. His high, broad forehead appeared dusky in the lamplight, which blurred the gray at his temples and in his black beard. At the sound of her step, he raised his eyes in anticipation. Seeing her, he put the beer tumbler on the table and said calmly, "You are in a rage, my dove. Come sit on my knee and tell me what troubles you." He held out his left hand to her, the half smile still playing on his strong-boned face.

She seated herself with kittenish movements, the long sleeves of his loose wool robe enveloping her. "Forgive your slave for her anger. She was taken by surprise when she saw the guard tonight. She thought you cared more for your humble dove than to let the man who attempted to molest her go free."

The royal eyebrows rose. "I have not set him free."

"I don't know who you arrested," she said, pouting, but slightly mollified. "I just know the villain stands outside my door, and I am afraid."

He stroked her hair. "You are with me, you have nothing to fear."

"Guard!"

Instantly, a guard appeared in the doorway, dropped to his knees and touched his forehead to the floor.

"Arrest the man who guards the lady's chamber. Bring him and the one you arrested the other night to my audience court in the morning."

The guard bowed and crawled backwards out the door.

"If the first man is innocent, I will let him go. Praise be to Marduk, I have been too busy with diplomats and arrangements for the coming festival to punish him."

"Yes, that is lucky. But I hope Your Majesty will not free the other one. He should die," she said vehemently.

"I will see both of them in the morning." He eased her off his knee and stood up. "Come! I will undress you. You like that."

14

*D*aid knew the king's guards would arrest him. He strained his ears for the heavy tread of leather boots. He squinted into the black mouth of the king's corridor. He stretched his hands around his neck. The sword would be swift. He pictured his head bouncing on the ground and shuddered. Motion caught his eye. Three guards, one in front, two behind, exited the king's corridor. He hadn't heard them at all.

His instinct was to run, but where? He stood at attention beside the concubine's door. The thump of the boots came from the stairs now. Nearer, nearer. They halted right in front of him.

"You're under arrest," said the lead man. "Fall in behind me."

They marched along corridors, down steps, along more corridors, and down more steps. The atmosphere became damp, river dampness. The stone corridor walls glittered with moisture in the light of the flares. In the final corridor, Daid counted four doors before they stopped at the fifth and thrust him in. The door banged shut and the bolt shot home, obliterating the light from the flares, but he had recognized Tishrata in the shadows of the small, dark cell.

He sat on the floor and rested his back against the slimy stone wall.

"Now isn't this clubby," said Tishrata sarcastically. "Perhaps you should suggest the whole guard division join us." He leaned over and yelled in Daid's face. "Can you tell me what the hell we're arrested for?"

"The Egyptian woman tried to seduce me."

Tishrata roared with laughter. "It wouldn't have been 'tried' with me."

Daid closed his eyes and imperceptibly shook his head.

"That's death for you, buddy. You can say your prayers to

Marduk all night for all the good it'll do you." Tishrata made gleeful little bubbling sounds.

"I didn't do it."

"So? King Hammurabi won't believe you." Tishrata sank into thoughtful silence, then said, "I didn't know why I was here. Now I can guess. That was the night you were sent to the kitchen." He yelled, "I'm in all this trouble because I had to guard that foreign hussy and watch over you."

"Why did you have to watch me?"

"Don't be stupid. In case you tried to run away."

"Where would I go? I didn't even know the way back to where we slept."

"How do I know where you'd go?" Tishrata's voice grew more strident. "You're dumber than I thought if you couldn't escape. That Egyptian woman would have helped you."

Daid sat up straight in amazement as the import of that percolated through his mind.

"I could kill you." Tishrata balled his fists.

"What good would that do?"

"It'd make me feel better."

"Then you'd die, too."

"I wouldn't get punished for killing a slave. You're nothing but a stupid peasant."

Daid pressed his lips tightly together to control himself. Any retort might start a fight, to no purpose.

"All right, I won't kill you," grumbled Tishrata, some of the edge off his anger at Daid's calm, matter-of-fact replies. "But you better get me out of here. It's all your fault."

"I certainly will get you out if I can. You had nothing to do with what happened."

Tishrata sneered. "What kind of a trick do you think you're pulling? You're going to try to save me and not yourself? I don't believe you. I sure wouldn't if I were in your place." Tishrata changed his position. "And another thing: You think King Hammurabi will believe you if you just tell him the truth? That's a laugh."

Tishrata put his hands over his face. "If only I could go back to the army. I was happy then, even if I was a slave."

"How did you become a slave?"

"I grew up in the mountains on a sea way north of here. I had lots of brothers and sisters. My father was a fisherman. Our life was hard. I always wanted to be a soldier, so I ran away from home when I was fourteen—I think—I don't really know how old I am. I went and joined an army. I didn't know whose army it was. And I didn't care. It was an army. But in my very first battle, against Babylon, I was captured."

"So you've been a slave a long time."

"Maybe seven years. It hasn't been bad—until you came along. I was lucky. I was part of the king's take. We got marched down here to Babylon, and I was made a guard." He snorted explosively. "For this."

"I'm sorry," Daid said, not knowing what else to say.

Tishrata became expansive, repeating what he heard from the guards he gambled with. "Kings send their daughters here to King Hammurabi as hostages for their own good behavior. Our king is a great king, and they're afraid of him. That concubine who has caused us all these problems is the daughter of the king of Egypt. But King Hammurabi'll tire of her like all the rest."

"I'm a soldier," he said after a short silence. "I wish the king would go on campaign again. I'd go with him. I'd pledge my life to him, anything he wanted, to go with him. But this hanging around the palace and watching his women is only for the gutless."

Tishrata had started on his usual tirade. Daid, bored, shifted his back to one of the great foundation stones and dozed.

Suddenly, light penetrated his eyelids and a foot nudged his buttocks.

"Are we getting out of here?" Tishrata scrambled to his feet.

"It may be worse; only the gods know," said a shadowy form holding a flare.

"Remember your promise," Tishrata whispered to Daid.

"Silence," commanded a guard.

In the corridor, four guards surrounded them. The guard holding the flare led, one immediately in front of Tishrata and Daid, two behind. That way, they marched up several flights of stairs and along a corridor. Suddenly, the corridor ended in one corner of the king's audience court.

The king sat on a red-and-gold throne set in the middle of an imposing, ten-foot long dais centered on one of the walls of the court. Capitals painted in colorful floral designs topped red pillars that supported the blue-and-gold canopy above him.

Daid grunted. The guard in front whirled and flashed his sword. "One more sound out of you and—"

Daid cowered and bumped Tishrata. Tishrata shoved him. The guard turned on Tishrata.

Moving slightly forward, Daid blinked at the light pouring into the open court. Its brightness obliterated the demarcation between the blue canopy and the blue of the cloudless sky.

"Forward and on your knees," commanded the guard. Handing the flare to a slave, he grabbed an arm of each prisoner and pushed them toward the dais.

Daid kept staring at the king, trying to read his mind.

Hammurabi had dark, penetrating eyes, slightly hidden by the projecting brim of his hat. He sat with one leg stretched before him, the other planted solidly on a red and gold footstool. His right elbow rested on the throne's arm and his chin rested on the knuckles of his raised right hand. He looked thoughtful, intelligent, masterful and regal. Daid quailed.

His chancellor stood at his right shoulder. Two scribes sat cross-legged behind the chancellor, two on the other side of the king. Each held a bronze stylus in one hand, wet clay in the other. Behind them stood three guards, straight and still against the wall.

Pushed from behind, Daid fell on his face and heard Tishrata's body hit the paving. Then nothing. He lay full length, his arms stretched over his head as he had flung them up to break his fall. The silence made him jittery. They must be plotting something awful. Yahweh, Yahweh, he pleaded.

Hammurabi observed the two prostrate figures on the floor below him. The one with the sloping eyes, a trait common to Sumerians, probably came from one of the cities in the delta. He was young, too, maybe sixteen or seventeen. His face had an innocent, open demeanor, and he had only a trace of a beard.

The other man, he judged to be older, maybe twenty-three or four. His blue eyes indicated a northern tribe. A stupid face, angry and frightened, bearded in the Babylonian fashion. This fellow would not have spoken to Nefert, his Egyptian kitten. She was so far above his station it wouldn't have occurred to him. The younger man, yes. But had he? The young man's face had expressed so much awe as he entered the audience court that Hammurabi doubted it. He would be shy around anybody so close to power, too nervous to speak to his kitten, let alone to seduce her.

Also, Nefert may have been seeking a young, energetic body. Being turned down would account for her rage.

He motioned a guard to approach him. "Which one was arrested last night?"

"The man on your right, Majesty."

"Take the other to the guards. Assign him to the city wall for
the moment."

The scribe nearest the king rapidly wrote on his wet clay and
handed it to the guard.

The king rose. As he passed his chancellor, he said, "Bring the
young fellow to me. I wish to speak to him alone," and disappeared through a door in the wall behind the throne.

Daid heard someone walk across the dais and jump. Steps
came near and someone said, "Get up."

He started to move.

A sandal poked him. "Not you."

He heard Tishrata rise and the soft shuffling of feet.

Next, somebody above him said, "Follow me."

Instantly on his feet, he found himself facing the sharp scrutiny of a man he judged to be his father's age, more elegantly
dressed than even King Idi-Sin.

The chancellor read Daid's eyes, smiled, and turned.

Head bent slightly, Daid followed him into a tiny, bright yellow room with painted miniature soldiers in reds and browns
marching around the walls. The king sat on the only chair, his
long, thin face serious, his arms folded in his lap, his feet on a
gilded foot stool.

In an instant, Daid imprinted on his mind a detailed picture
of Hammurabi: the yellow garment of the finest wool; from the
neckline, across his body to the floor and all around the hem,
delicate embroidery flashing brilliant colors; a double-stranded gold
necklace hung around his neck, the chain ending in a large gold
disk which lay against his chest; two female deities, sculpted on its
surface, held symbols that Daid couldn't make out in hands that
reached toward the sun god; the sun god's golden rays exuber-
antly fanned across the background, enveloping the two deities.

Unlike Idi-Sin's rounded hat brim, the hat Hammurabi wore
jetted straight out, dropped three inches at a perpendicular angle,
and jetted back. The stiff, dark fabric cast a shadow over the king's
face, giving him a distant, mysterious appearance.

The king of Ur never, never, never looked like this king. Daid
flung himself on his face.

Hammurabi chuckled. To Daid, a good-humored, pleasant sound, the sound of spring, abundant grain, and hope.

"Sit up," commanded the king.

As Daid bowed his legs under him, his skirt pulled over the pouch secured at his waist. He twisted, his hands trying to loosen the tension of the waistband and reach the pouch containing the remaining letter.

"You're seated. Don't squirm, slave."

"Majesty, forgive your humble slave, but read this letter." Daid held out the small piece of fired clay covered with cuneiform writing.

Hammurabi clapped. The chancellor appeared instantly.

"Call a scribe."

The chancellor opened the door and beckoned.

A stylus and wet clay in his hand, a scribe knelt before the king.

"Break that envelope and read the letter to me." Hammurabi pointed to the dried clay in Daid's hands.

Quickly removing the envelope, the scribe leaned close to the king's ear and read.

Daid watched the expression on Hammurabi's face change from polite interest to alert astonishment to intensity.

"Read that to the chancellor outside," said Hammurabi with a dismissive wave of his hand.

Turning to Daid, he said sharply, "Where did you get this?"

"I was employed by my lady, the high priestess of Nannar in Ur, to bring it to you."

"Valuable time has passed. Why didn't you bring it immediately?"

"I could not, Majesty."

"Why not?" in staccato. "Explain yourself."

"I was made a slave the day I arrived. I don't know why. My pouch with the letters was taken from me. There were three: one for the high priest, one to be read in your audience hall, one just for you."

"Where are the others?"

"Destroyed."

Hammurabi's narrowed eyes warned of danger.

"The one for the high priest was destroyed by a priest at the temple. I destroyed the one meant for a public reading in your audience hall. Since I could only carry one letter without it being detected, I thought it better to destroy that one."

The king watched Daid intently. "Young man, only because of the seriousness of this letter have I not punished you immediately for daring to assault my concubine. The request of the high priestess of Ur demands my immediate attention. If you value your life, you better start from the beginning and tell me everything that happened."

With lowered head, Daid related his employment by Nanshe, the boat ride up the Euphrates, his inability to see the high priest in the Temple of Marduk, his imprisonment, his slavery in the palace, the priest's return of the two letters, his encounter with Nefert, and his arrest. When he finished, Hammurabi sighed and clapped his hands twice.

A court official appeared.

"Ask my wife's nephew, the assistant high priest of Marduk, to come here, send my Egyptian concubine to the house of the women across the river, and send the chancellor to me."

Daid cringed. Being sent to the house of the women probably meant something awful.

The chancellor bowed before the king. Daid noted his dark blue garment, heavily embroidered around the bottom, and tried to imagine wearing a garment like that.

"You know the contents of the letter?"

"Yes, Majesty."

"See to it. The best we have. Give specific instructions."

As the chancellor started to back out, Hammurabi said, "I have decided to send the other prisoner with the troops leaving for the north. Tell the officer in charge."

From the forcefulness of the order, Daid sensed Tishrata would face hard work and have no free time, but Tishrata wanted to campaign. The king had ordered a punishment that would actually make Tishrata happy.

"Now," said the king when the chancellor had left them, "Do you know the content of those letters?"

"No, Majesty."

"Why?"

"They were sealed. And the high priestess didn't tell me, other than saying that the one addressed to the high priest of Marduk asked him to help me."

"Very well. You are an honest young man. I shall reward you."

Daid's heart leapt. Free. Rewarded. He would ask the king's help to get Hana-Ad released and go home.

"Majesty," he started.

"Silence." Hammurabi held up his hand. "I have not asked you to speak."

Again, he clapped for the chancellor. "See what you can find out among the guards about any men enslaved by my wife's nephew. He will sell no others into slavery to enrich himself. Identify who these unfortunates are so I can set them free."

"It will be done, Majesty."

"And have a guard take this man to the Temple of Marduk."

"You," he said to Daid, "find the priest who returned your pouch and bring him to me."

Copying what he had seen the scribe do, Daid crawled backward through the door. Outside the room, the chancellor waited, a guard beside him.

As before in the crowded temple grounds, priests carried slabs of clay covered with writing from one building to another. A slave staggered under the weight of piles of clothing. A group by Marduk's temple gesticulated at the top of the ziggurat. Daid looked to the left at the building where he had been imprisoned, the building where he had seen the assistant high priest. Emptiness. Nothing moved.

He frowned and casually glanced across the courtyard. Four young priests emerged from a building midway in the string of buildings from the street to the ziggurat. Seconds later, the priest he sought walked out alone.

He couldn't call; he didn't know the man's name. He rushed to him and stood grinning.

Not sure what to make of it, the priest smiled. "I'm happy to see you. What wonderful thing has happened that brings you here?"

"How do you know?" exclaimed Daid.

"Why else would you, a king's slave, run in here so excitedly?"

"He wants to see you."

"Me! No!"

"It's all right. He read my letter and wanted to know who returned it to me. He's pleased with you. So you must come."

"I'll inform my teacher."

Hammurabi received the two in the same room where Daid had left him.

"Rise," he said to the prostrate figures. "Priest, what is your name?"

"Sahar, Majesty."

"What are your duties in the temple of Marduk?"

"I'm a priest studying to be a physician, Great King," mumbled Sahar.

"You have shown responsibility and done me a favor. You will take the place of my brother-in-law as assistant high priest."

Sahar trembled. To hide his fear, he fell on his hands and knees, repeatedly touching his forehead to the floor.

"You," Hammurabi said to Daid, "will take the place of Sahar in the school of medicine."

"But—but—Great King," began Daid. He saw the king's eyes harden. He fell on his face.

"Go."

They crawled backward without looking up. On their feet outside the door, they faced the chancellor. "You are to go to the rooms of the high priest and await his arrival," the chancellor said to Sahar.

"And you," he said to Daid, "will be escorted to the school of medicine and told what to do."

"Sire," Daid said meekly, "why am I not allowed to go home?"

"The king chooses to honor you by making you a great physician. You will obey."

Still a prisoner. Yahweh, how long? Daid's very soul cried out in anguish.

An official of the court appeared and pompously ordered them to follow him. Together, they fell in behind. On the Processional Way, people swiftly cleared a path, bowed before the official, and slyly looked at the two men thus honored, one a priest, one a slave. Embarrassed by his slave's clothing, Daid kept his eyes down.

Inside the temple area, the official waved Sahar toward the quarters of the high priest and started in the opposite direction. Daid meekly followed his guide to the school building where the official handed him over to a pleasant-looking elderly priest with a shaved head and crippled left arm.

"We'll get you something decent to wear first," said the priest, starting along the line of buildings. "You'll meet the master tomorrow, early."

In a small room, the priest rustled through a pile of orange and yellow wool skirts like those worn by the priests of Marduk. "This will do," he said, extricating one. "Put this on."

Daid looked at the skirt uneasily, but fastened it around his waist. Then, another priest shaved his head and beard. A third showed him a mat laid against a bend in the corridor wall of the sleeping quarters, where to take his meals, where to find the library and the classroom. As the priest pointed to the classroom, he said, "Appear there at six in the morning," adding, *"Remember, you are a ward of the king."*

Daid lowered his head in submission.

Late that night, silent as a great cat, Sahar knelt beside Daid's mat and gently pressured his shoulder.

Daid opened his eyes, sensed the form hanging over him and sat up.

"Come outside where we can talk," whispered Sahar.

One behind the other, they exited the building, to stop in a shadowed corner where two walls joined at right angles.

"You want to go home?" said Sahar.

"Oh, yes."

"Well, you have the perfect way."

"What do you mean by that?"

"Think ahead. Our king is a brilliant administrator. He has placed you directly under the best physician in Babylon. I'm guessing that King Hammurabi wants to make you a good physician to send back to Ur. So if you want to go home, you better learn in a hurry. That's my judgment."

Daid rubbed his lips with his finger, turning his head from side to side. So—that was the way out and the perfect way into the palace at home. His excitement rose. He grabbed Sahar's shoulders.

"I'll work. I'll learn as fast as the master can teach. They'll be astonished."

"Not so loud," warned Sahar, amused.

Daid withdrew his hands. "And you? What about you, Sahar?"

"The high priest has already been exceedingly gracious and thorough. He met with me for three hours today. Then, he introduced me to the priests on his staff. One of them is the old fellow who took you down the hall to the cell. He ordered us to feed you. I don't trust him."

"I don't understand. You were in the medical school then.

How could he order you around when you weren't part of the administrative staff?"

"His position is such that he can order anybody to do what he wants. I was walking across the court. He grabbed me and ordered me to follow him."

"And the other priest, the one who used to come into my cell with you? Who is he? And what is his rank?"

"He has the same rank as I did. But he wasn't in the medical school. He works in the temple, helping with the animal sacrifices. However, there may be some connection there."

"You mean with the queen's nephew?" interrupted Daid.

"No, with the old priest. I'm not sure, though. But I have an uneasy feeling about it."

"Why are you afraid?"

"The queen's nephew controls a number of the priests on my new staff. The old priest is one of them. That's well known. Who the others are, I don't know. I need to find out and quickly."

"But the queen's nephew can't control them now."

"Unfortunately, I think he can. And he's a cruel, vindictive man."

Unable to think of anything helpful to say, Daid gave Sahar's arm an encouraging squeeze and crept back to his bed.

Morning came too early. Groggy, Daid felt someone shaking him. At the same time, a gruff voice said, "On your feet. Your presence is requested by our master."

He dressed and reached the courtyard before his eyes were fully open. He rubbed one, then the other. A middle-aged priest standing near the door laughed at him, a sensitive, kindly laugh.

"Come along," the man said. "The tablet house where we have classes is this way." He started at a rapid trot. "The second-best physician in Babylon will be your teacher. The best physician disappeared yesterday, just gone, nobody knows where." The priest scowled, shrugged, and charged on.

Daid ran alongside. "Don't we eat first?"

"No, not until the end of the first class. Then we eat while we discuss what happened in class."

They entered a room full of priests sitting on low, oblong slabs, two to a slab.

"You," the authoritative man standing at the end of the room indicated Daid. "Up here." He pointed to an empty bench right in front of him.

Daid hesitated.

"Come along," said the priest who brought him, starting down the side aisle.

Daid slumped onto the front bench, trying to look invisible. He surreptitiously eyed the man who now controlled his every move. The shaved head, the long, bony face with hooded eyes intimidated him. Plus the master exuded a slightly arrogant authority that unnerved him.

"The lecture today," said the master, "is on bleeding a patient." He began by explaining the sites on the body for different ailments. Then, using his own body, he designated the different sites.

Fascinated, Daid forgot his timorous fears and absorbed everything the master said.

After the lecture, the master said, "You will now practice what I have said by using leeches to bleed. I will announce a disease, and you will apply the leech in the correct spot."

The master walked up and down between the benches. His sharp tongue made the priests who balked at the leeches cower even more.

Daid slapped a leech onto the chest of his partner then deftly peeled one off his own wrist.

The master watched him. "Sit beside me at breakfast."

"Yes, sire."

At breakfast, the master commended Daid on his handling of the leeches. Daid explained that his family had large herds, that he cared for the animals, that they got sick, that he healed them when he could, but that he had no specific knowledge.

The answers seemed to please the master. He asked a few more questions before turning his attention to other students.

Daid grabbed at the chance to gulp down goat's milk, alternately with great bowlfuls of grain cooked with water, making it liquid, all the while stuffing pork into his mouth. The same kind of food he had had at home covered the table in abundance and tasted just as good.

After breakfast, the class learned incantations to sing along with the treatments. Bored, Daid's mind wandered to his parents, to his younger brothers doing the work, and to his chances of sending his father a message.

"Daid, you sang that incantation incorrectly. If you prefer to think of other things, instead of paying attention, you can return to guard duty in the palace."

"Forgive me, Master. I will pay careful attention, Master."

The master's eyes burned fire into his brain.

In the afternoon, the master talked about how people turned all red. How their skin felt as hot as fire. Or they turned pale and shivered. Water drops formed on their foreheads. Daid eagerly asked questions. He remembered every word the master said.

By the day's end, he found himself exhausted, but exhilarated. He couldn't believe his good fortune. He would go home as a temple physician. But wait. He looked down. He wore the skirt of a priest of Marduk. The temple at Ur belonged to Nannar. He believed in Yahweh. If only Apilsin were here to help him, steady him.

He designated a spot in his tiny sleeping area for Yahweh. Standing there, he suddenly remembered Hana-Ad's personal goddess. He had left his belongings in the cell where he had been imprisoned when he went to bathe. Maybe the statue was still there, along with the bundle of extra clothes, bits of soap, a knife, things he had carried with him from Ur.

With that, he faced the wall and had a long talk with his God.

He shivered as he stepped into the courtyard the next morning. A chilly wind blew. He scanned the sky. Hopefully, they might get a little rain to settle some of this dust.

Sahar emerged from the administration building and headed across the temple yard. Daid veered so their paths would cross. Hurriedly, he asked about his package and the small wooden statue.

"The statue is probably still there," said Sahar. "Even if the old priest retrieved the package after we took you out, he might leave the little goddess. I'll have a look."

Sahar hustled away. Daid didn't see him again until Sahar appeared at his bedside a few nights later. From his skirt's waistband, he drew Hana-Ad's personal goddess.

"Whoever took the package was afraid of this little goddess. Is it yours?"

"Yes. Or, no. I'm supposed to give it to a young woman."

Though perplexed, Sahar said, "The statue was standing in the corner."

Daid turned the little wooden female over and over in his hand. Now that he had it back, what should he do with it until he could give it to Hana-Ad?

"I'll put her against the wall at the foot of my bed," Daid said. "Maybe if I give her some grain, she'll look after Hana-Ad."

"Maybe," answered Sahar, noncommittally.

15

shnan flung her drape back dramatically. The seven girls on the floor playing dice looked up. "Somebody," she let her gaze insolently rest on each girl staring at her, "stole my gold loop earrings, the ones I wear all the time. I left them on my cosmetic table this morning."

The seven sat frozen in stunned amazement.

"Don't you understand what I said? One of us has turned into a thief. No—Let me take that back. I don't believe Shegunu is involved or Ninti, or Ninbar. And Girsu-Ad is too stupid."

Girsu-Ad drew up her shoulders and threw out her chest.

"That leaves five. Though I doubt Nin-Ad would bother to steal anything." Her glance deliberately rested on Uttu, swept to Kigal, Hana-Ad, and Nidada.

"Ashnan," said Shegunu, "you are making a serious accusation. Couldn't you have mislaid them?"

"No," said Ashnan with an upward thrust of her head. "And I'm going to start by checking Hana-Ad's alcove since she's the major troublemaker around here."

Hana-Ad's mouth dropped open. "I'm the major trouble-maker! I think you've got that backwards."

Kigal laid a hand on Hana-Ad's curled leg and whispered, "You'll only make her worse."

"I heard you, Kigal. Your alcove will be second." A few long, slow, attention-getting steps placed her in front of Hana-Ad's drape. With a flourishing arc of her arm, Ashnan swept aside the drape and stood at the entrance, her back to the mesmerized girls, still seated on the floor cushions. Then, she laughed with snide relish. "Come and see," she called. "Hana-Ad stuck my earrings under her pillow, but carelessly let part of one show."

All arms and legs, jumbled haste, they fluttered to their feet, flocked around Ashnan, and tried to see over her. Ashnan didn't move. Hana-Ad shoved her way past and looked at her bed. Slowly, she drew two gold loops from beneath the pillow, the strangest, unbelieving expression masked her face.

In a voice coming from a void, she said, "Are these your earrings?" and held up the loops.

"You stole them," said Ashnan coldly.

"No," Hana-Ad said, "I didn't. I don't know how they got here."

"You lie." Ashnan held out her hand. "Give them to me."

Carefully, deliberately, Hana-Ad laid the earrings in Ashnan's hand.

Regally, Ashnan turned, swished her bright red gown, and stalked back to her alcove.

In slow motion, Hana-Ad's head oscillated from side to side. "I didn't steal them. I didn't. I don't understand."

"I don't think you did, either," said Uttu.

"She has her earrings, so come." Shegunu took Hana-Ad's hand and drew her toward the cushions where they had been sitting. "She has made her point, whatever it was supposed to be. The rest of us don't believe her so let's forget it."

The first day of the next week, after they had played the harps all afternoon for the old queen, Ku-bau suddenly sat up, dangling a gold chain, and said too sweetly, "Hana-Ad, this was under your mattress. Where did you get it?"

Hana-Ad turned red. "My—my father gave it to me, Majesty."

"So you say." her glance swept the group. "Does this belong to any of you? Was it stolen?"

No one moved.

"Answer me."

"No, Majesty, it does not belong to any of us," said Shegunu.

"Therefore, Ashnan may have it since her earrings were stolen."

"No," escaped Hana-Ad.

"Call the guard," Ku-bau said to the court official at the foot of her couch.

"That one," she said, when the guard appeared, extending a jeweled forefinger toward Hana-Ad, "alone on bread and beer for five days."

Kigal noisily drew in her breath.

"Quiet," said Ku-bau. "Dismissed."

Nine girls filed out. Kigal's tender eyes clung to Hana-Ad as long as possible.

Hana-Ad stood quietly, the guard at her side. He flexed his muscles, ready to grab her if she moved. After the others had gone, he grasped her upper arm and led her to the opposite side of the garden from their usual route. He drew the bolt on the door of the room the old queen used for punishment, thrust her into the room, banged shut the door, and locked it.

She found herself in a small, dim room. A mat and yellow coverlet lay on the floor. Close to the ceiling, above the door, a long opening had been cut to let in dim light and some air.

For a long time, she stood just inside the door, her feet together, her arms hanging limply at her sides. She had no desire to move, no strength to do anything.

She heard the bolt withdrawn. Instantly, hope bubbled up. Emitting a tiny cry, she turned toward the door. Gula's scared face appeared. In her hands, the slave held flat, fresh bread and a cup of beer.

"Gula," begged Hana-Ad, taking the food, "I'm hungry."

Gula shook her head, produced a straw from her sleeve and darted to the door.

"Don't leave me. Please don't leave me." Hana-Ad started to cry.

Gula straightened her shoulders to steel her nerves, stepped across the threshold and closed the door.

Hana-Ad remained standing, bread in one hand, beer in the other, her head bent forward, sobbing. Her tears splashed on her bread. Holding her head up, she blinked back the tears. She sipped a little beer. Anger at the injustice, at Queen Ku-bau, and at Ashnan, burned in her like an all-consuming flame. She sat down on the mat and slowly ate the bread. Determination to get back at Ashnan simmered hotly through her brain.

The following afternoon, forlorn in her crumpled, messy orange gown, hungry, feeling abandoned, she became convinced nobody cared what happened to her. She lay on the mat and let tears ooze between her closed lids.

Outside the door, Nanshe paced back and forth. She didn't dare defy the old queen and call out any encouragement to Hana-Ad.

The third day, Hana-Ad lay on the mat, sleeping off and on, crying in between. She didn't move or speak when Gula laid beer and bread beside her. Each time Gula returned, she found the bread in a pile, untouched, the cups in a row.

Gula rushed to Temena. "She's dying." Gula stuttered in her own anxiety. "She's not eating."

"Queen Ku-bau won't let her die," said Temena. "That would spoil her funeral. Bring meat, milk and fruit to Hana-Ad's alcove. I'll go see the old queen."

Gula ran toward the kitchen, and Temena walked purposefully along the portico to Queen Ku-bau's room.

Ku-bau was sleeping. Temena sat on the floor where the old queen would see her the second she opened her eyes.

The old queen opened one eye. In a low voice, she said, "How is the girl doing?"

"Badly, Majesty. She takes no food. She will die by tomorrow."

"You're exaggerating, but get her out." Ku-bau went back to sleep.

Later, while her other charges entertained the old queen, Temena slipped along the walkway and drew the bolt on the door of the small prison room.

"Come." Temena pulled at Hana-Ad. The girl, limp and apathetic, wouldn't get up from the mat.

"I want to die."

"Queen Ku-bau won't allow you to die. So on your feet."

"No." Hana-Ad resisted.

"You'll come if I have to carry you."

Temena wanted to hold Hana-Ad and rock her, cuddle her, comfort her, but had to get her moving. "Uttu is not eating well. She's worried about you. And Kigal, too. They're all upset."

Hana-Ad got up unsteadily, knocking over three cups of beer.

A firm arm around Hana-Ad's waist, Temena guided her across the garden, through the empty recreation room, and deposited her on her bed.

Gula stood at the foot of Hana-Ad's bed, her pocked-marked face taut with worry. In her small hands, she held a bowl of the finest tidbits she could find in the kitchen. The two slaves hovered over Hana-Ad, urging her to eat, offering succulent bits of lamb, a gold straw to drink milk from a golden tumbler. At first, Temena supported her back while Gula popped the tasty meat tidbits into her mouth or held the tumbler while she drank milk.

Finally, Hana-Ad pushed away the food. Gula washed her face. Temena perfumed her body with a lovely fragrance kept for special occasions, bent and kissed her forehead. Hana-Ad smiled shyly.

She must have slept because darkness surrounded her. She felt weight pressing down on her bed. She couldn't move her legs beyond a certain spot. Somebody was sitting on her bed.

"Hana-Ad," whispered Uttu.

Hana-Ad pulled her arm from under the blanket and touched Uttu.

"I'm so glad." Uttu planted a little kiss on her friend's hand. "We've all been worried. Kigal is beside herself. Even Ashnan; she walks into our room, dragging her feet, not her usual swagger, her head bent, eyes on the floor, and goes directly to her alcove. She feels isolated, I'm sure. Everybody has ostracized her." Uttu huffed. "Serves her right."

"How did Queen Ku-bau get my chain?" whispered Hana-Ad, reviving rapidly.

"She sent guards to search your alcove after Ashnan accused you of stealing her earrings. They found it."

"I want it back."

"Not right now. Sometime Ashnan will trip herself up. You'll see."

Uttu patted her friend. "Temena told me you were here. The others don't know yet. You are to be brought in tomorrow, while we're playing the harps. Hold your head up and take your place as if nothing had happened."

Hana-Ad felt Uttu's weight shift, then she could move her legs freely.

"Sleep well." A fleeting draft of air entered the alcove, then silence.

Hana-Ad followed Uttu's advice. Escorted by Temena, wearing her most beautiful scarlet gown, she entered Queen Ku-bau's chamber, her head high, her face serene, and took her usual place. No head moved. The girls continued to play their soft, melodious music. The old queen was drowsing. Just as Uttu finished playing a short solo passage, Ashnan cried "Oh!" in a high, stifled voice, turned her back and vomited.

"Get her out of here," yelled Ku-bau. "How disgusting. Clean it up. Perfume," she demanded, fanning herself.

A slave dabbed her with a strong fragrance. "You," she said to a kneeling slave, "call the physician, the new one from Babylon, the one who lives in the palace." She shifted her gaze to the girls. "Get out, all of you."

Slaves ran hither and thither. The girls, two by two, trying to be sedate, leaving a wide space between themselves and a doubled over moaning Ashnan, rushed into the corridor, where a guard grabbed Ashnan and scooped her into his arms. The others slowed down and watched him until he and his burden disappeared into their room.

Just inside their own door, all nine stopped to stare. Ashnan lay on her bed, the drape pulled back. Temena and Gula hung over the moaning girl. Ashnan, arms wrapped around her abdomen, rocked from side to side.

"The gods are punishing her for what she did to you," Uttu said loudly to Hana-Ad.

"Maybe she won't get well until she gives back your gold chain." Suddenly brave, Kigal spoke just as loudly.

"Here's the physician," Ninti said, an odd look on her face.

Nin-Ad, Nidada and Ninbar glanced behind them then moved quickly out of the doorway to let the short, stocky Babylonian, wearing the orange skirt of a priest of Marduk, enter. He smiled, glancing from side to side.

From Ashnan's alcove, Temena beckoned him. "In here," she said.

In silence, the girls watched. They could hear his low rumble as he spoke to Ashnan and see her head nod or her hands move over her abdomen. But try as they might, they couldn't hear what was said. Then, Temena dropped the drape.

"Why is a priest of Marduk here?" asked Ninbar.

"I don't know. Maybe King Hammurabi sent him to Ur. In any case, I know he's treating the prince," Shegunu said.

"Is that why he stays in the palace rather than at the temple with the priests?"

"Yes."

They stopped talking to watch Gula run from their room and out the double doors. Other slaves came back with her. They carried cups and bark.

"What are they going to do?" said Girsu-Ad.

"He's going to make a poultice," Nidada said.

Behind the drape, his round face and intelligent eyes serious, Sumulael kneaded together the contents of the various cups: turtle shell, sprouting naga plant, salt and mustard. He ordered the slaves to wash the girl's abdomen with beer and hot water, then rub it with vegetable oil before applying the poultice. The slaves scrubbed and scrubbed, then applied the paste over the spot he indicated. Sumulael covered that with pulverized fir.

The moaning stopped.

"Now, lead me to the old queen," Sumulael said to Gula. He followed her out, past the girls clustered outside Ashnan's alcove. Great Marduk, he said to himself, his sharp eyes sparkling with delight, they are beautiful.

In Queen Ku-bau's chamber, he dropped onto his face.

"How is my dear child?" she said, adding, "You may stand up."

Rising, he said, "Sedated, with a strong poultice. I have ordered that she eat nothing. I ask permission to see her tomorrow." He waited to be asked for details.

The old queen picked up her golden tumbler and drew on the straw before answering. "Well, be sure and come to me afterwards. I don't want her starved."

"I won't allow that, Majesty." He hesitated. "If it please Your Majesty, one of your ladies is coughing badly. May I look at her?"

"Nin-Ad. I've told her to stop it many times."

"She may not be able to, Majesty."

"Very well. Do what you can—if anything." Ku-bau waved her hand dismissively.

He made no effort to move. Her glance sharpened.

"There is something else?"

"I beg your help, Majesty."

"In what way?" She said cautiously.

"I came as a visitor to spend a few days absorbing the ancient glory of Ur, Majesty, and compare notes with your physicians here in the temple. I have done that. Now I want to go home."

"Well, go," she said, knowing that her son, Idi-Sin, wanted him to treat the prince.

"The king has asked me to be court physician. He wishes me to attend to his family."

"You should be honored." She stalled, not wanting to commit herself until she had a chance to talk to Queen Nin-Anna.

"I will think about it and see." She toyed with her tumbler. "You may go."

In the morning, the old queen sent word that Sumulael was to attend Ashnan late in the afternoon, and that he should also examine Nin-Ad.

Ashnan was morose when he arrived, still in pain, but not as intense as yesterday. She answered his questions without looking at him. He ordered another poultice.

"I'm hungry," she said.

"Bread and beer," he told Temena.

"No," yelled Ashnan.

He ignored her. "Where is the other woman?" he said to Temena.

"Waiting in her alcove." Temena led the way.

Ashnan kept yelling, "No, no, no," as they crossed the room. Temena looked at Sumulael.

"Bread and beer," he said.

She nodded.

Sumulael examined Nin-Ad's lungs.

"It's called consumption," he told Temena, "You are to give her hot compresses every night. When you make the compress, wrap layers of linseed inside the cloth. She'll also need to get plenty of rest, drink lots of milk, and eat no garlic. Honey in warmed beer should help her cough."

Over the next three days, both girls improved. By the fourth day, Ashnan had recovered. Though she complained constantly, Sumulael kept her on bread and beer for another week. Each time he came, he checked one or two of the other girls. Temena ordered Uttu to her alcove first. She reappeared grinning. "I'm in superb health," she announced, flinging up her head.

"May I be next?" Girsu-Ad rolled to her knees and waved a hand at Temena.

"All right." Temena raised her hand to hide her grin, but her eyes twinkled.

Exiting her alcove, Girsu-Ad glanced over her shoulder at Uttu. "I'm in perfect health too."

Hana-Ad giggled at Girsu-Ad's smug expression and faked a cough.

Shegunu, Ninbar, Ninti and Kigal also announced that they enjoyed perfect health. Nidada hung back when Temena called her. "Nidada," said the slave, "tell him your problem. Maybe he can help you."

In her alcove, Nidada stood in front of Sumulael, twisting her fingers together, her head down. "I get sick often," she said.

"How?" said Sumulael.

"It comes irregularly. I alternate between burning with fever and trembling with cold. I have a lot of pain and perspire profusely."

He felt her forehead. "You're all right now?"

"Yes."

"Well, we'll see if we can help your chills." As he walked across the room to Hana-Ad's alcove, he stopped to speak to Temena. "Give her licorice root in water when she has chills," he said. "A lot of people have this. There isn't much we can do for it."

Hana-Ad bounced from her alcove followed by Sumulael. "Perfect," she said with sparkling eyes. Sumulael grinned.

He reported his findings on Nidada to Queen Ku-bau. She went into a tirade. "How can these girls possibly get sick when I shower them with luxuries?"

"Majesty, only the gods know which of their numbers the girls have offended."

Ku-bau turned to a slave. "Tell the high priest to send a priest every night to pray with those girls for their sins."

Sumulael waited, hoping the old queen would say he could go home. She simply dismissed him.

After he left, Ku-bau sent for her daughter-in-law.

Hurrying into the old queen's rooms, Nin-Anna said, "Majesty, are you all right?"

"Yes, of course."

Dropping to a cushion, Nin-Anna covered her annoyance.

"Ashnan is well; the other two are better." Said Ku-bau, "The Babylonian wants to go home. Why not let him? In spite of what you say, King Hammurabi must know about Shulgi. He certainly knows that Ibbisin, your second son, has been invested as crown prince. The Babylonian Ambassador was a prominent visitor at the ceremony."

She paused, waiting for comment by Nin-Anna. Nin-Anna, sitting on the cushion beside her mother-in-law, simply studied her fingernails.

"What's the point of keeping a priest of Marduk as physician in the palace?"

"I've changed my mind about the physician." To Queen Ku-bau's surprise, she casually added, holding up her right hand to observe the nails, "My darling boy is so improved I want Sumulael to continue his treatment."

Ku-bau straightened and stared at Nin-Anna's hand then at Nin-Anna. Nin-Anna blushed and placed her hand in her lap.

"Don't you think," the old queen said archly, "your favorite priest of Nannar could treat him as effectively?"

"Absolutely not," said Nin-Anna, a sly little expression appearing on her face. "Who knows? Besides—" she pronounced the last words like an edict from on high— "Idi-Sin wants the priest of Marduk to remain in the palace."

Ku-bau shrugged and squirmed down among her pillows, signaling dismissal to her daughter-in-law. She had at least made an effort on the physician's behalf. Perhaps it was just as well that he stay. He could be useful to her, too. Nin-Ad's coughing had lessened and, no, she didn't think it was her imagination that Nidada looked better. She even considered having him examine herself, but sloughed it off. She preferred the priest of Nannar who usually treated her son.

Ku-bau sent word to Sumulael that she didn't need to see him each time he visited the young women. Sumulael went to the Babylonian ambassador for help. He pleaded to be allowed to go home.

The man said, "If King Idi-Sin wants you here, you stay."

16

*T*he morning after the festival for the river god, a minor official of Hammurabi's court addressed the master at break fast. "Your student Daid is to report to the chief education administrator in the palace."

"I hope this doesn't mean Daid will be removed from the school," said the master.

"No. The king wants to know how he's getting along," answered the official.

The master turned to Daid, who sat beside him. "You have nothing to fear. You're doing extremely well."

As an aside to Daid, the official said, "Sahar also has to report to the palace. Delighted, Daid hurried to the administration building to wait for him.

"Sahar," Daid asked as they walked along the crowded Processional Way, "Do you like it?"

"Yes, I like it. The high priest complimented me the other day." Sahar smiled. "I was so pleased, I messed up a report. The high priest just laughed. He said, 'Don't let my praise go to your head, Sahar.'"

Daid chuckled delightedly.

"I have a totally blank memory of the last time we walked along this route," Daid said, looking around. "What's that black basalt thing over there among the flower beds? It's almost twice the size of a man." He indicated a pillar with two male figures on top, one standing, the other sitting.

"That's the king's law code. He had it written on that large stone and placed there so that whoever goes by can see it."

"Let's go read it."

Sahar hesitated. "We're supposed to go directly to the palace."

"It'll only take a minute. As that law code effects everyone in

Ur, I want to see it up close." Daid walked rapidly toward the basalt slab, Sahar following slowly, uncertainly, behind.

"Look at that," Daid said, pointing to the figures on top. "King Hammurabi stands in front of the seated sun god, Shamash, with his right arm raised in respect."

"And Shamash holds in his right hand the rod and circle of power."

"Look at the flames that rise from Shamash's shoulders."

"Yes. He's dictating the laws to the king."

"From the mountain top. No wonder the laws are so superb."

Daid lowered his eyes to the middle section.

"Listen," he said excitedly. "If a man be captured and there be maintenance in his house and his wife go out of her house, she shall protect her body, and she shall not enter into another house. If that woman do not protect her body and enter into another house, they shall call that woman to account, and they shall throw her into the water."

He shifted to another section of the pillar. "Here's some more: An officer, constable, or tax-gatherer shall not make over to his wife or daughter the field, garden, or house, which is his business, that is, which is his by virtue of his office, nor shall he assign them for debt. He may make over to his wife or daughter the field, garden, or house which he has purchased and hence possesses, or he may assign them for debt. A woman, merchant, or other property holder may sell field, garden, or house."

He turned to Sahar. "That happened in my city. One of our neighbors bought a garden from the tax-gatherer. But the tax-gatherer didn't say that the garden belonged to him only because of his office. Our neighbor had to forfeit his money and return the garden. He was furious and raised such a ruckus with the tax-gatherer that the man's wife gave him a garden that was hers. Everybody was satisfied."

Daid continued to scan the code.

"Oh, here we are. Listen to this, Sahar. This part concerns me." Daid began to read:

"If a physician operate on a man for a severe wound, or make a severe wound upon a man, with a bronze lancet and save the man's life; or if he open an abscess in the eye of a man with a bronze lancet and save that man's eye, he shall receive ten shekels of silver as his fee. If he be a freeman, he shall receive five shekels.

If it be a man's slave, the owner of the slave shall give two shekels of silver to the physician.

"If a physician operate on a man for a severe wound with a bronze lancet and cause the man's death; or open an abscess in the eye of a man with a bronze lancet and destroy that man's eye, they shall cut off his fingers."

"Ugh! I don't like that."

"It only happens if the physician is careless or the family seeks restitution," Sahar said.

Daid pursed his lips and shifted his eyes around, storing Sahar's comment in the back of his mind. He swallowed and continued reading. "If a physician operate on a slave of a freeman for a severe wound with a bronze lancet and cause his death, he shall restore a slave of equal value. If he open an abscess in his eye with a bronze lancet, and destroy his eye, he shall pay silver to the extent of one-half of his price."

"If a physician set a broken bone for a man or cure his diseased bowels, the patient shall give five shekels of silver to the physician. If he be a freeman, he shall give three shekels of silver. If it be a man's slave, the owner of the slave shall give two shekels of silver to the physician."

"That's enough," said Sahar. "You've convinced me the code is wonderful."

Daid grinned. "What do you think of that? The fees are all laid out."

Sahar laughed. "Come on. We better get our reporting over with before you can charge fees."

Daid's eyes sparkled, and he laughed, too.

"I haven't had a patient yet. So where's the fee?"

"In time."

They reached the audience court at the moment the king was ending the morning session. He rose and walked sedately through the rear door. Instantly noise erupted like the roar of the flooding river. Every man spoke at the top of his lung power as they moved toward the exit.

The chancellor left the dais and signaled to Sahar and Daid.

Pleased with their timing, Daid wiggled an eyebrow at Sahar behind the chancellor's back.

Sahar tried hard not to grin.

King Hammurabi sat on the same chair in the same small

room, exactly the same way they had seen him last. Only today, he had on a magnificent royal purple garment. The two young men fell prostrate on the floor.

"Rise," said the king. "You both look as if my decision agreed with you. Sahar, give an account of yourself."

"Majesty, the high priest has been most helpful and support-ive. I like the work and think I can do it. I deeply thank Your Majesty for this opportunity."

Sahar bowed low and stepped back.

Daid started to perspire, unsure of what to say.

"Daid." Hammurabi turned his head slightly and looked at Daid.

Taking a cue from Sahar, Daid said, "The master has shown me much favor. I have enjoyed his confidence in my ability—I mean, my progress." He gulped for breath, then rapidly said, "I like it very much, Majesty. I plan to be the best physician you have. Thank you."

He prostrated himself.

Hammurabi threw back his head and laughed. "I think you will be, Daid. I hear excellent reports of you—of both of you." He glanced at Sahar. "You have confirmed what I hear. I am pleased." He looked from one to the other. "You may go."

Again on the road, they laughed and poked each other in relief.

A few days later, during breakfast, a slave summoned the master for an emergency.

"Go to the classroom as soon as you finish eating," he said to Daid.

A priest hailed Daid as he left the dining room. "I guess once the king's slave, you're always the king's slave. You're to go back to the palace."

Daid paled.

Snickering, the priest continued. "The master said you are to bring henbane and accompany him."

Henbane? The request mystified Daid. If henbane was called for, someone had to be in severe pain. They had studied its anal-gesic property, discussing it along with things like mandragora, mulberry, alum, cypress, garlic, and onion.

He carefully chose some henbane from the storeroom, then placed his left hand on the mandragora. Should he take a little of that, too? No. They had about the same effect. He hurried to the master.

"One of the king's slaves is wounded," said the master. "You learn rapidly. It's about time you learned to deal with the sick."

"Me!"

The master read his face. "Don't be a stupid boy. It's only a slave. Besides, I'll be there. I won't let you do anything drastically wrong. However, I expect you to get it right," he ended emphatically. "While you treat him, I will sing the incantations. You never get any of them right."

At the palace, Daid panicked when he saw Tishrata lying on the mat, groaning with pain, a nasty red slash on his thigh. Only by biting his tongue, gripping his fists, and telling himself he was there as a physician, not a lowly slave, could he prevent himself from turning around and running from the room.

"How did you get this?" asked Daid, careful not to look Tishrata in the eye.

"During the campaign. I'm lucky to be alive."

Daid mixed the henbane. "This will help your pain." He raised Tishrata's head so he could swallow.

For a long time, Daid examined Tishrata's leg. Thick yellow fluid oozed from the wound.

"I think we should pack it with cow excrement," he said to the master.

"Excellent. And what incantations do we sing for this type of wound?"

Daid rolled his eyes. Disgusted, the master took a position at the head of the bed, ready to begin singing.

"We have nobody to stand at the foot," said Daid.

"That's really not necessary here."

Daid tried to think of incantations. He discarded the one for bleeding. The cut no longer bled. A deep, angry red covered the skin all around the gash. And when he held his hand over the spot, he could feel the heat.

"Fever," he said.

The master nodded. "As good a choice as any."

Daid worked at binding the cow excrement poultice on Tishrata's leg. The master droned on in uneven cadence. Tishrata looked hard at Daid. "I know you," he said. "But you weren't a

priest." He knit his brows. "And what are you doing to my leg?"
He tried to pull away, but Daid grabbed the leg.

"I'm your physician now. You do as I say. And I say you wear
this poultice until I come and change it."

"Leave me alone," screamed Tishrata. "You're a slave, a guard.
You're a fake. I'll go before the king."

"Go ahead. See what good it does you. The king made me a
physician, and you'll do as I say." He spoke with more authority
than he felt. Despite his insecurity, he looked defiantly at the ex-
guard and saw him withdraw in fear.

"You ought to be delighted to see me," said Daid. "Didn't
I do as I promised? Not only did you go free, but you were
allowed to go on campaign." He stretched the point, but he
didn't care. "You ought to be falling on your knees, thanking
me."

"Yes, well, you did get me in the army. How'd you do it?"

Daid busied himself with his bindings. "Never mind that. I
tell you all this so you will do as I say now."

"All right. All right." Tishrata made a special effort to lie
quietly.

Daid laughed. "Relax. I can't get the binding under your leg
if you keep holding yourself so rigidly."

"Well, don't scare me."

Daid finished his work in silence.

"I'll come again tomorrow," he said prestigiously, turned and
walked out. The master followed him. Daid didn't see the amusement on his face.

In the corridor, Daid stopped. "Master, was the way I talked
to him wrong?"

"No. You have to show your authority."

"Did I treat him properly? Will he get well? I want him to."

The master put a hand on Daid's shoulder. "Of course you
do, especially when it's your first case. But whether he gets well
is in the hands of the gods. That leg is pretty bad. Your treatment
was correct."

Two days later, nervous but appearing confident, Daid removed a second poultice from Tishrata's leg. The churning in his
stomach calmed. He poked the infected leg. The violent red had
now turned a washed-out pink. Less pus oozed, and Tishrata said
the pain up and down his leg had lessened. Acting as he had seen

some of the physicians do, Daid pulled at his chin and nodded his head. Tishrata watched every nuance in his facial expression.

"I'm better," he announced.

His chest slightly puffed, making his voice stern, Daid said, "Good. We will continue the treatment." He clapped for assistance. A slave appeared. Daid told him to prepare another poultice. "A strong one. Add a little myrrh to it. I will come back in three days."

"I don't have much money," said Tishrata gruffly.

Daid cut him off. "Don't worry. I'm doing it out of friendship."

On his next visit, Tishrata greeted him with a smile. "I feel good. When can I get up?"

"Not until the flesh around your cut has closed. Let's see." He removed the poultice. The wound looked so much better that he didn't know what to do. Another strong poultice seemed unnecessary. And yet, to have nothing covering the open gash seemed dangerous. To give himself time to think, he said, "You are to stay down. If I have to order you tied down, I will. You could split that cut wide open, in which case, I would have to amputate your leg."

"I will, I will," cried a terrified Tishrata.

Daid spoke to the slave who attended Tishrata. "Cover it with clean straw, dipped in pulverized pear and roots of manna. And change it every two days until I come back again."

"Yes, sire."

Daid tried hard to retain a superior exterior. The fellow had called him "sire." From now on, he must act like a great physician and not a shepherd from Ur.

"You make an all-fired better physician than prison cell mate," said Tishrata. "I'll do you a good turn one day."

Daid flushed with pride. That emotion didn't last long. His next patient died.

Humbled, Daid rushed to the master to report his failure.

The master said, "Tell me quickly his complaints and how you treated them. Unfortunately, I have been ordered to the home of one of the king's generals so I can't spend time with you."

"He alternated between being so hot he couldn't stand anything over him and so cold, he shivered uncontrollably. He complained about his breathing, but I made him lie flat. His family said they had to hold him down. He screamed and yelled that he couldn't breathe. The yelling made him cough blood. He had terrible pains in his chest."

"Not good, not good."

"I gave him a paste of sunflower ground up in honey and purified oil to swallow for the cough, followed by a drink of cold beer and honey. I put poppy in it for his chest pain. And a poultice of pulverized river mud kneaded with hot water. Before applying that, I rubbed his chest with black oil."

"The poultice was good. And what incantations did you use?"

"For bleeding."

The master shook his head. "His breathing difficulties were the most important thing. His lungs must have had a lot of pus in them. He should have been half sitting, not lying flat. I guess I shouldn't have let you go alone. You aren't ready yet."

"Oh, what can I do," cried Daid, his shoulders sagging. "The man's widow is screaming. It's my fault. I'll have to support the family."

The master shook his head. "From what you say, he probably would have died anyway. You must learn to accept failures. Our treatments don't always help. We do the best we can."

"Yes, master." Daid hung his head.

The master looked at him. "Come along with me. You can watch and if I decide incantations are necessary for this I'll ask you to sing." He looked askew at Daid. To his amusement, Daid grimaced.

The fluttery and nervous general's wife received them in the courtyard of her elegant home. "He lies on his bed the way the slaves placed him," she said apologetically, leading the way up the stairs.

"What happened?" said the master.

"We were eating our midday meal. He seemed nervous, more than usual. He was just picking at his food. That's not like him. He's a good eater. I said, 'What's the matter with you?' He said, 'I feel funny.' He got up and started across the courtyard. Suddenly, he swayed, staggered a few times and fell. I screamed. The slaves ran from the kitchen. They picked him up and set him on his feet. He slumped against them. Two of them had to carry him to bed. He was helpless. He couldn't answer us when we talked to him. I asked him to move to the middle of the bed. He couldn't."

At the bedside, the master felt the general's forehead. "I will ask you to do some things for me. Will you obey?"

The general moved his jaw.

"You cannot speak?"

The eyes pleaded.

"Well, that tells me where to begin."

He turned to the wife. "Has he been dizzy?"

"I don't know. He never tells me anything."

"Headache?"

He looked at her.

She stared back at him.

"I see you don't know." He shrugged. "Step outside."

For a few minutes, he studied the room and the bed's position in it. Light from a window high up cast a strong beam in the middle of the room.

The master turned to the corner where Daid sat quietly. "He has bleeding on his brain. I must open his skull. You might as well help me," he said holding out a jar.

"Ask a slave to warm that. Come right back and bring two slaves with you."

The minute Daid returned with the two, the master pointed at the slaves. "Move the bed into that pool of light." Quickly, they pushed the bed into the middle of the room, making the whole bed bright with light, and hurried out.

The master said, "Sit on the bed, Daid, behind him and brace his body against your armpit so his head is on your shoulder."

The master pulled the general's hair up and looked carefully around each ear.

"You see the little scar here above his right ear?"

"Yes."

"That's where I shall open his skull."

The shaving of his head finished, the master said, "Hold him so his head is slightly raised. I want to get some poppy juice down his throat."

From his position supporting the general, Daid placed a hand under the man's chin and raised his face. The master dripped poppy juice down his throat, careful not to gag him. Then, with Daid holding his head in a vicelike grip, the master drew the point of his knife from the right ear to the top of his head in circular fashion and back to the ear. Blood seeped along the cut. Nodding his approval, the master observed the area.

"That will do nicely," he said.

With that, he cut along the line of oozing blood. He laid the skin flap back over the ear, exposing the skull and picked up the trephan. Daid had seen the little circular saw before but didn't know its use. He watched the master turn the handle and saw a circle in the middle of the cut.

Daid quailed with each grating sound as the handle turned.

The master laid down the trephan, took the chisel and lightly tapped in the cut. Again, he used the trephan. Dexterous and swift, he loosened the circle of bone and gently pried it out.

A moist, quivering, red mass ballooned from the hole.

"Just as I thought," said the master and stabbed the balloon from underneath. Blood gushed over the bedding.

Daid gulped noisily and adjusted his grip on the inert body of the general.

From the edge of the hole, the master pulled the tissue that had held the blood straight up to examine it. Using a thin strand of animal gut, he put one stitch where he had exploded the bloody mass and stuffed the tissue back in the hole. As he replaced the bone piece, the master said, "I need the resin now." He looked at Daid holding the general.

"Never mind. I'll get it." From the balcony, he called for the jar of warm resin.

A young slave stuck his head inside the room, stared horrified at the general's open scalp, handed the jar to the master, and soundlessly closed the door behind him.

The master tested the temperature of the resin with the knuckle of his index finger. Using his knife, he smeared the warm substance around the bone circle, sealing the piece into place. Then, he replaced the skin flap and sealed that with resin.

"His wife can come in now," he said as he fitted a wool cap onto the man's head.

Daid eased the sleeping patient flat on the bed, then went for the woman. The two eldest sons, bearded and pompous, entered the room behind their mother to stand around the bloodied bed.

"We'll wait until he wakes," said the master.

They sat on the floor, the sons side by side, rigid and unblinking. The woman a little apart, where she wiggled around, ordered a slave to bring more cushions and fussed with her elaborate green dress. The master and Daid sat quietly together on the opposite side of the bed with a good view of their patient, and waited for what seemed an eternity.

Two hours later, the general opened his eyes and looked directly into the eyes of the master.

The master rose and leaned over the general. "Can you raise your hand?"

With intense concentration, the general managed to raise the index finger of his left hand slightly.

The master's eyebrows went up. "That's a good sign," he said to the family. "Don't let him out of bed or in a sitting position. And keep him warm. I'll come tomorrow."

Walking side by side back to the temple along the narrow, half empty, quiet streets around the palace, Daid said, "How did you know his brain was bleeding?"

"We see a lot of this among the military. It indicates that at some point, he either fell or was hit on the head. He will never be as supple as before, but if he recovers, he'll have some use of his arms and legs."

Feeling ill equipped and ignorant before the master's ability, Daid marveled at what a physician could accomplish.

17

Queen Nin-Anna smiled to herself as she entered the old queen's area. Daydreams spun around in her head. Wild, impossible, wonderful daydreams of power. She hesitated and peered into Ku-bau's room.

"Come in, Nin-Anna," said the old queen. "After receiving your request, I sent word you were welcome."

Nin-Anna settled herself on the yellow cushion beside Ku-bau's couch without comment, slowly arranged her red dress to her satisfaction, then raised her face to her mother-in-law.

"Majesty, your granddaughter, my daughter Shara, is to be married."

"Really!" exclaimed Ku-bau. "To whom?"

"The king of Lagash has requested her for his eldest son and heir. Ur-Ilum and the Lagash ambassador are negotiating at this very minute."

"Excellent. A good match," Ku-bau said, nodding her head vigorously. "My son is wise to marry Shara into the ruling house of that city-state."

Nin-Anna ducked to hide her grimace. "I don't think it so wise. I told Idi-Sin a long time ago I wanted her to marry an aristocrat from Ur."

Ku-bau raised her eyebrows. "An aristocrat can't compare to a future king. Whatever gave you that idea, Nin-Anna?"

"It's a long ways away. She's afraid."

"Oh, nonsense."

"Anyway," said Nin-Anna petulantly, "I have no say in the future of our children. At the completion of negotiations, she goes. Those are my husband's words." She tapped her chin with her forefinger. "Then, there's the question of Luga."

"Don't bring up Nanshe again. I won't be a party to that."

"I wasn't going to, Majesty. But now that you do, have you noticed that Nanshe doesn't look well lately?"

"No. She came to see me yesterday and looked perfectly healthy. I don't know what you're aiming at."

"I do hope I'm wrong because if anything happens to Nanshe and Luga marries Ur-Ilum, for instance—"

"Luga marries Ur-Ilum!" In her amazement, Queen Ku-bau fell forward. Immediately, two slave girls rushed to catch her under the arms and pull her up, rearranging the cushions.

"That's better." She looked intently at Nin-Anna. "Do you think the chancellor would make a contract with a child?"

"He might. It would make him part of the royal family."

Ku-bau carefully smoothed her green gown. The conversation had become ridiculous.

"In which case," continued Nin-Anna, "there would be no female member in the family to fill the position of high priestess if Nanshe became ill or—anything else."

"You're courting trouble." Ku-bau gave Nin-Anna a disgusted look. "There's nothing wrong with Nanshe."

Nin-Anna smirked. Each morning, alone in her bedroom, she performed, with rigorous care, the ritual to transfer terrible sins to Nanshe. She watched the high priestess intently, surreptitiously, at every opportunity. The last two days, she had thought Nanshe looked pale and walked as if in pain.

Ku-bau scowled as she watched Nin-Anna, eyes down, fingers playing with tufts of the rough woolen pillow fabric on which she sat, her voice sing-song. She didn't like it at all.

"If, by chance, Nanshe should die soon," Nin-Anna spoke hesitently, "Luga isn't old enough yet to handle the temple. It would need a more knowledgeable hand."

Ku-bau caught herself before saying, "You mean you would happily assume the power." Instead, she said, "I'll send for Nanshe and tell her you are worried about her, that you think she looks pale, and are fearful that she might die."

The queen paled. "Don't say anything to Nanshe, please. Please don't, Majesty."

Ku-bau smiled to herself. That settled that. They went on to talk of other things until the old queen tired. "It's almost supper time," she said.

"Forgive me, Majesty. I must fly. Idi-Sin will wonder where I am." She stood up, bowed and backed out.

Walking along beside the garden, Nin-Anna admitted she hadn't achieved any firm decisions, but she had planted some seeds and who knew where that might lead. She looked into the girls' social room to see what they were doing. As far as she could tell, most of them were doing nothing, just sitting around, a couple of them playing with dice.

"Now, what do you suppose she's up to?" Uttu said as Nin-Anna walked on.

"She's been talking to Queen Ku-bau a long time," said Ninbar.

"Hurry." Nin-Ad rolled the dice. "Dinner will be here."

The minute dinner arrived, Ashnan reached for the tastiest bits of meat and the largest hunk of bread and pushed Girsu-Ad away from the fruit bowl for trying to take a pomegranate.

The other girls, used to her behavior, waited while she took what she wanted. Uttu, Hana-Ad, and Kigal carried their bowls to the floor cushions in front of Kigal's alcove. Ninbar seated herself at a table next to Ninti. Bowl in hand, Ashnan strode up to Ninbar.

"I want to sit by Ninti," she said haughtily.

Ninbar glanced around. "Well, sit over there." She indicated a table behind Ninti.

"I want to sit here. Move." With her hip, she shoved Ninbar.

Ninbar rose, her face rigid and red, and walked slowly toward a floor cushion near Shegunu. For a few minutes, everybody busily ate the roast bass, peas and beans. The tension became unbearable.

Uttu laid her bowl on the carpet with controlled deliberation. Awkwardly, she rose and walked over to Ashnan. "Ninbar has as much right to sit here as you do."

Ashnan's chin went up.

"We live in godlike luxury with our queen. Why do you always have to cause such unpleasantness?" said Uttu scathingly.

"Go back and sit with Hana-Ad," Ashnan snarled.

"I will. Don't worry. I'm not planning to push you off the chair. But just remember, the rest of us are *sick* of you."

Ashnan raised a hand to strike her, but Uttu had turned away.

18

*H*olding her harp in front of her like a shield, Hana-Ad rushed into the tiny instrument room. From the doorway, she spotted Ninti on her knees in the far corner.

"What's the matter?" she asked as she set her harp in an empty space near the door, carefully balancing it so it wouldn't fall over.

"The bottom part of one of my earrings fell off," said Ninti, feeling around on the floor. "It must be here someplace."

"I'll help you look." Hana-Ad started across the floor.

"Oh." Ninti scrambled to her feet. "It was in my clothing all the time. See!" She dangled the carnelian loop.

"Come on, then. The others may have already started for the temple." Hana-Ad turned and ran from the room, Ninti after her.

Restless that night, Hana-Ad rose and walked barefoot through the darkened room to sit in the cool, sheltered walkway that surrounded the garden. She watched the brilliant night sky as she fondled an exquisitely carved gaming piece. The feel of the polished alabaster calmed her. With the passage of time, hope of escaping had begun to fade. The indolent, luxurious life she led, so different from milking goats and spinning, had become bewitching. Perhaps she might not settle easily into her old life again. Noise made her turn her head.

Returning from Queen Nin-Anna's suite, Uttu stormed along the passage, pounding the ground, so different from her quiet, light footfall. Her eyes snapping angry sparks, her body trembling, she stopped within a hair's breath of banging into Hana-Ad.

"My harp is broken," Uttu said in answer to Hana-Ad's baffled expression. She fled to her alcove and sprawled facedown on her bed.

Hana-Ad ran after her. Sliding gingerly onto the edge of the bed to avoid sitting on Uttu, she said, "Dear Uttu, don't cry." Her hand found Uttu's shoulder and caressed it.

"I'm not." Uttu rolled over, bumping into Hana-Ad. "I want to scream and wake everybody up."

"Tell me what happened instead."

"You know Queen Nin-Anna begged Queen Ku-bau to let me play at the special dinner for her daughter's betrothal. Just before I was supposed to go to the royal suite, I went to get my harp. It lay on the floor, broken."

"I don't understand. How did it get broken?"

"How should I know! When I picked it up, I just saw that its strings and pins had been pulled off, so that they dangled from the body."

"Somebody did it deliberately."

"That's what I think. The damage was too blatant to be an accident. And mine was the only one."

"Where had you put it?"

"In the far corner so it would be clear of anybody hurrying in and out of the instrument room."

Hana-Ad gasped. "Ninti was on the floor in that corner when I ran in. She said she was looking for an earring. Her back was to me, but I could see that she was feeling around on the floor."

"Ninti! She's too delicate. She couldn't possibly have pulled the pins. It would take a much stronger person."

"Maybe, but I did see her in the room by herself."

"When was that?"

"This afternoon, before we went to the temple. I placed my harp by the door because I was afraid of being late. I don't remember even noticing the instruments near me, much less those on the other side. I don't know whether any other was broken or not. And, of course, I couldn't see yours. That's where Ninti was crouching."

"It must have been broken then. We all went to the temple with Nanshe and came back together for dinner." Uttu hesitated. "Yes, everybody was here until I left to go perform for Queen Nin-Anna."

"How did you, since your harp was broken?"

"I grabbed the one next to it. What else could I do? There was no time." She added, "I don't know whose it was. I'll put it back in the morning."

"There'll be a to-do when everybody finds out."

"It'll be worse when Queen Ku-bau finds out. She's always so unfair when she punishes us, I'm afraid of what she'll do to me."

"Are you going to tell her?"

"I don't have to. I'll be without a harp. She'll have to give me a new one." Uttu paused. "I can't help wondering if Ashnan had anything to do with it."

"She's been furious with you ever since you told her we were all sick of her." Hana-Ad raised her hand like an angry cat's claw. "I'd like to bloody her face with my fingernails."

Uttu tried to suppress her laughter. "She'd make meat scraps out of you in return."

Hana-Ad smiled. "Maybe you're right." She bent to kiss Uttu. "Goodnight. Try to get some sleep. Tomorrow morning should be rather exciting."

Uttu snickered.

The broken harp caused such babble in the instrument room that Temena rushed in. "Be quiet," she said. "Queen Ku-bau is in a foul mood this morning."

Uttu groaned. "I'm really going to get a tongue-lashing," she whispered to Hana-Ad.

Hana-Ad studied each girl. All of them, even Ashnan, seemed truly upset. "I don't trust Ashnan," she said to Uttu, "but she acts just as upset as the rest of us. Either she's innocent, or she's good at acting."

Ashnan went to Uttu and handed over her harp. "Take it, please. You play so much better than I do, you should have it."

Uttu's head went up and she blinked rapidly, but gracefully accepted the harp. "At the end of the morning, I'll talk to Queen Ku-bau after the rest of you have left the room and tell her of your kindness." As she turned away, Ashnan's eyelids dropped slyly over her eyes. Uttu caught the motion and bristled. But, before she could talk to Hana-Ad again, they lined up to march into Queen Ku-bau's room.

Ashnan, being tall, stood in the back row. She held Uttu's broken harp close to her body and moved her hands and shoulders as if she were playing it.

For a while, all went smoothly.

The old queen pointed. "Sit down over there in the corner."

She watched them file across the room. "Ashnan, why is your harp unstrung?"

"It's broken, Your Majesty."

"As usual," said the old queen, "you've been careless. I suppose you expect me to give you a new one. Do you think I have an endless number of harps?"

"No, Majesty." Ashnan said, being particularly silky. "That's why I said nothing this morning when it was found broken."

"So," Ku-bau's eyes narrowed, "one of you did it and tried to cover it up."

Ashnan bit her lips to keep from smiling.

"Girsu-Ad, come forward," said Ku-bau.

Ninti's mouth opened. She exchanged glances with Nin-Ad and slowly closed it.

Girsu-Ad knelt at the old queen's side.

"Were you, at any time yesterday, alone in the room where the harps are kept?"

"No, Majesty."

"Can you prove that?"

"I think so, Majesty." Girsu-Ad, obviously flustered, looked guilty. Each word Queen Ku-bau said upset her even more.

"Your behavior belies your statements. We will hear the others. Ninbar, come forward."

"I was with Nidada, Majesty," said Ninbar, "when we laid our harps down. We left the room together and stayed with the group all evening."

"Nidada, is that correct?"

Nidada knelt beside Ninbar. "Yes, Majesty."

"All right," Ku-bau continued, "you two are excused. Shegunu, I don't imagine you had anything to do with this."

"No, Majesty, though I was in the room alone. The others had already left to meet Nanshe. I was held up because a guard stopped me with a message from my aunt. When I finally went to the instrument room, I put my harp away, but didn't look in the corner where Uttu's was."

"Uttu's harp! We're not talking about hers, but about Ashnan's."

"It's Uttu's harp that's broken," Shegunu said placidly.

Ashnan squirmed.

"Ashnan!"

"Majesty, I did not mean to imply that the broken harp was mine. This morning, when we found out about it, I insisted Uttu take mine because she's the better player." Ashnan bowed low, fawning, smiling sweetly, trying to flatter the old queen.

"That still doesn't solve the question of who did it." Ku-bau scrutinized the girls.

"Ninti, what do you know about this?" she demanded.

Immediately dropping to her knees, Ninti said, "Please, Majesty, I was alone in the room, looking for an earring. The carnelian dangles came loose and fell off. I felt them fall, but couldn't find them right away. Hana-Ad came in while I was there, and we left together."

"Hana-Ad, where were you?"

"By the door, Your Majesty. I was putting my harp against the wall when I saw Ninti in the back corner."

"By the broken harp?" Ku-bau addressed the question to Ninti.

"It was not broken then," said Ninti, "or I would have reported it."

"Enough of this," said Ku-bau, irritated. "Uttu, you shall have a new harp. All of you go to your room, except Girsu-Ad, and wait."

Slowly, they filed out. Girsu-Ad on her elbows and knees before the old queen, panic-stricken, her stomach heaving, let her head fall to the floor.

"Uttu," said Hana-Ad when the two had reached the garden, "I think Ninti lied."

"So do I," said Uttu. "And Girsu-Ad will be blamed."

"She's so lovely and so stupid," said Hana-Ad, exasperated. "She'll just get herself in deeper and deeper the longer the old queen questions her."

"Who do you think did it?"

"I don't know. But somehow, I think Ninti knows. She's covering up for someone."

"And that someone is Ashnan," said Hana-Ad flatly.

"Right. She's Ashnan's only friend." Uttu sighed. "But we can't prove anything."

Temena, carrying a new instrument, put a stop to the conversation. "I'm sure you'll want to try this out, Uttu."

Uttu took the harp and plucked its strings as she sauntered back to their social room with Hana-Ad. Temena followed them.

At the door, she said in a loud voice, "You are all to go back and play for Queen Ku-bau."

"And Girsu-Ad?" asked Uttu.

The others crowded around to hear what Temena would say.

"Girsu-Ad has been confined for three days."

They returned to the old queen's rooms in silence. Ashnan gnawed on her lip, sour-faced.

They could hear Girsu-Ad sobbing from across the garden. Every sound came through the air space above the cell's door. For the next three days, Girsu-Ad's every moan and sob reached the other girls. They ate in silence and moped around. Once, while serving them dinner, Gula said, "Snap out of it. She isn't being hurt."

The girls busily applied themselves to their cucumbers in sour cream and lamb, their faces serious, their mood heavy.

The day the guards released Girsu-Ad, she ran to Kigal for sympathy. "I didn't do it, I didn't," she sobbed in Kigal's arms.

"We know you didn't, Girsu-Ad."

"Everybody hates me."

"No we don't. We feel terrible. We think you were unjustly accused and shouldn't have been punished."

"You do?"

Kigal stroked Girsu-Ad's hair and scowled. She knew what Hana-Ad and Uttu thought. They had to be wrong. Ashnan had been so generous to Uttu that morning. The only possible culprit was Ninti. But Ninti couldn't possibly have broken the harp. A satisfactory answer evaded Kigal. She'd just try to be nice to everybody.

19

"It's almost the spring equinox. The New Year festival will be upon us before we know it." Nanshe lay in her husband's arms in their palace chamber.

"As usual, you'll be too busy to pay attention to me." A proud Ur-Lumma kissed her forehead.

"You know better than that," she said, giving him a playful slap. "The first five days are devoted to prayer and purification ceremonies. My part only involves a bit of time each morning. That's all. So, my loyal spouse, you have nothing to complain about."

"I won't complain as long as you keep looking so beautiful when you stand up there next to the high priest."

"Oh, you wonderful man." She planted a kiss on his shoulder, adding, "The first five days aren't exhausting for any of us. It's the last five that are so wearing on the king. I always agonize for Idi-Sin."

"And there isn't much we can do to help him."

"Not so long as the high priest keeps adding rituals that are performed in Marduk's temple in Babylon."

"He seems possessed with those rituals."

"I was standing close to the high priest in front of Nannar there in the main temple last year when he put his hands on Idi-Sin's shoulders and forced him to his knees."

"From the back of the packed room, I couldn't see what he was doing."

"He slapped Idi-Sin across the face. I don't think he meant to hurt him, but the blow made Idi-Sin jerk back. I could see he needed all his control not to put his hand on his face."

"Poor fellow. I can't imagine the high priest of Marduk slapping King Hammurabi like that."

Nanshe laughed in one burst. "The high priest said, 'Give me your insignia,' and held out his hand. Idi-Sin took it off and gave it to him, chain and all. After that, Idi-Sin repeated the formulas about not having done anything bad for Ur."

"I heard that. He spoke in a clear, strong voice."

"You know how long they feasted that night. I went to bed."

"It was *quite* a feast, I must say, and long. At one point, I almost fell asleep."

"I know the sacred prostitutes had a terrible time with the drunks. They shouldn't have to put up with that."

Ur-Lumma shrugged. "How do you stop it?"

"Other than closing their area, I don't know."

"You can't do that."

"I suppose not. But back to Idi-Sin, he didn't get a chance to rest for the next two days, either."

"He must have walked in front of the bullocks, dragging Nannar's cart, along every narrow, winding, street in Ur, picking his way through the filth and the chanting townspeople who kept throwing themselves in the dirt at his feet."

"You didn't walk the whole way, did you?" Nanshe raised her head to look at her husband.

"No. I only followed part of one day. The group of court officials kept changing as they came and went."

Nanshe was silent. "I think I'll indoctrinate Queen Ku-bau's ten virgins into some of the ceremonies."

"Not the one you perform with Idi-Sin, I hope," he teased.

"Brute." She laughed. "That would put an end to her dreams of music in the afterlife."

"Some of them might accept the challenge."

"At least two might."

"Really! Which ones?"

"Kigal and the most recent girl, Hana-Ad."

"I haven't seen her."

"Fortunately, I was able to talk to her before she did anything foolish."

"Praise Nannar for that. From what you've told me, Kigal was treated severely."

"Hana-Ad appears to have settled down well. She's popular with all the girls." Nanshe caressed her husband's arm before returning the conversation to her nephew.

"Sometimes, as you know, Idi-Sin doesn't perform as he's supposed to. Of course, I don't really care."

"The two of you are alone in the bedroom atop the ziggurat. Who's to know?"

"The only thing that matters is that—" She stopped.

"Is what?" he prompted after a minute.

Nanshe stroked his face. "I want another baby before we get much older."

"It's too risky." He tightened his arms around her. "We might have to give the baby away again. That's too hard on you."

"My arms still ache for that baby girl."

"I know, love." He kissed her.

"I could probably get Idi-Sin to perform."

"And if you can't, we'll have the same problem as the last time."

"We could wait until after the festival."

He chortled. "Then we wouldn't know whether the baby was mine or his."

"Oh, darling, don't. I don't want Idi-Sin's baby."

"The only way to prevent it is for you to get pregnant first, and I don't think that's wise."

"I could get rid of it if he doesn't perform."

"You wouldn't. You know that. In the end, you wouldn't."

"Please." She snuggled against him. "I need a baby."

"Are you willing to give up being high priestess?"

She drew back and squinted at him.

"You might have to make a choice, Nanshe."

"No. Being high priestess is my duty. To me, that comes first." She turned her face from him. "Besides, I do like being high priestess. And Nin-Anna is so anxious to make her daughter high priestess."

Ur-Lumma laughed. "You and Nin-Anna aren't exactly friends."

"She's a difficult and rather stupid woman. I don't understand what Idi-Sin sees in her."

"Remember, you look at her from a woman's point of view."

Surprised, Nanshe said, "Do you find her attractive?"

"Yes."

Nanshe was quiet.

"That doesn't mean, my sweet, that I could get interested in her. You simply asked me an impersonal question."

"Forgive me. When it comes to you, I'm touchy."

He kissed the end of her nose. "Nin-Anna is jealous of you; she always has been."

"I could cope with jealousy. What she feels toward me is deeper and uglier than that. When I'm around her, I always feel that I have to watch my back. She's so blatant about wanting my position. Sometimes when I pass her and her ladies, she stops talking. I always wonder what trouble she's planning for me."

"It's probably just gossip she doesn't want you to hear."

"No, I know she's plotting something. She may have sent Shara to Lagash as bride of the heir apparent, but now she's starting to push her second daughter."

"Luga?"

"Yes. She says Luga would be a perfect high priestess."

"Perhaps we could marry Luga to a prince in Babylon. That would really go to Nin-Anna's head."

"The girl is only ten."

"She's old enough for a marriage contract. Send her up to Babylon to be trained. King Hammurabi is known as a good family man. She would be well treated."

Nanshe smiled. "How do you propose we do this?"

Ur-Lumma paused. "I haven't figured that out yet."

"We might try to do it through the Babylonian ambassador."

"I'm sure Nin-Anna thinks you've done enough damage through him."

"What do you mean? She hasn't connected me with the Babylonian physician, or how he came to be here."

"Don't be too sure."

"Why should she?"

"I don't know. She might easily be suspicious. She's not exactly a beginner in the game of politics."

"In which case, she would have to admit that Sumulael has done wonders with the prince."

"Admitting that the prince is better isn't going to change her attitude toward you if she thinks you've whispered state secrets to King Hammurabi's ambassador."

Nanshe stirred in his arms as she thought about Nin-Anna's reaction. "She could make my life very uncomfortable."

"So you marry Luga to one of King Hammurabi's sons. She would be overjoyed."

Nanshe's lips reached for his neck. "You can easily drop hints to the ambassador. Then, if King Hammurabi sends a request for the girl, Nin-Anna will jump out of her skin with delight. She'll put on airs as if she were already the queen of Babylon."

Ur-Lumma's laugh was deep and sultry. "You want a baby?" He rolled her onto her back.

In ecstasy, she wrapped her arms around him.

Ur-Lumma didn't seek out the Babylonian ambassador. There would be plenty of time to meet him during the New Year feasting. Just before the festivities started, King Idi-Sin gave a large formal banquet in his audience hall. After dinner, the guests in their gorgeous new raiment sauntered around the hall, chatting. Ur-Lumma spied the Babylonian ambassador near the dais by the silver wine pot. He walked over next to him and dipped his long ceremonial silver-and-lapis straw into the pot. The Babylonian sucked in a long draught and turned to Ur-Lumma.

"Your lovely wife is always a joy to watch. She performs the duties of high priestess so beautifully."

Ur-Lumma smiled and bowed. "I'm sure the high priestess of Marduk also does a splendid job."

"Yes, King Hammurabi's daughter does perform her duties well, too."

"I hear he's searching for a suitable husband for his second daughter. He takes great care in dealing with his children."

"He's a wonderful father," said the short, wily ambassador with a broad smile that caused his chin to draw up so his face didn't appear so long and thin.

"Your royal family is large compared to ours," Ur-Lumma said.

"One day, Shara, King Idi-Sin's daughter in Lagash, will bear a child," said the ambassador, smiling. "Though the baby would only be a member of your larger family."

"However, the news would please the king. Unfortunately, Lagash is too far away for the queen to see the baby. That's what happens when girls marry. Even so," Ur-Lumma hesitated, "we want the girls to marry well. Our ten-year-old is big enough to send to a court with a king who would treat her well."

The Babylonian's eyes narrowed. "Is this an offer?"

"Absolutely not. King Idi-Sin hasn't authorized a marriage contract or even mentioned it. You and I were simply talking about royal families." Ur-Lumma went on to discuss preparations for the festival.

Ur-Lumma decided not to disturb Nanshe, sleeping in her temple chamber, as the deepest part of the night approached. In the morning, he sent a slave to ask if he could breakfast with her.

"Of course," she said to the slave. "Tell him he doesn't need to ask."

Holding a hand-painted bowl full of warm gruel in his hands, pieces of lamb with lentils, a pitcher of milk in front of him on the round wickerwork table, Ur-Lumma said, "I talked to the Babylonian ambassador last night. He snapped at the thought like a tiger with prey."

"Very good." Nanshe set down her bowl and crinkled up her eyes in delight.

"I had to back off quickly when he asked me if Idi-Sin was making an offer." He paused. "However, having planted the idea in the fellow's mind, I mentioned it to Ur-Ilum. I don't think it's gone any further."

Nanshe considered this for a moment. "I could easily have someone suggest the idea in front of Nin-Anna. She would pick up on it right away, and then make Idi-Sin think he'd had the idea all by himself."

Ur-Lumma chuckled. "Still, who knows what will come of it?"

"If," she hesitated, "King Hammurabi takes the child, and Idi-Sin doesn't perform, and I have a baby—"

"That's a lot of 'ifs.'"

She smiled coyly. "Anyway, if all those things, maybe we could persuade Idi-Sin to let me remain high priestess."

He sought her eyes and held them. "Nanshe, you know better than that. You know the stipulation made when you were given the position. It was very specific. You may not have a child by me. You aren't even supposed to have a human husband. Any child you have is Nannar's."

Her eyes were as intense as his. "This one isn't."

"Nanshe," he yelled. Jumping to his feet, he pulled her from her chair and gave her a lion's hug.

20

Daid lurked in the deep shadows cast by the glittering stars in the clear bright night, hoping to catch Sahar.

A shape exited a door at the end of the temple's right wing, the wing where he had been imprisoned. The figure emerged from the shadows and crossed the starlit courtyard. Sahar. Daid moved out of the dark jog in the building, motioned, and faded back into the shadows. Sahar joined him.

"Why were you way down there at the end of the building?" Daid whispered.

"The old priest you had the misfortune to meet the day you arrived in Babylon fell and broke his hip. He's behaving like a two-year-old. He won't stay quiet. I ordered the priests caring for him to tie him down. That's one more thing he'll hold against me."

"But you haven't done anything to him."

"He's obligated to the queen's nephew. I hear the nephew's sycophants informed him that I have replaced him. So he would like to see me ousted—one way or another."

"It isn't your fault that King Hammurabi threw him out and put you in his place."

"In a way, he thinks it is. He found out that I took the letter to you. He holds me responsible for everything that has happened as a consequence."

"How did he find out?"

"Who knows? I had the letter. The other priest who was with me when we brought your food knew I had it. Everyone knew I was ordered to appear before King Hammurabi. It's an easy deduction."

Daid blew out his breath. "And from what I know of the queen's nephew, he won't rest until he accomplishes what he wants."

"The old priest tells him everything that goes on in the temple."

"How come he has such a hold on the old fellow?"

"A number of years ago, the old priest accused a votary of wrongdoing. He couldn't justify his accusation and was hauled before the judges. He should have had his forehead branded, but the queen's nephew saved him. So now, every time dirty work needs doing, the old priest has to do it."

"Being tied down will put a stop to his activities for the time being."

"Yes and no. I mean, I don't know. I don't know how he passes the information to the queen's nephew. I don't know from what quarter an attack might come. I could make a thousand guesses, all of them wrong. But now with the New Year festival and all the extended festivities connected with that, I'm afraid about what might happen." Sahar shook his shoulders. "Enough of that. Let's not worry until we have to."

He searched Daid's face. "Why were you looking for me?"

"I'm to remove the opaque, white growth from an eye tomorrow. I just had to tell somebody. I wanted to tell you. I hope you don't mind."

"An eye! Great gods, you have made progress."

"I've been studying for over a year."

Sahar smiled at the slight bruskness in Daid's voice. "It's still great progress." He patted Daid's shoulder. "Get some sleep. It's wise to be rested for such a delicate operation."

Daid was deep in sound, dreamless sleep when a priest shook him. "Wake up. You're already late. You're due in the tablet house for the lesson on eye problems."

Barely awake, Daid had his skirt fastened before the man was out of the door. The master had just started lecturing when Daid fell into his seat. A scalding glance and a raised eyebrow greeted him.

"Excuse," he murmured.

The master went through numerous eye infections, yet the symptoms all seemed to be about the same—redness, swelling, muddiness in the white part of the eye, itching, blurred vision, burning. "The easiest way to keep the flies off the eyes," said the master, "is to bandage them. In fact," he added, "the best treatment for eye disease is to soak the bandage in cassia juice and put the patient to bed in a closed, darkened room."

The eye operation lecture, right after breakfast, explained exactly how to proceed. Two priests then worked together to learn the right position. One, acting as patient, sat on the bench. The other positioned a stool between the patient's knees so that his eyes were on a level with the blinded eye. Having stored everything the master said in his memory, Daid deftly reproduced it during his turn as physician.

The master watched. "Meet me at the street gate immediately after class," he said, turning away.

Daid walked to the gate with confidence.

"We go," said the master, "to the home of a member of the king's foreign service."

A bustling, self-important man met them at the door. "My father is ready for you," he said.

Daid's nerves suddenly jangled. He caught the master's eye and mouthed, "What's the punishment if I destroy the patient's sight?"

The master only gave Daid's arm a reassuring touch as they entered the small, square room where the old man sat on a chair. Behind him, his narrow bed occupied a corner. Sunlight poured in from a long, barred window on one side.

Daid humbly asked that the chair be turned so the old man faced the window. He then administered henbane, more than he probably needed, but he wanted to be sure the patient wouldn't move his head.

"Sir," he said to the official, "stand behind your father and hold his head to keep it steady."

Turning to a slave, he said, "Bring me *clean* water to wash the knife."

"And be quick about it," barked the government official.

Daid sat down on the stool he had placed between his patient's knees, rose and asked for a lower stool. The official snapped his fingers, and a slave ran from the room.

Sitting on the lower stool, Daid looked directly into a dense, white cloud covering the man's pupil. A cloud had also started to form on the other eye.

He laid the sharp obsidian blade of his knife in the bowl of clean water the slave had set on the floor beside him, held it there while he counted to ten, raised it and shook off the excess water.

Holding the eyelid up with his left hand, he cautiously positioned the point of the blade at the top of the cloudy membrane.

Gently, he exerted downward pressure. The cloud yielded. Down. Down. Slowly, slowly. Don't panic. Down, down. The black rim of the man's iris appeared. Almost finished. Just a little more. He pushed the cloud toward the inner part of the eye. Only then did he realize that he had been holding his breath.

"I will bandage the eye," he said to the official. "Darken the room and keep him in bed for four days."

The official bent his head toward Daid in thanks.

"You did well," the master told an elated Daid as they walked back to the temple. "The only thing I think I would do is give the patient a mouthcleaning tablet before you start," adding, "In case he should cough."

On the fourth day, Daid returned alone to the official's home and removed the bandage. In the semidarkness, the old man's face crinkled into a thousand spider's feet. "I can see," he crowed.

"Don't open the drapes right away," Daid said to the government official. "Let him get used to the light."

The official gave him ten shekels of silver as his fee. Away from the house, Daid skipped one step, then another. The master had said that he could keep whatever the man gave him. Clutching the silver so hard it left an imprint on his hand, he headed straight for a bead shop. For a long time, he had wanted a chain of blue beads. He had seen some pretty ones in a shop stall.

At the entrance, two men were discussing the pros and cons of five gold chains that the shop owner had arranged in size around his own neck for better comparison.

One said, "You don't need that in Lagash. Are you getting carried away with the glitter in Babylon?"

Daid looked at the beads. Was he beginning to be carried away by the glitter, too? He had to admit, he enjoyed living in the temple, studying with the master, tending the sick. And he liked the city, too, the excitement of wandering the streets, the market, talking to the laborers on the quays. He reminded himself that he had come to Babylon on a mission. So far, he had only carried out half of that mission, assuming that the school's great physician had gone to Ur. Looking longingly at the beads, Daid put his silver into his waistband.

He crossed the river and searched until he found a small temple.

"Where do I find your temple scribe?" he asked a priest replenishing the oil in the clay lamps.

"Outside, sitting on the ground at the left of the temple."

Daid left the temple and rounded the corner. There on the ground, his large belly making a mound of his wool skirt, sat a middle-aged priest using his stylus to scratch his head.

"I need a letter put in the correct form to present at the king's audience," Daid said to the scribe. "The letter should beg the king's help in freeing ten young women held prisoner by Queen Ku-bau of Ur. She plans to make them wait on her in the next life. That's the gist of what I want said."

A blank expression on his face, the scribe set to work. Daid stood behind and watched him swiftly and beautifully execute the cuneiform strokes. Carefully holding the damp, finished product, Daid read it through, nodding in satisfaction.

"Would you wrap this in an envelope for me and have it fired?"

The minute class broke for breakfast the next morning, Daid ran to the scribe for his fired letter, then hurried to the palace. In the audience court, a man was complaining that he hired a boat and boatman to carry his grain, oil and dates to Uruk. Through carelessness, the boatman wrecked the cargo by allowing dirty river water to flood into the boat. The man asked recompense from the boatman.

Daid spotted the chancellor leaving a group of men near the dais. Walking rapidly around one corner of the audience court, he planted himself where he could attract the chancellor's attention.

The chancellor saw Daid and motioned him to approach.

"I have a letter for the king," Daid said, timidly extending it.

"Stand on the left side," the chancellor said, taking the letter, "so the king can see you easily."

Hammurabi ordered the boatman to pay damages, then turned to Daid. "What brings you here?"

The chancellor stepped forward and handed Daid's letter to the king, which Hammurabi handed to a scribe to break the envelope.

After listening to the scribe recite the contents of the letter, Hammurabi took it and turned it over and over in his hand.

Finally, with as kind a voice as he could manage, he said, "Sad and unfortunate as I find this situation, I cannot interfere in the internal policy of Ur."

Daid's spirits sank.

"You had better pay attention to your studies. I suspect you have missed valuable instruction by coming here on a useless errand. I will not take kindly to bad reports." He turned to the chancellor for a moment before recognizing the next petitioner.

The chancellor caught Daid at the door. "Our king deeply regrets that he cannot help these young women. He realizes one must be important to you. He regards you as an asset to the school and hopes you can find happiness here in Babylon."

"Thank him for his kindness." Daid tried hard not to sound as miserable as he felt.

At the temple, out of breath, Daid rushed to the tablet house and slipped onto a back seat in the classroom, feeling about the size of a woman's clothing pin.

Class over, the master's voice rang out over the heads of the students rising from their benches. "Daid, report to me."

Daid came to a despondent stop in front of him.

Concern at the slow, indifferent manner, the sagging body, made the master knit his brow and purse his lips. "I looked for you at breakfast. Not finding you, I sent a slave to check your bed, thinking you might be ill. You weren't there. Where were you?"

"At the king's audience, Master."

Taken aback, the master said, "If you have dealings with the king, you come to me first. Do you understand?"

"Yes, Master."

"You are not to go rushing to the king unless given permission."

"Yes, Master." Daid remained with bowed head and drooping stance.

Unable to contain himself any longer, the master said, "What's wrong, Daid? Why did you go to the king?"

"I wanted to ask him," said Daid straightforwardly, "to order some imprisoned young women in Ur freed."

The master's face whitened. Did this boy have anything to do with the odd things that had happened at the temple about the time he appeared at the school? That very day, to his astonishment, he had been appointed master; no explanation. He had hurried to the home of the great physician he was appointed to replace. The man could not be found. Priests searched over the next two days. His wife was frantic. Then the queen's nephew had been ousted as assistant high priest and the student Sahar installed in his place. There had been explanations for that. The queen's nephew had been selling men who came to the temple into slavery. Daid came to the school as a slave of the king. Had he been sold by the queen's nephew? He had just admitted being from Ur, though in a roundabout way. Suddenly, the whole picture fell into place. The master knew what had happened in the temple and the school.

"And?"

Daid just stood there, saying nothing.

"What did the king say, Daid?"

"He couldn't interfere with the internal affairs of Ur."

Humbled by the extent of the politics he perceived and not wishing to inadvertently thwart the king's plans for Daid, the master said, "I had expected to have you do a leg amputation this afternoon."

"Forgive me," murmured Daid.

"Now, I think we'll put that off until another day."

"Yes, Master."

The master continued to observe the disconsolate stance, the lack of response to anything he said. "Daid, you are an exceptional student. You will do well in medicine. Remember that." No motion, no sound, no change. He sighed. "You may go."

Daid went to the corner where he talked to his God. No warmth came from Yahweh. He turned and looked at Hana-Ad's personal goddess. He found himself addressing her with the same intensity he used with Yahweh.

He lay on his mat, dozed and woke, dozed and woke. He pictured his lovely Hana-Ad dead beside the body of the old queen. He castigated himself for his enjoyment of what he was doing so much that he hadn't thought of home as often as he ought. He dozed.

Sahar woke him.

"You weren't at dinner. Are you ill? Shall I call the master?"

Daid jolted into a sitting position. "No, no."

"Hmm," commented Sahar. "What did you do wrong?"

Daid hesitated, then told him about Hana-Ad, what happened during his audience with the king, and the master's questions.

"Oh my, oh my," Sahar kept interjecting, his head moving slowly from side to side and his eyes getting larger and larger. When Daid finished, both men remained in drained silence, Daid sitting on his mat, Sahar standing.

In his quiet, supportive manner, Sahar finally said, "I'm so sorry, Daid, that our king refused. But I'm not surprised." He squatted beside Daid's mat.

"And the king won't let me go home."

"You must leave it in the hands of Marduk."

Daid sighed. "I don't know much about Marduk."

"I'll tell you." Sahar crossed his legs and sat, more comfortable than squatting. "In the beginning, Tiamat, the goddess of chaos, ruled. The other gods were afraid of her. They conferred together about how to fight her. Nobody volunteered. At last, the youth Marduk came forward. The gods were delighted. They promised him all their powers, which were considerable. He asked the winds to blow down her throat."

Daid whistled.

"Clever, isn't it? Anyway, Tiamat became so bloated she couldn't move. That made it easy for him to kill her."

Daid chuckled. "It sounds a great deal like the story of the creation I heard from my father, except Yahweh passed his hand across the deep to end the chaos, and no other god was involved."

After a short silence, he said, "How did Marduk get to Babylon?"

"Marduk was still a young god without much power when King Hammurabi became king. He wanted Marduk to rule in Babylon, but also knew that the young god needed status. The priests conferred and decided to name Marduk the god-who-came-forward-to-fight-Tiamat. The other gods endowed him with strength and wisdom, plus all the other powers in their possession. Then King Hammurabi installed him here in Babylon." Sahar looked at Daid seriously. "You should really consider Marduk's greatness. Maybe he could help you."

"Well," Daid hedged, "I'll give it some thought."

21

*D*aid cinched his skirt around his waist and hastened to the temple outer court. Flares moved to and fro as priests readied the gods' cart. Sputtering light from four flares jammed into buckets of dirt cast a smokey glow around the temple entrance. Shadowy figures, bent or erect, arms stretched sideways or up, constantly changing, struggled to get the great statue of Marduk through the door. His new golden garment glittered in light from the flares.

The darkness of the morning, the flares, the excitement in the air, thrilled Daid. Some priests carried lesser gods from the temple and set them in the courtyard. As soon as Marduk stood in his place in the cart, the other gods would be positioned around him.

The stars were winking out one by one and the flares didn't seem as bright as the deep, midnight blue in the sky gave way to cerulean.

A whisper passed swiftly. The king. The king. Daid spun around eagerly. Hammurabi, swathed in a dark cloak, accompanied by members of his staff, walked toward Marduk, now aloft in the cart. The high priest hurried to the king. The two spoke momentarily, approached the god, and went to their knees. Hammurabi raised his voice, asking blessing on the land for the coming year. With that, he rose and took his position before the cart. The high priest joined him, at the same time raising his hand in the signal to start.

Walking slowly, they left the temple grounds and started along the Processional Way. The rest of the priests in a mass that included the students studying to be physicians followed. At the river, gods and men boarded boats that took them to Akitu House set in a garden outside the city wall. Here, the gods, Hammurabi, and the high priest, along with certain others went into the house. Everybody else stood in the garden. They waited.

"What are they doing in there?" a young priest, a mere child, asked Daid.

"I don't know." Daid said and turned questioningly to another priest.

"It's a very important ritual having to do with the river flooding to nurture the earth, the growth of crops, and the fertility of the country for the coming year," said the priest.

Hours later, priests crying, "Praise to Marduk, Great is Marduk," carried the gods back to the boats. The moment the boats came into view of the city docks of Babylon, the silent, waiting crowds broke into cries of joy. Singing triumphantly, they danced alongside Marduk's cart as the plodding bullocks pulled him to his temple.

Excitement kept Daid awake a long time that night. He could hardly wait for morning when he would participate in the ceremonies.

In the pale light from a clear sky just before dawn, a line of naked priests snaked across the outer courtyard of Marduk's temple. The high priest, carrying a small jar of expensive incense, stood at the top of the staircase leading from the outer court to the ziggurat platform. With patience, he observed the scraggly line. Immediately in front of him, Sahar was arranging the administrative staff in proper order. Each priest carried a sacrifice. The lambs lay still, contented to be held. A few priests had trouble with squirming piglets. Other priests carried painted jars containing wheat, barley or wine.

Hammurabi, his green garment heavily encrusted in gold, ascended the stairs to the outer courtyard. He walked slowly, regally, toward the high priest. For a few minutes, they spoke together. Then the king moved to the enclosure set aside for the royal party, which included privileged palace functionaries and townspeople, garbed in brilliantly colored robes of scarlet, yellow or orange.

Below the temple platform, in the large courtyard of the temple complex, the men and women of the city, in their sheepskin skirts and heavy woolen cloaks, waited. Some knelt in reverence. Others stood with radiant, expectant faces. Still others clung together, fear on their faces.

Daid shivered in the morning's damp chill. The river surged

past the city in full flood. Its waters would turn the dull, withered stubble in the fields to green shoots, the dusty cart tracks into mud. This was the greatest festival of the year, the beginning of a new season, a renewal of life. Never before had he taken part in a New Year Festival. A titillating thrill passed through him as he stood with the other students near the middle of the snaking line of priests.

Today, culminating the eleven days of celebration, Hammurabi would unite with the high priestess. In their union, Marduk would bless the country in the coming year. The land would bloom in the exuberant surge of renewed life. Marduk's power and goodness had begun to impress Daid.

As he watched, a beam of light hit the temple on top of the ziggurat. Instantly a chant rose from somewhere at the head of the snake of priests and was taken up by coil after coil until the whole courtyard reverberated. Sahar had told him that there were one hundred steps to the first tier, one hundred more to the second tier, and more than that to the third tier, with the house of Marduk on top. He and his group of students were scheduled to stand on the second tier.

Slowly, the column started to mount the steps to the ziggurat platform. The high priest awaited them on the tower steps. Without really paying attention, Daid became aware that a priest had moved slyly to his coil from the coil to his right. Four priests separated him from the interloper. Then, just as his line started to inch forward, the priest slipped into the coil on his left. With a start, Daid realized that the man was the second priest who had fed him when he was a prisoner.

At that time, along with Sahar, he had carried out the wishes of the queen's nephew. Daid hadn't run into the man since. Sahar had told him that he feared the priest still did the royal nephew's bidding, at the command of the old priest. Even though Hammurabi had banished him from Babylon, making him the head of a temple a long way up the river toward Hattusa, the Hittite capital, the queen's nephew could still force priests to do his will.

Hardly aware of what he did, Daid slipped into the coil on his left and slid his eyes to the next coil on his left. The priest had half turned to speak to the priest behind him. He gesticulated in an apologetic way. Daid quickly looked straight ahead, fearful of locking eyes with the fellow, though with his shaved head and position as a student in the temple of Marduk, surely the priest wouldn't recognize him. He moved when the man moved, always one coil behind him.

Slowly, slowly, the line of chanting, naked men mounted the ziggurat stairs, higher and higher. Daid had never dared go near these steps. Only the highest ranking priests used them. Sacred tradition allowed no one else in the house of Marduk on top. Humbly walking up the steps, Daid thanked Yahweh that the urn of wine he carried wasn't heavy. Up, up, up. He climbed in the light now. Sweat on the bodies of the men in front of him glistened. He passed up to the second level, determined to keep near the other priest.

Sahar mounted the steps ahead. The man ascended, step after jaunty step, close behind him. Daid knew in his bones Sahar was his objective. Whatever the priest planned to do, he, Daid, intended to prevent it.

All at once, Daid perceived that he would be standing on the top level of the ziggurat. He caught his breath in trembling wonder.

Finally, they reached the level just below the god's house and fanned out on either side of the stairs. Sahar veered to the left. Other priests veered right. The high priest continued to the top. The interloper he followed planted himself to the left of and slightly behind Sahar. Daid managed to worm himself into line with that priest, a bit to the right of Sahar.

He straightened. For an instant, his breathing stopped. He looked out over the roofs of Babylon, its temples, even the palace of the king, the gardens and orchards, the winding river spilling over the fields. It flowed south to Ur. Could the priests on the other side see south? How far? His eyes moistened. He shook his head to clear his mind. How glorious the blazing light and cool, lilting breeze up here. Each leaf on the trees planted in deep rich soil spread over the terraces of the ziggurat fluttered gently, making a soft rustling sound. He shook his head in disbelief at the beauty spread before him. The hand of God.

The high priest entered the god's chamber. Daid tensed. Would Marduk be pleased and extend his favor for another year? A brilliant, simmering orange lit the sky. The intense light obliterated a lot of the view he had had a few minutes earlier. But now he could clearly see the people in the royal enclosure and the public below, all motionless, stiff, their expectant faces turned toward Marduk's house at the top of the ziggurat.

The sun burst above the horizon. An excited murmur rose. Daid raised his eyes to the temple just as the high priest appeared. Someone shouted. It became a massed cry that expanded and expanded in the light air. The high priest stood on the top step, his hands raised in thanksgiving. The swelling cry became wild joy. The people in the courtyard prostrated themselves. As they dropped, the priest Daid had followed lunged toward Sahar, hands stretched in front ready to push.

Daid grabbed Sahar's arm and yanked him back. Sahar fell into him. The other priest toppled over the low wall of the platform's edge.

Sahar let out an uncontrolled sharp cry, not loud enough to be heard in the wild euphoria of the moment. All faces blazed up toward the high priest in thanksgiving. Then everything on the ziggurat upper level returned to the way it had been. Daid glanced around. The priests seemed to be oblivious to what had just taken place. He relaxed. The high priest's sonorous voice intoned the final prayer. The fragrance of incense drifted past Daid. The New Year had begun. In babbling exhilaration, the priests put down their offerings and descended the staircase.

Daid pushed himself right behind Sahar. As they reached the second platform, each cast a sharp eye to the right. A motionless body lay across that low wall. Others noticed the body and murmured in surprise. The rumor spread that a priest in the ecstasy of the ritual had thrown himself off the platform, a living sacrifice to Marduk. People marveled at what he had done.

His family, notified of the magnificence of his sacrifice, came to the temple to thank the god for the great benefit they hoped for because of their son's gesture.

Daid paced uneasily that night in the shadow outside his sleeping quarters. He desperately wanted to talk to Sahar, to judge his reaction to the murder attempt, to listen to his worries, his plans. He fully expected Sahar would come. Head down, moving nervously, he didn't notice the slim figure running across the courtyard. He jumped when Sahar said, "He tried to kill me."

"Yes." Daid nodded.

"Thanks to you, I'm still alive."

"I've been offering prayers of thanksgiving to Yahweh ever since. Suppose I hadn't realized he meant to hurt you."

"Don't even think about it." Sahar placed his hand on Daid's arm.

"Do you think he was a go-between?"

"No."

"Why not?"

"His loyalty was to the old priest." Sahar thought a minute. "Yes, that's right. The old priest was the go-between. I suspect the queen's nephew ordered him to have me killed."

"But that old priest is dying."

"Somebody caring for him will undoubtedly tell him about the priest throwing himself off the ziggurat. He will somehow, and I don't know how, send a message to the queen's nephew that—"

"A priest sacrificed himself."

"Right. No names."

"He'll send the message assuming that priest was you."

Sahar nodded. "He'll die thinking he accomplished his task. So I'm safe until something comes up that brings me to the royal's attention."

Daid squeezed Sahar's shoulder. "I'm glad. I'd hate to have anything happen to you. You're the only real friend I've got."

"That goes for me, too. I know you want to go home, but I hope you stick around a long time."

Daid made a wry face as Sahar left him.

22

*A*shnan lost her grip on the bowl of hot food she carried, dropping the bowl on the floor and spilling the brown sauce and pieces of pork down the front of her gown.

"By the gods," she cried, whirling on Nidada, "You pushed me."

"I wasn't anywhere near you." Nidada stalked off, her face flush with anger.

"Now I have to change before Queen Ku-bau calls us back." Ashnan glared at the other girls. "That could be any minute." Her nose in the air, she held the soiled gown away from her body with a thumb and forefinger. Making a show of extending her other fingers, she headed for her alcove. Temena followed her.

"Queen Ku-bau isn't going to call us back any time soon," Ninbar whisered to Uttu.

Uttu snorted. "Ashnan'll have plenty of time to march around in whatever she puts on before the old queen wakes up."

A half hour later, Ashnan appeared in a stunning yellow gown. She walked arrogantly toward Girsu-Ad, Shegunu, and Hana-Ad sitting on cushions in the middle of the room.

"Oh, is that a new dress?" said Girsu-Ad. "It's lovely."

Shegunu nodded and smiled. "It looks beautiful on you."

Hana-Ad started to smile, then froze. From Ashnan's ears hung the carnelian dangles Ninti had picked up from the floor in the instrument room. Quickly ducking to prevent her face from giving her away, she pressed one fingernail into her wrist. The pain distracted her enough that she had time to compose herself.

Here, at last, Ashnan had stumbled. They had something tangible to link her to the broken harp. She couldn't wait to tell Uttu.

The afternoon seemed interminable. Ku-bau demanded music, then had them practice dance steps. Kigal, a clumsy dancer, placed her foot too close to Ashnan. Ashnan pirouetted, struck

Kigal's foot and sprawled. She rose awkwardly to her hands and knees before she could manage to stand up.

"Ashnan," said Ku-bau, "I'm trying to train you to be graceful, not to look like a lumbering dog."

"Yes, Majesty," said Ashnan, purple-faced. "I'll try. My humble apologies."

The girls could feel her mortification. Kigal wanted to cry out that she had made the error and beg forgiveness. Instead, she forced herself to line up with the others to start over.

The old queen became restless, fussed with her green dress, her gold neck chains, her pearl and carnelian bracelets.

The lead slave knelt beside her.

"You are tiring, Majesty," said the woman.

Queen Ku-bau looked at her slave, looked at the girls, sighed and said, "Dismissed."

Hana-Ad placed her harp in the instrument room and waited for Uttu. "Let's go into the garden."

"Now?"

"Yes." Kigal trailed a few steps behind them.

Once out of earshot, Hana-Ad blurted, "Ashnan broke your harp."

Uttu stopped short. Kigal, who had been examining one of the flowers, bumped into her, blushed, and apologized. Uttu took Kigal's arm without looking at her. She stared at Hana-Ad, her face puckered up in puzzlement.

"We've thought that right along. How do you know for sure?"

"I recognized the earrings Ninti found. Ashnan has them on tonight."

"I can't believe it."

"She waited long enough before wearing them," Hana-Ad said sarcastically.

"She's big enough and strong enough to yank out the strings and smash the wood," said Kigal. "But how mean. Why would she do such a thing?"

"It wasn't long after you told her off for pushing Ninbar out of the chair," Hana-Ad said, looking at Uttu.

"That's true."

"She's probably also the one who arranged to move my rouge shell into Kigal's alcove to get me into trouble because I'd crossed her."

"You mean, she's the one who put it in my alcove?" interrupted Kigal.

"I doubt she did," Hana-Ad said. "She probably bribed Ninti. Ninti's small and quick."

"But I didn't do anything to her," Kigal objected.

"You're my friend. She's trying to get back at me and make trouble between us at the same time." After a second, Hana-Ad said, "And Queen Ku-bau gave her my gold chain." Tears made her blink.

"We'll get it back, Hana-Ad. Don't worry," said Kigal.

"Ninti," said Uttu, "is Ashnan's only friend. She's the logical one to do it."

"Also, if Ninti is caught, Ashnan isn't implicated," Hana-Ad said, her expression thoughtful.

"That's terrible," said Kigal. "Ninti's a nice girl."

The other two smiled. "Dear Kigal," Uttu said, "you are kind to everyone and think no evil thoughts."

Kigal hung her head and blushed.

"I've thought about Ashnan all afternoon," Hana-Ad said. "The only thing I think we could do is corner Ninti and make her confess. She would, once we confronted her. What do you think we should do?"

"What we better do right now," said Uttu, "is go in to dinner or Ashnan will have devoured everything."

"She never does that," Kigal said.

Uttu laughed. "Come along, Kigal."

Uttu walked directly to the table where the huge basin of steamed fish and vegetables lay. She pointedly inspected Ashnan on the other side loading her bowl. The carnelian stones dangled from her ears.

Kigal picked up a bowl and shyly edged beside Ashnan.

"Kigal, keep away from me—now and in the future."

Hana-Ad, heading toward her alcove, turned to hear what else Ashnan was going to say.

"You're a rotten dancer anyway, and you're always in somebody's way."

"She isn't all that rotten," said Nin-Ad, who had just entered the room and heard Ashnan's last statement.

"She not only is the worst dancer I've ever seen, but she's stupid besides. It takes somebody inordinately stupid to mangle those steps and then to knock me down." Ashnan's face flamed in anger. "Queen Ku-bau yelled at me. Me! When it was your fault. You idiot."

"Leave her alone," Hana-Ad snapped as Kigal started to cry.

"Don't you tell me what to do," Ashnan turned to Hana-Ad.

"I will when you hurt somebody else," she said, slowly joining the group around the food.

"I'm the one who's hurt. This little viper just stood there and said nothing. Besides," Ashnan added, "what I say to her is none of your business."

"That's right, I don't bother when you're your usual nasty self." Hana-Ad stood her ground, suddenly quiet and assured. "But when you deliberately and unnecessarily hurt Kigal, it's my business and everybody else's business." She moved between Kigal and Ashnan. The others stood like statues, watching, scarcely breathing.

"All right," Ashnan sneered, setting her bowl precariously on the table's edge. "Our oh-so-goody-goody deserves a thrashing." She swung, catching Hana-Ad with a hard open hand across the face. The blow knocked her into Kigal whose body kept her from falling. For a stunned instant she stared into the black, furious eyes of Ashnan.

Her face cold, hard, and ugly, Ashnan said, "Next time, I'll hit you until you cry for mercy, or," she sneered, "would you like to do that now?"

Immobile for the moment, Hana-Ad stared at Ashnan. Blinding rage started in her toes and surged through her body like a hot flame.

Ashnan insolently snatched up her bowl and turned her back. The motion released Hana-Ad. She jumped, grabbed Ashnan's wig, tilting it over her eyes and brought her knee forcefully up into the end of Ashnan's spine. Ashnan shrieked. Her hands flew up, shooting the bowl across the table and spraying the contents over everyone.

Hana-Ad kicked the backs of Ashnan's knees, causing her to crumple, then jumped astride her. Using her clenched fists to pummel any part of Ashnan she could reach, she reduced Ashnan to a squirming, sobbing lump. The others closed in on them, silently cheering for Hana-Ad.

The three slaves, who had just come back from the kitchen with more food, descended like a whirlwind and separated the two. Temena led Ashnan, sniveling and deflated, to her alcove. Bitar and Gula kept a firm grip on Hana-Ad.

"I'm not hurt much," she said, shaking an arm free to feel her stinging cheek and trying to control her weak and wobbly legs.

She felt ashamed of her rage, ashamed of her behavior, her physical brutality, yet somehow elated, rather enjoying the admiring glances of the surrounding circle.

"You were wonderful." Kigal gazed at Hana-Ad with puppy adoration.

"Paid her back for some of her meanness," said Nidada.

"Yes, but still, I'm embarrassed by my behavior," Hana-Ad said.

"Don't be," said Uttu. "We've all wanted to do the same thing and haven't dared."

"You girls better eat," said Gula from her hands and knees, mopping up the fish and vegetables Ashnan had shot all over the rug. "And some of you need a change of clothes."

"After we eat," Uttu said calmly. She handed Hana-Ad a full bowl, took her hand, and led her to the finely textured wool floor cushions. She formally seated Hana-Ad in a place of honor. The rest followed Uttu's lead. They arranged themselves around Hana-Ad. The wet, soiled gowns forgotten, they soon became absorbed in happy chatter.

Hana-Ad noticed Gula take a small bowl of food to Ashnan's alcove. She glanced around the circle. Every face beamed. Even Ninti munched her chunk of bread and her fish with a contented expression.

In bed that night, Hana-Ad lay on her back a long time, listening. Everyone fidgeted. She heard the bodies flip over and over in the beds. At last. Stillness. She knew what she intended to do, what she had to do. She breathed slowly, deeply, willing herself to remain calm.

Soundlessly, in the dark, she tiptoed to Ashnan's alcove and pushed aside the drape.

"Ashnan, don't say anything," she whispered urgently. "I've got to talk to you."

"Get out of here, you—you—"

"Shush," commanded Hana-Ad trying to put her hand over Ashnan's mouth.

Ashnan shoved Hana-Ad's arm with enough force to knock her off balance. Hana-Ad fell across the bed. "Oh Ashnan," she said, squirming off the bed. "We can't go on like this. I don't like worrying about what you're going to do to me next. It would be so much better if we could be friends. Please Ashnan."

In the dark, Hana-Ad furrowed her brow and shook her head back and forth. Tentatively, she put a hand on the bed. Two of her fingers collided with Ashnan's arm. Ashnan stiffened and moved slightly away.

Sensing a softening in Ashnan, Hana-Ad, half afraid of a violent reaction, gingerly sat down on the edge of the bed. Ashnan didn't move.

Hana-Ad rose slightly and sat down more securely. Ashnan moved over, making room for Hana-Ad.

For a short time neither moved or said anything, but the air pulsated.

Finally, unsure of how to begin, Hana-Ad said, "Tell me about your family."

"I don't have a family," Ashnan burst out.

"You don't have a family?" repeated Hana-Ad, aghast. "I don't understand."

"I was sold when I was a baby. I was eleven before I found out my father, a date farmer, and my mother weren't my real parents. One night I displeased him and he shouted at me, 'Get away. You're not mine.'"

"What did you do?" Hana-Ad gasped.

"I stared at him, dumbstruck. All this time, even though they'd turned me into a drudge and I had to serve their four sons, I thought I was their daughter. I didn't know my treatment was any different than other girls.'"

"And—and your mother—"

"They said my mother was the concubine of a carpenter. His wife was furious when I was born, so she palmed me off on the family who raised me. She did it while my father was off doing his tax duty for the state. She had money in her own right, enough to pay for my upbringing. We—the family where I lived," she said bitterly, "were poor and needed the extra cash."

"Didn't your father object?"

"I don't know anything about that. But when he died, his wife stopped paying, saying she didn't care what happened to me."

"But—but your mother—" Hana-Ad wagged her head sadly. How terrible. Terrible. Poor Ashnan.

"His wife drove my mother out of the house." Ashnan shed quiet tears. "She would have loved me."

Quickly, before she cried herself, Hana-Ad said, "But the family didn't throw you out when she stopped paying them?"

"They were a little better off by then so they kept me as a slave. I remember looking down at my coarse, skimpy dress, when he told me who my real parents were, without any feeling—just a numb blankness."

"Why didn't you tell us, Ashnan?" Hana-Ad wanted to put her arms around Ashnan.

"I was ashamed. Shegunu was royal. The rest of you had happy homes. You were engaged."

Hana-Ad remembered that awful day when Ashnan had deliberately told her their fate.

"I never had enough to eat," continued Ashnan. "I was just lucky their sons didn't take my virginity or the old queen would never have chosen me. A couple of them tried. And when I complained, their mother laughed at me. She said, 'It's a learning experience.' It was awful. I was so afraid."

"But then Queen Ku-bau sent for you." Hana-Ad cuddled up against Ashnan, not daring to hug her. "How long ago was that?"

"Five years ago. I remember exactly. The old queen's cart arrived at the door, and the guards asked the farmer for me. His wife got really mad and told him they were stealing her slave. She even slapped me. And it wasn't my fault." She started to cry, using the blanket to mop her eyes. "They were so cruel."

For a short time, Hana-Ad patted Ashnan in silence. "No wonder you're happy here."

"I love it. I love the beautiful clothes, the jewels, the slaves to dress and undress me. I'll be with Queen Ku-bau in luxury forever."

With sudden resolve, Hana-Ad said, "Will you sit with me at breakfast tomorrow?"

Ashnan didn't answer.

Hana-Ad started to ask her question again when very softly, with a catch in her voice, Ashnan said, "Yes."

"We'll wait until some of the others have served themselves," Hana-Ad said, smiling to herself at the thought. "Then we'll walk up together."

"Maybe we can take our bowls to the garden," Ashnan said.

"Yes, let's. Morning is lovely in the garden." Touching Ashnan's cheek with her fingertips, Hana-Ad stood up.

"Wait. I want to tell you something."

Hana-Ad withdrew into herself, deadly quiet, expectant. Everything was going to come out.

"Girsu-Ad had nothing to do with the broken harp. She always acts guilty. So, of course, the old queen thinks she is. And

I'm sorry about your rouge shell." Ashnan reached out and took Hana-Ad's hand.

"That doesn't matter now. It's all over and forgotten."

"I had my earrings placed under your pillow, too."

So, she had made Ninti do it.

"I hated you because the others all liked you. I went to Queen Ku-bau. She gave me your gold chain."

Hana-Ad snatched her hand away.

"Oh, please," pleaded Ashnan.

Hana-Ad seized the drape, ready to leave, ready to cry. She wanted her chain, desperately.

"Don't go. I'll give your chain to you." Ashnan got off the bed. "I know you'll never be my friend now," she said sadly. She went down on her knees and fumbled under the mattress. Then, stretching her arm out, she swung it around in the dark until she found Hana-Ad's hand. She laid the chain on her palm and closed her fingers over the metal.

"Thank you, Ashnan." Emotion made speech nearly impossible.

In her own alcove, Hana-Ad shed happy tears. She slipped the gold over her head and felt the cool metal on her neck. Her hand still clutched it when she fell asleep.

At breakfast, Hana-Ad smiled and nodded at Ashnan.

Ashnan ducked her head, so happy she wanted to scream. She let Hana-Ad fill her bowl first and didn't fish for the most succulent pieces of meat. Amazed, the others furtively glanced at each other. They watched Ashnan and Hana-Ad start toward the garden with their full bowls, seemingly unperturbed by the stupefaction around them.

"Join us in the garden." Hana-Ad smiled at Uttu as they passed by her table.

"A-ah yes."

The astonished reply released a hubbub.

"Can you believe that?" said Girsu-Ad.

"Something must have happened last night after we went to sleep. Because the last time we saw them, they were ready to kill each other," said Ninbar.

Kigal scowled at the three in the garden. She didn't know whether to go out or not.

"Kigal," said Ninti, "will you sit with me? Ashnan has a new friend."

Kigal observed the girl's downcast eyes and tight mouth. "I'll be your friend, Ninti."

"You will?" Relief flooded Ninti's face. "You're such a nice person, Kigal. I'd like to be your friend."

"You'll be Hana-Ad's and Uttu's, too."

23

*D*ressed in gorgeous deep yellow, Nanshe walked sedately along the corridor leading to the king's audience court. The morning glittered. The new year had started propitiously. Now, two months later, she intended to announce to the king and the assembled morning's petitioners the god's favor to her.

At the corner of the court, she hesitated. Quite a crowd of people stood around. Good. The more, the better. By tonight, news of the god's child would have spread over the whole city, strengthening her position as high priestess.

Slowly in all her elegance, she started toward the dais where King Idi-Sin sat. Ur-Ilum and several officials of the court stood behind him, guards in their places on either side of the dais. A man noticed her and bowed low before the high priestess of Nannar. Others noticed. A pathway through the throng instantly opened. The chancellor whispered to the king who raised his hand in greeting. She knelt on one knee before him.

"Rise." He smiled. "What brings my royal aunt, the high priestess of Nannar, to this audience court?"

"I have news, fortunate, lucky news for our city."

"Say on." Idi-Sin's face shone like the morning radiance as he edged forward on his chair.

"At the New Year, the god planted his seed. In the fulfillment of time, there will be a child."

An excited cry rose from those in attendance. They dropped face down in homage before the royal priestess. Idi-Sin registered pleased amazement.

After again gracefully kneeling, Nanshe left the audience court.

At the conclusion of the session, the king hurried to the ziggurat to give his daily report to Nannar.

"Today," Idi-Sin said to the stately high priest of Nannar, "I will sacrifice a sheep. Nannar has unbelievably favored us. Not only is our land blossoming, but he has offered us a child by the high priestess."

"Praise, praise to Nannar," cried the high priest. He and all the priests within earshot fell prostrate on the ground.

"Let us proceed to the altar for the day's report," said the high priest, rising. He turned to his assistant.

"Order a sheep without blemish to be brought. This is a day for rejoicing."

The king's report on the welfare of Ur was a hymn of praise and thanksgiving. As he neared the end of his homage to Nannar, a priest laid the right leg, kidneys and a roast from the sheep before the statue of the god. Dates and bowls of milk were also set on the altar.

In all his ritual elegance, his hands raised in supplication, the wide gold bands on his upper arms and the gold medallion against his chest glittering, the long, orange, wool skirt of the priesthood hanging close on his slender body, the high priest offered the final prayer:

"A sheep, oh Nannar, we consecrate

A vow, oh Nannar, we dedicate

A first born, oh Nannar, we consecrate

A sacrifice, oh Nannar, we dedicate."

Then the king and the high priest, in an unusual move, led a parade of priests the full length of the Processional Way among joyful citizens before returning to the ziggurat. His official duties finished, the king almost ran to his quarters.

"Where's the queen?" he asked the first guard he saw.

"In your oldest son's court, talking to the physician, Majesty."

This time, Idi-Sin walked regally, careful not to show his excitement.

"How fortunate that you came just now," said Nin-Anna the moment her husband appeared. "Sumulael tells me that our son has made progress." She stopped talking to look at Shulgi bouncing up and down in a little red cart and drinking pomegranate juice.

Idi-Sin flushed. "This is good news, too. Ur will prosper greatly."

His reaction warning her, she hastened to say, "Unfortunately, not enough to change the succession."

Wonderful how Nin-Anna had accepted the investiture of Ibbisin, their second son. Everything seemed to be favoring Ur today. Even the sheep's entrails indicated good fortune.

"He has stabilized on the regime I worked out for him," said

Sumulael from the other side of the red cart. "I have trained his caretakers to follow it. At this point, he no longer needs me. So I ask permission to return to Babylon."

"We can't talk about that now," said Idi-Sin. "I will have to observe my son. I have to see what physician we have to replace you. It will take time. Now, I wish to talk to the queen."

Seething with frustration, stymied in every attempt to return to Babylon, Sumulael bowed and quickly backed from the room.

"Wonderful news, my dear." Idi-Sin burst with pride.

"We will go to our quarters," he said as the prince flung a tumbler of pomegranate juice on the floor.

In their bedroom, the queen turned to him eagerly. "Tell me. I can hardly wait."

Taking her hands, he said, "On the New Year, Nannar favored us."

"You mean—you mean Nanshe—" Nin-Anna stuttered.

He nodded.

Nin-Anna bowed low, a formal bow, to hide her anger. "Ur will again be as great as in ancient times," she said, resorting to hyperbole to cover any indiscretion in tone he may have noticed. "We will throw off the Babylonian yoke."

"My dear, we have pleased our god. Today has been auspicious. But I doubt it means we will throw off the Babylonian yoke."

"Of course we will free ourselves from the Babylonians. We will rule all—all." She flung her arms wide.

Idi-Sin looked skeptical. "It would be nice, but I think our success will be somewhat less than that."

"My love, think big. The god did." She wanted to pound his chest with her fists. "Nanshe is old—old." Nin-Anna clamped her teeth before saying something worse. The baby made Nanshe's position inviolate.

"Not that old." Idi-Sin smirked at the memory of the New Year's ritual. Nanshe was quite a woman.

Tossing back her head, Nin-Anna said, "My dearest, I must fly to your mother with this wonderful news."

In a flutter of waving arms and swirling wool, she ran from the room.

Purposely avoiding her court ladies, Nin-Anna hurried along the corridor. The more she bridled her temper, the more exciting visions surfaced before her eyes. She saw herself living in the great palace in Babylon. Idi-Sin ruled the whole southern delta. He gave the city-states the same independent rule they had, but he extracted more taxes. The god's seed born of Nanshe had been installed as Nannar's high priest in Babylon, taking precedence over Marduk. Her youngest son ruled Nannar's temple in Ur. Babylonian society bowed down to her. She received them regally, wearing the costliest garments and the finest jewelry.

By the time she reached Queen Ku-bau's quarters, her anger had dissipated. She glowed, savoring her soon-to-be exalted rank.

"Something pleases you," said the old queen, motioning to Nin-Ad to stop reciting from the Gilgamesh Epic.

"Yes, Majesty," Nin-Anna said, watching Nin-Ad discreetly withdraw to her usual position against the wall and wishing all ten girls were present. "Nannar has favored us with his seed at the culmination of the New Year festival."

Ku-bau sat up straight for the first time in months. "Nanshe is with child?"

"Yes, Majesty."

"Praise be," said Ku-bau. "What wonderful news. That portends great things for Ur."

The two women clutched each other's hands in ecstatic delight.

In the exuberance of the moment, they didn't notice Nin-Ad slip out the door. She raced along the walkway, signaling the two girls in the garden. "Everybody," she yelled at the entrance to their social room, "come listen."

The girls around the gaming board stopped playing. Others stepped from their alcoves.

"I was reciting poetry for Queen Ku-bau when Queen Nin-Anna came to tell her—"

"What?" interrupted Girsu-Ad when Nin-Ad hesitated.

"That Nanshe is—oh," she burst out, her eyes sparkling, "is wonderfully favored by Nannar."

Cries of joy rose as each girl dropped to the carpet in praise.

"Let's go to the garden and watch Queen Nin-Anna leave," Hana-Ad said to Kigal when they were on their feet again. "She's so lovely. And to be queen—" Hana-Ad broke off, awed by Nin-Anna's royal position.

They wandered off, leaving the others chattering wildly.

Soon Uttu and Ashnan joined them in the garden. Uttu, always practical, said, "Nanshe should curtail some of her activity now. We can help her more in the care of the god."

"Yes," said Ashnan. "I'm taller. I can do the stretching."

Hana-Ad smiled at Ashnan. A happy Ashnan smiled back.

"Queen Nin-Anna is spending a long time with the old queen," said Uttu.

Nin-Anna was walking slowly when she passed the girls, a beatific expression on her face. Her talk with Ku-bau had been most satisfying. She couldn't resist. She waved.

In the corridor, she began to walk faster. Suddenly, an intense pain stabbed her lower abdomen. With a terrified scream, she fell against the wall.

A guard rushed from his station at Queen Ku-bau's double doors to find her in a heap on the floor, writhing in pain.

"Get my ladies," she croaked.

He ran off, yelling, "Help! Help!"

A crowd gathered. Slaves lifted a wailing Nin-Anna from the floor and carried her to her bedroom. As they placed her on the enormous carved and amber-inlaid bed, she screamed and curled into a ball. The king sent for Sumulael, then shooed the court ladies from the bedroom and hovered over his wife.

After an extensive examination, Sumulael said to Nin-Anna, "Majesty, it is not your usual bilious attack. You have hard lumps in your kidneys. I will give you medication to try and dissolve them. You are to stay in bed."

"Why has this misfortune befallen me just when Nannar has favored us? What have I done?" she moaned.

"I don't know, Highness. Seek knowledge from your personal god."

She didn't even hear him.

"I have done nothing wrong."

"We will sacrifice, my dear one," said Idi-Sin. "It'll be all right. You'll see."

"But it hurts," she whimpered.

"Majesty," said Sumulael, "have you been troubled with your water?"

"Yes," she answered, embarrassed. "It has been difficult."

"How long has that been going on?"

"Off and on since the new year."

Sumulael pursed his lips. "You should have told me sooner. Now, I don't know what success we will have in dissolving the lumps."

"I—I thought it would go away."

"You will take saltpeter. The quantity should be about as much as your thumb down to the knuckle. Take that mixed with oil of turpentine and powdered ostrich eggs. Put this in beer. Drink it each morning when you rise and each night when you retire. You may also have a small dose of nightshade for your pain."

"And the poultice?" said the king.

Sumulael didn't think a poultice necessary, but if the king wanted one, he would have it.

"Pulverize the lees of the dried vine, pine tree, and plum tree. Add beer to this until it is a soft paste. Then rub the queen's lower back with oil and fasten this poultice to the spot."

Sumulael, head down, backed away. "I will come tomorrow."

The queen started to sniffle. "It hurts."

"The nightshade, quick." The king snapped his fingers at a slave. "And beer."

"May I have my personal goddess?" the queen begged. "I must pray to her. Somehow, I have displeased her. She sent this terrible pain to punish me."

"You are so sweet, you can do no wrong," the king said, distressed by the queen's pain. He crossed the room to the table where they kept their personal gods. He picked up a round-eyed, severe-looking goddess and laid it beside the queen.

"Goddess, mine," she said, "help me. Tell me what I have done to displease you." She stroked the goddess' head. "I will rectify my transgressions. I humbly beseech you to aid me."

A slave appeared with a cup of beer. The king said, "Help her drink it." The slave supported Nin-Anna's head and shoulders as she drank. She sank back against the pillows.

"Please ask Queen Ku-bau for Shegunu," said Nin-Anna. "Her presence soothes me."

A male slave arrived with the saltpeter brew. Despite the beer, the smell made the queen crinkle her nose.

"Ugh, this is horrible." Nin-Anna pushed the cup away.

"Drink, my love," ordered the king, fussing over her.

Holding her nose, she drank a little.

"I will help you, Majesty," said one of the court ladies who had returned when Sumulael left. She took the tumbler from the slave.

Nin-Anna tried to swallow another mouthful and gagged. "No," she said.

"Nin-Anna," the king said, taking her hands in his, "you must drink."

"I'll vomit."

"Drink."

She knew she had to obey when he used that tone with her. In five stages, she finished the draught. Several slaves immediately rolled her onto her stomach for the application of the poultice. She was getting sleepy.

Shegunu entered and went to the bed. "I have come, Majesty." Nin-Anna glanced at Shegunu, smiled, and closed her eyes.

Each morning and each evening, the queen objected to the medicinal draught. Each time, she swallowed it after much pleading and shifting of the court lady holding the tumbler. Eventually, she passed the little hard lumps.

"You have recuperated quickly, Majesty," said Sumulael. "But next time, tell me right away when you have an ailment. You may get up, but, to keep the problem from recurring, you will have to alter your diet."

His eyes swung to the corner of the room, his thumb and forefinger holding his chin. Nobody moved, all eyes on Sumulael. His glance shifted back to the queen. "You will drink only beer and a little water. You will eat sea bass with vegetables once a day and meat with vegetables once a day. No milk and best eat no onions or garlic."

"No," she said. "I won't give up onions, and I will continue to drink as much milk as I want. How do you expect me to exist if I have to give up all those things!"

His face a careful, innocuous mask to hide his irritation, Sumulael backed from the room.

Nin-Anna immediately got out of bed and padded on bare feet to the table where the little statues of the gods stood watching her. She placed her personal goddess in the middle of the front row next to Idi-Sin's god and conveniently forgot about her transgressions.

24

"*A*re you going to remove your clothes or shall I call a slave?" Nanshe scowled at Uttu.

The nine other girls, naked and scared, huddled close to the wall in Nannar's major temple receiving room. Uttu stood between Nanshe and the bunched girls, her head raised in defiance.

"I'm a virgin, and I intend to remain one," Uttu stated as regally as a royal.

"Virginity is not in question here," snapped Nanshe. "You are well aware that we are repeating here in Nannar's temple a ritual performed in the Babylonian temple of the god Marduk. We will give thanks to Nannar for the great favor shown Ur this past New Year. Nobody will see you."

"I have bared my body to no one, and will not do so now."

"We'll see about that." Nanshe clapped her hands twice.

A muscular temple slave, wearing only a short blue skirt and a matching cloth wound around his head, entered.

"Strip this girl." Nanshe's chin jerked up as she stared under lowered lids at Uttu.

The slave walked around the priestess. As he approached Uttu, she stepped backward, fear distorting her face.

Sensing that she might turn and dart away, he lunged, grabbing her arm with his left hand and her gown's fabric, where it flowed across her breast, with his right.

Her eyelids fluttered as she felt the pressure of the dress against her back. Then came the sound of tearing as the fabric gave way. She screamed.

The slave left as silently as he had come. The torn garment lay on the floor. The nine young women drew closer together, their eyes bulging. Uttu sobbed hysterically. The royal priestess sagged momentarily, her eyes riveted on the red birth mark on Uttu's upper left leg where it met her torso. Her body became rigid. The anger drained slowly from her face, leaving it a yellow, sickly pallor.

Uttu stood, shoulders hunched over, head down, gulping drawn-out sobs. The grouped girls stood immobile, hands clutched at each other, mouths slightly ajar. Except for Uttu's sobs, no sounds came from the living statues. Even the air hung motionless and still. Then Nanshe wobbled, her knees buckled, and she sank to the floor.

Kigal's grip on Hana-Ad's upper arm increased. Hana-Ad gently pried her fingers loose. Walking slowly and deliberately toward Uttu, Hana-Ad glanced at Nanshe, whose closed eyes gave her face the aspect of death.

"Here," she said, scooping up the dress that lay at Uttu's feet. "Wrap this around you." She gave Uttu a hug and hurried to the corner where they had dropped their clothes when Nanshe told them to strip. "We must dress quickly," she said over her shoulder as she searched for her things among the pile, "and call Mesile to care for Nanshe."

"Do you think she's dead?" asked Girsu-Ad.

Ashnan and Nidada tiptoed up to Nanshe. "She's breathing," said Ashnan.

In a weak, barely audible voice, Nanshe said, "Call my slave," and shut her eyes again.

Ninbar ran to the door, stuck her head out, and looked first left then right along the corridor. She spied Mesile leaning against the wall where the corridor made a right angle.

"Come immediately," she called, "and attend your mistress." Then, making a circle around Uttu to hide her torn dress, the girls walked as a group out of the room.

At the door, Mesile jumped forward and back, trying unsuccessfully to dart between the girls. As the last two girls cleared the doorway, she rushed in, uttered a cry of alarm and fell to her knees beside Nanshe. "Help me to my room," whispered Nanshe. Mesile slid an arm under Nanshe's shoulders and raised her to a sitting position. Then, her arms under Nanshe's armpits, she pulled her to her feet. A firm, sturdy arm grabbed Nanshe around the waist.

"Put your arm around my neck, princess," said Mesile. That way, slowly, shuffling, they quitted the room.

The bunched group of girls, on the other hand, moved swiftly down the platform staircase. "Shush, Uttu," warned Hana-Ad. "Our guards are nearby and have to lead us back along the Processional Way.

Uttu sniffed and gulped. Kigal carressed her arm. As their guards surrounded them, Uttu gave a final gulp, but let the tears continue to run down her cheeks and off her nose. They walked rapidly along the Processional Way, three girls in front, three behind, Ashnan alone directly behind Uttu, one hand loosely holding the torn dress against Uttu's shoulder. Kigal and Hana-Ad on either side of Uttu kept a firm grip on the front of her dress. Without meeting anyone in the palace corridor, they arrived at Ku-bau's double doors.

The palace guards raised their arms in greeting before Ku-bau's door guards, turned, and marched back to the palace guard room.

With sighs of relief, the girls flew into their room. Uttu flung herself on her bed, curled into a ball, and covered her head with her arms.

Hana-Ad sat down next to her. For a few minutes, she stroked Uttu's shoulders. Finally, she said, "Uttu, you must stop this. You were humiliated, yes, but it was your own doing. It isn't the end of the world."

Uttu mumbled, "You think it isn't! After everybody saw that horrible red birthmark on my leg!" Sobs started again.

"What birthmark? None of us saw it. Nanshe was the only one who could see it because you were facing her. So, see, it isn't so bad."

"It isn't so bad!" gasped Uttu. "Look what it did to her. She passed out."

"I don't think your birthmark caused her to faint. I think we are going to hear it had to do with something else."

Uttu sat up. "Her coming child?"

"Maybe." Putting her index finger against her cheek, Hana-Ad's eyes shifted into nowhere. "She must be old to have a first child, and she's in the beginning months. That might be why she fainted."

"If anything happened to her child, it would be awful for this whole city," said Uttu, consternation replacing humiliation.

"Yes, it would." Hana-Ad nodded in agreement, pleased that that had taken Uttu's mind off her birthmark. "I'll call Gula to bring you another dress. Then we can go see if there's any news of Nanshe's condition." She slid off the bed.

"By the way, doesn't Gula see the birthmark when she dresses you?"

"No. I'm careful to keep something draped across me. Gula probably thinks I'm overly modest." Uttu sniffed. "But I don't care."

Hana-Ad grinned and left the alcove.

Days went by. The only thing any of the girls heard was that Nanshe was ill. The old queen rarely summoned them to entertain her. When she did, she sat slumped and scowling. They tried to cheer her. They danced and sang. They thought up funny incidents to pantomime. They offered her special sweets. Nothing helped.

Terrified by what Nannar might do to Ur if Nanshe lost the god's seed, Ku-bau called a young slave to take a message to the high priest. "Tell him," she said, "I want him to attend me every day right after my light meal." She waved her hand at the little boy.

As he reached the door, she called, "And tell him he's not to send a substitute. I want him to come himself."

Every day, the high priest offered prayers and small sacrifices. Every day, the ten girls were obligated to join in the prayers and sacrifices. Every day, after the service, a slave girl walked to Nanshe's room to inquire after her.

Mesile would say, "Her Highness is resting." She refused to offer more information.

Ku-bau stewed and fretted. One day, when the slave returned from Mesile with the same short sentence, Ku-bau threw up her hands in frustration. "You!" She pointed at a slave leaning against the wall. "Go to my daughter-in-law, Queen Nin-Anna, and ask her to attend me." Ku-bau squirmed around on her bed. Suddenly, her gaze focused on the ten girls sitting on the floor. "Go." She waved an arm at them. "I've had enough music today." She turned to a slave. "Bring me some beer. No, wine." She hesitated. "I don't know. Just bring me something to drink."

The girls hurried from the room. As they neared their room, Queen Nin-Anna walked through the double doors, followed by Ku-bau's slave girl. The ten girls fell on their knees and remained that way until the queen entered Ku-bau's room. Rising to their feet, their heads automatically turned in the direction of Queen Ku-bau's door. Slowly, one by one, her slaves came out. They stood in a group, whispering and looking at the door. The lead slave stood against the wall as close to the open door as she dared, her ear against the door jamb.

Inside, in the center of the room, their heads together, Ku-bau and Nin-Anna whispered.

"Have you heard any news?" the old queen asked.

"Nothing more than you have."

"I don't like it. The portents are all bad. We could lose her and the child. That would be a real disaster."

Nin-Anna's eyes raked Ku-bau in disgust. "We have survived the loss of other high priestesses," she said coldly.

"Not while carrying the god's seed," countered Ku-bau. "No state could survive that."

That bothered Nin-Anna, too. Much as she wanted Nanshe dead, or at least ousted from her position, this wasn't the time to have anything happen to her. She saw all her dreams of glory in Babylon fading.

"Has Idi-Sin done anything to anger Nannar?" Ku-bau asked bluntly.

Nin-Anna shook her head slowly. "No, I don't think so. He's careful to perform the ceremonies correctly." Then, "Oh," she gasped. She doubled up, dropping her face into her hands.

"What's the matter?" cried Ku-bau.

"I'm so afraid," said Nin-Anna, by dint of willpower calming herself.

Ku-bau observed her, sure she hid something.

"Would you care to join us for prayer each day?" she said, hoping to lull Nin-Anna into a confession.

"No thank you, Majesty. I have been saying rituals alone in my bedroom."

Both women were silent. Nin-Anna, her scarlet gown tight across her chest and pulling against her thighs, looked unseeing at the carpet on her left, her face expressionless and still. Ku-bau as unmoving and mask-like, kept her eyes glued on Nin-Anna.

Finally, Queen Ku-bau said, "It's this waiting I can't stand. Have my son question Ur-Lumma."

Instantly alert, Nin-Anna's glance met Ku-bau's. "He has. Ur-Lumma is worried, too."

"If the worst happens, we could be headed for war."

"But with whom? We have done nothing to upset King Hammurabi. There's peace over the whole south. Nobody's threatening him."

"Threatening! What does that mean? Obviously Nannar is furious with us. To punish us, he might incite King Hammurabi to attack us."

A week later to the day, Ur-Lumma held a secret meeting with King Idi-Sin. Afterwards, the king, white-faced and frightened, called Nin-Anna to their bedroom and shut the door. Looking at his drawn face, she panicked. "What's the matter?" She grabbed his arms.

"Nanshe has lost the god's seed."

Queen Nin-Anna sank slowly, her hands moving down Idi-Sin's body, until she lay crumpled at his feet. He continued to stand, numb in body and soul, unable to fathom why the god was so angry or what horror might be in store.

In a weak voice, Nin-Anna said, "It's my fault."

The king started. Pulling his black eyebrows together, he squinted down at her. "What have you done?"

She squirmed on the floor.

"Answer me," he said, giving her a nudge with his foot.

"The chancellor's wife didn't commit adultery."

Idi-Sin staggered a step backwards. "You," he pointed a finger at her. "You fabricated all that? But why? Why?" Shock and incredulity spread across his face, followed by a realization that caused his body to slump forward. By great effort he prevented himself from falling on top of Nin-Anna. "You did it deliberately to have Ur-Ilum marry our daughter Shara, didn't you?" he squeaked.

She buried her face in his embroidered, green wool skirt.

"Didn't you," forcefully, he again used his foot.

"Yes," she sobbed.

"How can we possibly atone for that?" Gnawing fear followed numbness. "Was my mother in on this, too?"

"No."

"I will sacrifice in thanks for that. You have to find your own way to placate Nannar. I do not want war."

She nodded and rose slowly to her feet. Dejected and crushed, she gazed remorsefully at her husband. He seared her with an angry sweep of his eyes and left the room, banging the door behind him. Nin-Anna faced retraction of the weeks of rituals she had been performing. With panic, she realized she didn't know how to do that. Whatever her own desires, whatever her hatred of Nanshe, she had to pray, pray, pray, for her recovery.

Carefully arranging her orange skirt, she positioned herself on her knees, her spine stiff and straight. She locked her fingers together and held her arms down in front of her. Then raising her head, her eyes on the ceiling, she repeated all the formulas she had been saying every day, changing the words. Everytime she came to "death for Nanshe," she said instead, "Please, please, Nannar, watch over Nanshe. I didn't mean all those awful things I said about her. Make her well again so she can continue to be a wonderful high priestess."

Chewing the inside of his mouth in unison with the intensity of his thoughts, Idi-Sin marched directly from his wife to his mother. Other than a few slaves who hovered near her, she was alone, resting. He motioned to the slaves to leave them. Bending over her, he took her hand before telling her in a few terse words what Nin-Anna had done. She cried out in agony, remembering her talks with the chancellor and his wife. Idi-Sin knelt beside her and patted her arms and left shoulder until she quieted. For an instant, in their mutual agony, they clung together. Then he rose and left her.

The minute her son left, Queen Ku-bau closed herself in her inner room and sent again for the high priest.

"I wish you to sacrifice," she said when he stood before her, "a perfect goat each day for a week and say special prayers for the sins of Queen Nin-Anna."

"What sins?" The flash of Ku-bau's eye forbade any further question. He returned to the ziggurat, praying in thanksgiving that he had not given Queen Nin-Anna a vital portion of the ritual. He notified his chief of sacrifices that he wanted a perfect male goat prepared for a personal sacrifice.

Nin-Anna took to her bed. She called for Shegunu.

Not knowing the seriousness of her illness, Shegunu hurried to her. Nin-Anna lay in bed, her head covered up. Moans came from beneath the coverlet. Shegunu placed a hand where she thought the queen's arm might be.

"I am here, Majesty."

Nin-Anna tossed back the coverlet.

"My darling aunt," exclaimed Shegunu upset by her ravaged face. The queen flung her arms around Shegunu and sobbed.

Shegunu could only hold her.

"Nanshe has lost god's seed. The king blames me. What shall I do? What can I do?" She gripped Shegunu like a wild woman.

"Majesty, you're hurting me."

The queen released her grip, apathetically sank back against the pillows and closed her eyes.

"Why does he blame you, dear aunt? You haven't done anything to Nanshe."

"It's what else I did that displeases Nannar."

"Then, we must call a priest and sacrifice and burn expensive incense so the sweet fragrance will reach Nannar and he will be bathed in the lovely odor. He will stretch out his hand to grasp the fragrance. He will look to see where it is coming from, and then he will forgive you."

Nin-Anna sighed in relief. Shegunu was such a joy. She always had good, solid ideas.

"I think I'll get up," she said. "I can easily do that here in the palace. I'll get a slave to bring me myrrh. Nannar is obviously very angry. Tonight, I will go to the temple to spend the night praying and sacrificing. I'll do everything I can to help the king face this disaster."

Shegunu returned to the subdued and nervous girls, waiting to hear her news about her aunt.

"Is Queen Nin-Anna seriously ill?" asked Ashnan.

"No," said Shegunu. "She is concerned about Nanshe. Nanshe has lost the god's child. The king thinks it will mean war with Babylon."

Nine girls threw themselves down and repeatedly banged their heads on the floor in an agonized frenzy. They slowly got to their feet.

"How is Nanshe?" said Kigal.

"I don't know. Ur-Lumma told the king she had lost the child; nothing more."

During their evening walk in the garden, Uttu clutched Hana-Ad's arm. "I'm so ashamed. How presumptuous of me to think I was the cause of her illness. Poor Nanshe."

Hana-Ad shook her head sadly. "Nanshe must have felt terrible that morning. And none of us were helping."

Life slowly returned to normal. The king, the queen, and Kubau continued to make daily personal sacrifices, but on a more moderate scale. Nanshe remained in her temple room, resting. To the delight of the court, Ur-Lumma reported improvement and that she expected to take up her duties soon.

Nanshe had not yet taken up her duties the afternoon Uttu, biting her lip, jittery, stood in front of Hana-Ad's closed drape. "May I come in?"

"Of course." At her dressing table, Hana-Ad deftly added powder to her nose.

"I have been ordered to attend Nanshe in her temple bed chamber," whispered Uttu. "I'm scared. She's going to punish me. She must think I made her lose the child."

"I don't believe that. Undoubtedly, it was beginning before she saw any of us."

"Don't be too sure. She looked right at that birthmark. I saw her eyes fly wide open." Uttu furrowed her brow. "Oh, Hana-Ad, I made her lose the god's seed. My punishment is going to be terrible. But I deserve it. I have to sacrifice right away. But, oh—" Uttu's spread fingers hid her anguished face. "I can't afford to sacrifice correctly. I haven't any silver to buy the animal."

"Uttu, stop it. Wait and see what Nanshe wants."

"But—but—"

"Uttu—" Hana-Ad started.

"Uttu!"

"That's Gula calling." Uttu parted the drape and stuck her head out.

Gula hustled across the room to stop in front of Uttu. "The guard is here to lead you to Nanshe," she whispered.

Uttu turned back to Hana-Ad. "I have to go," she said, her voice shaky.

The guard led Uttu through the palace at a fast clip. She begged to slow down when they came to the temple. Breathing deeply, she rested a minute against a wall, trying to calm her nerves.

Mesile, stationed at Nanshe's door, smiled at Uttu.

"Princess waits," she lisped and opened the door.

Nanshe's room smelled sweetly of musk, mixed with the odor of a great basket of flowers that stood at the foot of the bed. In spite of her fear, Uttu stood, enthralled, just inside the door, rapidly surveying each object. Placed at an angle to the door, Nanshe's carved and gilded rosewood bed occupied the center of the room. From that position, Nanshe could look directly at anyone who came in.

To the right of the bed, against the back wall, an ebony table with lion's claw feet had cosmetics and jewelry strewn across its surface. Two ivory-inlaid chairs, placed near the table, and yellow floor cushions heaped close by the head of the bed completed the room's furnishings. The bright yellow drape on the wall to her left probably concealed a dressing room. Mesile squatted in a corner near the door.

Propped against pillows of finely woven yellow wool and covered by a delicate white wool blanket, Nanshe said, "Come close, child." Her smile lit her pale, thin face.

In slow motion with mincing steps, Uttu drifted toward the bed, head bowed, stopped and went down on her knees.

Nanshe smiling lovingly surveyed the frightened, groveling girl. "Sit on this cushion beside me," she said softly.

Nanshe waited while Uttu knelt on the back edge of the cushion and gracefully went down, tucking her legs beneath her. "Your refusal to disrobe is understandable, but you should have told me. I would not have asked you to strip off your clothes in front of everybody."

"Then I would not have made you—" Uttu started to cry.

"There, there, child. Don't cry. It's unfortunate, yes. But other things that you know nothing about were involved. So dry your tears."

She hesitated while Uttu mopped her eyes with the hem of her scarlet robe.

"Tell me something of your parents, your life as a small child."

Uttu looked up, completely distracted from her fear of being punished.

"Begin." Nanshe folded her hands on the coverlet. "Where did you live? What does your father do? Do you have brothers and sisters? That's enough to start you off." She watched Uttu closely.

Uttu observed the drawn, but beautiful face for a second and said, "My father—well, he really isn't my father."

Nanshe's large, dark eyes narrowed. "Explain yourself."

Her intensity made Uttu stutter. "I—I was—was a ti—tiny baby when I was given to my parents, a miller and his wife. When they took me, they also received gold to take care of me."

"And did they?"

"I—I think so. They had lots of children."

"You were all treated the same?"

"Yes and no. They were good to me, but made it plain that I wasn't theirs."

"What name does this miller go by? Where does he live?"

"Ur-Sin. They own the mill by the big wool market near the river, going toward the sea."

"Ah! Yes. I know it." She was silent for a minute, thinking. "You may go."

The guard had disappeared so Uttu started towards Queen Ku-bau's apartments alone. Her feet behaved peculiarly, as if too fatigued to move her forward. She ambled along close to the wall, at times trailing her finger against it. At other times, she stopped, her brow contracted. No matter how hard she thought, she couldn't understand. Nanshe had said other things were involved in the loss of the god's child, then just asked about the family who had raised her. Did she think the miller and his wife had brought her up improperly, neglected to teach her submissiveness?

adn't dis-

e's bright

 from the

ered, his
t you are

nted that
sfiguring
saw that

s so she

he must

ler who
her she

et, don't
 stir up

s hand.
-bau?"
 might
 know,
urt."
he was

ith her
young
ffering

st any

d, and

loved the old queen and intended
emanded her own life as an atone-

ed on a glorious royal ceremony
ch she would be the central figure,
ewels, sent to Nannar amid hymns
ts of the temple. That way, royal
he whole world would know that
Jr.

ent vision of herself, as she picked

he door behind her, Nanshe beck-
nd. Ask him to come."
n. Nanshe tossed aside the coverlet
d. Unsteadily, she rose.
ght her waist. "You are weak, High-

said the smiling Nanshe. "My new
ive me color."
ove behind the yellow drape. Nanshe
thump. Then her head went up in
. Bracing herself against the bed, she

ng his wife, he cried, "Nanshe," and
and fell into his arms. "What are you
ength first."
ing up." She giggled.
Vhy are you so giddy?"
 away from him enough to look into
our daughter."

gle, Nanshe gave him another hug.
u-bau's virgins."
 die."
I'll find a way."

"

e birthmark.

Scared, Nanshe caught his arm.

"You wouldn't have seen the birthmark if she
obeyed you. Insolence on her part."

"I guess you're right. She's rough in spots. But s
and has made great strides under Queen Ku-bau."

"Well, it's unimportant now. We must get her aw
old queen."

"And find her a suitable husband."

"Without admitting that she's ours." His face s
eyes taking on a sadness. "We must always remember t
not allowed to have a child by me."

Nanshe rested her head against his shoulder. "I w
little one so badly. I held her in my arms and loved her,
mark and all. It engraved itself on my mind. When
mark on Uttu, I thought I would suffocate."

Ur-Lumma led her to the bed, plumped the pill
could lean against them, and helped her seat herself.

"We can watch over her and guide her life, bu
never know she's ours."

"I asked her about her family. Apparently the
brought her up was good to her even though he to
wasn't theirs."

Ur-Lumma observed his wife thoughtfully. "My s
attempt to have the miller questioned. That would c
suspicion."

"All right," she murmured. She caught and kisse
"How are we ever going to get her away from Queer

"Offer her money. She grew up in a poor family.
enjoy having money to spend as she pleases. Or, I c
maybe she'd be interested in having a high position a

"Without telling her she's ours? She'd wonder w
singled out."

"There is one sure way."

Nanshe looked questioningly at her husband.

"Queen Ku-bau demands that the girls who journ
to the afterlife be virgins. Trick Uttu into sitting with
women ready for marriage who wait on the temple ste
their virginity to Nannar."

Nanshe reacted with imperiousness. "I won't all
man to take her."

"Ask the chancellor to do it. He's young, virile, wi

She thwacked the wall. She loved the old queen and intended
to die with her, unless Nannar demanded her own life as an atone-
ment now.

For a moment, she reflected on a glorious royal ceremony
with all the court present in which she would be the central figure,
robed in scarlet, covered with jewels, sent to Nannar amid hymns
of praise sung by all the priests of the temple. That way, royal
honor would really be hers. The whole world would know that
she had sacrificed herself for Ur.

She smiled at this munificent vision of herself, as she picked
up her pace.

The minute Uttu closed the door behind her, Nanshe beckoned Mesile. "Find my husband. Ask him to come."

Mesile ran from the room. Nanshe tossed aside the coverlet
and swung her feet off the bed. Unsteadily, she rose.

The returning Mesile caught her waist. "You are weak, Highness. You shouldn't."

"I must start sometime," said the smiling Nanshe. "My new
flame gown, Mesile. It will give me color."

The slave went to the alcove behind the yellow drape. Nanshe
sat down on the bed with a thump. Then her head went up in
determination. Again she rose. Bracing herself against the bed, she
let Mesile dress her.

Ur-Lumma entered. Seeing his wife, he cried, "Nanshe," and
hastened to her. She swayed and fell into his arms. "What are you
doing up? You need your strength first."

"I'll get strong faster being up." She giggled.

Confused, he asked, "Why are you so giddy?"

"My darling," she drew away from him enough to look into
his face, "I think I've found our daughter."

"No!"

With a low, happy gurgle, Nanshe gave him another hug.

"She's one of Queen Ku-bau's virgins."

"One of—then she will die."

"No. I won't allow it. I'll find a way."

"Which girl?"

"The one named Uttu."

"How do you know?"

She told him about the birthmark.

"That girl!"

"Don't you like her?" Scared, Nanshe caught his arm.

"You wouldn't have seen the birthmark if she hadn't dis-obeyed you. Insolence on her part."

"I guess you're right. She's rough in spots. But she's bright and has made great strides under Queen Ku-bau."

"Well, it's unimportant now. We must get her away from the old queen."

"And find her a suitable husband."

"Without admitting that she's ours." His face sobered, his eyes taking on a sadness. "We must always remember that you are not allowed to have a child by me."

Nanshe rested her head against his shoulder. "I wanted that little one so badly. I held her in my arms and loved her, disfiguring mark and all. It engraved itself on my mind. When I saw that mark on Uttu, I thought I would suffocate."

Ur-Lumma led her to the bed, plumped the pillows so she could lean against them, and helped her seat herself.

"We can watch over her and guide her life, but she must never know she's ours."

"I asked her about her family. Apparently the miller who brought her up was good to her even though he told her she wasn't theirs."

Ur-Lumma observed his wife thoughtfully. "My sweet, don't attempt to have the miller questioned. That would only stir up suspicion."

"All right," she murmured. She caught and kissed his hand. "How are we ever going to get her away from Queen Ku-bau?"

"Offer her money. She grew up in a poor family. She might enjoy having money to spend as she pleases. Or, I don't know, maybe she'd be interested in having a high position at court."

"Without telling her she's ours? She'd wonder why she was singled out."

"There is one sure way."

Nanshe looked questioningly at her husband.

"Queen Ku-bau demands that the girls who journey with her to the afterlife be virgins. Trick Uttu into sitting with the young women ready for marriage who wait on the temple steps, offering their virginity to Nannar."

Nanshe reacted with imperiousness. "I won't allow just any man to take her."

"Ask the chancellor to do it. He's young, virile, widowed, and rich." Ur-Lumma shrugged. "What more do you want? If she finds herself with child, he'll marry her, once he knows her lineage."

"How, if we have to keep it secret?"

"We'll have to tell him ourselves and ask him not to reveal it."

"Well!" Nanshe mulled over what her husband said. "That's possible. He would be a good match. He has royal blood himself, and she really is a beautiful girl. Don't you think so?" Nanshe sparkled at the thought of Uttu.

"Yes, I'll say that for her. She really is beautiful, like you, my darling."

Ur-Lumma paid a social visit to the chancellor at his home in the upper city. Adroitly, he led the conversation to Queen Ku-bau and the young women living in her quarters. Concentrating on his fingernails, he said, "One of those girls is my daughter."

Ur-Ilum almost dropped the beer tumbler he held. "Great Nannar." A second later, he said, "Are you inferring that years ago, you disposed of the child and have just discovered her as one of Queen Ku-bau's virgins?"

"I am."

"What makes you so sure?"

In low tones, head bowed, Ur-Lumma summarized what had happened in the temple room.

"No wonder Nanshe has been so ill," said Ur-Ilum.

"At one point, I feared for her life."

Both men were silent, thinking of Nanshe.

Ur-Ilum said, "Which girl is yours?"

"Uttu."

"Uttu! She's an absolute delight."

"You like her?"

"I do. She has character and style."

Ur-Lumma smiled. "That will please Nanshe." He continued. "Now that we've found her, the problem is getting her away from the old queen."

"She requires virgins," Ur-Ilum said simply.

"Would you deflower her?"

Ur-Ilum gagged, clutched his throat, coughed and noisily blew his nose.

"We couldn't think of another way to free her without telling our secret."

"In which case, Nanshe would have to resign, and the king would appoint Luga."

"That would mean disaster."

"That does put a different light on it." Ur-Ilum sighed. "Does Uttu know? Would she cooperate?"

"No, and I don't know, in answer to both questions."

"Well, I'll do it, though I don't like the idea of taking the girl by force."

"You have our deepest thanks. It's a rather delicate matter."

"Have you thought about how this can be accomplished?"

"Yes, but nothing that seems plausible. Let's throw out suggestions and see what's best."

"All right. Nanshe could invite Uttu to her room, and I could be hiding in her dressing area."

Ur-Lumma stared at the chancellor, but started to laugh when Ur-Ilum's mouth broke into a broad grin.

"Let's play a game with it, good and bad, serious and foolish." Ur-Ilum signaled a slave to replenish the beer tumblers.

"All right. You could pick her up and run out of the old queen's area with her."

Ur-Ilum roared. "That would cause a scene."

They laughed, guffawed, raced around the room, acting out the silly possibilities. At other times, they stood together in serious discussion.

Once having decided on what they thought would work, Ur-Lumma hurried back to his anxiously waiting wife.

"It's arranged." He drew a chair alongside her. "And, incidentally, he likes the girl."

"He does! I'm glad."

"He sees a good bit of her. Queen Ku-bau often has her play background music for them. He says she plays extremely well."

"What did you decide?"

"You are to have her help you examine the cubicles used by the prospective brides."

"Examine the cubicles?" Nanshe exploded, then laughed.

Ur-Lumma smiled. "It's a good ploy, and it will work. He'll follow her into one of them."

"Perfect. I'll let him know what day."

"He said afternoon would be best when the king spends time with his family."

"I'll see to it." Her eyes glazed happily as she thought of Uttu. "Once we free her, we can talk of marriage. He'll be a good husband."

At an appropriate time, while she and the ten girls were dressing Nannar, Nanshe drew Uttu aside. "I wish you to help me, Uttu. I haven't totally recovered my strength yet. I can't overdo."

"Of course, Highness. I'll do anything you wish."

The next afternoon, Nanshe entered Queen Ku-bau's quarters looking for Uttu. Kigal, Hana-Ad and Uttu sat on the fountain edge, their heads together, gossiping. Nanshe caught Uttu's eye and beckoned.

Uttu jumped up. "I have to help Nanshe," she said.

Nanshe led the way to the temple and descended to the first tier, the one used by the prospective brides. She scanned the narrow corridor to the left and to the right. Every few feet an open door broke the solid line of the walls. She counted four closed doors, occupied cubicles. Otherwise, no activity shrouded the hot afternoon.

"Good," said Nanshe, "No couples coming and going to bother us as we check the cubicles. You start here." She pointed to a cubicle on her right. "Look to see that there is a floor mat, make sure that nothing has been left lying around and move on to the next cubicle."

Feeling slightly apprehensive, she turned from Uttu and walked into a cubicle across the narrow corridor. Suppose Uttu fought like a wild boar. Would he try if she really fought? Her mind on Uttu in the other cubicle, she glanced around. How disgusting. Dirt and dried blood jumped at her from the mat. She backed out and saw Uttu gingerly slide into another cubicle. From her tiptoeing walk, Uttu must also have found the first cubicle revolting.

Nanshe stood uncertainly looking up and down the empty corridor, her ears straining for any sound. A door swung open. Quickly she stepped into the nearest cubicle and cocked her head, listening. She heard quick, soft padding of feet. Nothing more. She emerged just in time to see the back of Ur-Ilum as he pushed the door of a cubicle closed behind him.

She scurried to the door and leaned her back against the wall, her left ear against the doorjamb. Though the door closed poorly leaving a crack large enough to peer through, she sniffed disdainfully. No. She would not peek. She heard Uttu say, "Her Royal Highness, High Priestess of Nannar, will be here immediately to assist you in finding someone to serve you."

Nanshe's eyes widened. What was Uttu going to do? Ur-Ilum's calm baritone reached her ear.

"I need no assistance. You and I will take our pleasure before I let you out."

An abrupt "no" rang through the crack. Nanshe closed her eyes, a worried frown forming.

She heard Ur-Ilum's soothing tone, but she couldn't make out what he said.

"I'm *one of Queen Ku-bau's maidens.* You know what that—"

Nanshe heard scuffling and what sounded like a weight dropping. Uttu gasped. Nanshe's eyebrows flew up, her eyes sparkled and she smiled. Everything was working beautifully. Uttu screamed. Ur-Ilum groaned.

Quickly, Nanshe fled to an empty cubicle on the other side of the corridor, closed the door and flung a shining face up in a gesture of exultation. It was accomplished. She had won. Slowly, she counted to ten and left the cubicle.

The door of the cubicle Ur-Ilum had quitted was slightly ajar. Pleased, but worried about Uttu's reaction, she hastened to her.

Uttu lay on the mat, her face to the wall, making little crying sounds.

Instantly on her knees, Nanshe gathered the weeping girl into her arms. She rocked back and forth, whispering soothing nothings the way one would calm a child.

"I want to get out of here," whimpered Uttu.

Nanshe stood up. "Oh my! You're all bloody." She helped Uttu to her feet.

"And I thought he was an honorable man."

Nanshe brushed back Uttu's hair. "Did he say anything?"

"He said he'd marry me if his seed found fertile ground."

"He did? How wonderful for you."

Uttu shook her head. "I want to die with the old queen."

Nanshe gaped at Uttu in amazement. "The chancellor, the most powerful and wealthy man in the city, offers to marry you and you want to die with Queen Ku-bau? I can't believe that. You would live in luxury if you were married to Ur-Ilum. Playing the harp as beautifully as you do, you could give elegant banquets and play for your guests and have the best poets read their verses to entertain them. Even the queen considered him for her oldest daughter," Nanshe said, not quite sure of the truth of the statement, but considering Nin-Anna capable of suggesting the idea to the king.

"She did?" Uttu stopped crying and stared at Nanshe. "The one who went to Lagash?"

"Yes. So you see," Nanshe laid a gentle hand on Uttu's arm, "Nin-Anna found him acceptable as a husband for Shara."

Uttu hung her head.

"Besides," said Nanshe, smiling, "you will have already paid your debt to the god with your own husband." She put an arm around Uttu's waist.

"I want to die with the old queen."

"What a stubborn girl you are." Nanshe dropped her arm and gazed in amazement at the solemn, bleary-eyed girl. "Come along. We'll go to my robing room and clean you up."

Her arm around Uttu in case she stumbled, Nanshe led the girl up the stairs.

"Mesile," Nanshe called as they passed her temple chamber, "Bring a basin of warm water to my official robing room."

Over the shock, washed and her gown sponged, Uttu announced that she would return to the old queen's quarters by herself.

Nanshe raised an eyebrow, but quickly decided to let her do it. She bent her head in acquiesence. Trying to keep her love from spreading across her face, she watched Uttu, head down, back from the room.

Anger swelled in Uttu as she walked rapidly toward Queen Ku-bau's area. How dare he do that to her. In her temper, she couldn't refrain from telling Hana-Ad what had happened.

"I wish I had been the one he took." Hana-Ad sat on Uttu's bed. Standing in front of her, Uttu sputtered and fumed.

"Do you love him?" asked Uttu, surprised and not sure she liked that possibility.

"No. But then I could go home to Daid," answered Hana-Ad matter-of-factly.

"Oh, Hana-Ad!" Uttu plumped down beside her and took her hand. "I wish it had been you." After a minute, she added rather smugly, "And you would have paid your debt to Nannar with a fine man."

Hana-Ad stared at her.

25

"Ur-Ilum!" The king turned to the chancellor standing at his right behind the throne. "Ask my mother to lend me two of her best harp players. I want the banquet tonight to be particularly successful, as the ambassadors from Lagash and Mari, as well as Uruk, will be present."

"I'll ask, Majesty. But she was irritated the last time and refused, as you well remember."

"Tell her that important negotiations are involved." He added, "She'll be more sympathetic if you say that two of my players have developed bloody, loose evacuations. That might convince her. We've perfumed the courtyard well, but it would still be awkward and offensive if they played."

Ur-Ilum allowed himself a single smile. "You're right. *That* she would understand."

"Anyway, she's so enamored with you, she won't refuse."

Ur-Ilum laughed. "So you send me rather than go yourself."

"Sensible of me, don't you think?"

The king turned serious. "She won't forgive me for telling her to free those girls."

"She's determined to keep them?"

"So determined she won't even talk to me about it."

Ur-Ilum pressed his lips together in displeasure. "That does make it more difficult." He thought a moment before saying, "I'll do my best."

"I'll finish the few remaining petitions here, then report to Nannar at the ziggurat. Come to my private quarters after you see my mother."

Queen Ku-bau opened her eyes, fluttered her lids and let them fall over her eyes. She drew in a long breath, turned onto her side, tucked a hand under her cheek and prepared to continue her

214

nap. Her lids slowly rose again, and she looked into the eyes of Ur-Ilum who knelt beside her.

He smiled. "You are beautiful when you sleep."

She rustled on the couch. "Help me sit up."

He propped the pillows behind her under the watchful eyes of two of her slaves.

"That's better," she said. "Now I can see you properly."

She wiggled comfortably into the pillows.

"How is my son today?"

Sensing the gods with him, he spoke to her in a confidential tone. "He's worried about the banquet he's giving tonight for the ambassadors of Lagash, Mari, and Uruk."

"Oh, it must be important if he's worried."

"He hopes to get their cooperation against our common enemy."

"King Hammurabi?"

"You are perceptive."

She glanced at him flirtatiously, pleased with herself.

"Not only did Nanshe lose the god's seed, but the prince makes no further progress. Because of this, the king thinks Nannar is angry with him. And he doesn't know what he has done."

"It isn't my son's fault. It's Nin-Anna's."

Ur-Ilum's head snapped back at the rapidity of the response. So Nin-Anna caused the trouble. He must find out what she had done to better judge how to amelioriate their gods.

Ku-bau puckered her lips and smoothed her orange gown, wishing she hadn't said anything.

Noting her embarrassment and to prevent causing her further embarrassment, Ur-Ilum returned to his mission. "On top of everything else, two of his harp players are ill."

She snorted. "Somebody's always ill. What's the matter with these people? Make them play anyway."

He ducked his head and hesitated before speaking. "They have loose bowels, and the odor would be too unpleasant."

"Ugh. How inconvenient." Pausing for a minute, she said, "I suppose he wants me to lend him my players?"

"It would be nice, Highness."

"It's one thing after another with him," she grumbled. "He doesn't leave me in peace."

"That's because you are such a wonderful mother. He knows he can always depend on you."

"Humph." She turned her head away.

He waited in silence.

"Finally," she said, "Well, he can have two."

"He will be forever in your debt. Undoubtedly, he will come himself to thank you."

"He doesn't need to do that," she said, still miffed, but softening. "Bring Uttu and Nidada to me," she said to a slave.

Uttu arrived alone. Without letting Ku-bau see him, Ur-Ilum's eyes caressed Uttu.

She quickly looked away.

"Where is Nidada?" demanded Ku-bau.

From her knees, Uttu said, "Nidada is hot and cold and shivering, Great Highness. She's in bed."

"She does that just to thwart me. Weeks ago when I needed her, she did the same thing," Ku-bau said angrily.

Ur-Ilum shifted his position to attract Ku-bau's attention. He smiled encouragingly.

Ku-bau's eyes swung to him then back to Uttu. "Who else could play the harp with you?"

"Hana-Ad, Majesty."

"But she is new."

"She has been here almost four years. She plays well, Highness."

"Humph!" Ku-bau looked at Ur-Ilum. "Well, all right. Take her with you."

"My Queen," said Ur-Ilum, "you have been most magnanimous."

In one consecutive motion, Uttu sprang from the floor and out the door to avoid Ur-Ilum's attention.

"Hana-Ad," cried Uttu as she ran into the room full of waiting girls, "be ready to play at the king's banquet tonight."

Hana-Ad left the backless chair like a slingshot, grabbed Uttu and danced around the room. The others laughed and applauded.

"Get your steps right," teased Nin-Ad.

"Oh, how wonderful." Kigal threw her arms around Hana-Ad's neck. "Your hours of practice were worth it."

"Give us a detailed account when you come back," said Ashnan.

"We will," Hana-Ad said, ecstatically happy, sure she was not coming back, but would go home to her own bed.

"We want to know who was there, what they ate, how the king looked, if the queen was there, everything. Even what they wore," said Ninbar.

Uttu giggled. "We'll tell you at breakfast."

"We better try out what we're going to play," Hana-Ad said. "I'm beginning to feel a little nervous."

"Don't," said Uttu. "We'll go out in the garden and run through what we know. Ashnan, you're a good judge, come tell us what we do best."

"All right. Then afterwards you can play for the other girls as if it were for the banquet."

"Good idea."

While Ashnan arranged the chairs, Hana-Ad walked up and down the garden impatiently.

"Hana-Ad," said Uttu, "stop being so nervous. We won't be the only harp players. We may not even get to play alone. Come on now! Let's rehearse."

"All right." Hana-Ad stopped pacing and began to play.

Ashnan seated herself on the edge of the fountain. With her head slightly tilted, her face intent, she listened. Once, she said, "I think you ought to play this song first. It would be a lovely opening."

"Shall we do it all over?" Uttu asked.

"No, wait until you play for the others."

After three more pieces, Uttu turned to Hana-Ad. "That's enough for us to play alone."

Ashnan nodded. She stood up and waved at Girsu-Ad who was standing by the door of their room. "All of you come and listen."

They trooped out and, moving the chairs noisily, arranged themselves in a semi-circle before Uttu and Hana-Ad.

"That song makes a perfect opening," said Shegunu.

Hana-Ad flashed her a smile.

"That was beautiful," said Ninti when they finished.

From the doorway, wrapped in blankets and shivering, Nidada applauded.

The chancellor crossed the king's audience court, wondering about Uttu. Three and a half weeks wasn't enough time for her to know yet whether she was with child. Or at least be sure. He certainly hoped she was. He didn't want to skulk around on the floor used by the prospective brides a second time. That had been very disagreeable.

He wanted to marry the girl. If she were enceinte, he could

easily argue that he'd fathered the child and get Queen Ku-bau to approve their marriage. Uttu was ripe for children. There would be many of them. He wanted a family.

The king, returning from the morning ritual in the temple, hailed him.

Ur-Ilum nodded. The king heaved a relieved sigh.

"So mother agreed?"

"Yes."

"Is she sending Uttu and Nidada?"

"No, Uttu and Hana-Ad."

"I don't know that girl."

"Uttu recommended her." He added, "Nidada is sick."

"Too bad," Idi-Sin tossed off indifferently.

Ur-Ilum hesitated. "Your mother thinks Nannar is angry with Nin-Anna. Do you know why?"

A cautious expression stole over the king's face. "No," he answered, drawing out the word noncommittally.

Ur-Ilum tucked the cautious expression deep in the back of his memory.

The two men separated, Idi-Sin to join his family in the dining room, the chancellor to entertain the ambassador from Lagash.

In her cubicle, Hana-Ad fidgeted as Gula attempted to dress her for the banquet.

"Hold still," said the slave. "How can I straighten this dress when you keep jumping around?"

Hana-Ad tried hard to stand still, not totally successfully. She kept flinging her hands around, touching her hair, reaching for the mirror on the bed, causing her weight to shift.

"Playing the harp at a court banquet isn't all that wonderful," carped Gula, taking the mirror from her.

"It's my first time," said Hana-Ad, twisting her torso.

"The guards will be here to take you to the banquet before you're dressed at the rate we're going."

Hana-Ad stood stock still.

At twilight, the king's guards finally came for them. Uttu and Hana-Ad followed the guards to a small audience court in the king's quarters.

The soft, warm glow of the evening light filtered through a clear sky dulled the flickering flames from the profusion of little oil lamps. Two long tables extended almost the entire length of the open court.

"It's not a large party," said Uttu, quickly calculating the number of chairs.

Slave girls with both lyres and harps were already seated near one end of the tables, their chairs set between pillars. A guard motioned Uttu and Hana-Ad toward two empty chairs just in front of the slaves.

Hana-Ad frowned. Their seats had been placed opposite the corridor to the kitchen. She'd have to work her way around the table ends and across the courtyard, exposing herself longer before reaching the shelter of the corridor. She soundlessly kicked the chair leg in frustration as she sat down.

She cast a sweeping glance around the court. On the wall behind the king's throne, four donkeys, galloping among green trees, pulled a beautiful, bright chariot. The driver snapped a whip above them. How often she had seen that exact same scene on the outskirts of Ur. But those chariots had been dirty and the donkeys had smelled. Here, the chariot always retained its clear yellow color, and the scarlet on the walls would never stop glowing in the late afternoon light. The throne itself sat on a dais, a little table beside it. The dancing light from the lamps seemed a bit brighter than when she came and created shimmering shadows on the red pillar capitals.

Set a little apart from the throne a large lyre stood upright, a wickerwork chair behind it. She inhaled sharply, noiselessly, at its beauty. A golden bull's head emerged from the sound box. Above it, the wooden perimeter contained alternate bands of carnelian, with ivory and lapis lazuli inlay.

Intent on her survey of the court, she jumped when the slave girls began to play. Uttu joined in and nodded to her to do the same. Male courtiers started to arrive. They all lined up across from the girls, ready to prostrate themselves at the king's entrance. Then, with great pomp and slow steps, the king walked in, followed closely by the three ambassadors. Carefully leaving a space of about a man's height, the chancellor led in the other guests.

Hana-Ad examined the heavily embroidered yellow and scarlet wool garments worn by the three ambassadors. They looked new. She smirked; just as she thought.

While the king was seating himself on his throne, one of the last guests to walk in surreptitiously tried to pinch Uttu. The chancellor immediately leapt to her side. "She belongs to the old queen," he said. "You might be interested in one of the group behind." Uttu flashed him a silent thanks.

The man nodded and pointedly looked at the slaves.

The minute all the guests had taken a seat, a court official placed a gold bowl of barley soup before the king. Slaves set a silver bowl in front of each guest. The men stopped talking. Almost in unison, they raised the bowls and gulped their soup with a noisy slurping sound.

After that, the guests ate mutton and fish, cucumbers, peas and broad beans, flat bread and a dark bread, which they tore off the loaf in big chunks. Slaves continuously poured wine into fluted silver tumblers which the men drained through straws.

Hana-Ad's stomach rumbled. In her excitement, she hadn't eaten much. Now, she drooled at each new dish presented. She glanced at Uttu. In nonchalance, Uttu raised both shoulders and let them fall.

After the guests had finished the main meal, a poet recited verses. One of the slave girls accompanied him on the big, beautiful harp. But when the fruit was brought out along with the dessert made of grapes and figs, she and Uttu played alone. She was tiring. The banquet went on and on. At last, the king got up and disappeared through a door behind him. As soon as he left, the others rose, becoming noisy and talkative. Some of them stumbled unsteadily to the slave girls.

Hana-Ad slid off her chair and dodged behind a fat man ogling a tall, voluptuous slave. Glancing rapidly from side to side, she glided between two small knots of men, gesticulating, laughing men, and succeeded in rounding the ends of the tables. Her spirits rose. Another short distance and she would reach the corridor. But a short, empty distance. She eyed it. Nobody stood around in the space, nobody to shield her movements. She'd have to make a dash for it.

Just then, a leering member of the Mari contingent, dressed in a dark orange robe, lunged at her, his right hand extended. She jumped sideways, missing by a fraction his eager, reaching fingers and whisked behind the nearest pillar. She landed right in front of one of Queen Ku-bau's guards.

"Oh," she squeaked. She clapped a hand over her mouth and lurched back a step.

"I've been watching you. Just what do you think you're doing?" He looked very solemn.

"That—that man was trying to catch me."

The guard narrowed his eyes. "If it's escape you're after, it's
not wise to try." He stood looking at her, his right hand on his hip.

She simply shifted her feet, her head hanging almost to her
chest. In the tense silence, she wanted to scream.

"If I told the old queen, you would be severely punished."

"Don't, please don't," she pleaded, raising frightened eyes to his.

"I won't this time. But don't do it again, you hear?" He atten-
tively looked around the court. "Go back to Uttu. I'll watch so
don't try anything funny."

Hana-Ad choked back tears and held her head high. Trans-
formed into a perfect court lady, she walked across the banquet
hall.

"Hana-Ad," whispered Uttu, "what were you doing? Are you
crazy?"

Hana-Ad stooped to pick her harp from the chair. "Not now."

Their guard left them at Ku-bau's carved double doors. In the
dark and quiet social room, Hana-Ad ran to her alcove and dropped
the drape behind her.

Gula, napping on the floor, yawned, stretched, and hurried to
Uttu's alcove. Having finished undressing Uttu, she moved with
the silence of a wild cat to Hana-Ad.

Afterwards, Hana-Ad lay facedown on the bed. A hand
touched her hair, and a body pressed the bed beside her. She recognized Uttu's fragrance.

"Hana-Ad," whispered Uttu, "what is it? Would it help to talk?"

"I don't know," came the muffled answer.

For a time, Uttu just sat and stroked the black hair rumpled
over the pillow.

Eventually, Hana-Ad whispered brokenly, "I planned so carefully how I was going to escape."

The hand stopped. "Oh, Hana-Ad, you didn't."

"I did." Hana-Ad sat up. "I know, Uttu, that you truly want
to serve Queen Ku-bau forever. I don't. I don't mind going back to
spinning and housework and milking and everything. I want to
share it with Daid."

"Maybe if I had ever loved a man, I would feel differently,

too. But if I left the palace, I would have nothing but drudgery to go back to. And I couldn't stand that."

They fell silent. Ur-Ilum's image appeared in the darkness before Uttu's eyes. That might really be worth going to, instead of staying here. She remembered the warmth of his body, the enveloping smell of his embrace. She pushed the memory away.

"Hana-Ad, Queen Ku-bau will be furious when the guard tells her you tried to escape. Are you ready for the consequences? I don't know what she'll do other than the usual punishment. She'll put you in the locked room. But even that punishment will make the rest of us worry and grieve each day you're locked up."

"The guard won't tell. He said he wouldn't."

"If he keeps his word."

"I think he will." Hana-Ad added fiercely, "I hate that room. I hope I won't have to go there ever again. But if he does tell," she said with a sigh of resignation, "I suppose it will be longer than before."

"Much, much longer."

"Why are you so sure?"

"Years ago, she put Kigal in that room for five days for trying to walk out the door. She only permitted the slaves to give her beer. Kigal screamed and screamed. It was awful. She was hysterical when the old queen let her out. She ate so much that she threw up all night. She couldn't get up in the morning, which made Queen Ku-bau even angrier. She had Kigal dragged in and ordered her to play the harp all by herself for hours until Kigal fainted."

"Dear, dear little Kigal," sighed Hana-Ad. "So that's why she looks so scared whenever the old queen scolds any of us."

"If Kigal finds out what you did, she'll go into a state and cry."

"We won't tell her."

"All right, but don't try to escape again, at least not while Queen Ku-bau is alive. If you still really, really want to get away, the time to try is when she dies. In the confusion, you might succeed."

Hana-Ad threw her arms around Uttu. "You're so wise, Uttu."

"Our queen will question us tomorrow about the banquet. You need to be careful what you say." She passed through the drape as silently as she had come.

26

M esile entered Nanshe's temple room. "Highness, Uttu waits," she said from her knees.

Every muscle in Nanshe's body tensed. "Admit her." Hands hidden under the folds of her white robe, Nanshe gripped the chair seat.

"You wanted to talk to me, Uttu?" she said, noting the sad eyes, the downturned corners of her pretty little jewel-red mouth.

"Yes, Highness." Uttu shied a bit sideways, embarrassed. "Now that I'm here, I don't know how to say it." She lifted her eyes to meet those of Nanshe.

"Speak plainly." Nanshe smiled encouragement. "Sit here on this floor cushion beside my chair." She pulled out one hand and indicated the cushion.

Uttu seated herself with care, going through an elaborate stalling performance, before saying, "I'm with child."

Nanshe had difficulty controlling her laughter, she was so happy. "Are you sure?" she said quietly. "Not much time has elapsed."

"No, but I think so." Uttu ducked her head and twisted her fingers. "It's strange. There's nothing definite I can point to; I just know."

"I'm so glad for you." Nanshe's eyes caressed Uttu. A soft, loving expression made her face even more beautiful, a gentle curve on her lips. Instinctively, her right hand started to reach out. She snatched it back to lie still in her lap.

"But I want to die with Queen Ku-bau." Uttu started to cry.

"Uttu." Nanshe's eyes widened, her face blanched and her hand went to her breast. She shook her head sharply to compose herself. "Please don't cry, dear heart."

Uttu was too upset to notice the endearment. "She'll send me back to the miller, and I don't want to go." Uttu raised swimming black eyes.

"She won't do any such thing." Nanshe thought her beautiful

even with tears running off the end of her nose. "The chancellor will marry you. You'll have a full and happy life."

"Why would anybody as rich and handsome and interesting as the chancellor marry me?"

"Because—" Nanshe bit her tongue before blurting out, "you are my daughter." Instead she said, "Because you are a lovely young woman, well trained in court ways."

Uttu shifted her body. She knew Nanshe was just saying that about her being lovely to make her change her mind. She raised her head in defiance.

Nanshe smiled. "He said he would."

"He said that at the moment because he knew he shouldn't have done what he did," Uttu said with force.

Nanshe shook her head. "Surely you must realize that he is an honorable man, Uttu."

"Highness, please help me. I don't want the old queen to find out about the child."

"There's little you can do, Uttu, to prevent her knowing as your child grows."

Uttu crumpled. "I'll have to do something."

Nanshe straightened. "Uttu, if you ever try to get rid of that lovely little thing growing inside you, I'll tell Queen Ku-bau. Then, you will be sent back to the miller. Ur-Ilum will have nothing to do with you."

Trapped, Uttu put both hands over her face. Tears seeped between her fingers.

Nanshe observed her, sadness replacing the joy she had felt. Softly she said, "Dear child, I want you to find an opportunity—and you can do that when the chancellor comes to visit your queen—to tell him about your condition. I am certain that he will ask to have you withdrawn from Queen Ku-bau's quarters."

Uttu bowed her head submissively, but stubbornly determined to do no such thing.

"You may go now."

Uttu got awkwardly to her feet and bowed from the waist.

Nanshe stood up and hugged the unhappy girl. "Some day, you'll see how fortunate you are, once you're living in the chancellor's beautiful home with this child and a lot of other children around you." Holding Uttu by the shoulders, Nanshe smiled at the girl, then hugged her again, a great longing in her heart.

Uttu bowed and left. She walked slowly. Warm tears wobbled down her face. The high priestess of Ur had hugged her. She tried to push the memory out of her mind. Nanshe meant nothing by it.

Then she cried out and fell against the wall. How could she have been so inconsiderate, thoughtlessly babbling about getting rid of her child when Nanshe had recently lost the god's seed. Uttu castigated herself all the way back to Queen Ku-bau's quarters.

The minute Uttu left, Nanshe sent Mesile with a message for the chancellor. It wasn't long before he presented himself at her door.

She met him with outstretched hands and a radiant face. For an instant, he stood nonplussed, then his face broke into a wide smile. His hands went out to meet hers. "She's with child," he said.

"Apparently."

"I'll make arrangements immediately."

"Not so fast. I told her she was to tell you herself. Wait and let her do it."

"Suppose she doesn't."

"She better. If she doesn't, I'll tell Queen Ku-bau. She knows that."

"I'll give her every opportunity." He suddenly became bashful. "I'm quite pleased. Watching Uttu now, having held her in my arms, I realize I care for her deeply. I owe it all to you and Ur-Lumma."

"I'm so glad, Ur-Ilum." Her eyes acquired a moist sparkle. "I'll tell you a secret. She thinks you're handsome and interesting."

"She does, does she?" He burst into delighted laughter, and a red color suffused his neck. "Wonderful."

Nanshe laughed, too.

That evening, holding her full silver bowl with both hands, Hana-Ad sat down beside Uttu on the fountain ledge.

"Come to my alcove tonight," Uttu whispered as she saw Ashnan approaching. "I need you."

Hana-Ad's head bobbed.

Once the noise settled, the big room empty and still, Hana-Ad, wraith-like, appeared in front of the waiting Uttu.

"I'm so upset, I could die," Uttu whispered, moving slightly so Hana-Ad could sit beside her on the bed.

"What's the matter?"

"I think I'm carrying Ur-Ilum's child."

"But that's wonderful news." Hana-Ad put her arm around Uttu's shoulders. "Now you can leave Queen Ku-bau. You don't have to die." She added, "And he's such a fine man."

Uttu dissolved in tears.

A bit envious, perplexed and distressed, Hana-Ad ran her hand up and down Uttu's back.

"You said you didn't believe he'd marry you. Tell Nanshe. She knows it's his child. She can force the issue. She can go to the king." Hana-Ad became expansive as the words tumbled out.

"Force him to marry me? Never." Uttu smoothed the bed cover. "I talked to Nanshe this afternoon. I thought because I was with her when it happened that she'd help me get rid of it."

"Uttu, how could you?"

"She told me if I try, she'll go right to Queen Ku-bau."

Hana-Ad stopped trying to sooth Uttu. A fabulous life lay ahead of her, and she wanted to throw it away. She was blind, blind.

"I don't know how to go about it, Hana-Ad. Do you?"

"About what?"

"Getting rid of it."

"No," said Hana-Ad shocked. "You must not. Nanshe will tell Queen Ku-bau."

"The old queen will find out anyway, either from Nanshe or by looking at me. So help me think of something." She stuck out her lower lip.

Hana-Ad squirmed in resentment. "As your friend, I'll try, but I don't want to."

Uttu brushed at her tears. "If I don't do it soon, I'll start to show. Everybody will know. Queen Ku-bau will be furious. She'll make a scene like we've never seen before. Maybe she'll lock me up or—Oh! Maybe I should just tell her. The punishment might make me lose it."

"Even if you do, she'll know you're not a virgin."

"That's right. I forgot."

"You could feign sickness and get the physician to come see you. Maybe he'd help you."

Uttu thought for a moment. "That's worth a try. I could claim I was having bad stomach pains."

With the morning sun, Uttu hung over the side of her bed

and whimpered in pain. "My stomach, my stomach," was all she could manage to say.

Temena went to the old queen, and Ku-bau sent a slave for Sumulael.

"Where does it hurt?" he asked her.

"Here," she said putting her hands on her lower abdomen.

He carefully poked here and there. Sometimes she cried out; sometimes she simply lay there. When he finished, he ordered a draught of pulverized lees of dried vine, thyme, and plum mixed in beer. "If you aren't better by tomorrow, I will come again."

To her delight, the draught began to make her sick. But she noticed no blood on her bed linen and didn't feel any change inside herself.

She complained again the next day. Sumulael returned. She asked for a stronger dose, which he gave her. Ur-Ilum, who had been with Ku-bau, caught him as he left the girls' quarters.

"What's wrong with her?" he asked.

"I don't rightly know. I didn't find anything specific. It's almost as if she were making it up. I've given her an innocuous drink. I gave it to her yesterday, too. It may make her a little sick. She'll vomit, that's all."

Ur-Ilum went to Nanshe.

"Do you suppose she's trying to get rid of the child?" he asked.

"I'll go see her."

Uttu was sleeping when Nanshe arrived. Nanshe looked closely at her. The nose was Ur-Lumma's, the mouth hers. Somehow that pleased her.

"Uttu," she said quietly.

Uttu opened her eyes. "Highness." She tried to rise.

Nanshe's hand on her shoulder prevented further effort. "I hear you are in pain."

"Yes, Highness," she said in a low, agitated way.

"Uttu, it would be a tragedy both for you and for Ur-Ilum if you were to lose this child. Knowing about your condition would make him happy. I told you that the day you came to me."

Startled, Uttu looked at her. How did she know about what Ur-Ilum thought? Suddenly, Uttu distrusted Nanshe.

Nanshe continued, "Therefore, I'll tell the physician to make sure he takes proper care of you." She caressed Uttu's cheek.

Uttu lay on the bed, after Nanshe left, holding the cheek she had caressed. If Sumulael told the old queen, then surely she faced the rest of her life with the miller.

"Never," she exclaimed. For another minute, she lay still. Well, she might as well get up and say she was feeling better. She swung her legs off the bed and promptly threw up.

Temena and Gula immediately rushed to her side. They sent for Sumulael.

"You'll be all right by tomorrow," he said, smiling at her. "But you should have told me the truth."

Uttu turned bright red and twisted her hands. "Please, please," she begged, "don't tell Queen Ku-bau."

He looked at her in silence. "It will be between you and me and the high priestess," he finally said.

The next day, she resumed her place with the others. "I'm glad to see you are feeling better, Uttu," Ku-bau said.

That night, sitting next to each other in Hana-Ad's alcove, Hana-Ad tried to tackle the subject without upsetting Uttu. "You should tell Ur-Ilum. You like him, you know you do. Why are you so determined to die?"

"If I die with Queen Ku-bau, I'll live in luxury forever, whereas joy with him would only be momentary. Once he compares me with his aristocratic friends, he'll quickly tire of me. I'm not an aristocrat."

"But you've been here at the palace for years. You've learned a lot. You could run his home the way it should be run."

Uttu shifted her body and flung up her head.

"Uttu, you're my friend, my dear friend. But I simply don't understand you."

Uttu jumped up and left the alcove. Hana-Ad fretted in her bed most of the night, too disturbed to sleep. She'd have to make up with Uttu as soon as possible.

Temena noticed that Uttu's dresses were getting tight, not much, only enough to stretch the fabric. Her face looked fuller, too. The slave watched her at meals. Uttu was eating no more than usual. Without telling the other slaves, she let out Uttu's dresses, sure that nobody would notice.

"Uttu," Ashnan said one day, "you're putting on a little weight."

"I know. Isn't it awful?"

"I noticed it, too," said Nin-Ad.

The others began to comment. They watched what she took at meals. Aware of it, Uttu began to take less.

"I'm starving," she told Hana-Ad. "I have to eat."

"I'll take extra and slip it to you in the garden or when the others are occupied."

So far, the only one who hadn't noticed anything was Queen Ku-bau.

Uttu continued to gain weight. The girls teased her for getting fat. Though Uttu knew that someday her weight would be obvious for what it was, she refused to face the fact. She lived from day to day. She didn't tell Ur-Ilum about her condition, even though he gave her constant opportunities, visiting the old queen several times a week.

Discouraged, he talked it over with Nanshe. "She won't speak to me. Yesterday, I tried to encourage her by telling her that I was fond of her. That seemed to surprise her, but she didn't say anything. How can I get her to talk to me about our child?"

"I don't understand her," Nanshe said. "The bad part is that soon the slaves won't be able to cover up her weight. Queen Ku-bau will notice and fly into a tantrum. And whenever she's angry, she's unpredictable."

"We should have told her about it immediately. Then the situation would have been smoothed over."

"I don't know what more to do to make Uttu tell you." Nanshe threw up her hands. "Give her until she really starts to show. That may push her into action. If not, we'll have to act. You're right, we can't wait too much longer."

Eight days later, Ku-bau complained of not feeling well. Her temperature spiked. Too sick to pay attention to which girl was doing what, she wanted music, but didn't seem to care who played. Though she usually demanded that Uttu perform for her, days passed without a specific request. Hana-Ad and Nidada played most of the time, occasionally one of the others. Uttu didn't go in.

A full week passed with the old queen showing no improvement. The girls sat eating their evening meal in silence. Suddenly, Girsu-Ad asked loudly, "Do you think Queen Ku-bau'll die?"

The rest of them looked up.

"She's getting worse. She didn't recognize me today," said Nidada.

"If she dies, we'll die." Nin-Ad stared into her food bowl.

Kigal started to cry.

"We've lived each day happily in luxury," Nin-Ad continued, "without thinking much about," she stuttered, "what happens when our queen dies."

"I don't want to die," sobbed Kigal.

Ashnan, next to Kigal, drew her into her arms. "There, there, pet," she said, caressing Kigal's hair and shoulder.

Her face buried in Ashnan's neck, Kigal trembled in terror.

"I don't want to die either," Hana-Ad said, "and I intend to do something about it."

"I look forward to it," Uttu announced.

Nin-Ad glanced at Uttu and looked quickly away, a tense, unhappy expression on her face. "What are you going to do, Hana-Ad?" she asked.

"At this moment, I don't rightly know." Hana-Ad swung her eyes up and scanned the ceiling, her brow furrowed.

The following morning, she bumped into Nin-Ad leaving the harp room. "Oh, Nin-Ad, I want to talk to you."

Nin-Ad gave her a quizzical look.

"You intimated without really saying so that you didn't want to die. I intend to leave. We could go together."

"It's true, I don't want to die." Nin-Ad hedged and started to cough. "But I don't know where I'd go."

"Go home," said Hana-Ad matter-of-factly.

"I can't do that. My parents would feel humiliated after they gave me such an enormous send-off."

"Well, come with me then. I'm going to Daid. He'll be glad to see me, even if my parents aren't."

"Don't be so sure."

Hana-Ad shivered. The thought had never occurred to her that Daid might turn her away. She fought back tears.

"Will you try to escape or not?"

"No."

Kigal, on the other hand, proved eager to take the chance. "I'll try to see my father," she said. "I would really like to see him. If he won't have me, I'll come with you."

Hana-Ad flung her arms around Kigal. "We'll see what happens. Meet me at the door the second we hear the old queen is dead."

"I will."

27

"The astrologers are in a panic," whispered Sahar from where he sat on Daid's mat.

"Why?" Daid stopped pacing the narrow corridor and tumbled down beside him.

"They're afraid because there's a new object in the sky. It appears at dusk just at the right of the ziggurat and moves to the left until it disappears."

"How big is it?" Daid made a mental note to look for this strange floating object.

"It looks like a big, bright star. But it has a long feathery tail. It's getting brighter. All the portents are bad. They think something awful is going to happen."

A faintly audible whistle escaped Daid. "It can't be another flood. Yahweh promised Noah never to send another flood."

"Your Yahweh may have promised Noah, but that has nothing to do with what Enlil does."

"Anyway, men aren't as wicked as they were when Yahweh sent the flood." The remark reverberated loudly up and down the deserted corridor. "Oh," said Daid. "I hope that didn't wake anybody."

Both men tensed, listening. The snoring coming from the room near them continued at an even pace.

"I don't know what you mean by 'as wicked.'" Sahar picked up the whispered conversation. "The world is full of wickedness."

"A long time ago, the sons of Yahweh coupled with the daughters of men. The offspring were vile and beastly giants. No ruler could control their wickedness. That's why Yahweh sent the flood— to rid the earth of those monsters. The flood did that. So Yahweh promised never to send another."

"Of course," Sahar said thoughtfully, "we Babylonians think Enlil sent the flood because he was displeased with the way we humans served him. Enki, knowing what Enlil planned, whispered a warning to Utnapishtim, who saved himself and his family. Enlil was furious until Enki explained to him that there would have been nobody to serve him if he'd carried out his threat. In gratitude to Enki, a contrite Enlil gave Utnapishtim eternal life."

"You mean your gods don't care if men do wrong?"

"Sometimes the gods do wrong."

Daid couldn't argue that point; he knew they did.

As dusk descended the next evening, along with most of the temple priests, Daid stood in the open court in front of the ziggurat scanning the sky.

"There it is. There it is." Group after group took up the cry. In silence, they watched the brilliant white ball and flowing tail.

"What do you suppose it means?" whispered the priest standing next to Daid.

"I don't know," Daid whispered, "but it scares me."

"Me too. The way that tail flares and shrinks in size must mean Enlil is very angry."

"And it seems to sway from side to side," another priest said.

"What's most frightening is the waiting, not knowing what's going to happen," the first priest added.

They dispersed, uneasy, fearful of the future.

Weeks went by. Daid paid no more attention to the long-tailed star that still moved leftward in the sky. One afternoon, stiff from the long class session, he stood up and flexed his muscles. He noticed a strange priest hurriedly zigzagging his way between the classroom benches. Arrested by the priest's drawn mouth, wrinkled brow, and worried eyes, he waited near the master.

"Honored priest," said the stranger, bowing before the master, "the catastrophe foretold by the appearance of the long-tailed star has come. Sailors brought a delirious man to our temple across the river where he died. Now, three of our priests are dead, others are sick, and some of the children living around us are sick."

"Fever?" snapped the grim-faced master.

"Yes. And blisters."

"Lead the way."

Turning to Daid, he said, "You come with me."

They crossed the river and entered a badly lighted wattle and daub hovel behind a small temple. A raving little girl, covered with red sores, rolled on the floor. Once he saw her, Daid knew they had to deal with the pox.

"She'll die soon," the master said to the priest who brought them. "How many others live here?"

"Five, including their mother who's about to give birth. One of the other children is already hot and vomiting. She's lying over there." The priest pointed to a dark corner.

"Give her henbane mixed with myrrh and copper in a portion of beer," said the master. "And rub her with pig fat and river mud." He walked out. Daid and the priest followed.

"What are you planning to do with the bodies of those who die?"

The priest threw up his hands in a gesture of helplessness. "I think the sailor's body was dumped in the river. We buried the priests. And I heard that a couple of corpses have been found on the street."

"Burn them," yelled the master. He motioned to Daid and rapidly returned to the Temple of Marduk. In the schoolroom, he flung himself on a bench and doubled over in agony. Daid sat down on a nearby bench to wait.

"Brace yourself," the master finally said. "We're going to have to work all day and most of the night. I'll have no time to supervise you, so do your best. Give the ill henbane for pain. Mix it with myrrh and copper and mix that with beer. The pig fat and river mud are for blisters" He sighed. "Soon, the public will start panicking. So many people will die that there won't be time for burials. By morning, I think we'll find bodies piled up in the streets. Be ready for it. The stench will be vile. And it will be everywhere. You won't be able to escape it."

The master looked at Daid wearily. "Some of us will die. Others will recover but bear pockmarks for the rest of their lives. Eventually, the sickness wears itself out." The master shrugged. "The population will be so decimated, no one will be left to get sick."

A creepy sensation slithered over Daid's body, making him tremble.

True to the master's predictions, the sickness had taken on the appearance of an epidemic by morning. The following day, the healthy who ventured out had to pick their way around the corpses. Each succeeding day found more and more bodies tossed from the houses. Slaves dragged them to the fires outside the city but couldn't keep up as the number mushroomed. Terror-stricken people wandered the streets, begging Daid and any physician they passed to tell them how to save themselves. Others masked their fear in frantic activity. Daid tied a wet rag over his nose to avoid the stench. Then he had trouble breathing, so he abandoned the attempt.

Day followed day in an agony of work that seemed fruitless to Daid. "Is what we're doing helping? Are we really making a difference?" he asked the master late one afternoon as they sat in the school room comparing notes.

"The main help we give is having people think we can do something."

The answer satisfied Daid enough to rebuild his confidence in himself as a physician.

Mid-afternoon, two weeks later, a guard came to fetch the master to go to the home of Hammurabi's marshal, whose wife had fallen ill.

"Daid!" The master beckoned. "Come with me."

The marshal, his brow contracted in worry, led them to the bedroom. His wife lay on her back in the middle of a huge bed, a blanket tucked tightly under her chin. The master felt her forehead. "Fever," he said to Daid. "High fever." He tapped her shoulder. "Let me see your arm."

Slowly, trying not to uncover any of herself, she pulled out an arm. "I'm so cold," she whined.

"Blisters," said the master. Bending over, he started to pull down the blanket. His face grew wan, and he keeled over across the bed.

Screaming, the woman tried to push him off her abdomen.

"Get him out of here," yelled the marshal. His slaves, starting to howl, rushed to a corner where they clung together and continued to howl.

Daid began to lift the master off the bed. When his naked chest came into contact with the master's upper body, the heat of his teacher's flesh rattled him. For an instant, his grip loosened. He looked around for help. Redfaced and angry, the marshal pointed an index finger at the door. The slaves, quiet now, huddled together, exposing only their backs. He'd have to act alone. Collecting himself, he clasped the master tightly by the waist and raised him off the bed.

Awkwardly hoisting his teacher across his shoulders, Daid hurried to the temple as fast as his burden allowed. Thanks to

Yahweh, the master wasn't a big man. At the temple, loving hands eased their teacher from Daid's shoulders and into bed.

"I'll bring henbane," said one student.

"I'll rub him with pig fat," said another.

Yet another said, "I'll watch tonight."

The students took turns attending him. Temple physicians came and went. Two days later, in spite of all the care given him, he died.

The entire body of the medical school plus many priests from the temple gathered at the door of his austere room, while those who had been attending him massed inside. Daid, standing beside the bed, suddenly fell to his knees in intense prayer for the safe transport of the master to the luxury he deserved. Immediately, others followed his example and loudly called on Marduk.

A strident voice interrupted their prayers. "Get the body out of here. Get the body out of here. What's the matter with you?"

Still half absorbed in prayer, Daid stood up. He scanned the crowd in the room. Instantly, his mind cleared. Of course, the master's body had to be placed in the funeral piles for burning. Gently touching the shoulders of those nearest him, he said, "We must remove the body."

With loving care, they wrapped the body in the bedclothes and carried it away.

Sahar met Daid as he returned. They went to the classroom and sat on a bench next to each other, no longer careful not to be seen talking.

"Why is it some are stricken, and some not?" a sad and exhausted Daid said.

"Those who get it have either offended their gods, or demons have gained control over them," replied Sahar firmly. "Everything has life. You know that. This bench you are sitting on has life."

Daid looked at it uncomfortably. He moved forward trying to lessen his weight.

"I've been here four years," said Daid. "During all this time, I haven't yet met anyone who believes in Yahweh. My faith is starting to slip. I live in the temple of Marduk, and every day I see the faith and goodness of the priests here. I wish I could be like my father's friend Apilsin. Apilsin once told me he made a contract with Yahweh to pray only to him. Because of that, Yahweh talks to him and takes care of him. But I can't seem to achieve that myself." He started to walk around. "In the dead of night, tired as I am, I pray and pray. And still, Yahweh doesn't answer."

"Have you made a contract?"

Daid stopped in front of Sahar. "Actually, no."

"Then how can you expect him to answer you specifically?"

"I don't know." Daid paused. "I follow Yahweh because I was brought up that way. Also, I've always admired Apilsin and followed his example. Apilsin said Yahweh told him that I should come to Babylon." He gave a short ironical laugh. "That landed me in prison."

"But once you were released, you became a great physician."

"Will he get me home?"

"Perhaps Marduk will."

"Perhaps," Daid said uncertainly. "I've been carrying Hana-Ad's personal goddess in my waistband."

Sahar exclaimed, "Perhaps that's why Yahweh doesn't answer. Gods are jealous."

Startled in turn, Daid cried, "Should I hide it? I can't throw it away. It belongs to Hana-Ad."

Daid started to pace again. Worn out by the long hours he'd spent by the master's side and the demands of the ill, he began to stagger.

Sahar caught him. "You need some rest." Putting his arm around Daid, Sahar guided him to the small room he had been assigned and helped him into bed.

"I have some things still to do," mumbled Daid, trying to get up again.

"They'll wait." Sahar sat down on the floor beside the bed to prevent Daid from making another attempt to rise. Daid's body soon relaxed, and his breathing settled into the even sounds of deep sleep. Shortly afterward, Sahar walked quickly to his office across the temple yard.

His own work had doubled. The high priest was ill. Six of the staff were caring for him day and night. One of them was already sick. The king was frantic. He came to the temple every day to pray. Sahar had to attend him. Following the prayers, Hammurabi sacrificed a large animal. The meat was piling up. Surreptitiously, he had started to give it away to the hungry people. Supplies had become scarce. Nobody worked. Why should they? They could be dead tomorrow.

Daid slept heavily, longer than he should. Feeling guilty, he dove out of bed, but then remembered that he had to hide Hana-Ad's personal goddess. He stood the little goddess in the corner opposite the one he used for Yahweh, her face to the wall, and headed for the classroom.

Since the master's illness, the students had looked to him for guidance. He didn't understand why; he felt so inadequate. He had remonstrated vehemently when they pushed him into the role of master, but they had been adamant.

Every student sat, half-slumped, when he entered. He glanced at them sadly. They were all overworked and on the verge of collapse. Which ones would be missing by tomorrow?

"I don't know of anything more we can do than what we're doing," he said. "Try to get some rest whenever you can. You need your strength to keep fighting this epidemic, but I see no point in wearing yourselves out uselessly."

He lost count of the passing days. He did what he could for the sick, instructed the healthy, and counted the dead. He had become so used to the stench of the ill and the fumes from the fires on the edge of the city that he no longer noticed. He dragged himself through each day. At night, he threw himself on his bed to sleep a few hours.

Returning to the temple one evening, he felt too tired to walk to the dining room. Instead he turned his steps toward the administration area, needing the comfort of Sahar's quiet strength. Sahar's assistant sat writing.

"Where's Sahar?"

"Sick," came the emotionless answer.

"How long?" yelled Daid.

"Since yesterday."

"Why wasn't I notified?"

"Another priest saw him."

"Is he in his room?"

"Yes."

Daid rushed to the building that housed the administrative staff. Sahar lay inert, apathetic, weak from vomiting, burning with fever. Daid spent the night at his side. He administered henbane mixed with myrrh and copper. He wiped his body with pig fat and river mud. He gave him water and beer to drink. He tried to ease his discomfort.

Sahar smiled sweetly. "I am going to die, Daid."

"No," shouted Daid. He redoubled his efforts. But by morning light, Sahar died in his arms. Daid sat numbed. His teacher and Sahar, the only friends he had in Babylon, were dead.

In Ur, Sumulael, the Babylonian physician, headed for the morning audience. On seeing him, the king said, "What brings you here, Sumulael? Don't make a request to go home because I can't grant it."

"I have no request, Majesty, only—"

"Good." Idi-Sin settled back.

Sumulael hesitated. "—unfortunate news."

"My son?"

"No, majesty. The pox."

"The pox!" Idi-Sin sprang to his feet. "Where? How?"

"It probably originated with a ship coming from Babylon. Three ill sailors were dumped on the wharf. They are dead. Others are already sick."

"Tell the high priest," yelled Idi-Sin, "the temple physicians will have to care for the sick in the city."

"He knows," said Sumulael.

Idi-Sin turned to the chancellor. "Spread the word throughout the palace that nobody is to leave and nobody is to come in." He snapped his fingers. "This audience is over. All you applicants get out of here immediately."

Men rushed toward the exit, bumped into each other, tripped and fell. Guards tried to push them along. Idi-Sin himself hurried out through the rear door. He went directly to the royal quarters in search of his wife.

"Madam," he said to the seated queen, not caring how many of the court ladies attending her heard him, "Nannar has not sent King Hammurabi a war, he has sent the pox."

Her chin searched for her lap, her eyes widened and rounded, her skin turned an unpleasant color.

"Obviously, you were careless in your sacrifices. You had better placate him, and soon."

She jumped from her chair and ran toward him.

He glared at her, intentionally spurned her, turned, and left the room.

As Idi-Sin's back receded from view, Nin-Anna slithered to

the floor. Her horror and guilt, like hot flames in her brain, dulled her ability to move.

"Majesty, Majesty," said one of her attendants, kneeling beside her, "you mustn't lie here like this. Please let me help you get up."

"Tell the high priest that I need him."

At the queen's summons, the high priest entered the palace, despite the king's order. He found Nin-Anna on the floor. For seconds, he stood over her.

"Majesty, what is your wish?"

Nin-Anna raised her head and looked at his orange wool skirt. Then her glance glided back and forth, resisting upward motion, to the gold chain around his neck, the square chin, the unsympathetic black eyes under the shaved head. "Oh," she moaned, "he is going to make it hard for me."

She sat up. As she tried to regain her dignity, her eyes lit on the hovering, worried, court ladies. "Leave us," she said.

Alone with the high priest, slowly, faltering, with many pauses, she told him what she had done to the chancellor's wife.

Fortunately, she wasn't looking at him. He couldn't hide his consternation. He studied her anguished face with distaste. "You will sacrifice a small animal each day, and you will tell the chancellor what you did."

"No," burst from her.

"You may do it in front of me," he continued, "or in private."

"In private." She started to cry.

Without saying another word, he left, anger boiling in him at the evil she had brought on Ur.

In Babylon, the pox raged on. Despair entrenched in the depths of his being, Daid put Hana-Ad's personal goddess back in his waistband. Maybe it belonged to him now. Maybe it would help him.

Each day, he dragged himself through the same routine. He rose early. In the classroom, he and the students pooled the latest information they had gleaned from areas they had visited—where the epidemic showed signs of subsiding, where it was heaviest, the approximate number of dead, what medicines needed replenishing and where to obtain them. Then they fanned out over the city to help where they could.

How long he could go on, Daid didn't know. The king would

never release him now that he had become master. He just wanted to lie on his bed and do nothing.

In the intense heat of the noonday sun, after spending the morning in the area around the house of forgotten women, he headed back across the river. Unconsciously, he noted the glut of ships waiting to dock. On the other end of the bridge, a voice he vaguely remembered said, "Daid. Listen. Walk slowly." The individual close behind him continued to speak just above a whisper. "Walk along the river."

Slowly, Daid turned left. What difference would taking a detour make? He could always turn up one of the streets further along.

"Do you still want to go to Ur? I remember that's what you told me when we were in prison."

Daid tensed. Tishrata walked behind him.

"You cured my leg, for which I'm eternally thankful, even to the point of offering prayers to Marduk for you. Anyway, I've thought this out. I know of a ship that sails for Ur tonight. It'll leave as soon as the air freshens. Keep walking along the river, and I'll tell you which one it is. But you have to board now and lie hidden. I've arranged it with one of the sailors. King Hammurabi won't send guards after you. He'll just assume you died like everybody else."

Daid started to remonstrate, to turn around and face Tishrata. Then he hesitated. Waggling his head, weaving a bit, he slowed his gait. This probably was his only chance to go home. What a genius. Tishrata had worked it out so nobody would know.

"Here," said Tishrata.

Daid stepped onto the gangplank. He didn't look around. Only Tishrata heard him murmur, "You've been a true friend, Tishrata."

"Crawl among the bails in the stern."

Daid wormed his way among them, forcing two a little apart so he could lie down. The sun beat down on him, making the spot broiling hot. He didn't care. He lay exhausted on the ship's wooden planks. The sound of the water lapping gently against the ship lulled him to sleep.

At some point—Daid had no idea how long he had slept—three words, repeated and repeated, worked their way into his unconsciousness. He stirred. Again, he heard the words, "Are you awake?"

"I am now." Blackness enveloped him. The ship was in motion.

"You can come out. I brought you a little grain."

Daid slid out cautiously. In the brilliant starlight, he saw a sailor holding a bowl.

"Are you a priest?" asked the sailor, offering the bowl.

"It's a disguise." Hungry, Daid shoveled in a mouthful.

"Well, whatever you've done is no affair of mine. Your friend, the soldier, said you wanted to go to Ur. We'll put you off there. Stay hidden during the day. It's nice on deck at night. The air is cool, and the brightness of the stars makes everything on the banks visible. The river is in flood so we should make good time."

Daid couldn't keep track of how many days they sailed down the river. He slept most of the time, in the heat among the bails or on the cool deck at night. Periodically, the sailor woke him and gave him food.

Morning spread across the horizon, the sun a brilliant, sparkling orange, as the ship tied up at Ur. Daid wedged himself between two slaves unloading cargo and walked down the gangplank. On the dock, he hesitated. The city that had seemed so grand to the boy looked seedy compared with the splendors of Babylon. He stood a long time looking around. A few pleasure boats pushed out into the river, their bright sails fluttering. Men bustled around the docks, but didn't seem as busy. The warehouses didn't seem as prosperous. The palace still dominated this part of the city, but compared to Babylon—Well.

He started to walk toward the wide road running from the palace to the market gate. Few people were about. This surprised him. Suddenly, he recognized the familiar stench of disease and death in his nostrils. The pox. He groaned. He had become so inured to it that he hadn't noticed. That explained a lot of the city's desolate aspect. He began to hurry.

He passed a body lying in the street. The pox, the pox. He couldn't stand it. He hurried on.

He noticed that people stepped wide of him and lowered their eyes. He ran a hand over his shaved head and glanced down at his waist, then gave a silent, amused snort. To the surrounding people, he was a priest of Marduk. Actually, he realized, it was a fortunate break. The skirt would make his admittance to the palace easier. And after seeing his parents, he intended to head straight for the palace.

At last, he saw his home in the distance. As he drew closer, his sister, Buzu, opened the door and stepped outside. He waved wildly. She shaded her nearsighted eyes and squinted intently.

He started to run. He called, "Buzu. Buzu, it's Daid."

She screamed and disappeared into the house. In another second, his father hobbled out, followed by his mother and the servants. His mother couldn't contain herself. She rushed by Ur-Enlila and flung herself at Daid. With a cry, he caught her in an enveloping hug. Setting her carefully aside, he gathered his old father in his arms. Then everyone, his brothers and sister, the servants, all crowded around him.

Ur-Enlila drew him into the house. The family sat in a circle, the servants standing on the outer edge. Everybody wanted to know what had happened to him. "Well," he laughed. "The first thing that happened, I was thrown into prison."

"No," cried Ninlil, covering her mouth with five fingers.

"Wait," he said, holding up his left hand. "The way things turned out, it was the best that could have happened. That landed me in front of King Hammurabi who placed me in the school of medicine."

"Stop there," Ur-Enlila interrupted. "Tell me about King Hammurabi."

"It's a long story." Daid told about being made a slave which brought more cries from Ninlil, about Hammurabi's dove, her attempted seduction and his confrontation with Hammurabi, the king's rapid decision and his justice. Then Buzu wanted to know what Hammurabi's dove looked like and what kinds of clothes she wore.

"Buzu," remonstrated Ninlil.

Daid laughed. "Her shiny black hair hung to her waist. And her skin, a pale golden color, darker than ours, glowed. I thought her beautiful. She always wore a voluminous red cloak when I saw her that covered her from her neck down." He noted that his mother seemed fascinated.

Finally, after he'd answered all his family's questions, Daid asked about Hana-Ad.

Ur-Enlila shook his head. "The old queen may be alive. Nobody knows. The sickness has struck the palace. A long time ago, we heard rumors that a great physician had come from Babylon. But nobody knows any details."

So, Sahar's guess was right. The disappearance of the head of the medical school resulted from his finally delivering Nanshe's letter to King Hammurabi.

"Luckily, the pox has not struck our household."

"And Ur-mes?"

"Ur-mes is deteriorating. He made an amazing recovery after his stroke, but he dwells constantly on Hana-Ad and has never stopped worrying about what would happen to her. The family's slaves say that he asks at least five times a day whether the old queen is still alive."

Daid heaved a sigh. "I intend to bring Hana-Ad to him."

"You had better forget her, son," said Ur-Enlila.

Rather than become involved in that, Daid said, "Have you heard from Apilsin?"

Ur-Enlila ran his left hand through his hair and glanced at Ninlil. She raised her eyebrows and flipped up her palm in helplessness.

"He died soon after he reached Abraham," said Ur-Enlila.

Daid clutched his abdomen. Apilsin dead! When he could speak, he said, "I could use his strong faith."

"You haven't continued to follow Yahweh?" Ur-Enlila's head reared back. He stared intently, unbelieving, at Daid. "I thought you had a better grounding than that."

Daid threw up his hands. "You see what I wear. I'm torn between the two."

"You sadden me, my son. Once you're back taking care of the animals, you'll find the truth again."

Daid's eyelids flickered. After all he had related of his experiences, his father expected him to go back to tending cattle?

"No," he said as gently as he could, "That's impossible. Too much has happened in the interim. This afternoon, I will offer my services at the palace."

"No, my son." Ur-Enlila laid a trembling hand on Daid's arm. "The palace is not the place for you. You belong here; we need you here."

Daid covered the hand with his and smiled into his father's frightened eyes.

"Remember, dear father, I'm now a physician in the service of Marduk. I have treated the pox in Babylon. My help will be welcomed in the palace."

Ur-Enlila surveyed his son with a critical eye. The young

man who sat before him was a stranger. During the four-plus years since Daid had left Ur, he had become a different person. This man had authority in his face, in the way he held his head, in the sound of his voice. Suddenly Ur-Enlila was shy, a bit afraid. The life his son had lived in Babylon had gone way beyond his comprehension. Daid was now in command. Ur-Enlila dropped his shoulders and yielded.

Before going to the palace, Daid visited Ur-mes. With quiet joy, he greeted the old man. He noticed the tremor in Ur-mes' hands and head, the unsteady gait when he came forward. Daid took his arm to support him.

"Let us sit here in the guest area," Ur-mes said. After Daid had seated him, Ur-mes asked, "Why are you dressed as a priest of Marduk?"

Daid smiled. "It's too long a story to go into, but I'll tell you that although going to Babylon started as a disaster, it has turned into a great advantage. While I was there, I became a physician in the service of Marduk and now I'm on my way to the palace."

"To find Hana-Ad?"

"Yes, Ur-mes. I hope to bring her home to you."

"Please, please, do it soon, before I die." Ur-mes started to blubber.

"I will," Daid said with force.

While talking to Ur-mes, he had been positive that he would gain admittance to the palace. Now, facing the palace guards, he wasn't so sure.

"I'm a physician from the Temple of Marduk in Babylon," he announced with authority. "I have come to see the physician King Hammurabi sent to your king. Lead me to him."

The guard hesitated, then called his superior.

Daid repeated his request.

"Are you speaking of Sumulael?"

"Of course," bluffed Daid, who didn't know the physician's name.

"He is with the old queen. No other physician is allowed in her quarters." The superior turned on his heel.

Daid's breath caught. If the old queen had the pox, he had arrived just in time.

"I'm the head Babylonian physician for the epidemic," Daid said loudly to the superior's back.

The man stopped and mulled that over. "I'll take you to the king," he said, motioning Daid forward.

Quickly, Daid moved to his side. "Lead on."

They entered the audience court. Only a few men stood before the dais. So different from those days long ago when he had attended the king's audiences in order to learn what to do at Hammurabi's court. He wanted to cry out his desolation for his city. He sensed the stillness of the sickness here, too, as in Babylon.

He looked up at the king, on his throne, dressed in a scarlet robe, his feet on a footstool. Idi-Sin's face appeared fleshier than Daid recalled and so sad. It made his heart ache. The king clearly grieved for his people. As at King Hammurabi's court, his chancellor stood behind him.

"On your knees," said the guard.

Daid knelt, touching his forehead to the ground. He heard whispering, but couldn't make out the content.

"Rise and come forward," said the king.

Daid moved forward, keeping his head bowed.

"I am told you are the head physician for the pox from Babylon. If true, why are you here?"

Daid thought quickly. "I was told that I was to be made a slave."

Astonishment crossed Idi-Sin's face. "How can that be?"

"He enslaves men for himself and then sells them for profit." Daid paused.

The king remained still, waiting.

"Fortunately, a friend warned me in time. I dropped everything and escaped."

"I don't want King Hammurabi looking for you here," said Idi-Sin, irritated.

"Majesty, there will be no trouble. With the pox, nobody knows how many die or who. I could die here. Nobody would know or care. In the meantime, I could be of help to you."

The king looked at Daid and then through him, not quite sure whether to believe him.

Ur-Ilum bent and whispered in the royal ear. "It's plausible. He has the features of a Sumerian, probably from one of the city-states further north, living in Babylon."

"And the gods know, Ur could use help," Idi-Sin said hardly moving his lips.

"Guard, take him to the kitchen. We'll see how good a physician he is before we drag Sumulael away from my son."

Daid backed away, fuming. He shot a glance at the king who had cupped his chin in his hand, a worried expression on his face.

The kitchen. Why did Idi-Sin send him to treat slaves? Hana-Ad was in the old queen's quarters. Now, it would take him longer to find her.

Too soon, he was caught up with the sickness. A slave brought a delirious child covered with red blisters; a stricken mother held up a dead infant, pleading for him to help. He shook his head. The children were so much sicker than the adults. He could do little for them.

"Bring me copper and myrrh, pig fat and river mud," he ordered the guard.

He lifted the child from the mother's arms. "He is dead." The mother screeched and collapsed. Daid dumped the tiny corpse into a bucket. Handing the bucket to a slave, he said, "Burn this." Then he turned and set to work with the living. How long he worked, he couldn't tell. Suddenly, a gaunt, worn-out priest of Marduk stood at his side.

Daid straightened and looked down into deep-set, black eyes. "Sire," he said bowing his head, "My humble abilities are at your service."

"I don't remember you and I knew every physician in the temple, every student in the school. You were not one of them. Yet the king tells me you say you're the *head* physician."

"Sire, I was placed in the school during the furor over the disappearence of the head master."

Sumulael shook his head sadly. After a minute he said, "You were made master?"

"Oh no. I was studying." Daid's eyes slid sideways. "Until the pox."

Sumulael's face became rigid, his mouth slightly open. "A student?" he gasped. "I'm stunned."

Daid looked at the woman sitting on the floor near him. "The school has been decimated. The city is in shambles. Our master died of the pox, and many of the best physicians are also dead. We still have a long way to go, but the pox has begun to recede."

Sumulael heaved a sigh and looked around the kitchen. "It's a disaster here, too."

"You're the only physician in the palace?" asked Daid.

"Yes. The king allows no one else to treat the royal household. But now, with the pox, I can't keep up."

"I've seen what it has done to the slaves," said Daid. "Has it infected any one else in the court?"

"Yes, it has now struck the girls who attend the old queen." Daid's stomach contracted. "How many girls are there?"

"Nine. The queen, the king's wife, snatched her niece away to the royal quarters the minute the pox hit the palace."

"So there were ten?"

"Yes. I had just reached the old queen who is ill with consumption when a message from the king ordered me to come to his quarters. He sent me to the prince. Having been through the epidemic in Babylon, your abilities undoubtedly are honed, and the king won't object if you treat the members of his household. That's why I grabbed a moment to see you. But I must return to the prince. Please go examine the young women in my place. Do the best you can, but if we don't treat them right away, the pox could spread to the rest of the court. I'll come as soon as I'm able." He turned to leave.

"Sire, point me in the right direction," said Daid, pretending not to know the palace's layout, though he well remembered the discussion with his father.

"Of course," said Sumulael. "Forgive my thoughtlessness."

Daid bowed his head.

The two men walked through the corridors side by side, exchanging what information they had—what medications they used, what they did with the dead, how they thought it spread.

"The king's quarters are here," said Sumulael, indicating the area behind the audience court throne. "This is where I leave you. To get to Queen Ku-bau's quarters, keep following that corridor to the left until you pass through ornamented double doors. The girls are in the large room on the left."

Once he passed out of sight, Daid slowed down. He pressed his hand against his chest to still his pounding heart. Was Hana-Ad sick? Could he save her? His love for her welled up with such force that he stopped. For an instant, he leaned against the wall before walking on. Finally, the double doors. By force of will, he switched from being a lovesick boy to a physician. Assuming a look of authority, he walked through the double doors. On his left, just as Sumulael had said, he saw a large room. A beautiful young woman sat disconsolately on a cushion in the middle of the floor. She looked up as he entered.

"I'm a physician," he said. "How many of you are sick?" He glanced around at the closed drapes.

"The sickest is in there." She pointed to a drape.

Daid crossed the room, pulled aside the drape, then, starting to shake, gripped it, dazed. Hana-Ad sat on the bed with the head of a delirious young woman in her lap. She was bent over, smoothing a wet rag on the woman's forehead. He noticed the pustules covering the woman's face and neck, and the effort she made to stay alive. Her throat kept contracting as she tried to swallow.

A strong hand grabbed Daid's arm. "You can't go in there."

A shudder passed through him. Then, whirling, he snatched his arm from the grip of the middle-aged female slave. "I'm the physician, and I shall see each one of the ill girls. You get me some water and be quick about it," he snapped, raising a dismissive arm. "Perfume it heavily with plum blossoms." He turned back to the bed.

Hana-Ad stared at him with huge eyes, her mouth open, her face drained of color.

He moved his finger across his lips. His eyes smiled at her, caressing her. Hers filled with tears, and she lowered her lids.

"What's her name?" He motioned toward the young woman Hana-Ad held.

"Kigal."

Daid cupped Kigal's cheek with his palm. She moaned and thrashed around on the bed. He stripped the coverlet to check her body for blisters. Her legs and chest bore dozens of red marks. Fever consumed her.

"She won't live," he said softly to Hana-Ad.

"No, no." She flung her arm across her eyes. Daid drew her hands into his. "Get off the bed," he said. She resisted. His hand tightened on her arm, assisting her off the bed.

At that moment, the slave reappeared with the perfumed water.

"Why are you bringing that here, Temena?" asked a confused Hana-Ad.

Temena pointed to Daid. "The physician told me to."

Daid said quietly, "It isn't needed here now."

He turned to Hana-Ad. "Go sit with her on the floor." His finger pointed to the woman in the middle of the room.

Hana-Ad started to cry, but went to sit beside Girsu-Ad.

He watched her go, realized he was holding the drape open and let it drop. "She will die before nightfall," he said to Temena.

"Oh no," she cried, quivering.

Daid grabbed the perfumed water as it started to splash from the bowl. "Are others sick?"

"Yes." She retrieved the bowl.

"Where to next?"

Temena indicated a drape at the back of the room.

He strode across, Temena at his heels.

Uttu looked up as they entered. Ashnan's head lay in her lap. Healing blisters covered Ashnan's face.

Daid colored in anger. "Get out of here," he said to Uttu. "Go sit on the floor with the other two."

Uttu shot up from the bed. As she passed him, he caught her arm and felt her forehead.

"Normal." He looked at her sharply. Enceinte. She carried it well concealed. These girls were supposed to be virgins. He jerked his thumb toward the center of the room, indicating where Hana-Ad sat. She scuttled out.

"How many others are sick?" he demanded.

"Two," answered Temena.

"Does each of them have someone who's holding her head?"

"Yes." She sounded scared.

"Bring them here." He pointed to the floor in front of him.

She placed the plum-blossom water on the cosmetic table and hurried away.

He felt Ashnan's forehead. Her fever had abated. She tried to push his hand away with an arm that simply flopped back on the bed. She kept smacking her parched lips in an attempt to talk. She looked at him with sad eyes.

"You'll live," he said, smiling at her.

She smiled weakly and closed her eyes.

"Give her beer, lots of it," he said to Temena who had returned with Ninbar and Nidada. "Spread river mud on her pustules and send someone for copper and myrrh. Mix them in equal parts and add three pinches of the mixture to her beer."

He looked at the two girls Temena had brought to him.

"This is Ninbar and Nidada," she said. "Ninbar looks feverish, sire. Do you wish to examine her first?" Temena pushed the girl forward.

Daid felt Ninbar's head. "Go to bed immediately."

"No," she screamed. She clung to Temena. "I don't want to die of the pox. I won't have a life of luxury if I don't die with Queen Ku-bau."

Temena took her out of Ashnan's alcove and handed her over to Gula's care.

"I'll be in to see you shortly," Daid said over his shoulder, his hand on Nidada's forehead.

"Sit out there," he said, jabbing the air with his forefinger.

"Now," he said to Temena, "lead me to the two girls you said were sick."

"Yes, sire. Ninti and Nin-Ad are both in their alcoves at the other end of the room."

Daid made the rounds, the slave at his elbow.

Neither Ninti nor Nin-Ad looked as if they would survive. He ordered Temena to give them the same medication he had prescribed for Ashnan and to rub them with pig fat.

Making a mental note to obtain some henbane for them, he closed Nin-Ad's drape behind him. "Those two girls may not survive."

Temena brushed her face with her hands, drew her brows together, and made a gargled sound in the back of her throat.

"I think we can save the others," he said kindly. He advanced on the sober little circle of girls sitting in the middle of the room.

"You are to stay out of the sickrooms," he told them emphatically. "Do you understand?"

They nodded solemnly.

"The minute you don't feel well, you are to send for me. Do you understand that, too?"

They looked frightened and continued to nod.

For an instant, Hana-Ad's eyes locked with Daid's. Then he disappeared. A turmoil erupted in her. Outwardly, she sat in serene stillness, totally unaware of her surroundings. At last, Daid had come to help her escape. But he was a different Daid than the man who owned her heart. His body had filled out—she wasn't sure how—but more of a man's body. Love, blotting the sadness from his face, shone from his eyes when he looked at her. Temena jumped when he spoke. Everyone obeyed him without question. She shuddered, a bit afraid of this new Daid who walked with assurance in his step and authority in his manner. Yet, her soul sang with joy. She would be, she wanted to be, wedded to him for ever and ever.

Outside the double doors, Daid reached an empty corridor. Feeling weak-kneed, he leaned against the wall. So fast, he had found Hana-Ad. He gritted his teeth. He had to keep her healthy. How? He fisted his hands in determination.

That poor little thing that lay dying, how lovely she was. Kigal? Was that her name? He couldn't remember for sure, so stunned had he been to see Hana-Ad. But then, he reflected, Kigal would die anyway with the old queen. They all would—except Hana-Ad. Why was he going to try so hard to save them? Hana-Ad! She was more beautiful than he remembered, a fully developed woman now with the bearing and charm of a court lady.

His ear picked up footsteps. He started slowly along the corridor, pulling at his chin as though in deep thought.

Sumulael rounded the bend. Seeing Daid, he stopped and waited.

"How did it go?" he asked when Daid reached him.

"I saw nine extremely beautiful young women," throwing his eyes to the ceiling, and adding, "What a pity—five of them are sick; one may already have crossed the river. But I think two of them will recover. I don't know yet about the other two."

Sumulael said, "Thanks be to Marduk that you have arrived. You will be able to help me in the next couple of days. Please continue to treat the girls. I'm about at the end of my abilities between the pox, the crown prince, and the king."

"Is the crown prince sick?"

"No. He has other problems."

"Such as?"

Sumulael glanced at Daid. Should he say? Well, he was a physician, and he was from Babylon. "The crown prince is almost nineteen, but he has the mind of a five-year old. The queen won't accept that fact. She wants the boy cured, though there's nothing I, nor any physician, can do. It's tragic."

They neared the royal quarters.

"Come to my room," Sumulael said. "We can talk there while the slaves prepare a room for you."

"I'm to stay here?" asked Daid, not sure he liked that.

"I assume so. With the pox, there's much to do here."

They crossed the audience court. As they walked along, Daid said, "Where are we?"

"Just outside the quarters reserved for slaves of foreign dignitaries." Sumulael led him to a small room. "Here we are."

"A priest of Marduk in this area?"

"It's comfortable. And besides, it's close enough to the royal quarters so the king's slaves wait on me."

A woman carrying light-weight wool blankets, pillows, and a white linen cover went into the next room.

"I suspect that's where you'll be staying."

Inside his bedroom, Sumulael said, "Please sit." He indicated a cushion and seated himself on another.

"How is it that you came to Ur?" Daid said, wondering how much Sumulael knew of the circumstances.

"I was sent here by King Hammurabi four years ago."

"Why?"

"To treat the crown prince. Apparently, Nanshe, the king's aunt asked our great king for a physician. That's not common knowledge, though, so please keep the information to yourself."

Daid coughed to hide his face.

"I came here and did what I could for the prince. But now I am not allowed to go home. I've talked to Nanshe, who's a charming woman and who's a good high priestess, but she's in a tussle with Queen Nin-Anna and can't help me. The queen is determined to depose Nanshe in favor of her daughter. Palace politics here are as muddled as in Babylon."

Sumulael rose. "I'll introduce you to the prince."

"I must check on those girls first. When I left, the temperature of one of them was just starting to rise."

"We'll both go examine them," said Sumulael.

They found Kigal dead and Nin-Ad dying.

"Get the bodies out of here immediately," Sumulael said to Temena.

Ninti hovered between life and death. The men didn't know which way she'd go. As they left her alcove to go to Ninbar, Daid saw Hana-Ad enter an alcove third from the main door. All night, they held a vigil at Ninbar's bedside. She remained seriously ill, but toward morning, their other patient, Ninti, began to improve. A couple of times, hearing the muffled sound of crying, Daid stopped before Hana-Ad's alcove. A wild desire to slip behind the drape, to hold and comfort her, consumed him. He didn't dare.

In the morning, as he and Sumulael tore themselves from Ninbar's side, he saw Hana-Ad sitting with the three healthy girls. She was so beautiful, he shuddered through the depths of his being. He hurried away with Sumulael.

28

*D*elirious with fever, the crown prince lay on his tortoise-shell inlaid bed surrounded by hovering slaves. One held a silver bowl, ready to catch any vomit. One dipped a cloth into a golden basin of cool water, then wiped Shulgi's face. A third tried to keep the prince covered as he thrashed around. In the corner, a musician played lilting melodies on a lapis lazuli inlaid lyre.

Two terrified boys ran back and forth with messages to members of the court. The distraught king alternately paced the floor and railed at the hapless physicians. He retained a scorching anger against Nin-Anna, whom he blamed for the royal family's troubles. She scurried fearfully around the prince's bedside, constantly in the physicians' way, wringing her hands and crying.

"Please, Majesty," Daid finally said when she blocked his access to the bed, "forgive your humble servant, but it would be better if you and the king returned to your quarters. We will notify you the minute there's a change."

"How dare you tell me to leave my darling boy!" she sobbed.

"I need to give him liquid," Daid said with great care.

"Come here, my queen," called the king from his stand near the musician who, at his request, had begun to play a little dance tune that the prince loved.

Unwillingly, Nin-Anna joined her husband in the corner of the room where they listened with moist eyes as the musician played the lighthearted tune.

Sumulael and Daid tried to coax the prince to drink. Sumulael held the golden cup while Daid steadied the boy's head against his shoulder. The prince flailed his arms, knocking the cup from Sumulael's hand. The slave in charge of keeping the prince warmly covered rushed dry bedding into place.

The king started to pace, leaving Nin-Anna free to return to the boy's bedside.

"He won't survive the pox," Daid whispered to Sumulael during a huddled conference out of earshot of the royal parents.

"I know, but we must do something."

They ordered compresses. They sang incantations from the head of the bed, then the foot. They felt his forehead with each change of position. They inspected his arms and legs, then again retired to a corner to confer.

The prince screamed, high and drawn out. Then he giggled, wrapped his arms around his body and rolled from side to side.

Sumulael rushed from the corner to the bedside.

The king stopped pacing, to stand opposite Sumulael and stare at his son. He raised his eyes to the physician. Looking into them, Sumulael saw dull pain kindle into a spark of anger.

"If he dies, you die." The king turned and left the room.

With a cry of agony, the queen hung, tentative and undecided, over her son, then followed the king.

Daid looked at Sumulael's exhausted face. The demands of the royal couple consumed his energy. Together, he and Sumulael had done all they could.

"I'll return shortly," Daid said and hurried away.

Sumulael caught himself as he pitched forward over the bed. He wanted to sit down. Parched, he tried to wet his lips with his tongue, but his tongue stuck to his chapped upper lip. He could do nothing more for the prince. He had to face the possibility that he, too, might soon die. He looked around. A slave, struggling with an armful of bedding, entered the room.

"Bring me some wine," Sumulael said. At least, he might as well have a pleasant drink and rest while he waited for death. He sat on the floor beside the bed and ordered the slave playing the lyre to sing a love song. The silver wine tumbler felt cool between his trembling hands. He took a long sip and sighed. The prince quieted.

At first, Daid didn't see Sumulael sitting on the floor. Then he caught a glimpse of his head, eyes closed, bent back against the bed. He hurried around the bed and knelt beside him. "I've arranged for you to leave Ur," he whispered, "but you must go immediately. On your bed, you'll find a robe and a hat of a priest of Enki. Change into them quickly. After you've dressed, make your way as fast as you can to the part of the quay nearest the palace. Look for a large, gray ship with the red sail already up. It's leaving for Babylon within the hour. Once you've found the ship, ask for Ishbi-Erra. Hurry!" Daid gave him a push.

Sumulael squeezed Daid's arm and rushed out the door. Later, as the vessel rocked beneath him, he had no idea how he had gotten on board.

As soon as Sumulael left, Daid sat on the floor, sipped the cool wine and listened to the sad, haunting music. After a while, he got up and looked at the boy.

"The prince is dead," he said.

As one body, the slaves fell forward onto the floor.

Realization that he had to tell the king the prince was dead hit Daid like a falling mudbrick wall. He stepped over the prostrate body of a slave and walked slowly, deliberately, to the small guardroom by the audience court. "Where's the chancellor?" he asked the first guard he found.

"In the king's quarters."

"Tell the chancellor that the priest of Marduk needs to see him. I'll wait for him here."

Daid shivered. The king might easily guess why he wanted to see the chancellor. How fitting that he was already in the guardroom. It would be easy for the guard to arrest him. As that thought crossed his mind, the guard he had sent to the chancellor returned.

"Priest of Marduk, the chancellor is crossing the audience court," the guard said.

In a flash of swirling color, Daid dashed from the guard room. On the other side of the court, he spotted the chancellor headed toward the prince's rooms. Halfway across the audience court, Daid called, "Sire." Ur-Ilum stopped and turned.

"Ah," he said as Daid reached him, "you are the one I was looking for."

"The prince is dead," Daid said. "The king threatened to have Sumulael killed if the prince died. And I know my life is forfeit, too." Daid bowed his head. "I don't want to die."

Ur-Ilum clucked. "Right now, you are safe. The princess is vomiting. The queen is hysterical."

Daid's shoulders sagged. If the princess died, so would he. Then surely Hana-Ad would, too. With a deep sigh of resignation, he followed Ur-Ilum.

Light and color overwhelmed his senses the minute they entered the royal quarters. A delicate, indescribably sweet fragrance that he couldn't place drifted from the garden past his nostrils. After the stench of the sickness, he threw back his head in delight, inhaling the sweetness. A glance from Ur-Ilum warned him to hurry along toward the door in the far corner.

The princess' room was much like her brother's, though less spacious. She lay on a narrow bed, whose beautifully carved wooden footboard contained gold and ivory inlay.

"Where's Sumulael?" demanded the king.

"The prince is dead, Your Majesty." Daid tensely bowed from the waist.

The queen screeched. "No, no." She twisted her arms around her head and continued to screech.

"Guard," roared the king, "arrest Sumulael."

Daid hurried to the young princess before the king could question him. He felt her forehead. He said, "Stick out your tongue."

"Hmm," he said, observing the tongue. "Prepare the medication for the princess to drink immediately." He snapped his fingers with the authority of a priest of Marduk. The slave he addressed disappeared instantly.

He pointed at a second slave. "Bathe her slowly with sandalwood-scented warm water."

A sweet-faced little thing, the princess shivered with fever. He promptly ordered compresses of myrrh and mulberry, copper and garlic in beer for her arms and legs. To this, he added a tiny bit of poppy.

The king, distracted and upset, yelled everything Daid said to the slaves who started to run around pointlessly, too confused to execute the orders swiftly.

The guard returned with the news that Sumulael couldn't be found.

"Where is he?" The king bore down on Daid.

"Majesty, he left the prince's room moments before he died, and I have not seen him since."

"Find him," the king shouted at the guard. "He will die."

The night wore on. Daid persuaded the king and queen to retire after repeatedly assuring them that he would remain with the princess.

"She better not die," the king hissed in Daid's ear.

Every two hours during the night, Daid applied a new poultice. He lifted her shoulders gently and forced her to take medication. A slave constantly bathed her face. At regular intervals, she whimpered and asked for her mother.

He hoped it wasn't the imagination of an overtired man, but by dawn, she seemed better.

With the spreading light, the king arrived.

"She may be badly marked, Your Majesty," he said to warn the king and to head off any criticism of his medical care of her. "I've ordered warm saltwater compresses for her eyes."

"Lucky for you that she will live," growled the king. He looked at the sweating girl.

"You," he yelled at one of the female slaves, "bring a basin of cool water and bathe her."

The woman jumped and ran from the room.

Daid flicked his eyes at the king. Cool water could do no harm.

"Sumulael can't be found," announced Idi-Sin. "I've questioned the slaves. They saw him hurry from the room and never return. No one else has seen him. I'll find him if it's the last thing I do."

Daid hoped not. Once he reached Babylon, Idi-Sin couldn't hurt him.

A court lady hurried in and knelt before the king. Daid caught a sudden fear in the king's eyes.

"The queen doesn't feel well."

The king grabbed the bed to steady himself.

"She asks you to please come."

His voice husky, the king turned to Daid. "You come, too."

"Continue what we have done during the night," Daid said to the women helping him. "Give the medication slowly so she doesn't throw up. And try to give her a little gruel. I'll come back as soon as I can."

In the royal bedroom, the queen sat propped in a large ornate bed, surrounded by court ladies.

"Pray, ladies, wait outside," Daid said.

They looked at the queen. She nodded.

They filed from the room, glaring at him unhappily as they passed by.

The king was rhythmically patting her hand when Daid approached the bed. She looked gray. Somehow, she didn't look as sick as many he had seen. He felt her forehead. A little too warm.

"We'll have to start the medication," he said to the king. "May Your Majesty please stay with her while I supervise the preparation?"

The king nodded.

"Have one of her women bathe her, Your Majesty, and it would be well if you had the water scented heavily with lotus blossoms." Daid hurried out.

"Majesty," whispered the queen as soon as Daid left, "please send Ur-Ilum to me and leave us alone."

"Madam, I assume this is the penance you were told to perform some time ago. I thank you for complying at last."

She cringed.

The bath completed, the king ordered the slaves from the room and left himself.

Bowing, feeling uneasy, Ur-Ilum entered. "Majesty, we're worried about you."

"I have a confession. Please hear me out." She closed her eyes.

Nonplussed, he quietly took a position partway between the bed and the door.

"I caused Nannar to send the pox. I falsely accused your wife."

A muffled, agonized cry escaped him.

"I wanted you for my daughter, but the king thwarted me and sent her to Lagash. I humbly ask your forgiveness and as humbly ask what I can do to atone for my wickedness."

Unable to answer, Ur-Ilum kept gulping, trying not to weep. His lovely wife. He could think of nothing but that day when he sat on the cushion in their social room, holding her after the queen sent her home.

As he didn't answer, Nin-Anna opened her eyes. His were closed, the saddest expression she had ever seen on his face. Instantly, she regretted everything she had done to him and his wife.

"Please help me," she said.

He couldn't answer. He wanted to hide in some unused corner to nurse his misery.

"Tell me what I can do for the sake of Ur," she said reaching out toward him. "Is there something you want? Anything. I can get it for you," she pleaded.

"Majesty," he said, in a low, broken voice, "I would like to marry one of Queen Ku-bau's maidens."

She tensed.

"Help me get her away from Queen Ku-bau."

"Which one?" she demanded, snatching back her hand.

"Uttu."

Instantly, the queen hated the girl. "Oh—I'm not sure the high priest will let me change Queen Ku-bau's wishes."

He sighed, galled at having to defend his actions before this horrid woman. "She is not a virgin."

"How do you know that?" demanded Nin-Anna, her temper rising.

"She is carrying my child." Behind his back, he wound his fingers together in an iron grip lest he strangle the queen.

Beside herself, Nin-Anna sputtered, "How could you? How could you? I'll tell the king."

"I think that would be wise. He should know." Caught up in her own turmoil, she didn't catch his sarcasm.

Afraid she might refuse to aid him, he said, "This will help Nannar forgive you."

Fear overpowering her anger, she forced herself to say, "As soon as Queen Ku-bau dies, I will go to the girl and refuse to let her join the walk to the tomb. You can depend on my word. It is for the good of Ur. Nannar will accept it."

Bending before her as slightly as he dared, Ur-Ilum backed out.

Daid hurried toward the double doors that led into Ku-bau's area. As he approached, guards opened the doors for Nanshe. He had not seen her since his return.

She smiled. He bowed deeply from the waist, half afraid she would recognize him. Right after returning to Ur, he had felt guilty at not going to her immediately, to tell her all that had happened to him, before delivering her letter to King Hammurabi, of the pox and how he returned to Ur. Then, caught up in the demands of the palace sickness, of the royal family, of the prince, of the engulfing exhaustion of Sumulael and his own attempt to relieve the pressure on the senior physician, he had not contacted her. Now, he wished the time better chosen than this chance meeting.

"So," she said, "you are the second physician from Babylon. From what I hear, we are fortunate to have you in Ur." She moved on sedately.

He turned and watched her, longing to run after her. Instead, he hastened to Ninbar's alcove. He found her weak, but smiling. "No fever," he said, testing her forehead. "You're doing well. Shall I hook your drape back so you can see the others?"

"Yes, please."

He noticed Hana-Ad standing near the carved double doors. As he passed her, he murmured, "If you want life with me rather than death—"

"Oh yes, yes."

"—be prepared to escape." The doors closed behind him.

Days passed. The king gave up trying to find Sumulael, who had left only one clue: the palace slaves discovered his priestly robe tossed away on his bed. Ur-Ilum suggested that he might have thrown himself into the river. Under the circumstances, that seemed reasonable to Idi-Sin.

Daid continued to visit the girls' alcoves in the old queen's quarters each day. Those recuperating gained strength slowly, the listlessness hard to overcome.

The afternoon he heard music coming from Ku-bau's room, he found himself alone with the snoozing sick. He dropped Hana-Ad's personal goddess on her bed.

Dismissed by a weak, emaciated Ku-bau, the girls walked slowly back to their empty room. It smelled of the sickness. Hana-Ad dragged herself to her alcove and drew the drape. She missed Kigal. Her whole body ached for Kigal's gentle spirit, a cold emptiness lodged in her heart. And Nin-Ad, too. All the girls felt the loss. Their laughter had died, their dice games abandoned, their happy chatter forgotten.

Hana-Ad started to sit on her bed. Instead, with a tiny joyous cry, she fell to her knees beside it to grasp the small statue. It could only have come from Daid. Her father must have given it to him. So her family did know about her life at the palace.

She stood the goddess on her feet, holding her by the ankles. "Goddess mine, I've missed you. I've prayed. Did you hear me? I'm so glad to have you again. Surely, you've been helping me."

She made a space on her dressing table and balanced the statue so the goddess could survey the alcove. As soon as she finished eating dinner, she brought a bit of grain and beer and set it before her goddess. She better be good to her. She didn't want the goddess to become angry now that Daid was here to help her escape.

Daid sat on a cushion beside the princess' bed. She lay propped against pillows, weak, but recovering.

"Then," said Daid, "the man hugged and kissed his little daughter, so happy to have found her. Isn't that a nice story?"

He smiled broadly. Luga nodded, her eyes shining.

Ur-Ilum entered the room. "There you are," he said, his speech monotonous and dull. The chancellor's pained expression, his eyes dark with feeling, staggered Daid. He put out his hand as if to ward off a blow.

Quietly, simply, Ur-Ilum said, "The old queen is dead."

29

Nin-Anna, recovered from her minimal brush with the pox, stormed into the girls' area like a murderous tempest. "You are not to walk to the tomb," she yelled at Uttu.

Uttu fell to her knees, pleading, "Please, Majesty. Let me play the harp forever with Queen Ku-bau?"

"No, absolutely not," Nin-Anna looked with hatred at the disconsolate girl. "Go back into your alcove and get those clothes off immediately. Bring them to me. I won't have you getting into line the minute my back is turned."

"Move," she ordered as Uttu attempted to speak.

Tears streaming from her eyes, Uttu struggled off the floor.

Nin-Anna paced and fumed. "Hurry up," she called.

Two guards entered, saw the queen and prostrated themselves.

"What do you want?" demanded Nin-Anna.

"We are under orders to find Uttu," said one guard.

"If the chancellor sent you, tell him I am handling Uttu," she snapped, affronted. "Go."

They quickly backed out.

Uttu reappeared in a simple yellow gown. Squiggly lines of tear-smudged makeup stained her face, and she kept wiping her nose with the white dress clutched in her hand. The scarlet coat hung over her arm.

Nin-Anna snatched the dress and coat, whirled around and dashed from the room.

Uttu collapsed, sobbing, into Hana-Ad's arms.

Hana-Ad removed Uttu's jeweled wig and handed it to Ninbar. Then, still holding Uttu in her arms, she kept smoothing her hair and saying, "There, there."

The other six girls, shocked and upset, hovered, stroking Uttu's shoulders and arms.

Finally, Shegunu said, "We must get in line." With lingering sad looks and clucks of pity, the six started for the door.

"You must come, too, Hana-Ad," said Nidada, hanging a bit behind the others.

"In a minute. I'll catch up with you." Hana-Ad watched them leave, her eyes resting lovingly on each one of her dear friends. She would never see them again.

Uttu raised her head. "I need to repair my face and straighten my gown."

"Yes." Hana-Ad wiped some smeared kohl from Uttu's cheek. "I have some repairing to do also." She went to her alcove.

In the corridor, laden as they were with heavy clothing, excessive jewelry, wigs covered with gold leaves attatched to thin gold ribbons, and harps, the six girls tried to walk sedately toward the exit onto the main ramp. Every twenty steps, they stopped so the three still weak from the pox could rest.

They had finally reached the palace entrance when Ashnan said, "Oh, I forgot my silver hair ribbon. I have to go back."

"Do hurry," said Ninti.

The girls shuffled their feet, looking this way and that along the ramp, trying to decide where they were supposed to stand. Everything had happened so fast in the day and a half since the old queen died that they were unsure of what they were supposed to do. Right in front of them, slaves heaped flowers over the wooden sledge chariot and its wooden bier.

"Did you ever see anything so beautiful?" Ninti said.

"The red, white, and blue mosaic along the edges of the chariot frame is most distinctive," said Shegunu.

"But look at the lions' heads," gasped Girsu-Ad. "They're gold with lapis manes."

"With smaller gold heads of lions and bulls along the top rail and silver lionesses' heads on the front." Nidada shook her head in utter incredulity.

"Did you see the silver nose rings on the two asses for the reins to pass through and further back the double silver ring, that's attached to the pole between them, with the little gold donkey standing on it?" In her amazement, Ninbar flung up a hand to point.

"And the leather reins have silver medallions along them all the way to the driver's bench," sighed Girsu-Ad, overcome by the splendor.

A guard walked up to the wooden bier and tried to snap the thongs that strapped the bier tightly to the chariot. He nodded in approval when they didn't give way.

"We must leave the city by the sadness gate," he said to the driver, "and then follow along those bumpy cart tracks to the new tomb the old king, her husband, constructed outside the city." For a second, the guard blinked rapidly and tapped his mouth with a forefinger. "I guess he didn't want to be buried in the royal cemetery at the edge of the wall surrounding the ziggurat complex because it's full."

Further down the ramp, Nanshe exited the temple, followed by the highest echelon of priestesses. Solemnly, they walked to the head of the line where the marshal stood. He nodded to Nanshe and indicated that she was to walk directly behind him with the high priest, then signaled a group of priests to proceed behind Nanshe, followed by her ladies.

The new crown prince, Ibbisin, appeared. The marshal left his position at the head of the line and beckoned to the young prince.

"You walk directly behind the priestesses," he said. "The chancellor will walk with you, then the court officials and the queen's ladies. Their majesties will walk in front of the asses pulling the chariot."

"My younger brother and sister are to walk with the king?"

"Yes, right behind. Your sister isn't strong yet, so she may want to walk a short distance beside your mother, then have a slave carry her."

The marshal continued along the line, speaking to the court officials. He noted the crown prince's younger brother already in line. He checked the soldiers and the ass handlers grouped around the animals. Good. He sniffed and smiled. The flowers perfumed the lovely morning air.

Massed pink lotus blossoms vied with yellow swamp lilies, red berries, and white laurel in diffusing their sweet fragrance. Directly behind the chariot, a solitary court official, dressed in orange, carried the old queen's golden crown on an orange pillow.

The marshal noticed the girls. Motioning them to come to him, he stood behind the crown carrier, his index finger pointing to the ground. Their brilliant scarlet coats over white dresses making a splash of eye-catching color through the whole line, the girls hustled to him.

"You look beautiful," he said when they reached him and continued down the line.

The marshal nodded to everybody. After speaking to the ambassadors, foreign officials, lesser court officials and palace courtiers at the end, he returned to his position at the head of the line.

Watching him, Ninbar shoved the silver headband around her wig off her eyebrows. She felt weighted down by all the jewelry she and the other girls were required to wear.

"Where is Hana-Ad?" she whispered to Nidada.

"She was still soothing Uttu when we left," Nidada whispered.

"The queen was scary, the way she stomped in." Girsu-Ad forgot to whisper.

As she quickly looked around to see if she had been heard, the others shushed her. The whispering continued.

"I've never seen her so angry," said Ninti. "She walked straight up to Uttu and said in that loud voice, 'You have violated Queen Ku-bau's wishes. You are not a virgin.'"

"She was quivering, she was so angry," said Nidada.

"I felt sorry for Uttu," Shegunu said. "My aunt was really hard on her."

"Keep quiet," a guard yelled.

The huddle of girls separated, but they continued to fret.

Still seething, Nin-Anna joined Idi-Sin and her daughter at the edge of the audience court. She took the hand of the weak, but determined, Luga. Together, the three appeared in the doorway. Immediately, the soldiers stood at attention, people stopped talking and bowed. As the royal family walked by the five girls, Nin-Anna looked them over critically. She stopped.

"Where are Ashnan and Hana-Ad?" she said to Shegunu.

"They haven't come out yet, Majesty."

"Well, they better hurry." Nin-Anna moved on past the fragrant bier and took her place beside Idi-Sin.

Behind the chariot, the girls whispered in quick bursts.

"Hana-Ad didn't have her coat on yet when we left," Ninti whispered.

"Where is she?" Girsu-Ad fidgeted.

"And where is Ashnan?" continued Ninti. "She should be here by now."

"One of them will have to walk alone because there are seven of us," said Nidada.

Girsu-Ad fussed with her long strands of beads as she thought about the uneven number. "We can put her in the middle so her being without a partner won't be so obvious."

"That's a good idea," said Shegunu.

Girsu-Ad beamed at praise from Shegunu.

"The marshal will start the procession any minute," whispered Nidada.

"He won't start before the chancellor comes," Shegunu said.

"Why not?"

"Because, according to the funeral protocol, he has to walk with the crown prince."

"Silence," somebody yelled. The girls subsided, but cast wild glances at each other and at the open palace door.

Servants and slaves continued to pour out of the palace and stand four or five layers deep along the sides of the line. A short slave standing in the back complained, "I can't see a thing."

"Just be glad you're here on the ramp," commented his neighbor, "and not in the narrow, jammed streets below with all the townspeople."

In the girls' social room, Hana-Ad called, "Uttu!" She listened. "Uttu?" Ten empty alcoves stared back at her. "Where did she go?" Hana-Ad stood confused and indecisive in the middle of the room.

She squared her shoulders to counterbalance the weight of the short-sleeved scarlet wool coat, the cuffs embroidered with lapis lazuli, carnelian and gold beads, around her waist a belt of white shell rings fastened with a long silver pin.

"Kigal could never have worn all this," she murmured. The lapis-and-gold dog collar pinched her neck. Long necklaces of gold, silver, lapis and carnelian hung over her breasts, while large crescent-shaped gold earrings dangled close to her shoulders. Added to all this weight, twisted spirals of gold and silver wire kept the curls above her ears in place so they wouldn't disturb the gold and silver ribbons looped around her wig to hold the gold beech-leaf pendants hanging across her forehead. It had taken the three slaves hours to dress the girls.

"Where is Daid?" she muttered. "Why doesn't he help me?"

Ashnan rushed in. "Hana-Ad," she said as she flew by, "hurry up. We're about to start." She darted into her alcove, ran her hands over the bed, drew her brows together and pouted. "Where is it?" she mumbled. She looked around, becoming more and more agitated.

"Oh!" She stooped, made a grab at the floor by the leg of the bed and walked quickly past Hana-Ad. "I forgot my silver headband," she said, stuffing it into her pocket.

"Oh, where's mine?" Hana-Ad placed a finger on her chin and gazed at the ceiling.

"Well, hurry," Ashnan said. She leaned against the doorjamb a few minutes to gather her strength then disappeared through the door.

In slow motion, Hana-Ad returned to her dressing table, expecting to find the headband there. She pushed her cosmetics aside, looking both there and on the floor. No headband. She seized the bed-clothes and started shaking them, picked up the garments, flung them on the floor and again shook the bed-clothes. Her eye caught a silvery movement as the band tumbled over the blanket. She snatched at it and ran out the door. At the garden's edge, her feet slowed. She stopped.

What am I doing? I want to escape. But should I go live with Queen Ku-bau and my friends forever instead? The old queen is moving toward the reward she has earned for her greatness. I am privileged to go with her and be in luxury forever. Shegunu said little cups and a bowl of poison have been placed in the tomb for us.

Again in motion, she rushed pell-mell through the empty corridor. At the queen's chambers, she paused, muddled about where she was, what she wanted to do. What's the matter with me? This is my chance. But I'm not sure which way to go. I can't go out the front. Everybody's there watching the procession. I'll have to go through the kitchen.

I can't. I can't. I should go to the next world with the old queen.

Running steps sounded nearby. Hana-Ad whisked into a darkened room, saw Uttu, and popped out.

"Uttu." She grabbed Uttu's arm and drew her into the room.

"Hana-Ad." Shaking, her mouth working nervously, Uttu clutched Hana-Ad. "I just stabbed Ur-Ilum."

"You stabbed the chancellor! But— but— I thought—"

"I know. I know. I'm bearing his child. And, yes, I do love him."

"Then, why did you stab him?"

"I want to die with Queen Ku-bau, and he tried to stop me. I had my harp and was hurrying toward the door. He saw me and forced me into the king's little guardroom. A dagger was on the table...."

She brushed a hand across her eyes. "I don't want to think about it." After a second, she added, "I have to get outside to position myself in line."

"You can't join the procession dressed like that."

"I could walk along the edge and slip into the tomb."

"There might not be enough cups."

"I'd manage. Some poison would be left in the bowl."

Hana-Ad shook her head. "Uttu, Uttu."

"Come on." She pulled at Hana-Ad. "We're wasting time."

"I'm not going." Suddenly purposeful, Hana-Ad brushed off Uttu's hand. "I'm going home."

"You'll be found and killed."

"I don't think so. I'll go to Daid's family. Nobody will know where I am."

Uttu stared at Hana-Ad, blinking rapidly. "Then change clothes, quick."

"Right." Off came the beautiful coat and filmy white dress. The yellow wool Uttu handed her dropped over her head. It was too big, but she didn't care.

Uttu struggled with the white dress. "This dress is too tight. I can't get it over my stomach." She stopped yanking the dress. "My poor little unborn will die, too. Ur-Ilum would have loved him."

"Then don't go to the tomb."

"I must, I must," she almost sobbed. "I'd be disgraced." She wiggled, giving a vicious yank at the dress.

"Hold still. I'll try to rip the back. With the coat on, nobody will know."

Hana-Ad yanked, but the fabric didn't give.

"Pull down at the same time so there's pressure."

Uttu pulled; Hana-Ad yanked. The fabric gave way. It tore enough so that the dress dropped over Uttu's hips. Hana-Ad removed her choker, fastened it on Uttu, tossed the beads around her neck and handed her the earrings. Then she unpinned the wig, loosening it from the gold ribbons that held it in place, and settled it securely on Uttu's head.

"You're perfect," said Hana-Ad, eyeing her. "Here's the headband." She shook her hand rapidly. The band that she had wound tightly around her little finger fell onto Uttu's open palm.

"I'll put it on once I'm in line." Uttu slid the headband into her coat pocket.

They looked into each other's eyes for a long second before Uttu, sniffling a little, caught Hana-Ad in a strong embrace, careful not to disturb the wig.

With tears in her own eyes, Hana-Ad said, "You're the best friend I've ever had. I'll pray to you always in the beyond with Queen Ku-bau."

"And I'll watch over you and Daid."

Hana-Ad hugged her again.

"I must go," said Uttu, retrieving the harp she had laid on the floor. As she flew toward the king's audience court, she called over her shoulder, "Get out of here before someone finds you."

Hana-Ad ran her hands down the exquisite yellow wool gown. That would certainly attract attention. She'd have to find something else in the kitchen.

A dirty, ragged scullery maid looked up from the fire as she swooped into the kitchen.

Hana-Ad stuttered. "I—I need an old dress to go out and watch the parade. I can't go in this."

No more than a girl of eleven, the scullery maid stared as if she were seeing a vision. She didn't move, her mouth open, her eyes round, one arm half raised.

"Did you hear me?" demanded Hana-Ad.

"I have no other dress," the girl finally said.

"Find me something. I don't care what. Quick."

The girl didn't move.

Hana-Ad pointed to her yellow wool gown. "You may have this dress."

"What would I do with that? If anybody saw it, they'd think I stole it." Even so, her eyes greedily devoured the dress.

"Hide it. Cut it up. Make yourself something. Use it for—" Hana-Ad wildly searched for possibilities. "Please hurry. Find me something to wear. Anything."

The girl disappeared through a door and returned a short time later with a handful of dirty rags.

Searching through them, Hana-Ad grimaced. She extracted a

coarse grayish garment from the awful pile and held it against her body. It would do. She dropped it on the floor. "Help me get this dress off."

The slave took hold of the soft yellow gown and carefully pulled it over Hana-Ad's head. Slowly, she folded it, smoothing each crease, while Hana-Ad fussed with the rag she intended to wear.

"Put that down and help me," Hana-Ad ordered.

Sullenly, the scullery maid crumpled the rag, bunching it up from the hem to the round hole at the top of the garment, and tossed it over Hana-Ad's head. Hana-Ad kept getting her hand through a rip in one sleeve instead of through the sleeve itself. Finally, the scullery maid held it properly. The hem reached Hana-Ad's ankles. Feeling sufficiently disguised in the round-necked loose rag, she turned and fled through the open door of the exit pantry and out onto the building platform.

Trembling unmanageably, she cowered in a niche of the building crenelations that created a shaded area at each indentation, trying to control her shaking enough to walk. The only sounds came from the front of the palace. She peered up and down the platform and down the kitchen ramp. Nobody.

While Hana-Ad stood undecided about what to do next, Daid stalled. As a priest of Marduk, he was supposed to walk with the foreign officials. Instead of taking his place in the procession, he nervously prowled around near the front of the ambassadors' section to watch the girls. He had belted a large piece of cloth under his skirt, ready to throw over Hana-Ad's court clothing and race away with her.

The procession didn't start and didn't start. Daid saw Uttu slip into the line and the amazed reaction of the other girls who immediately pushed her into the center of the group. Still, the procession didn't start. People began to fidget. The king sent a guard for Ur-Ilum.

"Where is he?" grumbled the king when the guard returned without having found the chancellor. Finally, Idi-Sin lost patience and ordered the marshal to start down the ramp.

The straggling line moved forward by minute, unnoticeable distances. Daid edged along to where the seven girls shuffled in place and melted into the crowd of slaves standing on the sidelines. From that vantage point, he could scrutinize each girl. He noticed that Uttu walked unsteadily, surrounded by the others, and Ashnan didn't have a silver hair ribbon across her forehead. He didn't see Hana-Ad.

Again he examined the seven girls, thinking he might have missed her. Mystified, he glanced ahead at the barely moving line. He spotted Ur-Lumma loitering along the edge of the procession in the vicinity of the chariot with the old queen's body. Strange. Why wasn't he in line with the court officials? Fidgety, worried about Hana-Ad, Did walked slowly back to his proper spot. He turned just in time to see Ur-Lumma grab Uttu. She planted her feet solidly, refusing to budge. He pushed Nidada aside and yanked Uttu. She shrieked. Another yank and she fell against him. Holding her tightly, he whispered in her ear. Her head fell back, her eyes rising to his. The screeching stopped, her whole body rigid. Then, letting go the harp, she flung her arms around his neck.

Somehow, Uttu's reaction to Ur-Lumma's whisper catapulted Did into action. He darted from the funeral line and ran into the palace.

Hana-Ad must be hiding. But where? She could be anywhere.

He glanced cautiously around the king's audience court. Nobody. Hesitantly, he moved past the king's guardroom. He stopped and listened. Had he heard someone call for help? Yes. There it was again. Faint. He stepped inside the poorly lit room. A figure lay on the floor. Unable to stop himself, Did bent over the body. "Great gods," he exclaimed. Ur-Ilum stared up at him.

"What happened?" He fell to one knee beside the chancellor.

"I've been stabbed," murmured Ur-Ilum.

"Stabbed!" repeated Did, instantly ready to help him.

"I can't see in here. I'll have to drag you to where there's light. Grit your teeth."

The chancellor moaned. "All right," he said feebly.

"I'll be as gentle as I can." Did hooked one arm under Ur-Ilum's undamaged shoulder. Once the chancellor cried out, then fell silent. On his knees, Did inched toward the door, dragging Ur-Ilum behind him. Twice, he brushed sweat from his eyes.

As soon as he could see properly, he examined the wound. The knife had gone through a lot of flesh in Ur-Ilum's left shoulder. Sticky blood covered his chest and more oozed slowly from the wound, leaving a trail behind them.

At that instant, Uttu ran up, followed by Ur-Lumma. She dropped to the floor and pressed Ur-Ilum's head to her bosom. "My darling, forgive me."

"Stop that," yelled a startled Daid. "Get up."

To Ur-Lumma, he said, "I need a rag first, to stem the bleeding, and then a poultice."

"Here's a rag." Uttu's strong hands ripped a portion from the bottom of her white dress.

Daid wadded it up and pressed it on the wound.

Ur-Ilum gagged.

"Find a slave," Daid growled at Ur-Lumma.

And to Uttu, "I'll need more of your dress—a bigger piece."

Uttu ripped and wadded. Daid tossed aside the wet, red ball and pressed down on the wound with the new one.

Ur-Lumma returned with a palace guard.

"Bring me dung and wrappings for a poultice."

Saucer-eyed, the guard hurried off.

"Apparently, you're not squeamish," Daid said to Uttu. "I'll have to rely on you to put on the poultice. When it arrives, throw this bloody rag away. We already need a new one. Heap the dung on this spot," he pointed, "and bind his shoulder tightly with the leaves and straw. He'll need henbane, too. I can't wait now, but I'll come back later. Can you handle this?"

In answer, she tore off more of her dress and handed him the wad of fabric.

Daid replaced the wet one. Taking Uttu's hand, he guided her to apply the right amount of pressure on Ur-Ilum's wound. She gargled deep in her throat, nodded, and pressed down as he had indicated.

"I'll get some henbane," Ur-Lumma said.

Daid raced down the corridor toward the old queen's quarters, rubbing his hands together to try to wipe the blood from them.

There, he found only the silence of death. He called and called, "Hana-Ad! Where are you. It's Daid" No sound broke the silence. The kitchen! She might try to get out of the palace by going down the ramp off the kitchen.

As he bolted into the kitchen, the scullery maid quickly hid something behind her back, a guilty look on her face.

Guessing that her reaction meant Hana-Ad had been there, he said, "Which way did the woman go?"

She looked coy. "What woman?"

He approached her menacingly. "You know perfectly well. The court lady."

Terrified, she started to grovel. "I did nothing wrong. I didn't know. I—"

"That's enough. Tell me which way she went, and I won't hurt you."

Bringing one arm from behind her, she pointed to the exit.

He tore outside and ran a short distance along the wall, looking in each shadowed corner. Frantic, he returned to the ramp. She must have already descended it, in which case, she would head for home. In court dress? He shuddered. Even the stupidest peasant would recognize her. Would she take the main route? Wiser to take one of the narrow streets leading to the market gate, dressed as she was. Which to choose? How far ahead was she?

By taking the main route, he could reach the market gate quickly. Then he'd hang around, watching all the small nearby streets that abutted the gate. Old men sat at the gate as they had done years ago. Amused, he asked if they had seen a court lady. One had gotten lost in the crowds surrounding the funeral procession. This sent them into breathless laughter. A court lady? How would they know a court lady? But, no, they hadn't seen anyone who might be a court lady.

Daid walked around, peering at the passing throng as the old men continued to titter. Finally, he couldn't stand it. He walked out the market gate and started uncertainly along, intending to take the cart tracks leading to her home.

Hana-Ad had remained hidden in the shadows of the vertical crenelations until the music and shuffling noise from the front of the palace faded to a distant, unearthly cadence floating on the air before creeping apprehensively down the ramp. She ducked into a narrow street that ran parallel to the river to get away from the palace before turning toward the market gate. She poked along, fretting.

Why hadn't Daid come for her? Didn't he want her anymore? Would her father take her back? Would he be ashamed that she hadn't gone to live with the old queen?

Now that she had achieved her goal of escape, she wasn't sure she wanted it. What did life hold for her without Daid? She would just be tolerated at home like a servant. Hana-Ad stopped and thought about what she had done.

She shook her head. It was no use now; she had given her place to Uttu. She started walking again, one hesitant step after another. As she got close to the market gate, she turned onto the main road and mingled with the crowd. Nobody paid any attention to her. She became more confident and walked faster. But her feet hurt. She hadn't done much walking in four years. The hot sun beat down on her. She squinted. Way ahead, she spotted a man who resembled Daid.

She started to run, but stopped abruptly. No, if he didn't want her, she wouldn't force herself on him. She'd stay behind him until the turnoff for her own home.

For a while, they walked that way. Hana-Ad stumbled a number of times. Tears blinded her. Why didn't Ur's great god Nannar help her now? She had been in his room, helped dress him. She stepped on a stone and twisted her ankle. Looking up, she realized that Daid stood still.

Daid scanned the people on the roadway ahead as far as he could see. She couldn't have gotten this far. She must either be behind him or still at the palace. Suppose she had been captured and thrust into the procession while he searched for her in the palace? His shoulders sagged. He turned back. Should he go and question people at the palace? His lovely Hana-Ad. He couldn't imagine life without her.

He noticed a dirty girl in rags. How odd. She had shoes on. He stared. He started to run. The girl backed away and twisted uncertainly.

"Hana-Ad," he yelled. "It's Daid."

Again, she faced him. This time, he didn't hold back. He caught her in his arms. "Hana-Ad, Hana-Ad," he breathed into her ear. "I thought I had lost you forever."

"Oh, Daid." Happy tears smudged her face.

"My little one," he whispered, his voice breaking with emotion, "we'll go to my home. No king's guard will search for you there."

"I don't think a king's guard will search for me anyway."

"Why not?"

"I don't think anybody would realize I wasn't in the group with the others."

"Well, we won't take any chances. I must go back later and see the chancellor so—"

"Is he alive?"

"Yes."

"Uttu stabbed him," she said quickly.

"I know. Uttu rushed in with Ur-Lumma while I was helping the chancellor. That's what kept me from finding you. By the time I got away, you had left the platform."

"I waited for you."

"Well, I'll find out what happened later. Once you're with my family, I'll have to go back."

"No, Daid."

"I must check on the chancellor. I told Uttu how to put the poultice on. And if, for some reason, the wound turns bad, she isn't responsible. I am."

Hana-Ad said no more. Daid's arm went round her to support her. She limped along, trying not to put too much weight on her painful ankle. In silence, they reached his home.

Daid stayed longer than he felt he ought. He couldn't tear himself away. When he did reach the palace, he found Ur-Ilum in bed in Uttu's alcove, his eyes closed, his face relaxed. Uttu sat beside him, holding his hand. Gula and Bitar, while poised to give assistance or run errands, guarded the door of the main room.

"He's sleeping," Uttu whispered.

Daid checked the poultice superficially. "You've done a good job." He smiled at her. "You gave him some henbane?"

"Yes. Ur-Lumma brought it to Temena."

"Let him sleep. I must find Nanshe. I'll come back later."

Uttu nodded and turned her attention back to Ur-Ilum.

The first guard Daid encountered in the king's audience court told him the high priestess had returned and gone to her temple room. He flashed his eyes around, thinking. Ah yes. He smiled. After all these years, he remembered where it was.

Mesile sat in front of Nanshe's closed door. "Highness is resting," she said when Daid stopped in front of her.

"Tell her, please, that the shepherd she sent to Babylon more than four years ago would like to speak to her." Daid had trouble keeping his face in order as he watched surprise, astonishment, disbelief, and finally realization flow across Mesile's face. She couldn't stop staring at him.

"Go to your mistress," he said.

She jumped to her feet and disappeared through the door.

Seconds later, she flung it wide. Having changed her formal robe for something more comfortable, Nanshe sat in the middle of the room, facing the door.

One look at him and the eager smile on her face faded. "You!"

From his knees, Daid said, "Forgive me, Highness. I wanted to speak to you, to tell you all that happened to me and that I was, by accident, able to deliver your letter to King Hammurabi. But with the demands of the epidemic here and my identity—"

"Didn't you trust me with your identity? For shame. I trusted you with more at stake."

"Please believe me, it wasn't trust. I trusted you without question. Somehow the timing had to be right."

She studied him. "Well, we have all been through a terrible time."

"And it isn't over yet, but subsiding."

"Praise to Nannar for that."

"And Marduk and Yahweh."

She glanced over him sharply. "The innocent boy is still in you, but you have become an educated, well-mannered man at ease in court circles."

She pointed to a cushion near him. "Sit on that cushion and tell me what happened, what took you so long."

"It started tragically," he said, seating himself, "with an amazingly wonderful ending." In a precise synopsis, he outlined his years in Babylon and the unexpected escape.

"That's quite an incredible story. You are favored by Nannar."

"There's more. With the first money I earned, I had a letter written to King Hammurabi, asking him to force Queen Ku-bau to release those girls."

"You didn't!"

Daid examined the floor before continuing. "I'll confess to you alone the reason for all my behavior. I am contracted to Hana-Ad."

Nanshe leaned forward in consternation, her brow drawn into a straight black line. "But she died today in Queen Ku-bau's tomb. I saw those lovely, sweet girls drink the poison and lie down in pairs—pairs—There were only six. There should have been seven. Now I can't remember who was there."

She hesitated. "I was too busy checking that Uttu wasn't among them. Uttu is my daughter."

"Your daughter! But—but—"

"She's enceinte by the chancellor. And I'm having a second child by my husband." She laughed gleefully at the expression on Daid's face.

He tried to speak, couldn't find his voice, swallowed, and said, "I left Hana-Ad with my parents."

Nanshe stood up. Immediately, Daid was up, bowing.

"I think," she said, "we both better have a talk with my nephew. And we'll take Uttu with us."

Dark had long descended when Daid finally returned from the palace. To his surprise, his entire family had gathered uncertainly at the foot of the staircase. The faces turned toward him were momentarily immobile, then broke into wide grins. They all started to exclaim at once. His youngest brother rushed toward him. Laughing, Daid tossed him in the air.

Ur-Enlila broke from the group and went to greet his son. "It's so late, we thought you were staying at the palace. I ordered everybody to bed."

"You can go soon." Daid put his brother down on a step of the staircase. "I have a few things to say first."

"We will go back and sit on the mats. Bring your lamps," said Ur-Enlila, retrieving his from the floor where he had placed it when Daid arrived. He led the way to the courtyard corner where they had been sitting.

Daid took Hana-Ad's hand and smiled into her worried eyes. "It's all right," he whispered. "You are forgiven."

"Oh!" She ducked a blazing, happy face, at the same time giving his hand a squeeze.

"It's pretty extraordinary," Daid said in answer to the questions of his seated family. "After I made sure the chancellor was doing well, I went to Nanshe. I told her who I was with a quick synopsis of what had happened to me. She was utterly amazed." Daid's face dissolved into little amused gullies. "She sent Mesile to the king, asking that he receive her on personal business. He did, even though he had to leave his dinner table to do so. And we took Uttu with us because she's Nanshe's daughter."

"Her—" Hana-Ad stumbled. "So that's why Nanshe fainted that day she had Uttu stripped."

"Nanshe fainted!" said Daid.

"Uttu has an ugly red birthmark on her stomach or leg, I

don't remember which. I guess when Nanshe saw it, she realized that Uttu was her daughter."

"Ur-Lumma grabbed Uttu from the line. I saw that just before I entered the palace to look for you."

"He must be her father."

"Ur-Lumma!" Ninlil bridled. "She has no right to have a child by her husband."

"That's why she gave Uttu away, Mother," Daid said gently.

"I shouldn't have mentioned that birthmark." Hana-Ad said with chagrin. "I promised not to."

"It doesn't matter," said Ur-Enlila. "We won't mention it, and none of us will ever see her."

"I'd like to," said Buzu.

"You may very well," Daid said, emphatically.

"Really! At the palace?" Ecstatic, Buzu sounded as if she had joined the six girls living in luxury forever with Queen Ku-bau.

"Buzu!" said her mother.

Ur-Enlila smiled. "Let her dream."

Daid turned happy eyes on him, pleased with how well his father was taking everything.

"Uttu's going to marry Ur-Ilum."

"Is he all right?" said Hana-Ad.

"I think he will be. I'll keep close watch on him." Daid grinned. "So will Uttu. She sits beside him and holds his hand."

"I'm so glad," Hana-Ad said.

"Uttu wants us to sign and seal the tablet with the marriage lines at the same time in a double ceremony."

Hana-Ad clapped her hands together. "How lovely."

"It'll be quite a wedding," said Daid. "Nanshe can recognize Uttu by giving up the position of high priestess. And as she's having another child—her husband's," Daid looked pointedly at his mother, "She's going to do that."

"Who's going to be high priestess?" asked Hana-Ad.

"The king's second oldest daughter. I treated Luga. The epidemic left her badly pockmarked. The girl is in a slump. She feels that she has no future. She's afraid no one will want to marry her, now that she's scarred."

"How silly," said Ninlil. "She's a royal princess. All the king has to do is arrange for a marriage. Even pockmarked, she'll attract royal suitors."

"True. But at her age, she doesn't accept that. She keeps saying she wants to be beautiful like Shegunu."

Hana-Ad smiled and shook her head.

"Could she ever be as beautiful?" asked Buzu.

"It's impossible," said Hana-Ad.

"Anyway," Daid said, "Nanshe feels sorry for her and offered to let her be high priestess."

"As high priestess, she can't marry," commented Ninlil.

"Nanshe thinks the girl will adapt well to the position. Naturally, she'll oversee her for a long time so the temple will run as smoothly as usual."

"Nanshe really is a dear," said Hana-Ad, thinking of all the kindness Nanshe had offered her. "Luga will appreciate her help. Nanshe may have trouble with her mother, though." Hana-Ad had begun to understand the queen's desire for power.

"No. The queen is in disgrace. The king has ordered her to have no contact with her young daughter."

"How awful," said Ninlil. "It's her child."

"Wait. There's more," Daid said. "The king has ordered Nin-Anna confined to the royal quarters."

"But why?" cried Hana-Ad.

"I don't know the full story, but it has to do with the chancellor's wife."

"Oh, no." Hana-Ad covered her face with her hands.

Daid regarded her. "Well, you know more about that than I do."

Turning to his family, he continued. "Apparently the high priest accused the queen of murder."

"Murder," shouted Ur-Enlila.

"Yes," said Daid. "The whole court is in a hubbub. The queen has taken to her bed. That's all I know. We'll see what happens tomorrow."

Hana-Ad wiped a tear. "So many have died—Queen Ku-bau, the chancellor's wife, my dear, sweet Kigal," she sighed, "and Nin-Ad, then today the other six." Tears streamed down her face. "We lived together for four years. We were like a—a family."

Ninlil hurried to Hana-Ad. Kneeling behind her, she held the girl's head against her breast. "I know you miss them, but remember, they are living now in eternal luxury. Try to be happy for them. They would want you to." Her hands around Hana-Ad's head, she used her thumbs to wipe the tears from Hana-Ad's cheeks and kissed her.

"I'll try." Hana-Ad choked a couple of times, then said, "Is Nanshe going to stay in the temple with the princess?"

Daid put his arm across her shoulders. "No. Ur-Lumma and Nanshe will move into Queen Ku-bau's quarters. The area where you girls lived will be rebuilt for us." He gave her a little hug.

"Us! We're going to live at the palace?" Hana-Ad beamed. After helping Ninlil and the slaves with dinner, she wasn't so sure she wanted to settle back into the life she had formerly known.

"I'm to be court physician. The king insisted."

"I'm so proud of you, my son," said Ur-Enlila.

Daid flushed with pleasure, his eyes brimming with a close, strong, filial love.

"On my way home, I stopped by your house, Hana-Ad. I promised your parents that we would spend tomorrow with them."

Hana-Ad turned a deep rosy pink. "I'm glad. I wanted to let them know I was free and all right."

"I told them, and they're overjoyed. In fact, the news made your father so happy that he said he felt better and stronger than he had in ages."

Hana-Ad smiled lovingly. "My being with the old queen has been hard on him."

"On both of them. Ur-mes is frail. Having you back will be better than medication. Even your mother perked up. These years have taken their toll."

"We have all changed," she said simply.

Daid nodded.

"Time for bed," said Ur-Enlila, picking up the lamp he had set beside him on the floor. "Follow me."

"Hana-Ad, you sleep with Buzu. Daid, carry your little brother upstairs. All this excitement has put him to sleep."

Daid kissed Hana-Ad. "Until tomorrow, my love."

"Until tomorrow," she whispered.